STILLWATER

Published in 2025 by Bigfoot Robot Books

First US Edition

Cover design by John Parenteau
Some AI generation was used in the cover design

Paperback ISBN: 979-8-9990040-3-1

http://BigfootRobotBooks.com

*Dedicated to Maggie, who always tries to listen
first thing in the morning.*

STILLWATER

JOHN PARENTEAU

ONE

Fog clung to the forest floor, hiding the view of the pines that stood tall overhead. Dawn light barely reached through the trees as the sound of the Stillwater River churned it's way nearby, with darkness giving way slowly to morning.

Jackson McKenzie moved through the half-light on a path worn by years of use. At sixty-seven, his face was a map of wrinkles, skin worn from decades outdoors. His breath formed faint cumulus clouds in the cold air around his face as he climbed down a gentle slope, knees aching from the exertion. Remnants of a snow two weeks ago, most likely the last of the season, clung in spots beneath the trees and across the path, making each step a challenge.

Where there was no snow, the trail beneath his boots was packed earth, winding between rocks and fallen trees. Each step took him further away from the road, away from the noise and chaos of life. His retirement had been far too busy, and he relished his moments to escape, to enjoy the peace of his rod and reel, and the quiet of his game with the trout that lived in the river.

His fishing rod cast no shadow on the forest floor, the rising brightness of the sky still too dim. McKenzie ducked under a low branch heavy with dew. The tackle box in his left hand swung with a steady rhythm. A crow called from somewhere in the mist—a harsh sound that broke the morning silence.

The Stillwater River made itself known the closer he got to it—a steady murmur growing louder with each step. When the trees opened to show the water, he stopped at the edge of the clearing. The river flowed dark and fast, its surface broken by swirling patterns.

Jackson set his tackle box on a smooth boulder. The riverbank was littered with stones and driftwood bleached white by time. He pulled off his worn leather work boots and put on his waders, pulling the rubber overalls up over his jeans. They were newer than most of his gear, still stiff against his body.

As he fastened the suspenders, he noticed an old fence running along part of the bank. It leaned at an angle, the posts half-rotted and barely visible through the fog. Part of it stretched into the water, likely fallen during the winter floods. Jackson had seen worse debris in the river over his decades of fishing here.

The water covered his boots with cold as he waded in. April meant snowmelt, and the river ran cold enough to make his legs ache. The riverbed was slick with algae and uneven. Each step required care—a delicate balance against the current's push.

Just a few feet from shore, the water reached his thighs. Jackson angled upstream toward a narrow section of river, his favorite spot. The current pressed against him like an unseen hand.

As he settled in, adjusting his feet to find the right balance, the resistance came without warning—his left boot caught on something below. He shifted and pulled, expecting a branch. The boot stayed stuck.

Jackson stood still for moment, tense against the flow, then pulled harder, his balance uncertain as the water pushed at him. Whatever held him wouldn't let go. He leaned forward, trying to see through the dark water, but saw nothing beyond the shape of his legs.

His breathing quickened as he strained against the hidden snag. The fishing rod tilted in his grip as he fought to stay upright while pulling with growing desperation.

"Goddamn it!"

The words burst from him as Jackson summoned his strength for one massive pull. For a moment, he thought he'd freed himself—his boot seemed to lift.

Then came the sound—a deep crack, followed by the rush of disturbed water.

Jackson turned to see a large section of the old fence sliding into the river upstream, the first rotted post finally giving way after years of being undercut by the current. The wood snapped completely, the next two ancient fence posts in sequence breaking or tearing out of the soaked ground and falling toward him, dragging a metal mesh of old wire fencing on him, pushed forcefully down river by the current.

The rusty fence hit Jackson in the shoulder as he tried to turn, to move away, knocking him sideways into the water. His arms swung wildly, the rod torn from his hand. The weight of the fence and the force of the water pushed him down, rushing over his body, his boots yanked out from under him by the wire still tangled around his ankle.

His chest hit the riverbed, forcing air from his lungs. He was under before he could do anything, the cold water filling his waders and dragging him down harder. He looked through the churning water above, the morning light breaking into pieces. Jackson clawed at the heavy metal pressed against his body, his fingers slipping on the rust and algae that covered the ancient barrier.

The cold of the river threatened to fill his lungs as his struggles weakened. His attempts to fight his head above water, to breathe, were no longer effective, his gasps taking in more water than air. As his mind began to fade, Jackson thought of the countless times he'd passed that old fence, never giving it a second glance. The river had been his constant companion for decades, offering peace and purpose. Now, in some cruel twist of fate, it had become his tomb through nothing more sinister than time and neglect.

Above, the water flowed on, broken only by a few bubbles rising to the surface. The fishing rod drifted downstream, spinning slowly before stopping against the shore.

TWO

The morning sun crept over the eastern ridge of mountains that embraced Stillwater like protective arms. Carter Thompson pumped the pedals of his faded blue Schwinn, the plastic bag containing a half-gallon of milk swinging from the handlebars. Each rotation of the wheels sent small vibrations through the frame—the chain needed oil, the spokes needed tightening, but such repairs required money Carter didn't have.

At sixteen, Carter carried himself with the weary resignation of someone far older. His pale complexion suggested more hours spent indoors than out, though the lean muscles in his calves spoke of miles traveled on this same bicycle. His sandy brown hair fell across his forehead in an uneven cut, likely trimmed by his own hand with dull scissors. The jeans he wore were faded at the knees, the cuffs frayed and an inch too short. His flannel shirt hung loose on his narrow frame, the pattern faded from countless washes, the collar worn thin.

None of these clothes had ever belonged to Carter first. They weren't hand-me-downs from siblings—he had none—but rather castoffs from the church donation bin or items purchased from the thrift store on Pine Street. Carter didn't seem to notice or care about the origins of his wardrobe. Clothes were functional, nothing more.

The half-gallon of milk sloshed in its plastic container as Carter coasted down Maple Avenue. Mrs. Fulton at the corner market had been kind enough to put it on his grandmother's tab. The tab that grew larger each month, despite his promises to settle it when his grandmother's social security check arrived.

To a passing car or a casual observer peering through curtained windows, Carter was just another kid on an errand—perhaps enjoying the freedom of the early morning in this picturesque mountain town. Stillwater presented itself well in the golden light of dawn. American flags hung from porch columns, garden beds burst with early spring flowers, and freshly painted mailboxes stood at attention along the curb.

But Carter saw what others didn't, or chose not to.

He turned onto Birch Street, passing the Weber house with its immaculate lawn and gleaming white trim. Three days ago, he'd watched Mrs. Weber cleaning out flower beds with a trembling hand, her other arm held protectively across her midsection. When she'd turned to reach for the garden hose, her hair had shifted, revealing a yellowish bruise blooming across her cheekbone. She'd seen Carter looking and had quickly rearranged her hair, flashing a smile that didn't reach her eyes.

Today, Mr. Weber's BMW sat in the driveway, freshly washed and waxed. Carter slowed as he passed, noticing the deep scratch running the length of the passenger door—a jagged wound in the otherwise perfect finish. The scratch hadn't been there yesterday.

At the intersection, Carter waited for a pickup truck to pass. His eyes drifted across the street to the Johnsons' and Petersons' houses, which stood side by side on the tree lined street. The property line between their backyards was marked by a hedge that now resembled a battlefield. The hedge stood at six feet along most of the border between the two houses, but had been cut much shorter in areas, hacked down to half its height, exposing the bare, woody interior of the plants. Three years of disputes over property lines had culminated in this silent declaration of war. Carter could see into the Peterson's garage, two brand new gas cans sitting near the door.

Carter continued his journey. The plastic bag swung with the rhythm of his pedaling, the milk inside growing warmer by the minute.

Near the park, a group of younger kids huddled on the playground equipment. From a distance, it looked like innocent fun, but Carter recognized the posture of the smallest boy—shoulders hunched, head down, surrounded by three larger children. Carter had stood in that same position too many times to mistake what was happening. The boy handed something over—money, maybe, or a prized possession. The others laughed.

Carter pedaled faster, eyes fixed ahead. Not his problem. He had enough of his own.

The Anderson pharmacy stood on the corner, its windows plastered with cheerful signs advertising summer specials and sunscreen. Inside, Carter knew Mr. Anderson kept a baseball bat beneath the counter—had done so ever since the opioid thefts began last winter. The security camera above the door had been installed after the third break-in, its red light blinking steadily over the entrance.

As Carter turned onto his own street, he passed old man Guthrie sitting on his porch, rifle across his lap. The man stared at Carter, eyes narrowed with suspicion. The "NO TRESPASSING" signs nailed to Guthrie's trees had multiplied since spring, now numbering at least a dozen around the property perimeter. Some, Carter knew, were questionable symbols, that hinted to a much darker point of view.

Three houses down, the Millers' dog strained at its chain, barking furiously. The animal had once been friendly, often breaking free to follow Carter on his paper route, begging for pats and attention. Now it lunged with bared teeth, eyes wild with a rage born of neglect. An empty water bowl lay overturned in the dirt.

Carter's own house came into view—a small, gray two-story with peeling paint and sagging gutters. The yard was mostly dirt, with patches of stubborn crabgrass fighting for survival. Unlike the other homes on the street, there were no flowers, no decorative touches, nothing that suggested pride of ownership. It was shelter, nothing more.

He braked to a stop by the front steps, lifting the milk from the handlebars. Through the living room window, he could see the flicker of the television screen, its blue light pulsing against the faded curtains. No silhouette of his grandmother moving about, no shadow passing before the window. Just the TV, talking to a disinterested room.

The familiar sight sent a wave of anxiety through him. Yesterday, he'd found her staring into an open refrigerator, confused about whether it was time for breakfast or dinner. Last week, she'd called him by his father's name three times. Each morning was a gamble—would she remember to take her medication? Would she know what year it was? Would she remember who he was?

No one else knew. Not his grandmother's friends from church, who had stopped visiting when she began forgetting who they were. Not the neighbors, who attributed her occasional wandering to grief over Carter's parents. Not even Dr. Morris, who wrote her prescriptions but never asked why an eighty-year-old woman missed appointments or why her teenage grandson answered all the medical questions.

Carter knew something was wrong, terribly wrong, but he didn't have a name for it. He just knew that the grandmother who had taught him to fish, who had baked cookies every Sunday, who had never forgotten a birthday, was disappearing piece by piece. Some moments she was herself, sharp and present. Most other times she was lost in a fog, cooking breakfast at midnight or putting her shoes in the freezer.

He climbed the steps, careful to avoid the rotted third board. He knew if he startled her she might grow violent, mistaking Carter for an intruder. He listened carefully. No sound came from inside except the high-pitched laughter of a game show audience. Carter took a deep breath and pushed the door open.

Pausing, milk in hand, he looked back at the neighborhood spread out around him. From most people's vantage point, Stillwater was postcard-perfect—a charming mountain community nestled among towering pines, the kind of place tourists drove through and wished they could stay forever.

But Carter knew better. Behind every pristine facade lurked shadows—feuds that spanned generations, secrets that poisoned families from within, desperation masked by morning pleasantries at the coffee shop. Beneath Stillwater's picturesque surface ran currents as dark and dangerous as the river that gave the town its name.

He entered the house, stepping from one world into another, the weight of the milk nothing compared to the weight he carried inside.

Carter eased past his grandmother, ignoring the blaring TV, noticing she'd fallen asleep in her recliner again, the ancient La-Z-Boy that had belonged to his grandfather. Carter slipped into the kitchen and set the milk in the refrigerator, noting the sparse contents—half a loaf of bread, some bologna, a container of grape jelly. He'd need to stretch the social security check further this month somehow.

He crept back into the living room to check more closely on his grandmother, adjusting the afghan that had slipped from her lap. The television blared a commercial for denture adhesive. Carter lowered the volume and placed the remote within her reach.

"I'll be in my room," he whispered, though he knew she couldn't hear him.

Carter moved silently through the narrow hallway, then up the stairs to his bedroom. He slipped inside and locked the door behind him, his shoulders dropping as if relieved of an invisible burden.

The room was dark, the blackout curtains drawn against the morning sun, remarkably organized despite the chaos of its contents. A single desk lamp illuminated the space with a harsh yellow glow. The walls, once blue, were now barely visible beneath layers of paper—news clippings, printed articles, handwritten notes, and maps, all connected by red string that crisscrossed the room like arteries.

Carter crossed to a small desk positioned beneath the largest collection of papers. He pulled out a worn notebook from his backpack and flipped to a fresh page, then hunched over it, scribbling furiously. His handwriting was tight and precise, every letter formed with deliberate care, as if each one carried immense importance.

Above the desk hung what appeared to be a random collection of notes pinned to corkboard, but a closer look revealed an intense, methodical organization. The papers were arranged by neighborhood, date, and type of incident. Each note was coded with symbols in the margins—triangles, circles, and squares in different colors. Some had question marks, others exclamation points. Together, they resembled the investigation board of a detective working a complex case.

Bookshelves constructed from cinder blocks and planks lined one wall. Unlike the barren refrigerator, these shelves overflowed with volumes. "The Detective's Handbook," "How to Analyze People Like Sherlock Holmes," "The Field Guide to Law Enforcement," and dozens of true crime books filled the makeshift library. The books showed signs of constant use—dog-eared pages, broken spines, highlighted passages, and notes in the margins.

Carter finished writing, tore the page from his notebook with surgical precision, and stood. He pinned the new notes to the appropriate section of his wall, stepping back to review his work. The fresh notes documented what he'd observed on his bike ride:

"1504 Water Street: 10-16 Domestic Violence. Mrs. Weber, facial bruising, defensive posture. Mr. Weber's car scratched today, not present yesterday. Escalation likely."

"1646 Water Street: 10-14 Suspicious Person. Guthrie, rifle displayed openly, Possible Neo-Nazi symbol on property. Monitor for increased activity."

"Johnson/Peterson property line: Ongoing dispute. New gas cans in Peterson garage. Possible 10-66 (Fire risk) or 10-72 (Threat) situation developing."

Carter stood back, eyes scanning the wall, making connections invisible to anyone else. To an outsider, it might have looked like the work of a paranoid mind—conspiracy theories pinned to a bedroom wall. But to Carter, it was a system, a way to make sense of a town whose picturesque surface concealed dangerous undercurrents.

He glanced at his watch, a cheap digital timepiece with a cracked face. Almost eight. His grandmother would need her medication soon.

Carter moved to the door, pausing with his hand on the knob. For just a moment, his shoulders sagged, his face betraying the exhaustion of someone carrying burdens far beyond his years. Then, like a soldier donning armor, he straightened his posture, set his jaw, and stepped back into the hallway, locking his room behind him.

His sanctuary of secrets remained in darkness, waiting for his return.

THREE

Inside the Cain household, the aroma of fresh coffee and sizzling bacon wove through the air, a sensory alarm clock more effective than any electronic device.

Laura Cain stood at the stove, expertly flipping pancakes while monitoring the bacon's progress. Her dark hair was pulled back in a practical ponytail, blue scrubs already donned for her shift at Stillwater Memorial's emergency room. Twenty years as a trauma nurse had given her the ability to multitask with military precision—an essential skill both in the ER and in managing a household with a teenage daughter and the town's sheriff.

The wooden stairs creaked under Martin Cain's weight as he descended, uniform crisp and badge already pinned to his chest. At forty-seven, he maintained the solid build of his football days, though the hours behind a desk had softened his middle slightly. Silver had begun infiltrating his dark hair at the temples, lines deepening around his eyes—evidence of a career spent witnessing both the best and worst of their small community.

"Morning," he said, voice still rough with sleep. Laura glanced over her shoulder, a smile warming her features.

"Coffee's fresh. Breakfast in two minutes." Martin crossed to her, placing a gentle kiss on the nape of her neck before retrieving a mug from the cabinet.

"Smells amazing. What's the occasion?"

"Can't a wife make her family breakfast without an ulterior motive?" Laura teased, transferring golden pancakes to a waiting plate.

"In my experience as a law enforcement officer," Martin replied with mock seriousness, "unexpected kindness often precedes a confession or a request."

Laura laughed, the sound brightening the kitchen. "Well, perhaps I just wanted to enjoy a meal with my husband for once." She set the plates on the table and slid into her seat. "It feels like we've been ships passing lately."

Martin joined her, immediately reaching for the maple syrup. "Nature of our jobs, I suppose." He poured coffee for both of them from the carafe on the table. "County's been busy. Three break-ins last month, that fender-bender by the school..."

"Riveting criminal activity," Laura teased, her fork hovering over her plate. "Stillwater's crime wave keeps you working those long hours."

Martin chuckled, cutting into his pancakes. "Small town, small crimes. And I'm grateful for that." He paused, glancing up at her. "Been thinking about it, actually."

"About crime waves?"

"About stepping back. Maybe not going for another term."

Laura's fork stopped halfway to her mouth, surprise evident in her expression. She looked over to her husband, waiting for a sign it was all just speculation, like the last time, and the one before. But Martin wasn't flinching. "You're serious."

Martin nodded, his voice dropping slightly though they were alone in the kitchen. "I've put in my twenty-five years. Pension's solid. And honestly, Laura... I'm tired. Tired of those missed meals with you, tired of town politics, tired of being the face everyone brings their complaints to."

Laura reached across the table, covering his hand with hers. "You know I'll support whatever you decide. And believe me, this all sounds wonderful to me. But are you sure? You've been Sheriff Cain for so long, I'm not sure either of us remembers who Martin is without the badge."

"That's part of the problem," he admitted, turning his hand to squeeze hers. "Maybe it's time to find out."

"What about Mary?" Laura asked. "Have you talked to her about this?"

Martin shook his head. "Not yet. Let's keep it between us until I'm certain. No sense getting her hopes up about having a normal father around if I change my mind."

"A normal father?" Laura raised an eyebrow. "Is that how you think she sees it?"

Before Martin could respond, a whirlwind of activity announced their daughter's arrival. Mary Cain burst down the stairs and into the kitchen, her hair hastily pulled into a messy ponytail, still in her sleep clothes, a t-shirt and loose shorts. At seventeen, she had inherited her mother's warm brown eyes and her father's stubborn set to her jaw—a combination that had proven both beautiful and challenging.

"Morning," she mumbled, making a beeline for the coffee pot.

"No coffee," her father said, then grimaced, realizing these were his chosen first words of the day to his daughter. "Just go easy," he added. "Let's not stunt your growth." Mary didn't respond, but hesitated, then stopped her pour before filling her mug to the rim.

"There's pancakes too," Laura offered, gesturing to the stove where a covered plate waited.

Mary glanced at the clock on the microwave, grimacing. "No time. I told Amber I'd meet her before class to go over notes for the history test. I have to go get ready."

Martin frowned over his mug. "You're studying at school rather than at home? That doesn't seem efficient."

Mary rolled her eyes as she poured some milk into the mug. "It's called collaboration, Dad. Group study. Very effective learning technique."

"So effective you're rushing out without breakfast?" Martin's tone held the edge that had become increasingly common in their exchanges, a mixture of concern and disapproval that never failed to spark Mary's defenses.

"Martin," Laura warned softly.

Mary grabbed an apple from the fruit bowl, holding it up like evidence in court. "There. Breakfast. Nutritionally complete."

"The SATs are in three weeks," Martin continued, unable to stop himself. "Columbia's admissions department isn't going to care about your social life if your scores aren't competitive."

"Oh my God, Dad," Mary groaned, shoulders tensing. "It's seven thirty in the morning. Can we hold off on the future-of-my-entire-life lecture until later?"

"I'm just saying—"

"I know exactly what you're saying," Mary cut him off. "The same thing you say every morning. Study harder, focus more, remember that every decision has consequences." She mimicked his deeper tone with the practiced precision of someone who had heard the words countless times.

Martin set his fork down with deliberate control. "Your attitude isn't helping your case, Mary Elizabeth."

"Neither is your parole-officer routine," she shot back. "I have a 4.0 GPA, I'm on student council, I volunteer at the hospital with Mom. What more do you want?"

"I want you to take your future more seriously," Martin replied, his voice rising slightly. "I want you home by curfew, not rolling in twenty minutes late with excuses about Amber's car trouble."

"It wasn't an excuse—"

"I want you to understand that the choices you make now—"

"Martin," Laura interrupted, her tone sharper now. "Mary needs to get ready for school, and you need to finish your breakfast before it gets cold." Mary used the diversion to turn back to the counter, adding more cream to her coffee, avoiding locking eyes with her father. It was a practiced operation for Laura, strategically stopping a morning fight between her husband and their daughter, which seemed to happen more often these days. Laura was reluctantly getting better at it.

Martin's police radio on the counter chirped, but only crackled out an indistinguishable message, breaking up the heavy silence that lay over the kitchen. Before her father could start again, Mary broke the connection, pouring out the rest of her coffee and heading back upstairs.

"I'll see you later," was all she could say, directed at neither of them.

"Love you, honey," Laura replied as they watched her disappear back upstairs.

Mary's door slammed in the distance with more force than necessary, punctuating her exit with physical emphasis.

Laura sighed, pushing her half-eaten breakfast away. "That went well."

Martin ran a hand over his face, the gesture revealing the fatigue his carefully maintained professional demeanor usually concealed. "She's pushing every boundary, Laura. Testing limits, breaking curfew, being secretive about who she's with..."

"She's seventeen," Laura reminded him gently. "That's what seventeen looks like. You can't police her like she's one of your deputies."

"I'm not trying to police her. I'm trying to protect her."

"From what, Martin?" Laura challenged, leaning forward. "From making her own choices? From learning from her own mistakes? She's not a little girl anymore."

"I know that," he insisted, though the defensive note in his voice suggested otherwise.

"Do you?" Laura reached for his hand again. "Because from where I'm sitting, it looks like you're doing more damage than good with all these rules and expectations. You're pushing her away, not keeping her safe."

Martin opened his mouth to respond, but the sharp trill of his phone cut through the conversation. He glanced at the screen, professional mask sliding immediately into place as he answered.

"Cain." He listened for a moment, nodding. "Yeah, still not working. I thought Taylor found a way to boost the tower signal?" Another pause. "Ok, never mind for now. What's up?" Cain's weary face solidified into a darker expression. "I'll be right there. Secure the scene. Get ahold of Carol and the ME."

He ended the call, already rising from the table, breakfast forgotten.

"What is it?" Laura asked, the nurse in her immediately alert to the possibility of an emergency.

"10-32 out at Stillwater River, near the bridge" Martin replied, grabbing his jacket from the back of his chair.

"In English for the civilian, please?"

"Possible drowning." He bent to kiss her cheek. Then hesitated close, catching her eyes. "I'm sorry. Maybe retiring will fix this."

"Don't use retirement as a tool to improve your relationship with Mary. Just apologize to your daughter, listen to her. She loves you, you just can't tell these days." Martin nodded, added another kiss to his wife's forehead before turning.

Laura watched as he strode toward the door, and by the time he reached it the transformation was complete—no longer the frustrated father but Sheriff Cain, Stillwater's embodiment of law and order. The man who had just been contemplating retirement now moved with renewed purpose, shoulders squared against whatever waited at the river's edge.

As the door closed behind him, Laura sat alone at the table surrounded by the remnants of their family breakfast— plates in various states of abandonment, three conversations left unfinished. With practiced efficiency, she began clearing the dishes, her mind already thinking about her own upcoming shift at the hospital.

Two emergency responders under one roof, she reflected, and somehow the most urgent crisis remained the one they couldn't seem to resolve at their own kitchen table.

FOUR

The early spring sun had climbed above the hilly horizon, warming the quiet residential street where Deputy Sam Chambers stood on the sidewalk outside his newly purchased home. He checked his watch for the third time in fifteen minutes, glancing up and down the street for signs of the plumber who was now officially late.

Sam had bought the small Craftsman six months ago—a modest one-story with blue paint peeling at the corners and a yard that needed more attention than his work schedule allowed. The "For Sale" sign had barely been removed when his fellow deputies decided to "help", creating a running list of everything that needed fixing, from the sagging porch steps to the ancient boiler that groaned like a wounded animal whenever someone took a shower.

But it was his. After years of apartment living in Portland, dealing with each rent increase, Sam finally had something permanent. Something that couldn't be taken away with a thirty-day notice. The mortgage payments stretched his deputy's salary thin, but the pride of ownership made beans and rice for dinner worth it.

"Morning there, young man." The voice startled Sam, pulling him from his thoughts.

Margaret Holloway stood at the edge of her immaculately maintained lawn next door, gardening gloves covered in soil, her gray hair perfectly set despite the early hour. At seventy-eight, she maintained a vigilance over the neighborhood that made the Stillwater Sheriff's Department seem lax by comparison.

"Good morning, Mrs. Holloway," Sam replied, offering a polite smile. In the months since moving in, he'd learned that engaging with his neighbors was unavoidable, a mandatory toll for living on Maple Street.

"Waiting for someone?" she asked, eyes narrowing slightly as she surveyed him. Her gaze lingered a moment too long, most likely judging his dark skin, the silent assessment so familiar Sam barely registered it anymore.

"Plumber," he explained, deliberately ignoring her obvious appraisal. "Got a leak in the basement."

Mrs. Holloway nodded slowly, as if confirming something to herself. "Well, that's good. I saw you standing out here and thought maybe there was trouble. Can't be too careful these days, what with all these new people from the city moving in." She paused, then added, as if to soften the judgement, "I'm sure you see a lot of that at work."

Sam maintained his professional smile, the one he'd perfected during traffic stops with drivers who made similar veiled comments. "No trouble, ma'am. Just homeowner problems."

"You know, my grandson is very handy with plumbing," she continued, brightening. "He could have fixed it for you. Probably for half what those companies charge. They always overcharge, you know. Especially for people like you."

The implication hung in the air—that Sam, as a young black man, would naturally be taken advantage of by service providers. The assumption was wrapped in just enough concern to maintain deniability.

"I appreciate the thought," Sam replied evenly, "but the department has a recommended contractor list. Sheriff Cain insisted."

Mentioning his boss's name worked as expected. Mrs. Holloway straightened slightly, her attitude shifting. "Well, if Martin recommended them, they must be good. He's always been so particular about these things. Known him since he was knee-high to a grasshopper, you know. His mother and I were in the same bridge club for thirty years."

Sam nodded, having heard variations of this claim from nearly every elderly resident in Stillwater. Sheriff Cain existed in a web of connections that spanned generations—a stark contrast to Sam's recent arrival and outsider status.

A white van turned onto Maple Street, the words "Thomas & Sons Plumbing & Heating" emblazoned on its side in faded blue lettering. Sam felt a wave of relief as it pulled to the curb in front of his house.

"That's my appointment," he said, already stepping away. "Have a good day, Mrs. Holloway."

"You too, Deputy. And remember what I said about my grandson. For next time." She returned to her gardening, but Sam could feel her watchful gaze following him as he approached the van.

The plumber who emerged was a surprise—a woman in her forties with streaks of gray in her dark ponytail and arms corded with muscle from years of wrenching pipes. She extended a calloused hand. "Linda Thomas. You called about a leak?"

"Sam Chambers," he replied, shaking her hand. "Thanks for coming out. It's in the basement."

Linda retrieved a heavy toolbox from the van, following Sam up the walkway to his front door. "First house?" she asked as they entered.

Sam nodded, leading her through the small living room where moving boxes still stood in half-unpacked clusters. "That obvious?"

"You've got the look," Linda chuckled. "Part pride, part terror. I see it a lot."

"My friends convinced me buying was better than renting," Sam explained as they navigated toward the basement door off the kitchen. "Nobody mentioned how much maintenance was involved."

"Friends who recommend homeownership usually leave that part out," Linda agreed. She paused with her hand on the knob of the basement door. "Sort of like people who tell you having kids is great but forget to mention the sleepless nights and college tuition."

The basement steps creaked ominously as they descended, each wooden tread protesting beneath their weight. Sam clicked on the single bulb dangling from the ceiling, its weak glow barely penetrating the corners of the stone foundation basement. The cement room was mostly bare, lit sparingly by the small windows at the merger of the foundation and the walls, the glass covered with a wire mesh, most likely to keep animals out, Sam assumed. The creaky boiler moaned in the corner. A washer and dryer sat beside the boiler, old but serviceable.

"It's over here," he said, pointing toward the back wall where a thin spray of water arced from a copper pipe, splashing persistently onto the concrete floor. "Started yesterday. I put a bucket under it, but…" The bucket was overflowing.

Linda peered at the leak, examining it with practiced eyes. "Pin-hole leak in the copper. Not uncommon in these older homes. Minerals in the water eventually eat through. The public water here is pretty hard." She traced the pipe's path with her eyes. "How old's the house?"

"Built in 1937," Sam said, recalling the disclosure statement he'd signed without fully understanding the implications of buying a house that was older than most of Stillwater's residents.

Linda whistled low. "A lot of this looks like original plumbing." Her eyes traced back to the boiler in the corner. "That looks like a classic."

"It does," Sam admitted, suddenly feeling defensive of his purchase. "The inspector said it was in good shape for its age."

"Home inspectors," Linda muttered, shaking her head. "Nine times out of ten, they're former real estate agents who took a weekend course. They wouldn't know good plumbing from a garden hose."

Sam watched Linda work, her efficiency proof of her years of experience. She quickly identified the valve that fed the pipe, spinning it closed before returning to her toolbox.

She extracted a torch and some solder, working efficiently to patch the leak. As she worked, her eyes scanned the basement's infrastructure with professional assessment. "Your main issue isn't this pin-hole. It's that you've got mixed metals throughout the system—copper, galvanized steel, and some PEX near the water heater. Creates electrolysis, speeds up corrosion."

Sam tried to follow her explanation, but most of it sailed over his head. He'd spent years learning the intricacies of law enforcement, memorizing codes and procedures, but home maintenance remained a foreign language.

"How bad is it?" he asked, bracing for the answer.

Linda shrugged, focusing on the repair. "You're not in immediate danger, but I'd budget for replumbing in the next five years. Sooner if you start seeing more of these leaks."

Sam suppressed a groan. He could only imagine how much a project like that might cost, and on his salary he knew it would take years to cover, especially with property taxes and insurance constantly creeping upward.

"And your propane gas line isn't bonded," Linda added, nodding toward a black pipe running along the ceiling joists.

"Bonded?" Sam repeated, the term completely unfamiliar.

"Electrically bonded," Linda clarified. "Gas lines need to be connected to your electrical grounding system. Prevents static discharge that could ignite leaking gas. Especially important with propane—it's heavier than air, settles in low spots like basements."

The implication sent a chill down Sam's spine. "That sounds dangerous."

"No immediate danger, but it's not up to code," Linda said diplomatically. "I'd get it fixed soon. I'll give you a quote."

Sam nodded, mentally reshuffling his budget to accommodate yet another unexpected expense.

As Linda finished patching the leak, she glanced around the basement once more. "Got another way out of here besides those stairs? Building code requires two exits from basement spaces sometimes, depending on what you use it for."

"There's a storm door," Sam replied, pointing to the metal doors visible at ground level across the room. "But I haven't used it since I moved in."

Linda set her torch down, then crossed the basement, pushing up on the doors. "It's locked from the outside. Probably just someone padlocked it. You should get that fixed too—if there's a fire upstairs, you'd want another way out."

Sam nodded, adding it to his mental list of repairs. The list that had started with "paint bedroom" and "replace kitchen faucet" had now expanded to include items like "prevent potential gas explosion" and "ensure alternative escape route from fiery death."

Linda packed up her tools, having successfully stopped the leak. "Good news is, the pin-hole is fixed. Bad news is, there's probably more where that came from. Old pipes are like old people—once they start complaining, they rarely stop."

Sam followed her back upstairs. He cast a glance at the ancient boiler lurking in the corner like a slumbering beast, the maze of pipes disappearing into shadowed recesses. The storm door that offered no actual escape. The unbonded gas line. His sanctuary suddenly felt more like a money pit with malevolent intent.

In the kitchen, Linda wrote up an invoice, adding a separate quote for bonding the gas line. The figure made Sam blink twice, but he signed without comment. Some expenses couldn't be postponed, regardless of budget constraints.

"I'll call later and set a time to come do that gas line," Linda added. "It won't take long but I need different equipment."

"No problem, and thanks for coming out so quickly," Sam said as he walked her to the door.

"No problem. Always happy to help Stillwater's finest." Linda shook his hand with a sympathetic smile. "Don't let it get you down. Every homeowner goes through this phase. Eventually, you either learn to fix things yourself or marry someone handy."

Sam laughed despite his financial anxiety. "I'll keep that in mind for future dating criteria."

As Linda's van pulled away from the curb, Sam stood on his front porch, surveying his modest property with new eyes. The peeling paint on the eaves. The sagging gutter above the side window. The aging roof shingles that the inspector had described as "nearing end of service life."

Each observation represented future expenses, future weekends sacrificed to maintenance, future skills he'd need to acquire. For a moment, he questioned his decision—the apartment life suddenly seemed simpler, with its maintenance requests and property managers.

The crackle of his radio interrupted his spiral of homeowner anxiety. He reached for it instinctively, the transmission partially garbled by Stillwater's notoriously spotty radio coverage.

"—all units—10-32 at Stillwater River — bridge —" The voice faded into static before returning. "—respond—"

A drowning. Sam was already moving before conscious thought fully formed, training overriding all other concerns. He ducked inside to grab his keys from the entry table, homeowner worries instantly replaced by professional focus.

As he jogged to his department vehicle parked at the curb, Sam cast one final glance at his little blue house. Despite the leaking pipes, the ungrounded gas line, and the seemingly endless list of repairs, it was still his. His anchor in Stillwater, his commitment to this community he'd chosen to serve.

The cruiser's engine roared to life, and Sam pulled away from the curb, lights flashing as he responded to the call. Behind him, Mrs. Holloway watched his departure from her garden, shaking her head slightly at the abrupt exit of her new neighbor. Stillwater had always been a quiet town where everyone knew everyone else's business. The presence of this young deputy—so obviously from somewhere else, with his Portland education and city ways—represented change in a community that had remained largely unchanged for generations.

Whether that change would be for better or worse remained to be seen. But as Mrs. Holloway returned to her gardening, one thing was certain—Stillwater was evolving, and not everyone, herself included, was comfortable with the direction it was taking.

FIVE

The Stillwater River didn't care about the spectacle it had created. It continued its lazy morning journey around the bend, gurgling over rocks with the same indifference it had shown yesterday, before it had become a crime scene. Roadside, three police vehicles parked off the pavement, orange emergency cones had been laid out around the curve, a warning to slow down on a road known for its share of high speed accidents.

Sheriff Cain's boots crunched on gravel as he emerged from the Bronco, squinting against the morning light. He straightened his uniform shirt, tugging it down over his belt where it had bunched during the drive. The familiar weight of his badge caught the sunlight, throwing a small burst of gold across the ground.

Twenty feet away, Deputy Sam Chambers finished laying out the last cone on the road, his car idling nearby, lights flashing a warning to approaching motorists. The young deputy had only been with the department six months, and though his training exceeded even Cain's background he was still young, and the other deputies still gave him the menial jobs, including traffic duty.

"They got you on lookout?" Cain asked with a friendly smile. Didn't want to tease the new kid too hard; Sam was a good one. He had high hopes for the new deputy.

"Just got here myself. I'm trying to relay radio communications. Nobody is getting anything out from the river bank." Sam lifted the crackling radio in his hand, its static punctuated by unintelligible fragments of voices.

Cain nodded. The radios in Stillwater had been a going concern since his predecessor installed the tower on Bunker Hill. No matter how many budget appropriations he convinced the town council to give them, there was something about the geography around this river that made radio waves fail. The combination of iron-rich hills, the valley's peculiar bowl shape, and the dense tree cover created what the technicians called a "communication shadow" across half the county.

During budget meetings, Cain had explained it a dozen different ways—showing maps with the dead zones outlined in red, bringing in experts who used terms like "signal degradation" and "topographical interference." The council would nod, approve a modest increase for better equipment, and the problem would persist.

It was just one more challenge of policing Stillwater—a town where even technology seemed determined to keep its secrets. It made the sheriff's work that much harder, forcing his deputies to relay messages in person, use cell phones which managed more often than not to work when radios couldn't, or drive to higher ground just to report their findings. In emergencies, those extra minutes could make all the difference.

"That way?" Cain asked, nodding toward the narrow dirt path leading down to the riverbank.

Sam nodded. "Yes, Sir."

Cain gave a perfunctory nod, then glanced at the blind curve in the road just fifty yards away, and the cones laid out. "You put those cones out?" Sam nodded, sheepish.

"Yes, Sir. Hate to see some kids screaming around that bend and be surprised by all these cars parked here."

"Make that the last time you call me 'Sir'," Cain said, then, "good job." He turned away, heading toward the matted grass that constituted the start of the trail to the scene. Cain allowed himself a small smile. Enthusiasm hadn't been beaten out of the kid yet. That was something.

The path down to the river was steep and damp from the morning dew. Cain's boots slid slightly on patches of mud, forcing him to grab at saplings for balance. The sounds of activity reached him before he could see the scene – terse commands, the splash of water, the creaking strain of rope.

And then he emerged into the clearing by the riverbank and the tableau unfurled before him.

Two deputies—Dale Weathers and Mike Hargrove—were red-faced and straining against thick ropes that disappeared into the water. The object of their struggle was a section of old wire fencing that appeared to have been pulled down into the river. Beneath it lay the victim he assumed, though from this distance, all he could make out was a human form trapped in the shallows.

Deputy Carol Rivers stood thigh-deep in the river, her waders splashed with mud and river detritus as she tried to maneuver the body free. A few yards away, a boy and his father stood huddled together, looking shell-shocked. Deputy Louis Gantry was taking their statement, his pen moving steadily across his notepad.

"Come on, guys!" Carol shouted as the ropes suddenly started to slacken.

The fence shifted dangerously, nearly collapsing back onto her and the body. Dale and Mike lunged forward, regaining tension on the lines just in time.

"Sorry!" Dale called back, his face flushing darker.

Cain picked his way down to the water's edge, careful not to disturb any potential evidence. The image of the body hit him – the distinctive bloat, evidence that it had been in water for some time. No smell, the cold water keeping it at bay, with only the mineral tang of the river and the green scent of crushed vegetation in the air.

"Morning, Sheriff," Louis said, breaking away from the father and son. "Mark here spotted the body."

"Came down to smoke, didn't you," his dad mumbled, gripping his son's shoulder.

The boy—Mark—couldn't have been more than twelve. His face was ashen, eyes wide and fixed on the activity in the water, a new rod and reel laying at his feet, forgotten. His father had an arm around his shoulders, fingers digging into the boy's jacket as if he might float away without the anchor. Both protective and controlling, his anger masked by his concern for what his son had found.

"How you holding up, son?" Cain asked, ignoring his father's accusations.

Mark's gaze flicked to him, then away. "I just wanted to try out my new rod," he whispered.

Cain nodded, noting the boy's trembling shoulders. "That's a tough thing to see. You did the right thing calling it in."

A splash and grunt from the water drew their attention. Carol had managed to free the body from under the fence and was now guiding it toward the shore. The Deputies on the ropes maintained tension, ensuring the fence wouldn't collapse back into the river.

"Got him," Carol called, her voice tight with exertion.

The body emerged from the water like a grotesque parody of birth. Its skin had gone waxy and blue-white, bloated from days in the water, clothes—what remained of them—hung in tatters around the frame, except for a pair of rubber waders, which maintained their integrity.

Carol crouched near the body, her blue nitrile gloves stark against the mud as she carefully examined the fishing line still wrapped around the victim's boot. She tucked a strand of blonde hair back under her cap, her movements precise and methodical.

"Looks like Jackson McKenzie," she said, shaking her head softly as the sheriff moved over to look over hear shoulder.

Deputy Rich Mathews stood nearby, taking photographs from various angles, cataloging the scene. "Bet the fish are disappointed," he remarked, lowering his camera. "They finally had human on the menu and someone took away their lunch."

"Jesus, Rich," Carol hissed. "Have some respect."

Rich shrugged, his lean face breaking into the smirk that had earned him two divorces and more bar fights than he cared to remember. "Just saying what everyone's thinking. Lightens the mood."

"How long you think he's been here?" Cain asked.

Carol glanced at her watch. "Based on body temp and the lividity, I'd say since early Tuesday morning. ME will confirm, but figure 60, maybe 72 hours."

Sheriff Cain crouched beside her, examining the body without touching it. "Fishing accident?"

"That's what it looked like at first," Carol said, her voice dropping slightly. "He's got waders on, probably lost his footing. People have accidents every spring when the water's high and cold."

From the river, Dale held up a section of rusty fencing. "Look at this. I'm guessing it's what pinned him down."

Sheriff Cain frowned, his weathered face creasing deeper around the eyes. "Old fence gave way? Not surprising. There's farm equipment from the fifties still rotting out here."

Carol exchanged a glance with Dale before reaching for an evidence bag. "This is the fishing line that was caught around his boot." She held up the bag containing a thick, braided line. "It's not his. His rod and reel are standard fly fishing gear, lightweight monofilament. This is heavy-duty stuff, Sheriff. The kind you'd use for deep sea fishing, not trout."

"Could be from another fisherman," the Sheriff suggested. "That stuff gets tangled up in debris all the time."

"Maybe," Carol conceded. "But there's more." She pointed to the fence post still embedded in the mud near the victim. "Take a look."

Sheriff Cain moved closer, bending to examine the broken wooden post.

"See how it snapped?" Carol said, joining him. "Clean break, but if you look closely..." She pointed to the exposed wood grain. "It's been cut through most of the way. Just enough left to hold it upright until pressure was applied."

The Sheriff's eyes narrowed as he inspected the post. "You sure? Could be rot. Wood gets waterlogged, develops weak points."

Dale stepped forward. "I've repaired enough fences to know the difference, Sheriff. That's not rot. Someone took a saw to that."

A heavy silence fell between them. The implications hung in the air like the morning mist that still clung to the distant trees.

"And the fishing line was tied to the fence panel," Carol added quietly. "When he caught his boot and pulled hard enough, it triggered the whole thing. The fence was dragged right over him."

Sheriff Cain straightened, removing his hat, running a hand through his hair, then replaced it carefully.

"Let's keep this between us for now," he said, voice low and controlled. "No sense causing a panic before we're certain."

"Are you thinking what I'm thinking?" Rich asked, his typical smirk replaced by something more serious.

The Sheriff's jaw tightened. "I'm not thinking anything yet. We need facts, not theories." He turned to the group. "Carol, I want samples of that cut, the fishing line, everything. Rich, get pictures of it all."

"What about the ME?" Carol asked. "I called him on the way in. Should be here within the hour. Do I share any of this with him?"

"Let's not get ahead of ourselves. Could still be an accident— maybe someone started to cut that fence weeks ago for scrap or something, never finished the job."

Dale opened his mouth to respond but stopped abruptly, his eyes focused on something behind the Sheriff. "We've got company."

Sheriff Cain turned to see a man in his thirties making his way through the trees, camera slung around his neck, notebook in hand. He wore hiking boots and a flannel shirt with jeans, looking more like a local than a tourist, but the camera marked him clearly enough.

"That's Steve Wilson from the Stillwater Gazette," Dale muttered. "Must have heard the call on his scanner."

"Wonderful," Sheriff Cain muttered. He straightened his shoulders and raised his voice. "That's far enough, Wilson. This is a crime scene."

"Can we go now," the boy's father asked Louis. "He's missed half the school day already."

"Sheriff?" Cain glanced over and gave a slight nod before turning back to the conversation.

"Sure," Louis said, closing his notebook. "You're all good to go."

Mark stood, shouldering his backpack, still shaken from his gruesome discovery. He turned to his father. "Who's Jackson

McKenzie?" Then to the deputy, "It was an accident, right? He just fell in?"

Louis's round face remained neutral. "That's what we're here to figure out, son."

"Come on," the father urged, giving his son a gentle push forward. "Let's get you to school." They passed the reporter who moved to try and stop the father and son.

"Can I ask you a few questions," he blurted out but Cain grabbed his shoulder, steering him away from the father and son, who hurried back up the trail.

"We have a deceased male, identified as a local resident," Cain said, encouraging Wilson to write down the statement. "We'll release the name later, after next of kin are notified. Cause of death hasn't been determined. That's all I can share right now."

"Come on, Sheriff. I heard the kid mention Jackson McKenzie," the reporter said, writing the name down. "The guy who lives out on County Road 8, right? Retired from the lumber mill about a decade ago. Is that who it is?"

The Sheriff's expression didn't change. "We'll release more information after we notify next of kin. Don't print that, Steve. Let me confirm everything first, please." Wilson hesitated then nodded, scratching out the name, but he pressed on.

"Any signs of foul play," Wilson asked.

"As I said, the investigation is ongoing." Sheriff Cain's tone made it clear the conversation was over. "Now if you'll excuse me, I need to get back to work."

The reporter didn't move. "People have a right to know if there's a threat, Sheriff."

Something flashed in Cain's eyes—irritation, or perhaps something deeper. "What people have a right to is accurate information, not speculation. When we have facts, you'll get your story."

Behind them, Carol continued her methodical work, carefully cataloging pieces of fencing and post from multiple angles as Rich took pictures.

Sheriff Cain watched Mark and his father disappear into the trees, then turned his attention back to the reporter. "I'll call you when we have something official to release, Steve. That's the best I can do."

The reporter studied the Sheriff's face for a moment. "Off the record, Martin—should people be concerned?"

The Sheriff's expression remained impassive. "People should always be concerned. That's what keeps them safe."

SIX

The Fruit Loops swirled in Carter's bowl, a kaleidoscope of artificial color drowning in milk gone lukewarm. He jabbed at them mechanically, the tinny scrape of spoon against ceramic echoing in the empty kitchen. Morning light filtered weakly through yellowed curtains that hadn't been washed in too many years to count.

The plastic shopping bag from his dawn excursion sat crumpled on the table beside the milk jug, its contents already put away with methodical precision. Everything in its place. Order in a house that time was slowly dismantling.

Carter lifted another spoonful to his mouth, tasting nothing. The house pressed in around him—crowded with porcelain figurines collecting dust, surfaces covered with doilies gone gray, walls decorated with faded photographs of people he'd never met. The air hung thick with the unmistakable scent of elderly decay—mothballs, potpourri that had lost its fragrance years ago, and the medicinal undertone that followed his grandmother everywhere.

When he finished, Carter rose and carried his bowl to the sink. He turned the water to precisely warm, applied exactly three drops of dish soap, and washed the bowl with circular motions, moving from rim to base. He rinsed it thoroughly—twice—before placing it upside down in the plastic drying rack.

He dried his hands on the threadbare kitchen towel and headed for the living room, his footsteps light against the worn linoleum.

Eloise Thompson sat enthroned in her recliner, the leather cracked like the skin of her hands. She stared at the television where a man with too-white teeth enthusiastically demonstrated some kitchen gadget that promised to revolutionize vegetable chopping. Static rippled across the screen every few seconds, obscuring the image before reluctantly yielding again.

An oxygen tank squatted beside her chair like a sentinel, the clear plastic tubing snaking up to her nostrils. Each breath wheezed in and out, her chest rising with visible effort, but her expression remained placid. The struggle for air had become so constant that she no longer noticed its labor.

Carter approached from behind, his shadow falling across her thinning hair, once auburn, now faded to the color of weak tea.

"I'm going to school, gram." He pointed to the small plastic container on the side table. A single white pill sat forlornly inside. "You didn't take your pill. You need to take it."

Eloise's gaze remained fixed on the television. "I made you a lunch, Robert."

A muscle twitched in Carter's jaw. "I'm Carter. But thanks, gram."

He reached forward, his hand hovering for a moment before making contact with her papery skin. His fingertips barely grazed the archipelago of liver spots that mapped her hand.

With startling quickness, Eloise's fingers clamped around his wrist. Carter froze, caught off guard by the strength still hidden in those bony fingers.

She twisted in her chair, her rheumy eyes suddenly sharp with recognition. "Don't leave, Robert. Stay with me."

The plea filled the stale air between them. Tears welled in her eyes, transforming them into cloudy pools of desperation. For a moment, she was fully present, fully aware of something—someone—that wasn't there.

Carter's throat constricted. These flashes of lucidity were worse than the confusion. "Robert died, gran. I'm Carter, his son."

The words struck her like a physical blow. Her fingers went slack, releasing him as suddenly as they'd grabbed hold. She turned back to the television, expression vacant once more. It was as if the moment had never happened, though a single tear still clung to the edge of her eyelid, refusing to fall.

Carter stood motionless, watching her. The oxygen machine hissed. The infomercial host laughed at his own joke. The tear finally surrendered to gravity and traced a lonely path down Eloise's cheek. She didn't brush it away.

He shook his head and retreated to the kitchen.

The refrigerator hummed its monotonous song as Carter pulled open the door. Cool air billowed around his face. Between a jar of applesauce and a carton of eggs sat a brown paper bag, neatly folded at the top. His grandmother's handiwork from a moment of rare clarity.

He grabbed it, not bothering to look inside. Whatever was in there—a sandwich turning stale, fruit browning at the edges—he would eat it. It was easier than explaining why he couldn't.

He stepped outside, pulling the door firmly shut behind him. The lock engaged with a definitive click that was accompanied by a subtle yet perceptible ease in Carter's shoulders.

Carter stood on the path from his house, backpack slung over one shoulder, the weight of another school day already pressing down on him. He suddenly decided he should see, dropping his backpack off his shoulder and opening it up, unfolding the brown paper sack, and peering inside. A single slice of white bread stared back at him, slightly curled at the edges. No peanut butter. No jelly. Just bread.

"Shit," he muttered, rolling the top of the bag closed. His stomach growled in protest, but he stuffed the pathetic lunch into his backpack anyway. Since his parents' accident, food had become an afterthought in the Thompson household. His grandmother tried, but her memory wasn't what it used to be, and he rarely thought about it himself.

He exhaled a long breath that hung visible in the October air, shoulders slumping in resignation. Just another day.

"Morning, Carter."

The voice startled him. Laura Cain stood at the end of her driveway next door, wrestling a garbage can to the curb. Her brown hair was pulled back in a messy ponytail, her hospital scrubs covered by a loose coat cinched tight against the morning chill.

"Hi, Mrs. Cain," Carter replied, forcing his voice to sound normal. How long had she been watching him?

Laura dragged the can into place, then crossed her arms against the cold. "You heading to school?"

"Yeah." He shifted his weight, uncomfortable with the attention. The concern in her eyes made it clear she'd seen enough to know something wasn't right.

"Everything going okay over there?" She nodded toward his house.

"Fine," Carter said too quickly. "Gran's just sleeping in."

Laura took a few steps closer, lowering her voice. "You know, if you ever need to talk about anything, our door's always open. A hot meal, too."

The kindness in her voice threatened to crack something inside him. Carter straightened his spine, armoring himself. "Thanks, but we're good. Really."

"Well." Laura rubbed her hands together against the cold. "Do you see Mary much at school? I hardly ever hear her mention you these days."

Heat crawled up Carter's neck at the mention of Mary Cain. Seventeen, a year older than him, with her mother's brown eyes and a laugh that made his chest hurt. He'd known her since elementary school, but his own life's tragedies had erected invisible walls between them.

"Not really," he mumbled, studying the sidewalk cracks. "We run in different circles."

"And what circle do you run in?"

Carter shrugged. "They don't make a circle for one."

Laura decided it was best to change the subject. "How's that detective agency of yours going? Mary mentioned you were solving something about missing lunch money?"

At this, Carter's eyes lit up. The heaviness lifted momentarily from his shoulders.

"It's not really an agency," he said, a hint of animation entering his voice. "More like... I notice things. The lunch money thing was easy once I figured out the pattern. Someone was hitting lockers during fourth period gym, but only on Mondays when —"

"Mom!" A sharp voice called from the Cain's front door. Mary stood framed in the doorway, her hair a work in progress for the day. "Phone call! It's work!"

Laura sighed. "Coming!" She turned back to Carter, already retreating. "Sorry—we'll catch up later, okay? Don't be a stranger."

"Sure, Mrs. Cain," Carter said, but she was already halfway up the driveway.

He watched her disappear inside. The brief spark of connection extinguished as quickly as it had ignited. The familiar cloak of isolation settled back around his shoulders.

Carter turned away, grabbing his bike from where it lay on the browning lawn. The chain still needed oil. The frame squeaked in protest as he swung his leg it. One pedal was missing its rubber grip, the metal rough against his worn sneaker.

As he pushed off toward school, the silent houses of Stillwater stared back at him, windows like vacant eyes. As a younger boy, the town had seemed vibrant and exciting. Now it was lifeless to him, just he and his grandmother holding on to the edges of a life that kept threatening to unravel completely.

He pedaled harder, the cold air stinging his eyes. The pathetic lunch and Mrs. Cain's pity faded behind him as he focused on the road ahead—cracked, neglected, but still leading somewhere. At least for now.

Laura Cain closed the front door, shutting out the morning chill and Carter's retreating figure. The phone call from the hospital lay waiting, the handset still askew on the counter.

"This is Laura Cain," she said. She nodded in response, acknowledging. "I'm headed in now." She hung up and paused, trying to take even a minute of silence before her own day exploded into medical emergencies.

She moved to the bottom of the stairs, listening to the chaos of Mary's morning routine—drawers slamming, music thumping, muttered curses that Laura pretended not to hear. Seventeen looked different than she remembered. More anger, less forgiveness.

"Mom!" Mary's voice crashed down the stairwell. "Where's my blue blouse? The one with the buttons?"

Laura exhaled slowly, counting to three before responding. "Did you check the laundry basket in the hall? I folded it yesterday."

Only silence answered her. Then the thunder of footsteps as Mary appeared at the top of the stairs, hair wild around her shoulders, eyes narrowed with frustration. She wore jeans and a white bra, feet bare against the hardwood.

"It's not there," she stated flatly. "I need it for my presentation."

Laura climbed the stairs, each step a deliberate choice to remain calm. The house felt too small these days, as if the walls had inched closer while she slept. Or perhaps it was just that her daughter seemed to take up more space with her mood than her physical presence.

The laundry basket sat exactly where Laura had left it—on the hall table outside Mary's bedroom. A neat stack of folded clothes waited for their return to drawers and hangers, casualties of a teenage schedule that never included putting things away.

"Right here," Laura said, extracting the pale blue blouse from beneath a pair of jeans. She held it out, careful to keep accusation from her voice. "Third item down."

Mary took it from her mom with a grateful look, retreating into her bedroom while wrestling her arms through the sleeves. "I swear I looked," she responded, the words barely audible. Laura smiled. Just like her father.

She paused in the doorway, surveying the battlefield of her daughter's room. Clothing draped every surface, textbooks splayed open on the desk, makeup scattered across the vanity like casualties of war. The walls were plastered with posters of bands Laura had never heard of—angry young men screaming into microphones, their faces contorted with emotions too raw for their age.

She watched as Mary buttoned the blouse with quick, efficient movements. Her daughter's hands were beautiful—long fingers, clean nails, knuckles that still dimpled when she made a fist. Those hands had once reached for hers without hesitation. Now they seemed perpetually busy with other things.

"I saw Carter outside," Laura ventured, picking her way through the invisible minefield of teenage sensitivity. "He looked tired."

Mary's fingers stilled momentarily on a button before resuming their work. "Yeah?" The word carried no particular inflection, which made it more dismissive than any tone could have.

"Just wondered if you see much of him at school these days."

Mary's shoulders tensed, subtle but unmistakable. "Not really. We have different classes."

"I remember when you two were inseparable," Laura continued, leaning against the doorframe. "All those hours building forts in the backyard. And that detective club you started in fifth grade." She smiled at the memory. "You made me buy you those little notebooks with the spiral tops."

"I remember," Mary said, a tinged of sadness in her voice. She reached for a hairbrush, attacking her tangled hair with unnecessary force. "But that feels like a million years ago."

"Three years isn't exactly ancient history."

Mary met her eyes in the mirror, brush suspended mid-stroke. "What do you want me to say? We're not friends anymore. People change."

Laura crossed her arms, studying her daughter's profile. The stubborn set of her jaw—that was all Martin. The flash of defensiveness in her eyes—that came from somewhere deeper in the genetic pool, perhaps Laura's own mother.

"I'm not saying you have to be best friends again," Laura said carefully. "But it wouldn't hurt to be kind to him. After what happened with his parents—"

"I know what happened to his parents," Mary interrupted, her voice tight. "Everyone knows. It's Stillwater." She resumed brushing, each stroke more aggressive than necessary. "It's not like I'm mean to him or anything. We just don't talk."

Laura watched her daughter's reflection, noting the flush that had crept up her neck. Guilt, perhaps. Or something more complicated. "It would mean a lot to your dad if you made an effort."

The brush clattered onto the vanity. Mary spun to face her mother, eyes suddenly alive with indignation. "Why does it always comes back to Dad? What would make Dad happy? What would make Dad proud? What would help Dad's image in this stupid town?"

The vehemence in her voice startled Laura. "That's not what I —"

"Why do I always have to be the model citizen for him?" Mary continued, her voice rising. "It's not like he's running for president or something. He's just the sheriff!" She snatched her backpack from the floor, stuffing a textbook inside with enough force to bend its cover. "And he's never home anyway, so what does he care who I'm friends with?"

Laura took a step back, suddenly unsure of her footing in this conversation. "Mary, that's not fair. Your father works hard for this town."

"Yeah, well, maybe he should work a little harder at being a parent, and a husband." Mary pushed past her mother into the hallway, backpack slung over one shoulder. "I've got to go. Amber's probably waiting."

Laura followed her to the top of the stairs. "We're not finished with this conversation, Mary Elizabeth."

Mary paused on the first step, one hand on the banister. "Yeah, we are." She descended quickly, each footfall a punctuation mark in her escape.

Laura remained at the top of the stairs, listening as the front door opened and slammed shut. The house settled back into silence, the kind that rang in her ears like an accusation.

She moved to the window overlooking the driveway, watching as Mary stormed toward her friend Amber's waiting car. Her daughter never looked back.

A heaviness settled in Laura's chest as she turned away from the window. The flash of anger in Mary's eyes had revealed something more than teenage rebellion—something closer to genuine hurt. When had that happened? When had Martin's absences graduated from disappointment to damage in their daughter's eyes? Laura took some comfort knowing that their daughter wasn't just angry. Like a diagnosis, there was a cure, and Martin's admission this morning, his seriousness about retiring, might just be the cure they all needed.

Laura made her way downstairs to the kitchen, where the phone lay in its cradle, her fingers lingering on the plastic. She should call Martin. Tell him about this outburst. Warn him that the fragile peace in their household was fracturing in ways she couldn't control.

Instead, she pulled her hand away and reached for her own keys, her final motions before heading to work. Some conversations could wait. Others, she was beginning to realize, had already waited too long.

SEVEN

Carter's breath condensed in the early morning air as he pedaled along the river path, his old bicycle humming beneath him. The decision to take the longer route to school had been spontaneous—a response to his grandmother's confused state that morning, which had delayed his departure by fifteen minutes. The direct route would get him to Stillwater High just before the first bell rang, but the river path offered something more valuable than punctuality: solitude.

The Stillwater River curled through the town like a dark artery, bisecting it between the hillside where most residences perched and the flatter commercial district. Once the lifeblood of local industry, the river now served mainly as a tourist attraction for summer kayakers and a reminder of the town's logging heritage.

Carter's wheels crunched over loose gravel as the path curved alongside a stretch where the riverbank widened into a gravelly beach. Through gaps in the riverside foliage, he caught glimpses of color that didn't belong to the natural landscape—blue tarps stretched between trees, the orange glow of small fires, flashes of movement as people emerged from makeshift shelters.

He slowed, curiosity overriding his schedule. The homeless encampment had grown since he'd last traveled this way. What had been three or four tents a month ago had expanded to at least a dozen structures of varying permanence—everything from proper camping tents to improvised lean-tos constructed from discarded materials.

Carter stopped completely where the path crossed Maple Street, dismounting to walk his bike across the cracked asphalt. On the corner stood Foster's Auto Body, its concrete walls decorated with fading murals of classic cars. The shop wouldn't open for another hour, the parking lot empty except for vehicles awaiting repair.

He leaned his bike against the shop's chain-link fence, extracting a small notebook from his backpack. The elevated vantage point offered a clear view of the encampment, and Carter began making notes—number of tents, visible occupants, recent additions to the community. His precise handwriting filled the page with observations others might consider trivial but which formed part of his ongoing documentation of Stillwater's evolving landscape.

"Spare any change?"

The voice startled him, though he managed not to flinch. Carter turned to find a man standing a few feet away, close enough for conversation but maintaining the careful distance of someone accustomed to being considered a threat.

The man appeared to be in his mid-thirties, though weather and hardship had aged his face beyond his years. His face was scruffy but not unkempt, his clothing worn but deliberately layered against the morning chill, a frayed naval airman's flight jacket under a longer coat. Carter noticed his eyes—bloodshot and tired, with pupils contracted to pinpoints despite the dim morning light. His hands trembled slightly as he rubbed them together, whether from cold or something else, Carter couldn't immediately determine. A distinctive scar adorned the back of his left hand, a detail Carter stored away subconsciously.

"Sorry," Carter replied, closing his notebook. "Don't carry cash."

The man shrugged, producing a half-smile that revealed surprisingly well-maintained teeth, though his gums appeared inflamed. "Worth a shot. Got any pills? Oxy, Vicodin? Anything for pain?"

The directness of the question suggested desperation—a miscalculation of Carter as a potential source rather than calculated risk-taking. Carter noted the man's twitching fingers and slight sheen of sweat despite the morning chill.

"No," Carter answered simply, his tone neutral.

"Right, right. School kid. Of course." The man grimaced, rubbing at his lower back. "Sorry. Bad morning. Back injury from construction work. Doctors won't prescribe anymore, say I've had enough." He extended a slightly trembling hand. "James Kilgore."

Carter hesitated only briefly before shaking the offered hand, noting both its coldness and the surprising strength of the grip. "Carter Thompson."

"Thompson," Kilgore repeated, as if testing the name. His attention sharpened momentarily through what appeared to be a fog of discomfort. "Any relation to Robert Thompson? Used to work at the mill before it closed?"

A small crease appeared between Carter's eyebrows—the only visible indication that the question had affected him. "My father," he said after a pause. "He died. Three years ago."

"Sorry to hear that," Kilgore said, and seemed genuinely so despite his distracted demeanor. "He was a good man. Helped me out once when I was working construction and needed some timber that had been earmarked for scrap. Didn't ask questions, just looked the other way." His hand moved to his side, pressing against his ribs as if containing pain there.

Carter absorbed this new information about his father, filing it away with the meticulous organization that characterized his mental processes. "Were you a pilot?" He motioned to the flight jacket.

"Almost," Kilgore confirmed, swallowing hard. "I was an NFO. Like a flight specialist. F-14's. Always wanted to fly, but shit happens. That's when I first hurt my back. I kinda became a jack of all trades, master of none, as they say. Or I did, until this." He gestured vaguely at his back. "Fell from scaffolding. Third story. VA doctors got me walking again with the help of Oxy, then decided I liked it too much." A bitter laugh escaped him. "Can't imagine why anyone would get attached to not feeling like their spine is on fire."

Carter glanced at his watch, calculating travel time against the school schedule. "I should go."

"Sure, sure. Don't want to make you late." Kilgore stepped back, shoving his trembling hands into his pockets. "Nice talking to someone who doesn't look at me like I'm just another junkie." He turned, moving to the river.

Carter mounted his bike, adjusting his backpack straps with practiced efficiency. He hesitated, an uncharacteristic moment of social uncertainty crossing his features. "The clinic on Park Avenue has a pain management program," he said to Kilgore's back. "No questions asked. They might help."

Kilgore stopped and turned, focused back on Carter, surprise briefly flickering across his weathered face at the unexpected suggestion. "Yeah? Might check that out." The gratitude in his voice seemed genuine, though both knew the likelihood of follow-through was minimal at best.

Carter nodded then pushed off, pedaling with renewed purpose as he continued along Maple Street toward school. After a few hundred yards, he glanced back over his shoulder. Kilgore still stood at the corner, watching him, one hand wiping sweat from his brow. Beyond him, the river continued its steady flow past the encampment, carrying fallen leaves and occasional debris toward the open waters beyond Stillwater's boundaries.

Carter turned forward again, mind already processing the interaction, categorizing it among the countless observations he collected daily. James Kilgore—former construction worker, acquaintance of his father, currently homeless and addicted to prescription painkillers, opioids. A vulnerable population with specific needs and potential leverage points. A data point worth noting.

The school building came into view as Carter rounded the final corner, its brick facade illuminated by the strengthening morning sun. He increased his pace, calculating that he had exactly four minutes to chain his bike and reach his first-period class before the second bell rang.

As he navigated through the morning traffic of students congregating outside the main entrance, Carter's thoughts returned briefly to the river, to the growing encampment, to James Kilgore with his pinpoint pupils and trembling hands. There was something there—a pattern forming, perhaps, or simply another thread in the complex tapestry of Stillwater that Carter was methodically documenting.

Either way, it warranted further investigation. And if there was one thing Carter Thompson excelled at, it was thorough investigation of things others overlooked.

EIGHT

Mary Cain slammed the passenger door of Amber Wilder's Honda Civic, her backpack tumbling onto the floor mat at her feet. The car smelled of vanilla air freshener and the lingering ghost of cigarettes Amber thought no one detected.

"Whoa," Amber said, eyebrows rising above her heavily mascara'd eyes. "Who pissed in your Cheerios this morning?"

Mary slumped against the seat, crossing her arms over her chest. "Just drive."

Amber shrugged and pulled away from the curb, one acrylic nail tapping against the steering wheel in time with the radio. At seventeen, she wore her rebellion more comfortably than Mary—black lipstick, a nose ring she thought her parents still hadn't noticed, and an advanced placement in chemistry that confused everyone who judged by appearances.

"Seriously, what's up?" Amber asked, flicking a glance at Mary's scowling profile. "You look like you're planning a murder."

"My dad," Mary said, the words heavy with teenage disdain. "He's on the same message. 'You don't think about your future! You should be a perfect robot of a daughter!' And then my mom is suddenly on this kick about me being friends with Carter Thompson again. Like we're still ten years old or something."

"Carter?" Amber frowned. "That weird kid who's always writing in those notebooks?"

Mary's jaw tightened. "He's not weird. He's just... different."

"Uh-huh." Amber's tone made it clear she wasn't convinced. "Isn't he the one who was asking all those questions about Coach Brenner last semester? Something about suspicious behavior during basketball practice?"

"That was actually legit," Mary said, surprising herself with the quick defense. "Coach was selling prescription pills to some of the seniors. Carter figured it out before anyone else."

Amber shot her a skeptical look as she turned onto Main Street. "And how exactly do you know that?"

Heat crept up Mary's neck. "I just heard about it."

"Right." Amber dragged the word out, infusing it with doubt. "So why does your mom care if you're friends with Nancy Drew?"

Mary sighed, watching as the storefronts of Stillwater slide past the window. The hardware store with its faded awning. The diner where her dad used to take her for breakfast on Saturdays, when he wasn't called away to some emergency. The boarded-up video rental place that had closed three years ago and still stood empty.

"It's not about Carter," she admitted finally. "It's about my dad. She thinks if I'm nice to Carter, it'll make Dad look good or something. Like the sheriff's daughter befriending the orphan boy is some kind of political move."

Amber snorted. "Small town politics. So stupid."

"She actually said it would 'mean a lot to your father,'" Mary mimicked, her voice rising in a poor imitation of her mother's. "As if he gives a shit about anything I do."

"Parents," Amber agreed, though her tone lacked conviction. Her own mother and father maintained a safe, suburban distance from her life—neither intrusive enough to provoke rebellion nor absent enough to cause damage. They existed in a different orbit, making it easy for Amber to dismiss them, something she found she appreciated about them.

Mary's situation was more complicated. Her father's position meant everyone in town knew who she was, which vices she had tried, which parties she had attended. Being Sheriff Cain's daughter came with a spotlight she never asked for and couldn't escape.

"It's just..." Mary hesitated, searching for words that wouldn't make her sound pathetic. "He's never there, you know? But everyone expects me to act like I'm so proud of him. Like having a dad who's never home is some kind of achievement."

Amber turned into the school parking lot, navigating between rows of cars toward their usual spot near the back fence. "At least your dad does something important. Mine sells insurance."

"Yeah, but he's home for dinner every night, isn't he?"

The question hung between them as Amber parked and cut the engine. In the sudden silence, Mary could hear the distant shouts of students gathering on the front lawn, the bass thump of music from a nearby car, the rhythmic tick of the cooling engine.

"Look," Amber said finally, turning to face her. "If it bugs you so much, just tell your dad. He can't fix what he doesn't know is broken, right?"

"It's not that simple."

"It never is, Mary." Amber reached for her purse in the backseat. "But you could at least try talking to him before you take it out on everyone else."

Mary stared at her friend, stung by the casual accuracy of the observation. "I don't take it out on everyone."

Amber raised an eyebrow. "You've been biting my head off for weeks."

"It's not you."

"Sometimes it's hard to tell." Amber opened her door, letting in a rush of cool spring air. "All I'm saying is, I love you, Mary. But maybe try using your words with the actual person you're mad at, instead of spreading the joy around to the rest of us." Amber stepped out of the car, slamming the door before Mary could reply.

Mary felt a flash of anger then, with a leaden feeling that settled in her stomach the anger dissipated, leaving her heavy with the recognition that her friend might be right. She had been more irritable lately, quicker to snap, slower to apologize. The resentment she carried toward her father had become a poison she unwittingly shared with everyone around her.

The first bell rang in the distance, its shrill warning cutting through the morning air. Students began moving toward the building, a reluctant migration of backpacks and youthful faces. The driver side door opened again.

"You coming?" Amber asked, leaning in.

Mary nodded, gathering her backpack from the floor. She climbed out of the car, falling into step beside her friend as they joined the stream of students heading for the main entrance.

They were halfway across the parking lot when Mary spotted him—Carter Thompson, chaining his battered bike to the rack near the side door. His shoulders were hunched against the morning chill, fingers fumbling with the lock. Even from a distance, she could see the frayed edges of his jeans, the worn canvas of his backpack.

For a moment, Mary saw him as he'd been at twelve—gap-toothed grin, endless questions, boundless energy that had both exhausted and exhilarated her. They had been a team once, solving imaginary mysteries in a town too small for real ones.

Then his parents' car had gone off Sawmill Bridge Road, and overnight, Carter had become someone else—quieter, watchful, wrapped in grief like an invisible cloak. And Mary, unable to navigate the new terrain of their friendship, had retreated to safer ground.

"Earth to Mary," Amber waved a hand in front of her face. "You're staring."

Mary blinked, pulling her gaze away from Carter. "No, I wasn't. I was just thinking."

"About what your mom said?" Amber's voice had softened, the earlier irritation replaced by something closer to concern.

"Something like that." Mary adjusted her backpack, feeling the weight of more than just textbooks on her shoulders. "Come on, we're going to be late."

As they climbed the steps to the main entrance, Mary glanced back toward the bike rack. Carter had finished with his lock and was heading for the side door, head down, moving with purpose. For a fraction of a second, she considered calling out to him, bridging the distance with a simple hello.

Instead, she turned and followed Amber into the building, letting the metal door swing shut behind her with a hollow clang that echoed in the empty hallway. Some distances, she was learning, were harder to cross than others.

NINE

The fluorescent lights of Stillwater High's English classroom buzzed overhead like trapped insects, casting a sterile glow over thirty desks arranged in precise rows. Mr. Jennings paced at the front of the room, his wire-rimmed glasses sliding down his nose every few sentences, forcing him to push them back with an index finger stained blue from dry-erase markers.

"So the green light at the end of Daisy's dock represents Gatsby's hopes and dreams," he intoned, voice pitched to the exact frequency guaranteed to induce drowsiness in teenagers. "It's a beacon you see, but also a symbol of everything just beyond his reach."

In the third row, fourth seat from the left, Carter Thompson appeared to be the model student. His copy of "The Great Gatsby" lay propped up on his desk, pages dog-eared and worn. His notebook displayed neat rows of writing, pencil moving steadily across the lined paper. To the casual observer —Mr. Jennings included—Carter was engaged, absorbing the nuances of Fitzgerald's masterpiece with appropriate academic diligence.

The reality, hidden by careful positioning and years of practice, was quite different.

Tucked behind his open book sat a worn paperback with a lurid title: "Blood Evidence: How DNA Revolutionized Crime Investigation." Carter's pencil wasn't capturing insights about

Jazz Age symbolism but rather making notes on blood spatter patterns and the persistence of DNA in adverse environmental conditions. His highlighter marked passages describing how investigators had used luminol to reveal blood washed from a kitchen floor in a 1987 murder case.

While Mr. Jennings droned on about the hollowness of the American Dream, Carter absorbed details of how maggot development could establish time of death. His mind constructed timelines and evidence chains, mentally cataloging techniques he might someday apply to the unsolved mysteries of Stillwater—like who had really broken into the pharmacy last winter, or why Mrs. Davidson's car had been found abandoned by the river five years ago.

"The eyes of Doctor T.J. Eckleburg watch over the valley of ashes," Mr. Jennings continued, sketching a crude pair of glasses on the whiteboard. "They represent the eyes of God, looking down in judgment on the moral wasteland of—"

Carter barely registered the words, lost in a paragraph describing how investigators had matched soil samples from a suspect's boots to a remote grave site. The science of it fascinated him—how the smallest details, invisible to most, could reveal the truth that others wanted to conceal.

"Mr. Thompson."

The silence that followed the teacher's voice took a moment to penetrate Carter's concentration. A sharp kick to his ankle jerked him back to the present. Brandon Miller, slouched in the desk beside him, had delivered the warning blow.

Carter looked up to find Mr. Jennings staring at him, arms crossed over his chest, one eyebrow raised in the expression of a man who has caught precisely what he was fishing for. Thirty pairs of eyes swiveled toward Carter, some gleeful at the prospect of witnessing public humiliation, others wincing in sympathy.

"Welcome back to English class, Mr. Thompson," Mr. Jennings said, sarcasm dripping from each syllable. "I was just asking which character serves as Fitzgerald's most effective commentary on the emptiness of wealth without purpose."

Carter's mind raced. He hadn't been listening. Hadn't even been pretending to listen. The forensics book sat exposed on his desk, its spine creased to stay open to a page featuring grisly crime scene photos. There was no way to hide it now, no plausible deniability.

In the painful silence, he could hear the clock ticking on the wall, each second marking another moment of his impending academic execution. A few students shifted in their seats, the collective tension building as Mr. Jennings waited, triumph already gleaming in his eyes.

"Well, Mr. Thompson?" the teacher prompted again. "Since you were so engrossed in our discussion, I'm sure you have an insightful answer."

Carter closed the forensics book carefully, his face betraying nothing of the panic rising in his chest. This was the part where he was supposed to stammer an apology, admit he hadn't been paying attention, and accept whatever punishment Mr. Jennings deemed appropriate. Detention, probably. Extra homework at minimum.

Instead, Carter looked directly at his teacher and spoke with calm certainty.

"Myrtle Wilson," he said, the name firm on his lips. "She's destroyed by her desire for Tom Buchanan's wealth and status. Her death is literally caused by the gold car—the physical manifestation of Gatsby's fortune. She reaches for something that was never meant for her, and it kills her. Unlike Gatsby, who at least had an idealized love to pursue, Myrtle wants only the trappings of wealth. That emptiness makes her the most effective commentary on how material pursuit without meaning leads to destruction."

The classroom fell silent again, but for a different reason. Mr. Jennings stood frozen, mouth slightly open, clearly unprepared for a response so articulate and accurate. He pushed his glasses up his nose, buying time as he reassessed his target.

"That's... correct," he conceded finally, the admission clearly costing him. "Though I would argue Gatsby himself also represents that emptiness, as his entire fortune was amassed solely to impress Daisy."

Carter nodded once, neither agreeing nor disagreeing. "Their deaths are parallel. Both reached for something unattainable and were destroyed by it."

Mr. Jennings narrowed his eyes, sensing a challenge in Carter's response but unable to find fault with the analysis. "Indeed," he said after a pause, turning back to the class. "As I was saying about the symbolism of the valley of ashes..."

As the teacher resumed his lecture, Carter felt a small surge of satisfaction warm his chest. Not triumph—he took no particular pleasure in showing up Mr. Jennings—but the quiet vindication of being underestimated and proving that assumption wrong. He had read "The Great Gatsby" three times, dissecting it with the same methodical attention he applied to his crime studies. Literature was just another puzzle to solve, another set of clues pointing toward hidden truths.

Brandon leaned over slightly, whispering from the corner of his mouth. "Damn, Thompson. How'd you pull that out of your ass?"

Carter didn't respond, merely allowing the faintest smile to touch his lips before returning to his forensics book. He positioned it more carefully this time, angling the textbook to provide better cover. The smile faded as quickly as it had appeared, replaced by his habitual expression of cold concentration.

These moments of small victory were rare in Carter's life— brief flashes of light in days otherwise filled with responsibility and worry. They weren't enough to change anything. His grandmother would still be sitting in her recliner when he got home, possibly having forgotten to eat lunch. The bills would still be piled on the kitchen counter, their red "PAST DUE" stamps multiplying like a disease. The crack in the bathroom ceiling would continue its slow creep toward the wall.

But for now, for this single moment, Carter had won a tiny battle against the expectations that defined him. Not the troubled orphan. Not the kid with the "situation at home." Just a student who knew the answer when others thought he wouldn't.

He turned a page in his forensics book, immersing himself once more in the science of death and evidence, leaving Gatsby and his green light behind. In Carter's experience, hope was the most dangerous thing a person could possess. Better to deal in facts, in the concrete reality of what could be proven. Dreams, after all, were for people who could afford disappointment.

Carter ignored the occasional glances from classmates and the hollow feeling in his stomach that reminded him lunch was still two periods away. One problem at a time. One page at a time. One moment at a time. That was how survival worked.

And Carter Thompson was nothing if not a survivor.

TEN

The bell rang at 12:15, releasing a flood of students into Stillwater High's hallways. Bodies pushed and flowed like water finding the path of least resistance, voices rising in a cacophony that bounced off metal lockers and linoleum floors. Carter moved against the current, hugging the wall as he made his way toward the library instead of the cafeteria.

The single slice of bread in his lunch bag wasn't worth the social exile of eating alone in a crowded room. Better to find a quiet corner among the books, where solitude was expected rather than pitied, a regular practice for Carter.

He slipped through the library doors, nodding to Mrs. Phelps at the circulation desk. The librarian returned the gesture with only a glance up from her computer, long accustomed to Carter's daily appearance. Their silent agreement—he wouldn't disturb anyone, she wouldn't ask why he preferred books to the company of his peers—had been established long ago.

Carter navigated through the stacks toward his usual spot at a small table tucked between the reference section and a wall of outdated encyclopedias. No one ever came here, not even during finals week when every other surface was claimed by desperate study groups.

He set his backpack on the worn wooden chair and extracted the pathetic lunch, staring at the single slice of bread as if it might somehow multiply under his gaze. His stomach growled in protest, a hollow ache that had become as familiar as the weight of his responsibilities.

"That doesn't look very filling."

Carter startled at the voice, nearly dropping the bread. Mary Cain stood a few feet away, her own lunch tray held in her hands. She wore a blue blouse with jeans, her brown hair pulled back in a simple ponytail. No makeup. No jewelry except small silver studs in her ears. Nothing like the carefully constructed appearances of the popular girls she usually surrounded herself with.

"It's fine," Carter said automatically, his defenses rising. He crumpled the paper bag, shoving it back into his backpack. "I'm not that hungry anyway."

Mary took a step closer, her expression unreadable. "Mind if I sit here?"

The question hung between them, loaded with history and implications Carter couldn't fully decipher. Why now? Why today, after three years of careful distance? Was this some kind of prank? A dare from her friends?

He glanced past her, half-expecting to see Amber or Heather lurking between the bookshelves, giggling behind their hands. But the library remained empty except for Mrs. Phelps and a freshman using the copier near the entrance.

"Suit yourself," Carter replied finally, his tone carefully neutral. "It's a free country, or so we're led to believe."

Mary set her tray on the table and slid into the chair across from him. The plastic tray held the standard school lunch—some kind of salad in clear sauce, a tuna sandwich, an apple, and a carton of milk. Not great, but several orders of magnitude better than his solitary bread slice.

They sat in awkward silence for a moment, the years of estrangement stretching between them like a physical barrier. Carter stared at his backpack, wishing he could extract his forensics book without drawing attention to it. Mary picked at her salad with a fork, separating the wilted lettuce as if conducting an autopsy.

"So," she said finally, "I heard you got Mr. Jennings good in English today."

Carter shrugged. "Not really. I just answered his question."

"That's not how Brandon tells it. He said you were reading something else the whole time, then dropped a perfect analysis of Gatsby out of nowhere."

"Brandon talks too much," Carter muttered, uncomfortable with being the subject of hallway gossip.

Mary took a bite of salad, grimacing slightly at the taste. "What were you actually reading?"

For a moment, Carter considered lying. Making up something less revealing, less potentially weird. But some remnant of their old friendship—the trust that had once existed between two kids who shared comic books and secrets—made him reach into his backpack and extract the forensics book.

He placed it on the table between them, its cover facing up. The title "Blood Evidence" stood out in bold red letters against a black background. Below it, a stylized crime scene photo showed a room illuminated by ultraviolet light, fluorescent blue stains vivid against the darkness.

Mary stared at it, fork suspended halfway to her mouth. "Light bedtime reading?"

Despite himself, Carter felt the corner of his mouth twitch upward. "It's interesting."

"It's morbid," Mary countered, but there was no judgment in her voice. She set down her fork and picked up the book, examining the cover more closely. "Though I guess it makes sense."

"What does?"

"You were always into solving mysteries." She flipped the book over to read the back cover. "Remember that detective club we had in fifth grade? You made us take fingerprints of everyone in class for your 'database.' I'm sure there was something ethically questionable that the teacher let you do that. "

The memory surfaced unexpectedly—Mary and him crouched behind Mrs. Prentice's desk after school, dusting the surface with cocoa powder "borrowed" from the cafeteria, giggling as they lifted smudgy prints with Scotch tape. They'd been caught, of course. Given detention and a lecture on discretion that neither had fully understood at the time.

"I remember," Carter said quietly. "You were the only one who didn't think it was stupid."

Mary set the book down, her expression softening. "It wasn't stupid. It was just... you."

Something shifted in the air between them, a momentary clearing of the awkwardness that had built up over years of silence. Carter looked at Mary—really looked at her—for the first time in a long while. The girl he'd known was still there in the curve of her smile, the slight furrow between her eyebrows when she concentrated. But there was something else too, something new. A sadness, perhaps, or a weariness that hadn't been there before.

Before he could analyze it further, Mary reached to her lunch tray and picked up the apple. She set it on the table in front of him, then lifted one half of her sandwich and placed it beside the fruit.

"Here," she said simply.

Carter stared at the offered food, a confusing mix of emotions rising in his chest—gratitude, shame, defensiveness. "I don't need—"

"I know you don't need it," Mary interrupted. "But I'm not going to eat it all, and I hate wasting food." She took the apple, held it out him. "Consider it payment for letting me invade your space."

Carter hesitated, pride warring with hunger. The apple gleamed under the fluorescent lights, its red skin promising sweetness and sustenance. His stomach clenched painfully, making the decision for him.

He took the apple, his fingers brushing against hers for the briefest moment. "Thanks."

Mary nodded, returning to her salad as if sharing her lunch with him was the most natural thing in the world. As if three years of silence had never existed between them.

Carter bit into the apple, the sharp sweetness flooding his mouth. He couldn't remember the last time he'd had fresh fruit

—maybe two months ago, when he'd splurged on a bag of apples that had been on sale. The sensation was almost overwhelming, a simple pleasure made extraordinary by its rarity.

They ate in silence for a few minutes, the awkwardness gradually dissipating into something almost comfortable. Not friendship, exactly, but perhaps the possibility of it. A tenuous bridge being constructed over a chasm neither fully understood how to cross.

"So," Carter said finally, breaking the silence. "Why are you really sitting here? Your friends kick you out of the cool kids' table?"

Mary snorted, nearly choking on her milk. "God, you sound like a bad teen movie." She set the carton down, wiping her mouth with a napkin. "Maybe I just wanted a change of scenery."

Carter raised an eyebrow, not buying it for a second. "Right. And it has nothing to do with your mom cornering you this morning."

Mary's head snapped up, surprise clear in her expression. "How did you—"

"I saw you after first period," Carter explained. "You had that look."

"What look?"

"The one you always got when your mom made you do something you didn't want to do. Like that time she signed us up for ballroom dancing lessons in seventh grade."

A reluctant smile tugged at Mary's lips. "Those were the worst three weeks of my life."

"You stepped on my feet every chance you got."

"You counted the steps out loud like a robot!"

They both laughed, the sound strange and unexpected in the quiet library. Mrs. Phelps glanced over, eyebrows raised in warning, and they ducked their heads like co-conspirators.

The moment of levity faded, leaving an opening for honesty. Carter took it. "I saw you watching me when I was locking up my bike. You don't have to sit with me because your mom told you to be nice to the orphan boy."

Mary's face fell, guilt flickering across her features. "That's not —"

"It's fine," Carter cut her off. "I get it. Your mom means well." He took another bite of the apple, chewing slowly to mask the sudden tightness in his throat. "But we're not kids anymore, Mary. You don't have to pretend we're still friends."

Mary leaned forward, her voice dropping to an intense whisper. "I'm not pretending anything. Yes, my mom mentioned you this morning. But I'm sitting here because I wanted to, okay? Because maybe I miss talking to someone who doesn't just care about who's hooking up with who or what party is happening this weekend."

Her vehemence surprised him. Carter studied her face, looking for signs of deception, finding none. "What about Amber? And Heather? And the rest of your crowd?"

Mary sighed, slouching back in her chair. "They're fine. They're just... I don't know. Sometimes it all feels so stupid, you know? Like we're playing at being adults without any of the actual responsibility. Just the drama."

Carter understood that better than she knew. He'd been playing at being an adult since his parents died—cooking meals, paying bills, making decisions no sixteen-year-old should have to make; but he felt the responsibility. But that wasn't what Mary meant. Her version of growing up still included football games and parties, just with an added layer of awareness about their artificiality.

"So what, you're having an existential crisis in the middle of junior year?" he asked, trying to keep his tone light.

Mary tilted her head, considering him. "Maybe. Or maybe I just miss having a friend who calls me on my bullshit."

The word "friend" hung between them, fragile and tentative. Carter wasn't sure how to respond. Part of him—the part that remembered building forts in the Cains' backyard and trading comic books on summer afternoons—wanted to grasp that offered thread of friendship and pull it taut again. Another part —the part that had learned to expect disappointment—warned against hoping for anything lasting.

Before he could decide, the bell rang, signaling the end of lunch period. Mary gathered her tray, stacking the empty containers neatly.

"I should go," she said. "Chemistry test next period."

Carter nodded, returning the half-eaten apple core to his paper bag. "Yeah, I've got history."

They stood awkwardly for a moment, caught between the easy farewell of acquaintances and the warmer goodbye of friends.

Finally, Mary shifted her tray to one hand and reached out with the other, touching his arm lightly.

"See you another time?" she asked, the question casual but her eyes searching his face for a response.

Carter hesitated only briefly before nodding. "Sure. If you want."

"I want," she confirmed, her smile uncertain but genuine.

He watched her walk away, tray balanced carefully as she navigated between the tables. At the door, she glanced back, catching him watching. Instead of the embarrassment he expected to feel, Carter found himself raising a hand in a small wave. Mary returned it before disappearing into the hallway.

Carter gathered his things slowly, mind working to process what had just happened. Three years of careful distance bridged in a single lunch period. Not completely—there were still gaps, questions, unspoken histories between them. But a beginning, perhaps. A tentative step back toward something he'd thought was lost for good.

As he headed for the library door, Carter pushed down the hope rising in his chest. Experience had taught him that good things rarely lasted in Stillwater. People left. They changed. They disappointed you when you needed them most.

Still, as he merged into the river of students flooding the hallway, Carter found himself already thinking about the next lunch period with Mary. For the first time in a long while, he had something to look forward to beyond mere survival. The feeling was as unfamiliar as it was dangerous.

But maybe, just this once, it was worth the risk.

ELEVEN

The afternoon sun hung low over Stillwater, casting long shadows across Main Street. School had ended thirty minutes earlier, releasing its captive population into the small mountain town. Most students had scattered to homes or part-time jobs, sports practice or the diner where teenagers congregated over milkshakes and complaints about homework.

Carter pedaled his bike with single-minded determination, weaving between parked cars and around potholes that town maintenance never seemed to fix. His backpack weighed heavy against his spine, loaded with textbooks and the half-finished forensics paperback. Each push of the pedals sent a soft squeak through the frame—the chain still needed oil, another repair relegated to the "someday" list that grew longer with each passing month.

The Stillwater Sheriff's Department occupied a squat brick building wedged between the courthouse and the volunteer fire department. Its façade had been renovated five years earlier, the only visible result of a county bond measure that had promised modernization of law enforcement facilities. Gleaming glass doors had replaced the weathered wooden ones, and a handicap ramp now zigzagged up to the entrance, but the faded lettering carved in stone above the doorway remained unchanged—"STILLWATER SHERIFF DEPT."—a testament to the building's, and the town's, resistance to complete transformation.

Carter coasted to a stop at the bike rack, his front wheel hitting the metal bar with a soft clang. He dismounted, unwinding the chain lock from the frame and securing his bike with practiced movements. The sheriff's Bronco sat in its designated spot, which meant Sheriff Cain was inside. Good. Carter needed someone with authority if his plan was going to work.

He stood on the sidewalk for a long moment, mentally rehearsing what he would say. The approach needed to be professional. Mature. Not the eager rambling of past attempts that had earned him sympathetic smiles but little actual respect.

A group of adults exited the building, their conversation halting briefly as they passed him. Carter recognized Mr. Peterson, still complaining about his neighbor's hedge even here, in the shadow of law enforcement. The older man glanced at Carter, recognition flickering across his features before his gaze slid away, dismissive.

Drawing a deep breath, Carter squared his shoulders and pushed through the glass doors into the station's lobby.

The interior smelled of industrial cleaner and stale coffee. Fluorescent lights buzzed overhead, casting a harsh glow over the worn linoleum floor. A waist-high counter separated the public area from the department's inner workings, behind which sat Deputy Louise Garrett, phone cradled between ear and shoulder as she typed on an ancient desktop computer.

Carter approached the counter, gripping the straps of his backpack to stop his hands from fidgeting. Deputy Garrett glanced up, recognition immediately replacing her professional smile with a look of barely concealed exasperation.

"I'll call you back," she said into the receiver before hanging up. "Carter Thompson. Twice in one week. To what do we owe the pleasure?"

Carter leaned forward slightly, keeping his voice low and steady. "I'd like to speak with Sheriff Cain, please. It's about the incident at Stillwater River."

Louise's eyebrows lifted slightly. "The incident," she repeated, voice flat. "You mean the drowning accident."

"Is that the official determination?" Carter pressed, careful to keep his tone neutral. "Because I've been researching similar cases, and the pattern suggests—"

"Carter." Louise cut him off with practiced efficiency. "The sheriff is extremely busy today with actual police business. Whatever theories you've cooked up from your detective books will have to wait."

Heat crept up Carter's neck, but he maintained his composure. "This isn't from books. I've observed specific details that warrant investigation. If I could just have five minutes—"

"Not today." Louise's tone softened slightly, closer to how one might speak to a persistent child. "Why don't you leave your notes with me, and I'll make sure the sheriff gets them?"

They both knew the offer was hollow. Carter had left "notes" before—detailed observations about suspicious activities around town, meticulously documented leads on minor crimes. Those notes invariably disappeared into desk drawers, forgotten or dismissed without consideration.

"These observations need context," Carter insisted. "I'd prefer to explain them personally."

Louise sighed, her patience visibly thinning. "Look, I understand you're trying to help, but we have trained officers handling the investigation. The sheriff doesn't have time to—"

"I'll wait," Carter interrupted, gesturing to the empty chairs along the wall. "Until he's available. It's important."

Louise stared at him for a long moment, weighing the effort of continued argument against the path of least resistance. Finally, she nodded toward the chairs. "Suit yourself. But I can't promise he'll see you today. Or tomorrow. Or this week."

"I understand," Carter said, already moving toward the waiting area. "Thank you for your consideration, Deputy Garrett."

He settled into the molded plastic chair farthest from the entrance, slipping his backpack onto his lap. Through the interior windows that lined the wall opposite the counter, he could see the bullpen—four desks arranged in the center of the room, two occupied by deputies focused on paperwork. Sheriff Cain's office door remained closed, the frosted glass revealing only a silhouette moving inside.

Carter extracted a notebook from his backpack—not his school notes, but a smaller, leather-bound journal reserved for his investigations. He flipped it open to his latest entry, reviewing the observations he'd compiled about Jackson McKenzie's death. The timing of the "accident." The location—isolated enough to minimize witnesses. The victim—a man known for his routine, his predictability.

These weren't musings. They were data points forming a pattern, if only someone would take the time to see it.

Across the bullpen, behind the glass partition, Deputy Sam Chambers glanced up from his desk, dark eyes settling on

Carter through the window. At twenty-two, Sam was the newest addition to the department, his uniform still creased in all the right places, his badge still catching the light when he moved. Unlike most of Stillwater's law enforcement, Deputy Chambers was African American—a fact that made him stand out in a town where diversity existed mainly in tourism brochures.

Sam watched Carter for a moment, curiosity evident in his expression. He leaned toward Deputy Dale Weathers at the next desk, asking something Carter couldn't hear through the glass.

Dale looked up, his weathered face creasing into a familiar smirk when he spotted Carter. He said something back to Sam, gesturing dismissively with one hand before returning to his paperwork.

Carter pretended not to notice the exchange, focusing instead on his notes. He'd learned long ago that appearing oblivious often revealed more than direct observation. People spoke freely when they thought no one was listening. Sam's interest was new, though. Worth noting.

Minutes stretched into a half hour. Carter remained still, occasionally turning a page in his notebook to maintain the illusion of productive waiting. The station's routine flowed around him—phones ringing, deputies coming and going, Louise handling walk-ins with practiced efficiency. No one spared him more than a passing glance. He had become part of the furniture—the persistent kid with the notebook, harmless and easily ignored.

At 4:45, fifteen minutes before the front desk officially closed to the public, Louise's phone rang. She answered it, glancing toward Carter as she listened to whoever was on the line. After a brief exchange, she hung up and beckoned to him.

Carter approached the counter, hope rising despite his efforts to temper it.

"Sheriff Cain is tied up with an emergency call," Louise informed him, her tone professionally apologetic but her eyes relieved. "He won't be available for the rest of the day. You should head home before it gets dark."

Disappointment settled in Carter's stomach, heavy and familiar. He nodded, tucking his notebook back into his backpack. "I'll come back tomorrow."

"Carter..." Louise hesitated, something like genuine concern flashing across her features. "Don't you have homework? Friends to hang out with? Normal teenager stuff?"

The question hit harder than she'd likely intended. Carter adjusted the straps of his backpack, his expression carefully neutral. "This is important."

Louise sighed. "So is being sixteen. Just... think about it, okay?"

Carter nodded without committing to anything, turning toward the exit. As he pushed through the glass doors into the fading afternoon light, he allowed his shoulders to slump slightly. Another day, another dismissal. The pattern was predictable enough that he should have stopped hoping for different results, yet here he was, repeatedly throwing himself against the same wall.

He unlocked his bike, frustration making his movements jerky and imprecise. The chain slipped from his fingers twice before he managed to coil it around the bike frame. Part of him knew Louise was right—normal teenagers didn't spend their afternoons waiting in sheriff's stations with notebooks full of observations about suspicious deaths. Normal teenagers had friends, activities, lives uncomplicated by responsibility and obsession.

But normal teenagers hadn't watched their parents die in front of them. Normal teenagers hadn't learned at thirteen that the world was fundamentally unsafe, unpredictable, and indifferent to their pain.

"Hey! Thompson!"

The voice startled Carter as he prepared to mount his bike. Deputy Sam Chambers jogged across the parking lot toward him, one hand raised in greeting. Unlike the other deputies, whose faces had long ago settled into masks of professional detachment, Sam's expression remained open, his eyes reflecting genuine interest rather than practiced tolerance.

"Deputy Chambers," Carter acknowledged, straightening to his full height, which still left him four inches shorter than the officer.

Sam reached him, slightly out of breath. "Call me Sam. I was hoping to catch you before you left."

Suspicion flickered through Carter's mind. New deputies sometimes thought it was funny to humor him, to pretend interest in his "detective work" before sharing laughs with the others later. He'd learned to recognize the subtle mockery in their questions, the condescension masked as encouragement.

"What can I help you with?" Carter asked, keeping his tone neutral.

Sam glanced back toward the station, then nodded toward the edge of the parking lot. "Walk with me a minute?"

Curiosity overrode Carter's initial wariness. He wheeled his bike alongside Sam as they moved away from the building, stopping at the far corner where a large oak offered both shade and privacy.

"How long have you been coming to the station with your observations?" Sam asked, leaning against the tree trunk.

Carter studied the deputy, searching for signs of the usual dismissal. Finding none, he answered honestly. "Two years, three months."

Sam whistled softly. "That's dedication."

"It's necessary," Carter corrected. "There are things happening in Stillwater that no one is investigating properly."

Instead of the expected eye-roll or patronizing smile, Sam nodded thoughtfully. "Like what?"

The question caught Carter off-guard. No one had ever asked for specifics before—they'd always been too busy finding polite ways to dismiss him.

"Like Jackson McKenzie's death," Carter said cautiously, testing the waters. "It wasn't an accident."

Sam's expression remained neutral. "What makes you say that?"

"Pattern recognition." Carter unzipped his backpack just enough to extract his notebook. "McKenzie was the third drowning in Stillwater River in two years. All three victims were men over sixty. All three were found in locations they frequented regularly, at times consistent with their normal routines."

He flipped to a page covered in neat columns of data—dates, times, locations, details that most would consider insignificant. "The statistical probability of three accidental drownings with these specific commonalities is extremely low."

Sam studied the notebook, brow furrowed in concentration. "You've been tracking all this?"

Carter nodded, watching the deputy's face carefully for signs of mockery. "I document everything. Patterns reveal truth."

"That's solid detective work," Sam said, and the genuine respect in his voice made Carter blink in surprise. "But you know we can't just launch an investigation based on statistical analysis, right? We need concrete evidence."

"I understand procedure," Carter replied, unable to keep a hint of defensiveness from his tone. "The first two deaths are hard to quantify. The evidence was limited, and not consistent with a crime, at least as far as I could make out. But no one's even looking for evidence on McKenzie's death because everyone's already decided it was an accident."

Sam handed the notebook back, his expression thoughtful. "You might have a point there." He glanced toward the station again, seeming to make a decision. "Look, I can't promise anything about the drownings—that's well above my pay grade. But there is something you might be able to help with."

Carter's attention sharpened. "What is it?"

"We've had a series of bicycle thefts outside the library over the past month," Sam explained, lowering his voice slightly.

"Nothing high-value enough to justify significant resources, but it's becoming a pattern. Six bikes in four weeks, always between 3:30 and 5:00 PM on weekdays."

Carter's mind immediately began cataloging the information, fitting it into patterns. "That's when the after-school program runs. Kids inside, bikes outside, minimal supervision in the parking area."

Sam nodded, a smile tugging at the corner of his mouth. "Exactly. We've increased patrols, but we can't keep an officer stationed there indefinitely for bike thefts, and the perpetrator seems to know our schedule."

"You want me to watch the library," Carter surmised, excitement building in his chest despite his efforts to remain professional.

"Just observe," Sam emphasized. "Take notes on anything suspicious—unfamiliar vehicles, adults hanging around without apparent purpose, that sort of thing. But—" he held up a warning finger, "—no confrontations. No following suspects. No breaking laws to get information. Real detectives work within the system, not outside it. And no skipping school. This is not something we will give you a hall pass for."

Carter nodded solemnly. "I understand. Observation only, outside of school hours."

"If you notice anything, bring it to me directly," Sam continued. "Not to the front desk, not to any other deputy. Just me." He handed Carter a small business card with his name and direct line. "Can you do that?"

Carter accepted the card, studying it for a moment before tucking it carefully into his notebook. "Yes, sir."

Sam straightened from his lean against the tree, glancing at his watch. "I should get back. But I mean it, Carter—observation only. Promise me."

"I promise," Carter agreed, unable to contain a small smile. "Thank you for the opportunity, Deputy Chambers."

Sam nodded, already turning back toward the station. "Just be careful. And remember—"

"Observation only," Carter finished for him. "I've got it."

As Sam walked away, Carter mounted his bike, a new energy coursing through him. Finally, someone was taking him seriously. Giving him a chance to prove his abilities. A real case—small, perhaps, but real nonetheless.

TWELVE

The late afternoon had begun to cast shadows across the kitchen as Carter watched his grandmother prepare what she believed was his favorite meal. Eloise Thompson moved with glacial slowness, her once-precise hands now trembling as they spread mayonnaise across bread in uneven strokes.

He should stop her, take over the task himself. The sandwich would be another disappointment—she'd forget the meat again, or use the moldy cheese he'd been meaning to throw out, or add pickle relish though he'd told her a thousand times he hated it. But interrupting her would only trigger confusion, perhaps even tears. Better to let her complete the ritual, to preserve the illusion that she was still capable of this small act of caregiving.

"Got something to show you, gran," Carter said, extracting a folded paper from his backpack. He smoothed it against the table, positioning it where she couldn't miss it once she turned around. World History, B+, circled in Mrs. Winters' distinctive red pen.

Eloise placed two pieces of bread together, cutting the sandwich with mathematical precision into perfect triangles. Her movements in this one task retained the muscle memory of decades. "There you go, sweetheart. Just how you like it."

She set the plate before him with a flourish, her face brightening with the satisfaction of a job well done. Carter glanced down. Just as he'd expected—bread, mayonnaise, nothing else. He swallowed the correction rising in his throat.

"Thanks, gran." He nudged the test paper forward. "Look what I got on my history exam."

Eloise's eyes drifted to the page, then back to his face, her gaze sliding past the paper as if it were invisible. "That's nice, dear."

"It's an A," Carter lied, the words burning his tongue. "Mrs. Winters said it was one of the best in the class."

His grandmother patted his hand, her skin papery against his. "Of course it is. You were always so smart. Just like your grandfather."

Not his father. Never his father anymore. In her mind, the generational lines had blurred, time folding in on itself until Carter existed in multiple eras simultaneously—grandson, son, some amalgamation of the men who had populated her life and then abandoned her through death.

"Aren't you going to eat?" she asked, frowning at the untouched sandwich.

Carter picked up one triangle, taking a dutiful bite of mayonnaise-soaked bread. "It's great. Just wanted to finish my homework first."

She nodded, already losing interest, her attention drawn to the window where early evening light played across the yard. In these moments of quiet distraction, Carter could see glimpses of the woman she had been—sharp-eyed, observant, capable of noticing the smallest details in her environment. Now those moments of clarity came less frequently, windows closing before he could reach her through them.

"I'm going out for a while," he said, rising from the table. "Library research. For school."

Eloise didn't turn from the window. "Don't be late. Your father worries."

Carter swallowed the familiar ache that rose at these moments of confusion. "I won't be."

He gathered his backpack, slipping the test inside without further comment. What was the point of trying to impress someone who couldn't remember who he was from one moment to the next? The lie about his grade sat sour in his stomach, more pathetic than the half-eaten mayonnaise sandwich abandoned on the plate.

At the door, he paused. "Your pills are on the table by your chair. The two white ones. Take them after dinner, okay?"

She nodded without turning, a vague acknowledgment that he knew meant she wouldn't remember. He'd find the pills untouched when he returned, would have to coax her into taking them then, hours past when they should have been administered. Another failure in a growing list of medical oversights that he concealed from the outside world.

"I'll be back before dark," he added, though the sun had already begun its steady decent toward the horizon.

This time, she didn't respond at all.

Carter closed the door softly behind him, resisting the urge to check if she'd locked it after him. She wouldn't. He'd double-check when he returned, just as he checked the stove knobs and unplugged the iron and made sure the space heater was a safe distance from anything flammable. All the little precautions that had become second nature since her decline had accelerated.

His bicycle leaned against the porch railing. Carter secured his backpack on his back—binoculars, notebook, pens, the camera he'd bought at a yard sale last summer. The tools of investigation. Of purpose.

He mounted the bike and pushed off down the driveway, leaving behind the house with its peeling paint and silent ghosts. Ahead lay Stillwater, sprawled in the valley like a a victim awaiting discovery. Hidden beneath its surface, secrets and patterns waited for someone to find them. For him to find them.

Mason's Country Store stood at the crossroads where Stillwater proper gave way to outlying farms and wooded properties. Its faded clapboard exterior and rusting metal roof had weathered nearly seven decades of mountain seasons, the white paint now more suggestion than reality. A hand-painted sign promised "GROCERIES • HARDWARE • AMMUNITION" in letters that had been retouched so many times they'd developed a dimensional quality, rising from the wood like small mountain ranges.

Carter propped his bike against the front porch, wedging the front wheel between a bench and a stack of firewood bundles for sale. The floorboards creaked beneath his weight as he crossed to the entrance, the screen door hinges protesting with a metallic groan as he pulled it open.

Inside, the store existed in a perpetual twilight state, illuminated by fluorescent tubes that buzzed and flickered overhead. The air smelled of coffee, leather, sawdust, and the faint mustiness of a building that had absorbed decades of living. Narrow aisles brimmed with an eclectic inventory—

canned goods alongside fishing lures, work gloves neighboring homemade jams, ammunition locked in a glass case above children's candy.

At the rear counter, Ed Mason leaned forward on thick forearms, deep in conversation with a customer whose back was to Carter. Ed's face was a topographical map of wrinkles, his white hair cropped close to his scalp, body still solid despite his seventy-plus years. He'd run the store since before Carter was born, a fixed point in Stillwater's ever-shifting landscape.

"—telling you, Ned, those old fuses won't handle the load," Ed was saying, his tone suggesting this wasn't the first time he'd delivered this particular lecture. "That wiring in your place dates back to the forties. It's a fire waiting to happen."

Ned Miller—Carter recognized him now—shook his head stubbornly. The older man's shoulders hunched beneath his worn flannel shirt, his spine curved like a question mark from decades of physical labor. "Don't need rewiring. Just need fuses that work."

"They work fine. It's your wiring that's shot." Ed sighed, reaching behind him to a pegboard hung with small cardboard packages. "But suit yourself. How many this time?"

"Six oughta do it." Ned's voice carried the distinctive gravel of a lifelong smoker. "Carol's got that new iron. Blows the fuse every time she plugs it in."

Ed placed the packages on the counter, shaking his head. "At least let me send my nephew out to look at that junction box. He's certified, won't charge much."

"Don't need anyone messing with my house." Ned slapped a ten-dollar bill onto the counter with finality. "Been changing my own fuses since before your nephew was born."

"Man your age shouldn't be climbing anything higher than the front porch steps."

Ned stiffened, pride visibly wounded. "I ain't dead yet."

"Just trying to keep it that way," Ed muttered, making change from the ancient register. The drawer shot open with a metallic clang that echoed through the store. "You're what, seventy-four now? That old wooden ladder's probably older than you are."

"Seventy-six," Ned corrected, pocketing the fuses and his change. "I'll see ya, Ed."

As Ned turned to leave, Carter stepped aside, nodding a greeting. The old man returned the gesture curtly, his eyes narrowing slightly with the instinctive suspicion many of Stillwater's elderly harbored toward the younger generation. Moments later, the screen door slammed shut behind him.

Ed beckoned Carter forward. "What can I do for you, son? Your grandmother needing anything?"

Carter approached the counter, setting his backpack beside him. "Just me today. Need to pick up some film for my camera."

Ed raised an eyebrow. "Film? Christ, kid, nobody uses that ancient technology anymore. Everyone's gone digital."

"My camera's older." Carter unzipped his backpack, extracting the secondhand Nikon he'd purchased for fifteen dollars at Mrs. Dawson's estate sale. "Takes 35mm."

"Huh." Ed examined the camera with something like respect. "Solid machine. They don't make 'em like that anymore." He turned toward a dusty display case behind the counter. "Think I've got some film back here somewhere. Expired, probably, but might still work."

As Ed rummaged through drawers, Carter glanced around the store. No other customers at the moment, just the two of them surrounded by the accumulated necessities and odd treasures of rural life. Through the front windows, he could see Ned Miller climbing into an ancient pickup truck, its once-blue paint now a patchwork of rust and primer.

"So what's the occasion?" Ed asked, returning with a yellow box of Kodak film. "School project?"

Carter hesitated, calculating how much to reveal. In a town like Stillwater, information was currency, and Ed Mason was a primary exchange hub for local gossip. But pride won out over caution.

"I'm on a stakeout," he said, straightening slightly. "Investigating the bicycle thefts at the library."

Ed's bushy eyebrows lifted. "That so? Working with the sheriff's department?"

"Sort of." Carter's chest swelled slightly at being taken seriously. "Deputy Chambers asked me to observe the area. I'll be tracking suspicious activity for a few days."

"Deputy Chambers, huh?" Ed slid the film across the counter, his expression revealing nothing. "That young fella from Portland? Still wet behind the ears."

"He's a good cop," Carter defended. "He listens. Takes things seriously."

"I'm sure he does." Ed rang up the film. "That'll be $8.50. Film ain't cheap these days, what with nobody using it anymore."

Carter counted out the bills from his wallet, the transaction depleting most of his remaining funds for the week. The sacrifice was worth it. Documentation was essential for any serious investigation, and he needed evidence to prove his worth to Sam—and to the sheriff.

"You be careful with that stakeout business," Ed cautioned as he handed over the change. "People around here don't take kindly to being watched. Especially by teenagers carrying cameras."

"I know how to stay hidden," Carter assured him, pocketing the film. "I'm trained in surveillance techniques."

Ed nodded, a smile tugging at the corner of his mouth. "Of course you are." He leaned forward, lowering his voice conspiratorially. "Just between us professional investigators, I'd keep an eye on the bench by the west entrance. Seen some characters hanging around there lately. Not locals."

Carter absorbed this information with the solemnity of receiving classified intelligence. "Thanks for the tip, Mr. Mason."

"Anytime, Detective Thompson." Ed winked, his tone carrying a hint of indulgence that sailed straight over Carter's head. "You solve this case, maybe the sheriff will finally give you a badge."

Pride bloomed in Carter's chest at the suggestion. Not a real possibility, of course, but the acknowledgment of his potential felt like water on parched soil. "I'll do my best, sir."

As he turned to leave, Ed called after him. "And Carter? Make sure to say hello to your grandmother for me. Haven't seen her in ages."

The reminder punctured Carter's momentary elevation, bringing reality crashing back. "Yes, sir. I will."

Outside, the sun was all but gone behind the hills surrounding the town, the sky painted in soft blue and orange. Carter loaded the film into his camera with meticulous care, his fingers moving through the process with practiced precision. He secured his backpack once more and mounted his bike, pushing off toward the library with renewed purpose.

Suddenly, a sharp gunshot sound rang out, making Carter turn in panic, instinctively ducking slightly, as if ready to take cover. Behind him, Ned Miller's truck accelerated out of the parking lot, the backfire of the ancient engine still echoing through the trees, a plume of exhaust hanging in the air. Carter, his heart beating fast, took a breath, calming himself, as he climbed on his bike and pushed off toward town.

The Stillwater Public Library squatted at the edge of the town, a blocky concrete structure whose 1970s brutalist architecture clashed with the surrounding Victorian buildings. Its front door faced east onto Main Street, the harsh lines of the building silhouetted by the full intensity of the setting sun, which now painted the asphalt in shades of burnt amber and blood orange.

Carter positioned himself on a bench across the street, partially concealed by the drooping branches of an ancient oak tree. From this vantage point, he had clear sight-lines to both the main entrance and the bicycle rack without being immediately visible to those entering or exiting the building.

He arranged his tools with methodical precision—notebook open to a fresh page, pen uncapped, binoculars resting on his knee, camera ready with newly loaded film. The approaching evening had brought a chill to the air, but Carter barely noticed, his attention fixed on the task at hand.

For thirty minutes, he documented every movement with clinical detachment, his pen scratching across the paper in his distinctively tight handwriting:

5:15 PM - Male, approx. 60, gray hair, tan jacket, enters library carrying briefcase

5:17 PM - Female, teen, red backpack, exits library, retrieves blue mountain bike

5:23 PM - Library staff (Ms. Lewis) exits side door for cigarette break, returns at 5:29

5:30 PM - Black sedan parks in handicapped space without permit. Female driver remains in vehicle.

Each observation is categorized, timed, detailed—fragments of ordinary life examined for the patterns that might reveal themselves only when viewed collectively. This was what the others failed to understand. The meaning wasn't in individual moments but in their relationship to each other, in the negative spaces between events.

At 5:42 PM, the library's main doors swung open, releasing a burst of female laughter that carried across the square. Carter looked up from his notes. Mary Cain emerged flanked by Amber Wilder and Heather Davis, their heads bent together in conversation, Mary's brown hair catching the remnants of light from the darkening sky.

Carter's heartbeat accelerated, his hand instinctively reaching for the camera. Through the viewfinder, he framed the three girls as they descended the library steps, but his focus remained fixed on Mary—the way she tucked hair behind her ear, the slight lift of her chin when she laughed, the careful grace of her movements.

He pressed the shutter button, capturing the moment. Then another. And another.

The rational part of his brain supplied justification: documentation of all individuals in the vicinity during investigation hours. Standard procedure. But beneath this professional veneer lurked something more personal, more desperate—the desire to possess, if only in frozen moments, what remained perpetually beyond his reach.

Mary paused at the bottom of the steps. She extracted her phone, lit up with an incoming call, then, looked up to her friends, saying something that Carter couldn't hear. Amber and Heather continued toward the lot, Mary remained behind, raising the phone to her ear, a smile lifting the corners of her mouth.

Carter adjusted the focus, zooming tighter on her face. The viewfinder filled with Mary's profile, her features transformed to stark contrasts in the evening light. He pressed the shutter again, the mechanical click oddly loud in the quiet street. The conversation she was having brought out a glow in her, the effects of someone who made her happy. Carter frowned, wishing he was on the other end of the call.

Mary glanced up suddenly, as if sensing observation. Her gaze swept across the square, passing over Carter's position without pausing. Still, he ducked lower, heart hammering against his ribs. The moment stretched, taut with potential discovery, before Mary returned her attention to her phone.

The sudden flash of red and blue lights shattered the moment, reflecting off building facades and washing across the library steps in electric waves. Carter looked up as the Sheriff's Bronco pulled to the curb directly in front of the library. Sheriff Cain emerged from the driver's side, his uniform crisp despite the late hour, his face set in lines of barely contained irritation. He didn't notice Carter across the street, his attention fixed on his daughter, who had stiffened at his arrival.

"Mary Elizabeth!" The sheriff's voice carried across the street, pitched to command rather than request. "I thought you were studying?"

Mary quickly ended the call, then shoved her phone into her pocket, her body language shifting from relaxed to defensive in an instant. "We just left," she said, motioning to the parking lot where Amber and Heather were talking beside Amber's car. "Were the lights necessary?"

"I thought you were studying at home tonight." Cain ignored her question, already set on his path of disapproval. "That was the agreement."

"No, you had a decree," Mary corrected, the edge in her voice audible even at a distance. "I don't remember agreeing to anything."

Across the street, Carter remained motionless, camera forgotten in his lap. He should leave, slip away before either noticed him. This was private, not meant for observation. Yet he found himself unable to move, absorbed by the collision of worlds unfolding before him—Mary's life intersecting with the official authority he so desperately sought to access.

"Where's your car?" the sheriff demanded, glancing toward the parking lot.

"I rode with Amber. She was going to drop me home after we finished our research project." Mary's arms crossed, her tone not of apology but defiance.

"What time was that supposed to be? You know your mother and I expect you home before dinner."

Mary's shoulders squared, her stance widening slightly as if bracing for impact. "I'm sorry my academic responsibilities are inconveniencing your schedule, Sheriff. Next time I'll just fail the assignment to make sure I'm home in time for your inspection."

Sheriff Cain's spine stiffened at the title—"Sheriff" instead of "Dad," a deliberate distancing. His voice dropped, too low now for Carter to hear clearly, but his rigid posture and jabbing index finger conveyed the essence of the reprimand.

Mary stood her ground, arms crossed over her chest, chin lifted in fixed resistance. Even from a distance, Carter could see the familiar flush rising in her cheeks—not embarrassment but anger, the same color that had appeared when Billy Hoffman had pulled her hair in fourth grade and she'd responded by blackening his eye. Carter smiled at the memory, of Mary's strength, even at a young age.

Their argument escalated, voices rising and falling in familiar patterns. Carter couldn't make out individual words, but he didn't need to. This was clearly a well-rehearsed conflict, positions established and defended through countless previous engagements. The sheriff gesturing toward his cruiser. Mary's hand slicing through the air in rejection. The push and pull of authority challenged and reasserted.

Finally, Mary turned toward the parking lot, shoulders hunched in defeat or rage or some combustible combination of both. She called to Amber, who waited by her car, waving her friend off, then stalked back to her father's SUV, yanking open the passenger door with unnecessary force.

Before entering the vehicle, she paused, trying to swallow her rage, or brace for a new round inside the vehicle. This time, her gaze didn't pass over Carter's position but locked directly onto it, as if she'd known all along exactly where he was. For a suspended moment, their eyes met across the distance—hers narrowed with recognition, his widening with the shock of being seen.

Then she ducked into the Bronco, slamming the door hard enough to make the sheriff wince. Moments later, the vehicle pulled away from the curb, lights extinguished.

Carter remained frozen on the bench, camera clutched in suddenly sweaty hands. She'd seen him. Seen him watching, photographing, documenting a moment she'd thought was private, at least from the prying eyes of someone like Carter, despite the public setting it had occurred in. The realization burned in his stomach like acid, shame mingling with an odd defensiveness. He'd been conducting an investigation. The fact that Mary happened to have a fight with her father in front of him was coincidental, not calculated.

Even in his own mind, the justification rang hollow. He could have left, turned away. But he didn't.

He slipped the camera into his backpack, suddenly eager to be elsewhere. The bicycle thief could wait for another day. Right now, he needed distance, perspective, the safety of his room where he could process what had just happened without scrutiny.

As he gathered his belongings, Carter's gaze fell on his notebook, open to the page of observations. Among the clinical notations of strangers' movements, a single entry stood out in its detailed specificity:

5:42 PM - Mary exits library with A.W. and H.D. Blue sweater, jeans, brown boots. Hair down. Laughing.

He stared at the words, seeing them suddenly through imagined outside eyes—not the documentation of a detective but the fixation of something altogether different. Something unhealthy. Unwelcome.

Carter snapped the notebook shut and shoved it into his backpack. He was a detective. An investigator. His observations were professional, necessary, part of a larger purpose that would someday be recognized by those who mattered. By those who could finally see his true value.

The fact that his camera contained six consecutive frames of Mary Cain and none of the suspected bicycle thief was an oversight he would correct tomorrow.

He mounted his bike and pedaled away from the library, the weight of Mary's gaze following him like an accusation he couldn't quite defend against.

THIRTEEN

The Miller property sat two miles beyond the town limits, a five-acre plot that had been in Ned's family for three generations. The farmhouse crouched against the hillside, weathered clapboard barely distinguishable from the dark forest surrounding it. In the pre-dawn gloom, a single window glowed yellow against the lingering darkness—the kitchen, where Carol Miller had risen at 4:30 AM as she had every day for forty-three years of marriage, to prepare her husband's breakfast. She used to enjoy sending him off to work each morning, the ritual portion of life to which they had grown accustomed. He had been retired for almost 20 years now, but she still woke him with breakfast each morning, a habit hard to break for either of them. These days Ned had little to do after the meal, the reward of retirement seemingly more punishment as the years ticked on.

Carol navigated around the various projects she and Ned had started on his retirement, the unfinished repair on the toaster oven, the partially knitted sweater for their grandson. The house, both inside and out, was filled with partial projects that seemed so important and fulfilling early on, but now sat languishing as part of the home decoration. Ned had amassed a similar long list of undone projects outside, from the partially rebuilt deck railing to the rolls of fencing now overgrown with weeds. While the intention and purpose for each was still valid, with each year of age came a dampening of enthusiasm, or a physical limitation that made completing the projects more challenging.

At 5:17 AM, the lights in part of the Miller farmhouse surrendered to the lingering pre-dawn darkness. The power flickered once, twice, then extinguished completely. The electric clock on the kitchen counter froze at 5:17, its red digits fading to black. The refrigerator's steady hum ceased, leaving a silence broken only by Carol's startled exclamation from the kitchen.

"Ned? Power's gone!"

Ned Miller grunted from the bathroom, where he'd been shaving by the weak light of a bare bulb. He grunted, looking toward the kitchen, the razor poised against his half-stubbled cheek. "Fuse again," he called back, setting the razor aside and wiping his face as he headed toward the door. "Damn iron of yours."

"Wasn't using the iron," Carol protested, her voice muffled as she rummaged through a drawer for the flashlight they kept for such occasions.

Ned didn't bother responding. It was always something with the electrical system in this house—the iron, the microwave, the television, the new washing machine Carol had insisted on buying though the old one worked just fine. Modern appliances, too greedy for the ancient wiring that threaded through the walls like varicose veins.

The beam of a flashlight bobbed through the darkened hallway as Carol met Ned, illuminating the cramped space in sharp contrasts of light and shadow. She handed the flashlight to him.

"Be careful," she said, the words more ritual than actual caution after all the times they'd enacted this particular scene. "Don't need you breaking a hip out there."

Ned harrumphed, taking the flashlight. "My hip's just fine. It's the wiring that's broke." He shuffled toward the mudroom, Carol trailing behind. "Shouldn't take but a minute to replace the fuse."

"I'll make coffee the old way," she said, already turning back toward the kitchen. "Percolator still works on the gas stove."

Ned grunted acknowledgment as he pulled his work coat from its hook by the door. The house already felt colder, the darkness seeming to consume the warmth like a vampire. He shoved his feet into insulated boots, not bothering with the laces, then shoved the new fuses he had bought from Ed into his coat pocket. Quick out, quick in. No need for Carol to worry about him catching cold on the back porch.

The wooden door creaked as Ned pushed it open, ancient hinges protesting their first use of the day. Ned tugged his coat tighter and stepped onto the porch, boots crunching through a light frost that still lingered in the late spring. The cold struck his old lungs like a physical blow, the air sharply cooler in contrast to the warmth of the house. Seventy-six years in these mountains had taught him respect for weather's deadly potential, especially as he got older. He knew it didn't have to be freezing to be impacted. Get the job done and get back inside where his aging body preferred.

Ned glanced to the sky. Dark clouds had started rolling in, promising rain soon. He doubted it would fall before he was done, but he hurried just the same. He had no interest in being cold and wet in one morning.

The electrical box had been mounted high on the exterior wall when the house was first wired in 1947, a placement that hadn't even been a consideration at the time, but had proved increasingly inconvenient as decades passed and Ned's joints stiffened with age. Now the seven feet up the wall, requiring a ladder to access, was a treacherous positioning that seemed less viable with each passing year. The deck he had put in beneath it over twenty years ago created a gap between house and surface where he could post the ladder. The deck was still partially dismantled, another project that was waiting for a warm summer to complete, its top rail removed leaving only the steel balusters sticking up from the floorboards. He moved a few old metal buckets, heavily rusted and useless, onto the deck to make room for the ladder.

Ned directed the flashlight beam toward the corner of the porch where the ladder leaned against the railing. The wooden extension ladder had belonged to his father, solid oak construction with wooden steps reinforced by steel rods, built in an era when objects were made to outlast their owners. Its surface was scarred and weathered, darkened by decades of use and exposure. Several rungs were cracked and worn, something that Ned had been meaning to repair for months, though the ladder had held his weight without complaint, except for groans and creaks, the last dozen times he'd climbed it.

With practiced movements slowed by both age and cold, Ned lifted the ladder with a grunt and moved it to rest beside the box. The wooden legs settled into shallow depressions worn into the ground from repeated placement in exactly the same spot.

Ned shook the ladder with one hand, a habit formed from years of working construction in his younger days. It shook slightly but held firm. Good enough. He rotated the flashlight in his left hand, pointing the light up, then began to climb, each step accompanied by a subtle protesting creak of wood bearing weight it had carried hundreds of times before. The flashlight beam danced against the wall like a Hollywood searchlight at the latest premiere.

One step. Two. The third rung groaned beneath his boots, the sound almost human in its distress. Ned paused, suddenly aware of his vulnerable position—an old man on an old ladder in the dark.

For a moment, Ed Mason's voice echoed in his memory: "That old wooden ladder's probably older than you are." Maybe Ed was right. Maybe it was time to reconsider his stubborn insistence on self-reliance, to acknowledge that age brought limitations along with its hard-earned wisdom.

The moment passed with a grunt of refusal. The ladder was fine. He was fine. Ned climbed the last few rungs, the electrical box now at shoulder height. He braced one hand against the wall for stability, the flashlight in it rotated to point to the box, while the other hand worked the rusted metal latch that secured the box's cover. His fingers, already stiffening in the cold, fumbled with the mechanism before finally coaxing it open.

The interior of the box was a museum of obsolete technology—ceramic fuses screwed into sockets, cloth-wrapped wiring, components manufactured before the concept of planned obsolescence had taken root in American industry. Ned directed the flashlight beam across the row of fuses, searching for the blown one that had plunged the kitchen into darkness.

There. The tiny filament inside the glass fuse had ruptured, the break visible even to his aging eyes. He unscrewed the blown fuse carefully, mindful of the potential for electrical shock. He hadn't even considered turning the main power off, his old habits denying any potential for danger. The old fuse came free and Ned pocketed it—waste not, want not, though what use a blown fuse might serve eluded him at the moment.

Ned reached into his coat pocket for one of the replacement fuses, his movements awkward as he tried to maintain balance on the ladder while extracting the small object.

The new fuse felt cold and smooth against his fingers as he positioned it at the socket entrance. A simple task, one he'd performed countless times over the decades. Just a quick twist to secure it, then down the ladder and back to the warmth of the kitchen where Carol's coffee would be percolating on the stove.

Ned began to screw the fuse into place, applying gentle pressure to avoid cross-threading or an electrical arc. Beneath him, the ladder shifted almost imperceptibly, adjusting to a subtle redistribution of his weight as he leaned to the side. A hairline crack in one of the legs, one of many in the aging wood, widened by fractions of an inch, wood fibers separating along a break that hadn't been formed by natural stress alone.

The fuse screwed into place tightly. Ned allowed himself a small grunt of triumph; the kitchen lights flickering back to life. He began to turn, preparing for descent, when the weakened ladder leg, stressed by his weight as he shifted, finally surrendered to the forces acting upon it.

The snap was like a gunshot in the early morning stillness— sharp, definitive, echoing across the frost-covered yard. Ned felt the leg give way beneath him, the wood structure twisting and bending on the remaining leg, his body suddenly untethered from solid support. For an instant, he hung suspended between earth and sky, between life and what waited beyond it. His mind registered surprising clarity in that frozen moment—that he'd left his razor in the sink, that the chickens needed extra feed in this cold, that he'd never get around to fixing that broken hinge on the garden gate.

Then gravity reclaimed him. The opposite leg, unable to support Ned's entire weight, sheered and shattered. Ned's body twisted, then fell sideways, arms windmilling in a futile attempt to grasp something, anything that might arrest his descent. The ladder collapsed beneath him, wooden components separating along age stressed connections, exacerbated by joints deliberately tampered with and weakened. Ned tried to brace himself as he fell, instinct trying to protect vital areas as reason told him the height was not necessarily fatal.

What waited below made the difference.

The partially finished porch railing loomed beneath him, the vertical metal balusters exposed until he could find time to install new railing. The project, like many undertaken by aging hands, had stalled with the job half-complete. Now those steel rods stood like spikes driven into the porch floor, their tops jagged where the top rail had been removed, their exposed ends like unyielding spears.

The side of Ned's body struck the row of rods with horrible precision, the steel penetrating in three places from just below his left shoulder down to his thigh with enough force to continue through his chest cavity, stomach and leg. The impact drove the air from his lungs in a wet gasp, his mouth opening in a silent scream as the posts impaled him completely, the weathered steel now slick with spreading crimson that gleamed in the growing sky glow.

The human body contains approximately five liters of blood. When catastrophic damage occurs to major vessels, that volume can evacuate with astonishing speed. Ned Miller's life drained onto the porch boards in steaming rivers, creating a macabre tableau that would greet the first responders when they finally arrived hours later.

In the kitchen, Carol had smiled as the lights had flickered back on, but had heard the crack of breaking wood, followed by a heavy thud that rattled the dishes in their cupboards. She paused in the act of pouring coffee, head tilted toward the sound.

"Ned?" she called, already moving toward the door. "What's going on out there?"

No answer came. Just a light breeze picking up from the east, cold and damp, and the soft hiss of percolating coffee as she set the pot back on the stove in front of her.

"Ned?" Louder now, concern threading through her voice as she approached the mudroom.

The lack of response accelerated her movements. Carol pushed through the door into the mudroom, fumbling for the spare flashlight kept on a shelf by the coats. Her hands closed around it and she yanked open the exterior door, flipping on the light despite the slowly brightening sky.

"Ned!" she shouted, pulling the door shut behind her. The blast of cold air surprised her as she pulled her light coat tighter around her body. She felt the first drops of a coming rain strike her face, gently at first, then with more intensity. As she turned the corner of the house she forgot the cold and damp at the sight that greeted her on the porch.

The scream that tore from Carol Miller's throat carried across the yard, echoing off the barn and pond before dissipating into the vast indifference of the early morning. Inside the newly re-illuminated house, the electric clock on the kitchen counter reset itself, digital display blinking 12:00 in steady pulses that matched the rhythm of blood still pumping weakly from Ned

Miller's body, mixing with the falling rain as new rivulets were formed, disappearing between the boards of the deck.

On the porch, partially obscured by the collapsed ladder and Ned's splayed legs, the evidence of deliberate sabotage presented itself with terrible clarity—the ladder leg showed not the jagged edges of natural breakage but the clean, precise lines of a thin saw blade's passage, cutting nearly through the wood before stopping just short of complete separation.

Not an accident. Not chance. Not fate.

Murder, poorly disguised as misfortune, had claimed another victim in Stillwater.

FOURTEEN

The ambulance sat axle-deep in mud, tires spinning uselessly in the muddy driveway leading to the Miller property. Sheriff Martin Cain guided his SUV past the stranded vehicle, his heavy-duty tires efficiently navigating the slippery terrain. He killed the engine at the bend in the driveway and stepped into the rain.

"Call for the tow truck," he ordered into his radio before trudging up the slick path.

The farmhouse porch had transformed into a crime scene. Paramedics huddled in conference on the deck. Deputy Louise Garrett guided a wet and shell-shocked Carol Miller away from whatever lay beyond the doorway. The remnants of blood, most washed away by the rain, streaked the weathered boards in brown-black patterns. The mood was dark, just like the blackened skies and the heavy rain falling across the Miller property.

Cain stamped mud from his boots as he mounted the steps. The lead paramedic nodded grimly and stepped aside, revealing Ned Miller's body pinned to the porch floor by the metal balusters that had impaled him through the body in three places.

"He was gone before we arrived. Couldn't have survived this."

Cain stepped over to examine the body without touching it. "Time of death?"

"Based on the wife's statement, around 5:30 this morning. She heard the ladder break, came out to find him like this."

Cain's eyes narrowed on the collapsed ladder nearby. "Who moved these pieces?"

"We cleared access to assess the victim. Standard procedure."

"Anyone photograph the scene before you moved things?"

"I believe Deputy Rivers took pictures when she first arrived."

Cain nodded. "Where's Carol now?"

"Kitchen. Deputy's making her tea. She refused transport to the hospital."

Something about the broken ladder caught Cain's attention. He crouched, examining the fractured leg without touching it. The wood hadn't splintered chaotically—looking closer, he could see saw blade marks, discreet but obvious. It had been cut, deliberately weakened so any significant weight would complete the separation.

"Get me evidence markers," he ordered Deputy Chambers, keeping his voice low. "And call Forensics. This isn't an accident." Chambers nodded, turning away to open his cell phone.

The grim reality settled over him. Second suspicious death in a month. Both victims elderly men. Both deaths staged as accidents. Both occurring in isolation, with minimal witnesses.

Pattern. Intent.

Chambers returned to the sheriff. "Tow truck's coming for the ambulance. Forensics will be here within the hour."

"Set up a perimeter. No one in or out except emergency personnel." As Deputy Chambers set about following his instructions, Cain turned to the house. He took a deep breath, steeling himself for the next conversation, then climbed the step to the mudroom.

Inside, the farmhouse kitchen stood in stark contrast to the horror outside. Carol sat at the table, hands wrapped around an untouched mug of tea. Deputy Garrett stood nearby. Cain nodded at her and she slipped out, leaving him with Carol.

"Martin," she said. "They won't let me see him. Won't let me cover him up."

The familiarity complicated things. Cain wasn't just the sheriff; he was Martin, the boy who'd once helped Ned repair fences in exchange for fishing lessons. He sat beside her.

"I'm sorry, Carol. We need to examine the scene before we move him." She nodded, not understanding but not willing to fight. She gripped the tea cup tightly. Cain looked at her white knuckles, worried the mug would break.

"Can you tell me what he was doing? I'm sorry to ask, but…"

"He was just changing a fuse. Same as he's done hundred times before."

Cain listened as her story emerged in halting fragments—the power outage, Ned changing the fuse, the crack of breaking wood, her terrible discovery.

"The ladder," Cain prompted. "Had it given Ned any trouble before?"

"It's old. Been in the family forever. Ned knew it needed fixing —there was a crack in one leg."

"When was the last time anyone besides Ned used it?"

"Must've been last summer. My nephew helped paint the shutters in August."

"Anyone else been to the house recently? Workmen, delivery people?"

Carol's eyes narrowed. "What are you getting at? You think someone did something to Ned's ladder?"

Before Cain could respond, Chambers appeared in the doorway, motioning the sheriff to join him. Cain patted Carol's hand. "I'll be right back," and he followed Sam to the mudroom.

"Forensics is stuck behind an accident on Route 16. At least another hour."

Cain suppressed a curse. "You and Rivers continue documenting the scene. I want that ladder leg preserved exactly as it is."

"What about the body? Can't leave him out there in this rain."

"Thirty more minutes. Then we move him, forensics or no forensics."

Returning to the kitchen, Cain gently reclaimed his seat across from Carol. He waited a moment, reaching out and holding her hand briefly. Then, cautiously he asked, "had Ned mentioned any concerns recently? Anyone who might have wished him harm?"

Carol's laugh held no humor. "He was seventy-six years old. He's probably insulted half the town. But who'd want to harm an old man?" Cain smiled softly at the memory of Ned's crusty personality, and his kind heart. The chances of Ned having any real enemies was distant. If anybody in his circle wanted to do him harm, it would not have been easy to hide. He stood, touching Carol on the shoulder.

"We'll figure this out, Carol," He gave her shoulder a squeeze, then headed back outside.

Cain stepped on to the deck, surveying the activity—deputies marking evidence, photographing the scene, securing the perimeter. Rain pattered down on his lid, the plastic covering creating a staccato beat that sounded like a drum solo. Looking down, water streamed off the brim, and his gaze locked on the broken ladder leg. The cut was unmistakable now that he had seen it.

Two deaths, both possibly staged. Cain wasn't sure this was more than bad luck, his mind not ready to truly consider the worse case possibility.

Could Stillwater have a serial killer?

FIFTEEN

Spring gave way to summer quickly, the remnants of winter finally surrendering to a warm sun and the flock of tourists that invaded Stillwater every June. Like locusts, they would consume, and to the town's delight, spend through August, and like they arrived, they would depart, giving the town back to the residents.

For most, summer meant an opportunity to leave town, unless you owned a business, and most locals often escaped to other cities, descending on another community almost in retribution. Despite the flush of tourists, Stillwater seemed calm, almost peaceful over the summer months. Sheriff Cain was always happy to trade the crime of locals for that of tourists. A drunken college student or a fender bender at Main and Water street was almost enjoyable to the darkness that seemed to be building up in the town.

For Carter, the summer was a time of escape. No school, no forced interactions with people he could care less about. Only his grandmother to watch out for, and his research. He spent hours over the summer simply reading, true crime stories by the volume, police reports from old cases, anything he could find using his ancient computer and the dial up internet he was forced to endure.

By the time late summer arrived, the tourists gone and the locals returned, the town seemed to fall back into its old habits. The still hot sun began to cast its late afternoon shadows across the Stillwater Public Library as Mary stepped out of Amber Wilder's Honda Civic parked across the street. Summer had been uneventful, and now back at school, none of them were in the mood for homework. Heather Davis emerged from the backseat, already complaining about the history project that had dragged them to the library on a perfectly good Thursday afternoon.

"Two hours of research," Heather groaned, shouldering her backpack. "Like we couldn't just find this stuff online."

"Mrs. Winters specifically said we needed to cite book sources," Mary reminded her, though she privately shared the sentiment. "Something about learning to use actual references instead of copying from Wikipedia."

Amber locked the car, her attention already drifting to her phone. "Let's just split up the sections and get it over with. I have practice at five."

Mary nodded, suddenly distracted as she caught sight of a familiar figure across the street. Carter Thompson was securing his battered bicycle to the rack near the library's side entrance, his movements efficient and precise. He wore the same faded green jacket he'd had for years, his backpack bulging with what she assumed were notebooks rather than textbooks. Mary hadn't seen Carter all summer. In truth she hadn't been home, gone for a lot of the time, off on a trip to visit her grandparents, which she complained about but secretly enjoyed. Escaping the constant criticism of her father alone made the plastic covered furniture of her grandmother's precious sitting room worth it.

Now, seeing Carter again, she felt like she wanted to say hi, to try and continue their renewed friendship. Not for her father, but for herself.

"You guys go ahead," Mary said, a sudden impulse taking hold. "I'll catch up."

Amber glanced up from her phone, following Mary's gaze. "Seriously? Thompson?"

"I just want to say hi," Mary said defensively.

Heather exchanged a meaningful look with Amber. "Your funeral. We'll be in the reference section when you're done with your charity case."

Mary ignored the comment, waiting until her friends disappeared through the main entrance before crossing the street. Something about seeing him alone, focused on his own world, made her miss the easy friendship they'd once had—before his parents' accident, before high school's invisible boundaries had separated them into different social territories.

She was halfway across the street when she noticed a man approaching Carter from the alley beside the library. Tall, unkempt, with a scraggly beard and clothes that had seen better days—unmistakably one of Stillwater's growing population of homeless. The man moved with the furtive urgency of someone desperate for something, his gaze darting nervously between Carter, the street and the library entrance.

Mary slowed her pace, concern flaring. The man looked exactly like the type her father warned her to avoid—possibly drunk, definitely unstable, the kind who might hassle a teenager for money or worse.

She was about to call out when something in Carter's body language gave her pause. Rather than appearing threatened, he stood perfectly still, watching the man's approach with what looked almost like expectation. There was no fear in his posture, no tension suggesting imminent flight.

The man reached Carter, speaking rapidly, his hands gesturing with clear agitation. From this distance, Mary couldn't hear their exchange, but what she saw confused her. The disheveled man wasn't threatening Carter—if anything, he seemed almost afraid of the teenager, his posture deferential despite his larger size and age.

Carter responded with a calm that bordered on coldness, his face impassive as he listened. Then, with a slight nod, he gestured for the man to follow him around the back of the library.

Mary hesitated at the curb, indecision rooting her in place. Common sense dictated she continue to the library, join her friends, forget the strange interaction she'd witnessed. But curiosity—the same curiosity that had made her Carter's willing partner in childhood investigations—pulled her in the opposite direction.

Before she could reconsider, Mary changed course, moving along the library's perimeter toward the rear of the building. She kept close to the wall, grateful for the landscaping that provided intermittent cover. The library's back lot was a neglected space, used primarily for staff parking and dumpsters, bordered by a wooded area that separated it from the neighboring residences.

Mary crept along the building's edge until voices reached her. She crouched behind an overgrown rhododendron, peering through its branches to where Carter stood with the disheveled man in the shadow of the building's rear entrance.

"—told you next week," Carter was saying, his voice carrying just enough for Mary to catch fragments. "You haven't done what I asked yet."

"Come on, man, I need it now." The man's voice trembled with barely contained desperation. "I did the bike thing like you said."

"Not enough." Carter's interruption was soft but carried unmistakable authority. "I need more than just actions, Kilgore. I need credibility."

Mary shifted slightly, trying to get a better view without revealing her position. A twig snapped beneath her foot, and she froze, heart pounding. Neither Carter nor the man—Kilgore, apparently—seemed to notice. She strained to hear the conversation.

Carter reached into his backpack and withdrew a small baggy, holding it up where Kilgore could see it but keeping it just out of reach. The man's eyes fixed on it with naked longing.

"OxyContin," Carter said, giving the bag a small shake. "Thirty milligrams, just like you like."

"Please," Kilgore whispered, his earlier deference deepening to something like supplication. "I'm hurting bad, kid."

"Then give me what I need." Carter's voice remained steady, emotionless. "When the sheriff questions you, you tell him exactly what we discussed. You were watching the library for bikes to take. You were at the river, saw McKenzie hiking down to the river, and you saw Ned Miller the day before, buying fuses at Mason's."

"Ok, I will." Kilgore was nervy, scared, but clearly willing to agree to anything.

Mary's breath caught in her throat. McKenzie—the elderly man who'd drowned in the river months ago. Her father's case. What was Carter doing? And Ned Miller, another death. Mary desperately wanted to understand, but her gut instinct told her Carter knew things that maybe he shouldn't, and maybe she shouldn't either.

"I don't know, man." Kilgore's voice dropped lower, tinged with genuine fear. "That's police business. If they catch me lying—"

"They won't catch you doing anything if you stick to the script." Carter pushed the baggy to Kilgore who took it quickly, worried it was just a trick. "A down payment. You get the rest when you deliver. I need you to play your role for medication, Kilgore. That's our deal. Take it or leave it."

Kilgore nodded, defeat washing over him, the humiliation of being subdued, controlled by a teenager the final nail.

"Sell the story. Make it believable or the deal is off." Carter's voice carried the finality of dismissal. "Now go. Use the back path through the woods. I don't want you seen here."

Mary pressed herself deeper into the bushes as Kilgore shuffled past her hiding spot, disappearing into the trees that bordered the houses behind the library. She waited, barely breathing, as Carter remained standing alone, his expression thoughtful as he stared after the departing man.

The Carter she observed in that moment was a stranger to her —cold, calculating, yes, but manipulating a clearly vulnerable man for purposes she couldn't begin to comprehend. This wasn't the quiet, awkward boy who shared lunches with her in the library. This was someone else entirely.

After what felt like an eternity, Carter checked his watch, zipped his backpack, and headed back toward the library's side entrance, moving around the other side, his movements as measured and controlled as they'd been before the encounter.

Mary remained hidden until she was certain he was gone, her mind racing to process what she'd witnessed. Carter was using prescription drugs—stolen or otherwise obtained—to manipulate Kilgore into giving false information about a drowning death.

But why? What possible reason could Carter have for inserting himself into her father's investigation?

She extricated herself from the bushes, brushing leaves and dirt from her jeans with shaking hands. Her friends would be wondering where she was, but Mary could barely focus on that concern through the thundering questions in her mind.

As she made her way back toward the library's main entrance, Mary felt as though she'd glimpsed something she was never meant to see—a side of Carter Thompson that existed beneath the familiar surface, something cold and purposeful that sent a chill through her despite the afternoon warmth.

The history project forgotten, Mary pushed through the library doors with a single thought echoing in her mind: What was Carter really doing?

SIXTEEN

The afternoon breeze filtered through the trees and across Carter as he pedaled away from the library, his mind already methodically sorting the interaction with Kilgore into its proper place within his larger plan. The transient was proving useful, if unreliable—a tool requiring frequent adjustment and calibration. Today's discussion had accomplished its purpose; the next piece would soon fall into place.

Carter cut across Maple Street, turning down the narrow alleyway, shaded from tall trees hanging across it from the backyards of the bordering houses. The rough roadway served as a shortcut between the commercial district and the residential neighborhood, and was little more than a service lane behind businesses, dumpsters lining one side, wooden fences marking residential boundaries on the other. Few people used it except for delivery trucks and locals who knew its value as a thoroughfare.

The shade was a welcome respite from the heat as Carter navigated around puddles and debris. He mentally reviewed his timeline, calculating how much time he had before his grandmother would need her medication. Enough to transcribe his latest observations into his notebook, perhaps even update his presentation for the sheriff.

"Hey! Thompson!"

The shout interrupted his thoughts. Fifty feet ahead, three figures had entered the alley from the opposite cross street, spreading across the narrow passage like a blockade. Carter recognized them immediately—Jason Mercer, Dylan Foster, and Eric Tanner. Seniors. Athletes. Members of the same social ecosystem as Mary, though several levels down the hierarchy from her position.

Carter didn't slow his pace, steering a course straight through the middle of their formation. They wanted intimidation; he would deny them the satisfaction.

"Look who it is," Jason called. "The freak who's been stalking Mary Cain."

Carter came to a stop in front of them, expression neutral as he stared them down. "Move," he said simply.

The boys exchanged amused glances, making no effort to clear a path.

"We saw you watching her in the library," Dylan added, crossing his arms. "Pretty creepy, even for you."

"I wasn't watching anyone," Carter replied, voice flat. "Now move. I have somewhere to be."

"Hear that, guys?" Eric smirked. "Detective Dipshit has important business." Carter began to pedal again, trying to break through the barrier. Eric's hand shot out, grabbing Carter's handlebar. "We're talking to you."

Already off balance from pedaling, Carter's momentum carried him forward as Eric yanked the bike sideways, sending him sprawling onto the asphalt. The impact tore through his jeans, skin scraping against rough pavement as the bicycle clattered to the ground.

"Oooh, wipeout," Jason laughed, delivering an ineffectual kick to the fallen bike.

Carter rose slowly, dusting himself off. His knee burned where the skin had torn, blood beginning to well up through the denim. He assessed the situation with cold precision—three opponents, physically superior, minimal escape routes, no witnesses.

"That was unnecessary," he stated, moving toward his bike.

Eric stepped into his path. "Know what's unnecessary? You creeping around Mary. She's nice to you because she feels sorry for you. Get it through your head—you're a charity case."

Carter's expression remained unchanged, though something flickered behind his eyes. "You don't know what you're talking about. Now, for the last time, move."

"Or what?" Dylan challenged, stepping closer. "You'll bore us to death with your little detective notebook?"

"You don't know anything about me." Carter's voice remained level, but a dangerous edge had crept in, barely perceptible.

"We know enough," Dylan countered, his own anger visibly building. "Everybody knows about Weird Carter Thompson, the freak whose parents drove off the road."

The silence that followed was absolute, broken only by distant traffic sounds and the sudden sharp intake of Carter's breath.

"Probably on purpose," Dylan continued, encouraged by Carter's reaction. "One look at their weirdo kid and WHAM!"

He slammed his fist into his palm for emphasis. "Right into a tree just to get away."

Something shifted in Carter's demeanor—a subtle change that failed to register as warning signals in the boys' primitive brains. His stillness became something different, his eyes focusing with an intensity that made Eric take a half-step backward despite himself.

"You should walk away now," Carter said, each word precisely carved from ice.

"Or what?" Dylan stepped forward, shoving Carter's shoulder. "What are you gonna do, freak?"

Carter's hand moved toward his backpack, and despite the disparity in their sizes, something in that movement made all three boys tense.

"HEY!" The bellow came from over the wooden fence to their right. "What the hell's going on back here?"

A man in his fifties leaned over the fence, scowling at the group. "You kids fighting in my alley? I'm calling the cops right now!"

The interruption broke the strange tension that had built in the narrow space. Dylan and his friends exchanged quick glances, the calculation obvious—a police report would mean suspension from upcoming games, possible disciplinary action.

"Whatever," Dylan muttered, backing away. "Stay away from Mary, Thompson. This isn't over."

As the three continued down the alley, Carter retrieved his bike, brushing dirt from the seat with methodical precision.

The man who had interrupted continued to watch from his fence.

"You okay, kid?" he called, concern replacing his initial anger.

Carter straightened his backpack, mounted the bike, and looked at the man with empty eyes. "Fine," he replied flatly, pushing off.

He pedaled steadily, ignoring the burning pain in his knee and the warm trickle of blood now soaking into his sock. The physical discomfort was irrelevant, cataloged and set aside. What remained were Dylan's words, vibrating in the echo chamber that Carter kept sealed from conscious examination.

Probably on purpose. Right off a bridge just to get away.

Their deaths had been an accident. Black ice on Sawmill Bridge. The police report had been unambiguous, most likely a botched investigation. The sheriffs department failing at their job. Carter had memorized every detail, every measurement, every conclusion.

But as he emerged from the alley onto Cedar Street, a different thought surfaced from somewhere deep and carefully contained: What if they had wanted to leave? What if they had recognized something in him that others were only beginning to see? The dangerous thought, fleeting and insubstantial, still managed to linger at the edges no matter how hard he tried to push it away. A possibility he often considered, but rarely admitted, even to himself.

Carter coasted to a stop in front of his house, the peeling paint and sagging gutters a familiar sight. Inside, his grandmother would be waiting, possibly confused about the time, about his identity, about her own location in the flow of past and present.

As he chained his bike to the porch railing, Carter noted the blood now crusted on his knee with detached interest. Physical evidence of an encounter he had already begun reframing in his mind—not as humiliation but as intelligence gathering. New information about potential obstacles, weaknesses to exploit, contingencies to prepare for.

He climbed the steps to the front door, backpack secure over his shoulder, plans shifting and reforming with each deliberate movement. Whatever doubts had momentarily surfaced in the alley were submerged once more beneath the cold certainty of purpose.

After all, a true detective understood that variables were inevitable. The difference between amateur and professional was simply a matter of adaptation.

SEVENTEEN

The Stillwater Sheriff's Department hummed with the quiet energy of a small police station on a fall morning. Fluorescent lights flickered overhead, casting the waiting area in an uneven glow. The clock above the reception desk ticked forward with audible precision, the only sound besides the distant ringing of telephones and the soft whir of ancient computer fans.

Carter Thompson occupied the vinyl chair farthest from the entrance once more, legs bouncing with nervous energy beneath a binder clutched tightly on his lap. The binder's edges had frayed from constant handling, its once-blue cover mottled with stains and the overlapping impressions of countless notes scribbled atop it. Rubber bands strained to hold the excess materials stuffed between its covers—newspaper clippings, printed articles, handwritten observations that spilled from its confines like evidence refusing to be contained.

Next to him, his tattered composition notebook balanced precariously on the chair's edge, its pages dogeared and dense with Carter's precise handwriting. Three hours had passed since he'd arrived, insisting on seeing Sheriff Cain personally. Three hours of being alternately ignored by the front desk deputy and assured that the sheriff would return "any minute now."

Carter checked his watch for the nineteenth time in the past thirty minutes. The school day had begun two hours ago. Another absence added to his growing collection, another conversation with the counselor inevitable. It didn't matter. What waited in his binder carried more significance than whatever meaningless busywork his classmates were completing in AP English.

His leg bounced faster, heel tapping against the linoleum floor. Through the glass partition separating the waiting area from the bullpen, he glimpsed movement—a flash of the sheriff's distinctive silhouette passing between offices. Carter sat straighter, gathering his materials in anticipation of finally being summoned.

The sudden motion dislodged his notebook, sending it tumbling to the floor. It landed with a soft slap, pages splaying open in a fan of exposed information. Between the sheets, several photographs scattered across the worn linoleum—4x6 prints developed at the corner drugstore from the film he'd purchased at Mason's Country Store.

Carter lunged forward, scrambling to collect the images before anyone could examine them closely. Too late. Deputy Garrett glanced up from the reception desk, her eyes narrowing as she registered what lay on the floor.

The photographs showed Mary Cain and her friends exiting the library, captured in the grainy quality of cheap film. Several featured Mary alone, framed in tight focus, her profile highlighted by the setting sun. In one particularly intimate shot, she tucked hair behind her ear, unaware of being observed.

Carter's face burned as he swept the prints into a stack, shoving them back between the notebook pages with fumbling fingers. When he dared look up, Deputy Garrett was watching him with an expression that mixed disapproval with something more calculating.

"Sheriff won't be much longer," she said, her tone neutral but her eyes conveying a clear message: I saw that.

"Thanks," Carter mumbled, clutching the recovered materials against his chest like armor.

Through the interior glass, movement caught his attention again. The sheriff had entered the bullpen, followed closely by Deputy Sam Chambers. Even through the barrier, their body language telegraphed conflict—Cain's shoulders rigid with authority, Sam's hands gesturing with the passionate conviction of youth.

Carter couldn't hear their words, but the pattern was clear: Sam advocating, the sheriff resisting. Twice, Sam pointed toward the waiting area, presumably indicating Carter. The sheriff shook his head each time, hands planted on a desk as if physically anchoring himself against persuasion.

The argument crescendoed with Sheriff Cain throwing up his hands in surrender, his "OK, OK!" audible even through the glass partition. Sam's posture immediately relaxed, victory apparent in the set of his shoulders as he turned toward the door.

Moments later, the young deputy emerged from the bullpen, pushing through the swinging half-door that separated official space from public.

"Come on," Sam said, beckoning with a tilt of his head. "Sheriff will see you now."

Carter gathered his materials, pulse accelerating with vindication. Finally, someone was listening. Someone was taking him seriously. He followed Sam through the bullpen, ignoring the curious glances from other deputies as they passed.

Sheriff Cain stood behind his desk when they entered, his expression locked in the neutral mask of professional law enforcement. No welcome, no acknowledgment of the three-hour wait, just the appraising stare of a man who measured every interaction for potential threat or value.

"You've got five minutes," he said without preamble. "Deputy Chambers seems to think you have information worth my time."

Sam closed the door behind them, taking a position near the wall as Carter settled into the chair opposite the sheriff's desk. The binder felt suddenly inadequate in Carter's hands, the culmination of months of preparation reduced to a cheap office supply stuffed with amateur analysis.

No. Not amateur. Methodical. Precise. Valid.

Carter steadied himself with that conviction as he opened the binder. "I've been tracking suspicious activities around Stillwater for the past fourteen months," he began, voice steadier than he'd expected. "Particularly focused on potential connections between seemingly unrelated incidents."

The sheriff's expression didn't change, but something in his eyes sharpened—attention engaging despite his apparent reluctance. Carter sensed the shift and pressed forward, extracting a series of photographs from the front pocket of the binder.

"These were taken at the library over a three-week period," he explained, laying the images in sequence across the desk.

"Multiple angles of the bicycle rack where thefts have occurred."

The sheriff glanced at the photos without touching them. Each showed the library's exterior from various vantage points, timestamps meticulously recorded in the margins. Interspersed with general surveillance shots were closer images of a man, Kilgore, who appeared in multiple frames—mid-thirties, unkempt beard, worn clothing that suggested life on society's edges.

"In these images," Carter continued, pointing to a sequence taken on June 3rd, "the subject approaches the bicycle rack at 4:17 PM. Note his position here—bent over the lock of a blue mountain bike. Note the scar on the back of his left hand. Three minutes later, the bike is gone, and so is he."

Sam moved closer, examining the images over Carter's shoulder. "That's good documentation," he commented. "Clear shots of his face from multiple angles."

The sheriff held up a hand, silencing his deputy without looking at him. "I can see what the photos show. What I don't understand is why you're bringing this to me now, months later, and without any images of the actual theft."

Carter's momentum faltered. "Because it's connected to the other incidents. The pattern—"

"What pattern?" Sheriff Cain leaned forward, hands flat on his desk. "Be specific, Carter. What exactly are you suggesting?"

Carter hesitated, suddenly aware of how tenuous the connections might sound when voiced aloud. But he'd come too far to retreat now. "The bicycle thefts were just the beginning. They establish a presence in specific locations at specific times. Surveillance. The same surveillance approach was used before Jackson McKenzie's death."

The sheriff's expression tightened, almost imperceptibly. "And how would you know anything about the circumstances of Jackson McKenzie's death?"

"I observe," Carter replied, flipping to another section of his binder. "I document patterns that others miss. The fence that trapped him wasn't weakened by natural deterioration. The cut marks were deliberate, just like—" he stopped abruptly, realizing his mistake too late.

"Just like what?" Sheriff Cain's voice had dropped to a dangerous quiet.

Carter swallowed. "Just like the ladder at Ned Miller's house."

Silence crashed into the room like a physical force. Sam straightened from his relaxed position, shock evident in his expression. The sheriff remained completely still, only his eyes moving as they reassessed Carter with disturbing intensity.

"How do you know about Ned Miller?" he asked finally. "We haven't released any details about his death. It hasn't even been classified as suspicious in any public statement."

Carter's mouth went dry. "I heard it on the scanner."

"The scanner didn't mention anything about a ladder."

Trapped. Carter's mind raced for an explanation that wouldn't sound incriminating. "I... I've been tracking patterns of curious activity among elderly residents. Miller was on my list. He was very… independent, never asked for help. He often complained about issues with his house, ones he refused help in fixing. When I heard about his death this morning, I made the connection." Carter hesitated, then, "and I went and visited Mrs. Miller after you."

Sheriff Cain exchanged a glance with Sam, some silent communication passing between them. Then he turned back to Carter, his expression unreadable. "You're telling me you predicted Ned Miller might be at risk because of a hunch?"

"Not predicted," Carter corrected. "Observed. The same way I observed the bicycle thief. I notice things others don't."

A long pause followed as the sheriff studied him, weighing something behind his impassive gaze. Finally, he nodded toward the photographs of the bicycle thief. "You have an ID on this individual?"

Relief flooded through Carter at the shift back to more solid ground. "James Kilgore, 37, residence unknown but possibly squatting in the abandoned Campbell property off Route 16 by the Falls. Prior arrests for possession and petty theft in Clark County. Arrived in Stillwater approximately eight months ago."

Sam whistled softly. "That's detailed intel."

"Public records," Carter explained. "Plus observations from multiple sources around town."

Sheriff Cain gathered the photographs into a neat stack. "And you believe this James Kilgore is connected to Jackson McKenzie's death? To Ned Miller's?"

"I don't have conclusive evidence linking him directly," Carter admitted. "But his presence establishes a pattern of surveillance that precedes both incidents. He was observed near the river path three times in the week before Mackenzie died. And he purchased hardware supplies at Mason's the day before Miller's death."

The sheriff leaned back in his chair. "That's circumstantial at best."

"Patterns matter," Carter insisted, frustration bleeding into his voice. "Connections matter. Most people don't see them because they're not looking."

"And you're looking." Not a question but a statement, tinged with something that might have been a touch of sarcasm, or might have been suspicion.

"Always," Carter confirmed, ignoring the tone, and accepting the statement.

Sheriff Cain studied him for another long moment before pushing back from his desk. "I'll check out this Kilgore character. See if there's anything to your theory."

Victory surged through Carter, so unexpected he nearly missed the conditional nature of the commitment. "I'd like to come along. I can identify—"

"Shouldn't you be in school?" The sheriff cut him off, already reaching for his jacket. "It's nearly noon on a Wednesday."

Carter's momentum faltered. "This is more important."

"Not to the state education board, it isn't." Sheriff Cain nodded to Sam. "Deputy Chambers, see young Carter here to his bike and make sure you see him pedaling off in the direction of the high school." He stood, moving around the desk and toward the door.

"But I can help—"

"You've helped enough for one day." The sheriff's tone left no room for argument. "We'll take it from here." He nodded to Chambers and left the office.

Carter remained seated, frustration and disappointment warring in his chest. So close to being taken seriously, to being included, only to be dismissed like a child who'd delivered a homework assignment.

Sam approached, placing a reassuring hand on Carter's shoulder. "He's right, you know. You should be in school. But this—" he gestured to the binder, "—this is good work. Really good."

Carter looked up, finding genuine respect in the young deputy's eyes. Some of the sting of rejection faded, replaced by grudging acceptance that some acknowledgement was better than none.

"I'll make sure he actually checks out Kilgore," Sam said, "He won't admit it, but he was impressed with your intel."

"He didn't seem impressed," Carter muttered, gathering his materials.

"That's just Cain. Doesn't show much." Sam grinned, lowering his voice. "Trust me, if he thought you were wasting his time, you'd know it. The fact that he's following up at all means he sees something worth investigating."

As they stood to leave the office, the sheriff reappeared in the doorway."The photographs and information stay here. We'll make copies for the file."

Not a request but an order. Carter hesitated, his instinct to protect his research battling with the desire for official validation. Finally, he nodded, removing the relevant pages from his binder and placing them on the desk.

"There's more," he said. "Other connections I've documented. If you want to see those too—"

"One thing at a time," Sheriff Cain interrupted. "Let's see if your bicycle thief has anything to do with actual crimes before we go down the conspiracy rabbit hole." To Sam he nodded to the door. "See Mr. Thompson out. I've got to drop in on a council meeting next door, then we can head out to the Campbell place. 20 minutes?" Sam nodded.

As Carter was guided out of the office, he cast one last glance at the photographs remaining on the sheriffs desk—evidence of his methodical surveillance, his attention to detail that others lacked.

Behind them, Sheriff Cain watched as Carter was led into the waiting room, his expression thoughtful as he looked at the teenager's retreating back. Something in the boy's certainty nagged at him, a conviction too solid to dismiss entirely despite its unlikely source.

Patterns. Connections. The invisible threads linking seemingly random events into something more sinister.

The sheriff turned away, headed for his meeting, but his mind already planning his approach to James Kilgore—a man who might be nothing more than a bicycle thief, or might be something far more dangerous.

EIGHTEEN

Gerald Cooper wiped sweat from his brow, the sleeve of his flannel shirt coming away damp. The midday sun, unseasonably warm for early Fall, was almost too much for him. At seventy-three, every task required more effort than he cared to admit, but pride and an ill temper kept him from asking for help. The old Farmall tractor—a machine nearly as ancient as he was—had developed a persistent oil leak that needed tending before he could prepare the east field for the winter.

He'd parked on a slope overlooking his property before the machine had quit on him, putting the tires on the elevated furrows in the old dirt road, the position affording just enough elevation to slide beneath the tractor's undercarriage. The incline wasn't steep enough to worry about, especially with the parking brake engaged, a flat rock wedged for good measure behind the rear wheel closest to the downslope.

Gerald's farm sat two miles outside town proper, close enough for convenience but far enough to preserve the solitude he'd grown to value since Martha's passing three years ago. The quiet was a comfort now, broken only by birdsong and the occasional distant rumble of a passing truck on the county road.

Gerald lowered himself to the ground, joints protesting with a symphony of pops and creaks. An overnight rain had filled the ruts in the old fire line road, the still-damp earth immediately began soaking through his overalls, but he ignored the discomfort. Just a quick fix—locate the leaking line, figure out what needs to be replaced, and he'd be back in the warmth of his kitchen with a cup of coffee before the dampness settled into his bones.

He wiggled his way under the tractor, tools arrayed beside him. The Farmall had been his father's before him, a machine whose every bolt and part he knew intimately. Gerald had learned to drive on the tractor. He knew it well. The oil leak was likely coming from—

A soft metallic ping interrupted his thoughts. Not loud, but distinctly out of place.

Gerald paused, cocking his head to listen. Something shifted above him—a subtle redistribution of the tractor's weight that sent a faint vibration through the frame. The ping sound came again, slightly louder. It took Gerald a beat to process the information, the sound so distinct yet not immediately obvious. But then it came to him with a shock that made his aged body tense in panic.

The brake line.

Realization dawned a split second before reaction. He glanced quickly to the cable that held the parking brakes in position. A frayed section was coming apart before his eyes. It was only at that instant that Gerald could tell that the brake line had been partially cut.

He moved to roll clear, but seventy-three-year-old reflexes betrayed him. In a split second the rock behind the rear wheel shifted, dislodged in the muddy ground by the tractor's almost imperceptible initial movement. The wheel rolled slightly, the rock slid to the side, the massive tire now held back only by the remnants of the wire that held the Farmall's parking brake intact. Then suddenly, a final ping, a cable breaking, and the weight of the massive machine, no longer restrained, yielded to gravity's inexorable pull.

The Farmall lurched backward.

Gerald screamed a guttural sound as the the machine began to roll. The left rear wheel immediately rolled into a deep rut in the road, dropping the chassis of the three ton tractor onto Gerald's chest, trapping him beneath the tractor's underbelly. Gerald's scream was pushed from his lungs as the weight broke his ribs, then twisted him against the soft ground, rotating him underneath the machine. The tractor continued its terrible journey down the slope, dragging Gerald with it, his fingernails carving desperate furrows in the wet earth as he tried and failed to arrest his movement.

The tractor gathered momentum, bouncing over the uneven ground, each impact driving jagged components deeper into Gerald's flesh. His consciousness flickered between blinding agony and merciful darkness as he was pulled over rocks, through mud, his body becoming a grotesque plow cutting a crimson furrow across his own field.

When the tractor finally came to rest at the bottom of the hill, Gerald Cooper's mangled form lay motionless beneath it, eyes fixed on the brilliant blue sky he would never see again.

NINETEEN

The abandoned Campbell property squatted at the end of a rutted dirt road three miles outside Stillwater proper. The private piece of land was now surrounded on three sides by state park. The Campbell house was built by the former first residents of the small logging town as a country getaway. The once beautiful cabin had enjoyed easy access to the head of the Stillwater Falls, the jewel of Stillwater, which bordered the property. Now, generations later, the Campbells had moved on, leaving only the decaying home as a reminder. Its peeling clapboard and sagging porch had once housed five generations before the last family chose to leave the town. Now it stood as a monument to exodus—empty windows like vacant eyes watching the quiet forest in silent vigil.

Sheriff Cain guided his SUV along the overgrown driveway, gravel crunching beneath heavy tires. Beside him, Deputy Sam Chambers surveyed the property with the alert focus of someone expecting trouble.

"No vehicle visible," Sam observed.

Cain nodded, scanning the abandoned house and dilapidated outbuildings that dotted the property—a collapsed barn beyond the house, a garage listing dangerously like a Drew Englander painting, a storage shed whose roof was sagging heavily from decades of harsh winters.

"Let's start with the house," he decided, bringing the vehicle to a stop thirty yards from the front porch. "You take the back in case he bolts."

Sam unclipped his seatbelt, already reaching for the door handle. "You think the Thompson kid is right about this guy?"

Cain considered the question as he checked his sidearm and radio. "Carter's documentation of the bicycle thefts is solid. But let's find some evidence."

"I was honestly surprised you agreed to follow up on this."

"I follow up on all credible leads," Cain replied evenly. "Regardless of their source. And right now, James Kilgore is the only name we have connected to two potential murder scenes. That makes him worth talking to."

Sam acknowledged the point with a slight nod before stepping out of the vehicle. He moved to circle wide, approaching the house from the rear. Cain watched him disappear around the corner before beginning his own advance toward the front entrance.

The porch steps protested beneath his weight, wood groaning warnings of structural weakness from decades of exposure. Cain paused at the front door, listening for movement inside. Nothing but the whisper of wind through broken windowpanes and the distant call of a bird from somewhere in the trees.

He knocked firmly, the sound hollow and final in the fall stillness. "Sheriff's department. James Kilgore?"

No response. Cain knocked again, louder. "Mr. Kilgore? Stillwater Sheriff's Department. We'd like to ask you some questions."

The silence that followed implied an empty property, but something in Cain's instincts—honed through years of law enforcement—suggested otherwise. A feeling, perhaps not immediately inside but somewhere on the property. Cain turned around, looking out into the woods, then around the property from the front porch, half expecting to see someone there, but there was nothing. He turned back to the house.

Cupping his hands around his eyes, Cain leaned close to a front window, peering through glass clouded by years of dust and grime. The interior revealed little—furniture draped in sheets, floors scattered with debris blown in through broken windows, walls streaked with water damage from a leaking roof.

But there, in the corner of what had once been a formal dining room, sat evidence of use—a sleeping bag unrolled on a bare mattress, empty food containers stacked neatly beside it, a battery-powered lantern standing by.

Someone was staying here, recently enough. Nothing in the small collection was coated in dust like the rest of the house.

Cain stepped back from the window, keying his radio. "Sam, I've got evidence of occupation inside. No visual on the subject. What's your status?"

The radio screamed static, the signal even weaker this far from town, even though Sam and Cain were within fifty yards of each other. Finally, the signal crackled briefly before Sam's voice came through ragged. "Checking the —- out—-. Nothing yet in the—wait." The transmission paused, then resumed with increased urgency, this time coming through clear. "Movement in the storage shed. Stand by."

Cain's hand moved to his sidearm, touching the butt of his gun, a firearm he had not had to draw in nearly three years. He keyed the radio. "Do not engage alone. Wait for backup."

No response came through, only static. Cain cursed under his breath, moving with increased speed toward the rear of the property where the storage shed stood. The structure looked even more decrepit up close—its wooden walls warped by exposure, roof missing several shingles, door hanging at an angle that suggested broken hinges.

As Cain rounded the corner of the house, he caught sight of Sam approaching the shed, weapon drawn but pointed downward in the ready position. The younger officer paused at the partially open door, positioning himself to one side as training dictated. He glanced back, making eye contact with Cain who paused in position, covering Sam from the corner of the house. Cain gave him a nod, ready.

"James Kilgore?" Sam called out, voice carrying the practiced authority of law enforcement despite his youth. "This is the Stillwater Sheriff's Department. Come out with your hands visible."

Movement sounded from within the shed—the shuffle of feet on dirt, something metallic clattering to the ground. Then silence again, heavy with potential.

Sam glanced back, making sure Cain heard the motion, before returning his attention to the shed. "Mr. Kilgore, we just want to talk. No one's in trouble here."

A voice finally responded from within—male, wary, with the slight slur of someone either just waking or chemically altered. "Don't got no reason to talk to cops."

"We just need to ask a few questions. Easier to do this the simple way, sir."

More movement inside, closer to the door now. Cain drew his weapon, moving closer, ready to back up his deputy, creating a crossfire position that would discourage any attempt to flee.

"I haven't done anything wrong," the voice insisted, closer now. "Haven't been to town in weeks."

"Then this will be a quick conversation," Cain responded, his tone conveying confidence rather than threat. "Step out where we can see you, Mr. Kilgore. Show us your hands."

A long pause followed, filled with the calculation of a man weighing limited options. Finally, dirty fingers appeared around the edge of the door, followed by a palm, then a wrist. The door creaked wider, revealing James Kilgore in stages—hands, arms, torso, face.

He matched Carter's description and photographs with depressing accuracy, Cain thought—mid-thirties but weathered to look a decade older, beard untrimmed but not unkempt, clothes worn and layered. His eyes held the wariness of someone accustomed to negative interactions with authority, darting between the two officers with practiced assessment.

"Hands on your head, please," Cain instructed, keeping his gun pointed down. "Deputy Chambers is going to check you for weapons. Standard procedure."

"I don't have any weapons," Kilgore mumbled, but complied with the resigned efficiency of someone familiar with the process. Sam holstered his weapon and carefully patted him down. "This about trespassing? Old man Campbell said I could stay long as I helped clear brush in the spring."

"Old man Campbell died three years ago," Cain noted, watching as Sam performed a quick but thorough pat-down. "His son owns the property now. Lives in Pittsburgh."

"Huh." Kilgore absorbed this information with a shrug. "Guess I've been talking to ghosts then."

Sam completed the search, stepping back with a slight shake of his head to indicate no weapons found. "Clear, Sheriff." Kilgore lowered his hands, but kept his palms up, fearful any gesture might be seen as dangerous.

Cain holstered his weapon, maintaining a cautious distance but shifting to a less confrontational stance. "Like we said, Mr. Kilgore, we're looking into some bicycle thefts in town. A witness place you near the library around the times bikes went missing."

Kilgore's expression remained carefully neutral, but a muscle twitched in his jaw—the involuntary response of someone hearing accusations that hit too close to truth. "Don't know what you're talking about. Haven't been to any library."

"We have photographs," Sam interjected, "of you examining bike locks outside the Stillwater Public Library on multiple occasions. Most recently on August 3rd."

"Lots of guys look like me," Kilgore countered, but the defense lacked conviction. "Beards are common these days."

Cain studied the man. He could see a Navy flight jacket peeked out from under a longer overcoat, a prized possession. There was a background here, a former version of Kilgore that played an important role in the world. He could see a measured look in Kilgore's eyes. There had been a version of the man that had existed in the past that was smart, calculating. But all of that had been dulled by drug addiction, and the years of living marginalized at the edges of society.

The cool forest breeze kicked in, making both Kilgore and Cain shiver, wrapping their jackets closer. Cain saw it as an opening, a reasonable request.

"Why don't we continue this conversation at the station?" Cain suggested, the question framed as a courtesy that was actually a command. "Warmer there, and we can clear up any misunderstandings. If you're not the person in our photographs, you'll be on your way quickly enough."

Kilgore shifted his weight, glancing toward the treeline beyond the shed as if measuring the distance against his chances of outrunning two armed officers. The calculation must have come up unfavorable, because he sighed, his shoulders slumping in a gesture of resignation.

"Fine. Whatever. But I ain't riding in the back cage like some criminal. Not if this is just 'asking questions.'"

Cain nodded his agreement. "You have to sit in the back seat. That's just procedure. But no cuffs, and my Bronco has no screen, so it'll just be a normal ride." Kilgore accepted the terms reluctantly, moving toward the Bronco following a gesture from Cain.

Sam lingered behind, and took a moment to slip through the door to the shed. Inside, framed by the scattered beams of light that penetrated the decomposing building were bike frames, stripped of parts, many of them very old. He let his eyes adjust to the dim light, looking into the corners of the shed. The room was a series of piles, debris collected over many years, from farm tools to old wine casks. Sam pulled out his flashlight, shining it into corners with a quick, practiced eye. Most piles of debris were ancient and untouched, but off to one side, nearly covered by old wooden apple crates, sat a pile of stained shop rags. Sam grabbed a long stick, then moved the fabric aside carefully, revealing several rolls of thick fishing line and an old finishing saw half rusted, though the teeth were bright from recent use. Sam gently replaced the rags and backed out, letting the door close behind him before catching up to the two men.

As they walked back toward the SUV, Cain led the way, mind already formulating the approach for the upcoming interview. The bicycle thefts were merely pretext—a legitimate reason to bring Kilgore in for questioning while they built a case for the more serious allegations.

If Carter's suspicions proved correct, if this man had any connection to the deaths of Jackson Mackenzie and Ned Miller, Cain would need more than circumstantial evidence of his presence near the crime scenes. He would need motive, method, opportunity.

He would need a confession.

As they reached the vehicle, Sam caught up, pulling open the back door for Kilgore. "Have you lived in Stillwater long, Mr. Kilgore?"

"A couple years, maybe," Kilgore replied, settling into the seat with the false casualness of someone trying to appear cooperative. "Work's been scarce since my back injury."

Sam closed the door then stood up in front of Cain. His face away from Kilgore he whispered the words softly. "There's evidence in the shed." Cain nodded, but Sam continued. "Fishing line, a saw…" Sam dared not delay any longer, he moved past the sheriff and slid into the passenger seat.

"You worked at the lumber mill?" Sam asked as he positioned himself in the passenger seat, turning sideways so he could see their subject.

"Nah. Construction mostly. Day labor when I can get it. Not much building happening around here these days, even if I could manage it."

Cain slid into the driver's seat and started the engine, mind latching onto every detail. Construction. Ladders. Tools. Skills that might include knowledge of how to strategically weaken structures to ensure catastrophic failure under specific conditions.

"What kind of construction? Residential? Commercial?"

Kilgore shrugged, gaze fixed on the road ahead as they pulled away from the Campbell property. "Whatever pays. Done it all at some point."

The conversation continued in this vein as they drove back toward town—Cain asking casual questions about Kilgore's background and activities in Stillwater, the suspect providing answers just detailed enough to seem cooperative without revealing anything substantive.

As they approached the outskirts of Stillwater, Cain's radio crackled to life. Dispatch's voice cut through the interior of the vehicle, breaking the pattern of question and evasion.

"Sheriff, we've got a situation at 3495 Cypress Road. We've got an 11-44. Deputies on scene requesting your presence immediately."

Kilgore's head turned sharply at the code, recognition flashing across his features before he could suppress it. Cain noted the reaction without comment. He picked up the radio mic with calm professionalism despite the adrenaline now surging through his system.

"Copy, dispatch. En route. ETA ten minutes." He turned to Kilgore.

"Sorry, Mr. Kilgore. I hope you don't mind a quick detour. But please stay in the car. For your safety." Cain turned away, his focus on accelerating the Bronco, and trying to analyze what he was about to walk into.

Cypress Road. The Cooper address. 11-44— possible fatality.

Cain accelerated, tires gripping the winter-slick road as the vehicle picked up speed. Behind him, Kilgore sat in calculated silence, but his body language had shifted—tension radiating from his frame, eyes now tracking their surroundings with increased attention.

"Problem at the Cooper place?" he asked finally, leaning forward, the question too casual for the circumstances. "Hope that old man is ok."

Cain kept his expression neutral despite the alarm bells now ringing in his mind. "Why would you say that?"

Kilgore hesitated, realizing his mistake too late. "Just, you know, he's old, and stuff happens. Like what happened to McKenzie and Ned Miller."

"We haven't released any details about Ned Miller's death," Cain pointed out, watching Kilgore's reflection in the rear view mirror. "And you said yourself you haven't been to town in weeks."

The man's fabricated nonchalance crumbled visibly, replaced by the tight focus of someone trying to recall a script, a story that his drug worn mind had trouble following. "I saw McKenzie at the river, he liked to fish at that spot," Kilgore said, trying to remember the words Carter had insisted he say, but in the back of his mind he knew something was wrong. "I told him it was dangerous, with those old fences and stuff." Kilgore's heart began racing, though he couldn't stop himself from finishing what he had started. "And I saw Ned buying fuses at the store —" Kilgore stopped himself, seeing the pattern that had been laid out for him by that damn kid.

Kilgore had just incriminated himself in two, maybe three murders.

Cain gripped the wheel tight, his knuckles white from tension. Sam leaned subtly toward Cain, lowering his voice. "He's uncuffed."

The quiet reminder acknowledged what both officers now recognized—their subject had just inadvertently revealed knowledge he shouldn't possess, transforming a person of interest into a potential suspect in multiple homicides. The calculus of the situation had changed significantly.

"I know," Cain replied quietly, maintaining even pressure on the accelerator as they approached a curve in the road. "Mr. Kilgore, I need you to sit back and —"

The impact came from nowhere—Kilgore slammed the edge of his right hand into Sam's throat with unexpected force, catching the deputy by surprise before he could react. The younger officer made a strangled sound, hands instinctively flying to his injured airway.

In the second motion, Kilgore lunged, grabbing the steering wheel and wrenching it sharply toward the ditch that ran alongside the road. The SUV swerved violently, tires losing traction on the damp surface. Cain fought for control, muscles straining against the combined forces of momentum and Kilgore's desperate strength.

"Let go of the wheel!" Cain shouted, his right hand pushing against Kilgore's body while his left hand maintained a grip on the steering wheel, trying to keep the vehicle on the road.

The Bronco fishtailed, rear end swinging in a wide arc as Cain pumped the brakes, trying to regain traction without sending them into a full spin. Kilgore continued to fight for control, his face contorted with the realization that his options had narrowed to escape or imprisonment.

Sam gasped for air, his left hand holding his throat while his right reached for his gun. As Sam leaned forward to release it from his holster, Kilgore slammed his elbow into Sam's face, an audible crack followed by a muffled yell. Blood began to pour from his nose.

Sam abandoned his gun, and instead grabbed at Kilgore's arms, yanking them away, slamming a single, vicious punch to his face, making him weaken enough to let Sam pull him away from the wheel.

The SUV continued its barely controlled slide toward the roadside ditch. Cain managed to steer into the skid, gradually bringing the vehicle back under control as it slowed, half on the shoulder and half on the asphalt.

Before the SUV had fully stopped, Kilgore made his final desperate play—he pulled his right hand away from Sam's grip, then drove the heel into Sam's face, striking his already damaged nose. With a grunt of pain, Sam's grip loosened reflexively, giving Kilgore the opening he needed to wrench the door handle and throw himself from the still-moving vehicle.

He hit the ground in a controlled roll that spoke of past training, coming up in a runner's stance and sprinting toward the dense tree line that bordered the road. Cain slammed the SUV into park and vaulted from the driver's seat, drawing his weapon as his boots hit the frozen ground.

"Kilgore! Stop or I will fire!"

The fleeing man never slowed, already fifteen yards from the road and accelerating toward the protective cover of the forest. Cain raised his weapon, sighting on the center mass of the retreating figure, finger tensing against the trigger.

Time compressed to a single instant of decision—take the shot and potentially kill a man whose guilt remained unproven, or allow a suspect in multiple homicides to escape into wilderness he clearly knew better than they did.

Before Cain could commit to either option, Sam staggered from the vehicle, blood streaming from his broken nose down the front of his uniform. Despite his injury, the young deputy had drawn his own weapon and now tracked Kilgore's retreat with unwavering focus.

Sam's shot rang out, the bullet striking a tree just a foot from Kilgore's head, but then he was gone, lost in the dense woods.

Cain holstered his weapon. Sam was already reaching for his radio."Call for backup," Cain said. "And alert all units we have a dangerous suspect fleeing westbound from mile marker 47 on County Road 16."

As Sam relayed the information through his radio, Cain assessed the situation. Kilgore had a head start but would be leaving tracks in the damp forest floor. The temperature was dropping as evening approached, making extended exposure in the damp and cold forest potentially fatal without proper gear. All roads out of the area could be monitored by deputies and state patrol.

This wasn't an escape. It was a temporary evasion that would end either in Kilgore's capture or his death by exposure if he remained in the woods overnight.

Sam moved to the back of the SUV and began shoving shells into a police issue shotgun. Cain put a hand on his shoulder.

"You aren't going after him" Cain said, noting the younger man's unsteady stance.

Sam used his sleeve to wipe blood from his face. "He's not getting away."

"No, he's not. But we're headed to Cooper's place. And you can clean yourself up."Sam nodded, and Cain offered him a tissue. "Put some pressure on that."

Deputy Hargrove's patrol vehicle pulled up and, with a brief update on Kilgore's escape, Cain and Chambers left him, the SUV pulling back onto the road once more, headed to the Cooper property, to investigate another possible death. Cain fought the feeling that he was about to identify murder three in the recent gruesome series. His own training told him not to jump to conclusions, but he was quickly finding that no training could prepare him for what horrible game someone was playing in his town.

TWENTY

The Cooper farm lay under a gloomy sky, its quiet tranquility shattered by the commotion of emergency vehicles. Red and blue lights pulsed silently across the weathered barn, the family's modest farmhouse, and the gentle slope that had become a crime scene.

At the bottom of the hill, a vintage Farmall tractor lay partially on its side, its massive wheels still and silent after their lethal journey downhill. Yellow police tape fluttered in the afternoon breeze, creating a stark perimeter around the scene. The earth behind the tractor told the grim story—a long furrow of disturbed soil and blood marking the path where Gerald Cooper had been dragged to his death.

Deputy Carol Rivers crouched beside the tractor, her experienced eyes methodically cataloging evidence while she dictated notes into a small recorder. Her gloved hands moved with practiced precision, taking samples of fluids that had leaked from the machine's undercarriage, measuring skid patterns, photographing the point where the farmer's body remained partially pinned beneath the tractor's weight.

"We need the county wrecker to lift this thing," Deputy Weathers said, his face tight with frustration. "Can't process the body until we get the tractor off him."

"Wrecker could disturb the scene," Deputy Rivers countered, the older officer's rounded features set in stubborn lines. "Need to document everything before we move anything. That's procedure."

"Procedure won't help us if the evidence gets contaminated while we're standing around waiting for equipment," Weathers shot back. "It's already been two hours."

"And Cooper's been dead longer than that," Rivers replied grimly. "Another hour won't matter to him."

Their argument was interrupted by the arrival of a Police Bronco, its tires shedding dried mud as it came to a stop at the edge of the police line. Sheriff Cain emerged, the tight set of his jaw revealed his recognition of the gravity of the situation. From the other side of the vehicle Deputy Chambers joined him.

"What happened to you," Weathers asked loudly, suppressing a laugh. "Looks like at least three rounds."

"A suspect used his face as a punching bag," Cain responded. "Get that ambulance to wait a minute so they can check him out." Weathers, his smile fading, stood and ran back up the road, waving at the ambulance that was about to pull away. "Go with him," Cain said to Sam. "That might be broken." Sam nodded, hesitating only slightly, wanting to know about this latest "accident". But he decided it better to follow orders, turning away to follow Weathers, who had managed to stop the paramedics.

"What have we got?" Cain asked Rivers, ducking under the tape and approaching the deputy.

"Gerald Cooper, 73," Rivers reported, standing to meet him. "Apparent accident with his tractor. Looks like he was working underneath when it rolled down the hill. Dragged him about thirty yards before coming to rest here."

The sheriff nodded, glancing over the entire scene with practiced eyes. "Time of death?"

"I'm estimating between 11:30am and 1:30 this afternoon," Rivers said. "But the ME might have other ideas." She motioned with her eyes to a middle-aged woman off to a side, watching tearfully from a distance. "His daughter found him when she came to deliver groceries around 2:15."

Sheriff Cain circled the tractor, careful not to disturb the evidence markers Rivers had placed around the scene. "Anyone touch the machine yet?"

"Just enough to confirm he's deceased," Rivers responded. "We've been documenting everything before attempting to recover the body."

"Good." The sheriff crouched near the rear axle, studying something beneath the tractor that had caught his attention. "His daughter mention any mechanical problems? Reason he'd be working on it on a slope instead of level ground?"

"Said he mentioned an oil leak yesterday," Rivers replied. "Nothing major. Routine maintenance."

Sheriff Cain gestured for Rivers to join him, pointing toward something beneath the tractor's undercarriage. Rivers knelt beside the sheriff.

"Look at this," Cain said quietly, indicating the brake assembly.

Rivers leaned closer, careful not to touch anything. "The cable," she observed, her voice dropping to ensure only Cain could hear. "It's been partially cut."

"Not broken from impact," Cain confirmed. "See how the wire strands frayed where they snapped on their own? This half is a clean cut."

"That's not normal," Rivers agreed, meeting the sheriff's eyes with dawning understanding. "Someone deliberately tampered with it."

Sheriff Cain straightened, a muscle working in his jaw as he surveyed the scene again, now through the lens of potential homicide rather than tragic accident. "Third elderly man in Stillwater to die in what appeared to be an accident."

Their common realization darkening their expressions. Rivers nodded in grim agreement. "All made to look like accidents. All involving mechanical failures that could have occurred naturally, unless examined closely."

"A little too obvious," Cain added. "It feels like someone is toying with us, challenging us to find these. Someone thinks they are smarter than us." He glanced toward Weathers and Chambers at the ambulance, then back to Rivers. "Keep this between us for now. Document everything about that brake assembly. I want the tractor transported to the county garage for forensic examination once the body's recovered."

Rivers nodded, already reaching for her camera to take close-up photographs of the tampering.

"And Carol," the sheriff added, his voice pitched for her ears alone, "check Cooper's background. Any connection to McKenzie or Miller. Church groups, social clubs, medical providers, anything they might have shared."

"You think we have a pattern killer," she stated rather than asked.

Sheriff Cain's gaze swept across the peaceful farmland that had become a murder scene, his expression grim with the weight of recognition. "I think Stillwater has a problem we've been too slow to recognize."

TWENTY-ONE

Late afternoon sunlight slanted through the venetian blinds covering the windows in Sheriff Martin Cain's office, casting striped shadows across the worn wooden desk where decades of Stillwater's darkest secrets had been processed, filed, and sometimes buried.

Carter Thompson perched on the edge of the visitor's chair, perfectly still except for the rhythmic tapping of one finger against his knee, his backpack resting against the leg of his chair. He'd persuaded Deputy Garrett to let him wait here—a combination of persistence and the unexpected arrival of a minor emergency that had drawn her attention elsewhere. She'd agreed with clear reluctance, leaving the door pointedly open so she could monitor him from her desk across the bullpen.

"Just don't touch anything," she'd warned. "Sheriff Cain hates people messing with his stuff."

Carter had nodded solemnly, the very picture of compliance. For ten minutes, he maintained that image, sitting motionless except for occasional glances toward the bullpen to ensure Louise remained occupied with her radio calls and paperwork.

When her attention was fully diverted to a heated phone conversation, Carter allowed his gaze to roam the office with new intensity. The space revealed little about its occupant—no family photos, no personal mementos, just the institutional furnishings of rural law enforcement. A filing cabinet against one wall. Commendations and certifications framed with utilitarian simplicity. A map of Stillwater County pinned with colored markers whose significance only Sheriff Cain would know.

And there, on the desk directly in front of him, a closed manila folder, its contents partially sticking out.

Carter glanced toward the bullpen. Louise remained engrossed in her call, back half-turned to the sheriff's office. The moment stretched, pregnant with possibility and risk.

Decision made, he reached down to extract his notebook from his backpack, then rose silently from his chair and circled the desk, movements fluid and precise. He flipped open the file, and found it contained exactly what he'd hoped—case notes on Jackson McKenzie and Ned Miller, handwritten in Sheriff Cain's cramped, all-caps style that spoke of military training never quite abandoned.

"PROBABLE MURDER," screamed one notation, underlined twice with such force the pen had torn the paper.

"PREMEDITATED ACTIONS" appeared beside a photograph of what appeared to be the ladder leg from Miller's porch, notes and arrows indicating the saw marks Carter had predicted would be found.

But it was the other photographs that truly commanded attention—stark, clinical documentation of death stripped of dignity. Jackson McKenzie's body bloated from days in river water, skin mottled with the distinctive marbling of advanced decomposition. Ned Miller impaled on the porch railing, diluted blood black against weathered wood, eyes fixed in the permanent surprise of violent death.

Carter's breath quickened, not in horror but something closer to fascination, or sexual excitement. He paged his notebook open. His pen moved across the page in tight, precise script, capturing details only visible in the official photos—the exact angle of the impalement, the pattern of blood spatter on the porch boards, the precise location of the cut marks on the ladder leg. He wanted to examine the whole file, to consume all this new information. His heart raced, his pen losing just a small amount of its precision as he wrote quickly.

His attention was so completely absorbed that he nearly missed the approaching footsteps—heavy, purposeful, accompanied by multiple voices growing louder as they neared the office. Carter snapped the file closed and slid back around the desk, dropping into the visitor's chair and pushing his notebook back into it's appointed slot in his backpack, all in a single fluid motion that ended mere seconds before Sheriff Cain appeared in the doorway.

The sheriff filled the frame with his substantial presence, uniform now rumpled and mud-stained, a streak of dirt across one cheek. Behind him, Deputy Sam Chambers looked even worse—his usually pristine appearance marred by a swollen nose crusted with dried blood despite his efforts to clean it. A wadded tissue pressed against one nostril suggested the bleeding hadn't completely stopped. His throat was bruised, as if he were strangled.

Both men radiated the peculiar energy of physical exertion followed by unresolved tension—the aftermath of a chase or a fight, police action that had sent adrenaline through their bodies.

Behind them, through the glass partition, Carter glimpsed another deputy half-dragging a handcuffed man toward the holding cells. James Kilgore, his face bruised and expression murderous, caught Carter's eye for a fleeting moment as he passed. Something in that gaze—recognition, perhaps, or simple hatred for the source of his current predicament—sent a ripple of satisfaction through Carter that he carefully kept from his face.

Sheriff Cain entered the office without acknowledging Carter's presence, dropping heavily into his chair while Sam took a seat beside Carter, wincing slightly as he dabbed at his nose with the bloody tissue.

"You're back," the sheriff stated flatly, eyes narrowing as they assessed Carter across the desk. "Thought I made it clear you should be in school."

"It's 3:30, sheriff. School is out. And I hoped you could share anything you discovered about Kilgore." He glanced over his shoulder at the receding form. "I guess you found a lot."

The sheriff nodded, begrudgingly. "Your information about Kilgore was accurate. What I'm curious about is how you came by it. You mentioned you were interested in the stolen bicycles. What does that mean?"

The question came loaded with subtle suspicion. Carter felt a thrilling tension—the familiar dance of concealing truth while presenting plausible alternatives, of testing how much this seasoned investigator could actually discern.

"I got a tip," Carter clarified, glancing briefly at Sam before continuing. "I decided to observe. It's been going on for almost a year now. Multiple victims reported similar circumstances. Their descriptions of suspicious persons matched, so I began surveillance."

"Surveillance," the sheriff repeated, the word neutral but his tone carrying an undercurrent of something darker. "On your own initiative."

"I have an interest in investigation," Carter replied, keeping his voice even despite the satisfaction blooming in his chest. "When I had enough documentation, I brought it to Deputy Chambers, who agreed it warranted attention."

"After initial hesitation," Sam added, wincing as he shifted the tissue to a fresh spot. "But the kid's methodology was sound. Good camera work, consistent note-taking, pattern recognition."

Sheriff Cain leaned back in his chair, fingers steepled in front of him as he studied Carter with unsettling intensity. His expression froze, as if his brain was processing data, and hadn't decided how to react yet.

Then, surprisingly, his expression softened marginally. "It was good work," he conceded. "Unorthodox and definitely not something I encourage civilians to undertake, but thorough. Kilgore matched your description down to the detail about the scar on his left hand."

Pride surged through Carter, all the more powerful for being unexpected. "Thank you, sir."

"Don't thank me yet," the sheriff cautioned. "We still don't know if Kilgore has any connection to the McKenzie or Miller cases beyond circumstantial presence in the area. His escape attempt suggests guilt of some kind, but not necessarily murder." Cain chose not to mention the potential evidence Sam had found in the shed, nor the reaction Kilgore had in the Bronco.

"But the pattern—" Carter began.

"Patterns can be misleading," Sheriff Cain interrupted. "They can also be manufactured or misinterpreted. Right now, we have a suspected bicycle thief who ran from questioning. That's all we can definitively say."

Carter nodded, careful to display appropriate deference while disappointment churned beneath the surface. So close to recognition, to finally being taken seriously, only to have the sheriff retreat into professional skepticism.

"Of course," he agreed, forcing his voice to remain steady. "I just thought the construction background was significant, given the technical nature of both... incidents."

Something flickered in the sheriff's eyes—a reluctant acknowledgment that the point had merit. "We're pursuing all angles," he said after a moment. "Including the possibility that Kilgore had accomplices or was working for someone else."

The implication hung in the air between them—that Kilgore might be merely a tool rather than the architect of these deaths, a pawn in a larger scheme they had yet to fully comprehend.

Sam cleared his throat, breaking the tension. "Sheriff, the paramedics said to get this nose checked out. And Carter needs to get home before his grandmother worries."

The mention of his grandmother sent a brief spike of genuine anxiety through Carter.

Sheriff Cain nodded, pushing away from his desk to stand. "We'll continue this conversation another time, Carter. For now, I want to be clear—your assistance with identifying Kilgore is appreciated, but this is now an official investigation. No more amateur detective work, understood?"

Carter rose from his chair. "Understood, Sheriff."

"Good." Cain extended his hand in a gesture that surprised Sam as much as Carter. "You've got sharp eyes, son. Use them wisely."

Carter accepted the handshake, feeling the callused strength of the sheriff's grip—a gesture of respect between men, not the patronizing acknowledgment of a teenager's hobby. The validation sent warmth spreading through his chest, a sensation so unfamiliar it took him a moment to recognize it as genuine pride.

"Thank you, sir," he managed, voice steadier than he felt. "I just want to help."

"I know you do." Something in the sheriff's tone suggested he understood more than he was saying—about Carter's motivations, his need for recognition, perhaps even the deeper currents that drove his obsessive attention to Stillwater's darker corners.

As they filed out of the office, Sam placed a hand on Carter's shoulder. "I'll walk you out. Make sure Louise doesn't give you the third degree on your way to the door."

The gesture seemed friendly, collegial even, but Carter noted the subtle pressure directing his movement, the positioning that kept him slightly ahead of the deputy rather than beside him. Supervision masked as accompaniment. The professional skepticism hadn't entirely vanished, then, despite the sheriff's apparent approval.

They navigated through the bullpen, past curious glances from other deputies and the openly suspicious glare of Louise Garrett at the front desk. Sam maintained his grip on Carter's shoulder until they reached the main entrance, only releasing him when the glass doors slid open to admit the cold evening air.

"You did good today, Carter," Sam said, offering a slightly blood-stained smile. "The sheriff doesn't give compliments easily. That handshake? That meant something."

Carter allowed himself to return the smile, carefully calibrated to display appropriate gratitude mixed with youthful eagerness. "I'm just glad someone finally listened. Those bicycle thefts were just the beginning of the pattern. There's more—"

"One thing at a time," Sam interrupted gently. "Let us handle Kilgore and whatever he might tell us. There's proper procedure for these investigations." He motioned for Sam to step through the doors, but continued to follow him toward the bike stand.

"Of course," Carter agreed, the perfect image of reasonable deference. "I understand."

He couldn't see what Carter kept carefully hidden beneath the surface: The obsessive passion for patterns that revealed the chaos underneath.

But most importantly, Sam couldn't see the pages in Carter's notebook now filled with new details gleaned from the sheriff's confidential case files—details only the investigating officers and the killer would know.

TWENTY-TWO

S am walked Carter to his bike, both of them stopping beside it.

"I meant what I said back there," Sam said, lowering his voice. "Not many people—adults included—would have put together what you did with Kilgore."

Carter nodded, careful to maintain the appropriate balance of pride and humility. "Just observation. Connecting dots others missed."

"That's what makes a good detective," Sam replied. He hesitated, seeming to wrestle with something before digging into his pocket. "Speaking of which..."

Carter watched, curious, as Sam extracted a small leather shape from his uniform pants. The leather was worn with age, the corners smooth from handling. Sam extended it toward him with a slight self-consciousness that suggested personal significance.

"Here, I brought this for you.. unofficially," he urged Carter to take it.

Carter took the shape, its weight substantial in his palm. He turned it over carefully, revealing a silver badge nestled in black leather. The emblem was clearly old, but the design professional, the surface shined to perfection. The words

"APPRENTICE DETECTIVE" were molded in its face. A thin chain was connected to the leather.

"Had it when I was about your age," Sam explained, a nostalgic smile softening his features. "Back when I first decided I wanted to be a cop. Found it while cleaning out my mom's attic last month."

Carter ran his finger over the surface, feeling every ridge and imperfection in the metal. The gesture was unexpectedly meaningful—recognition of shared purpose rather than patronizing indulgence. The badge might be a child's toy, but the sentiment behind it acknowledged something deeper.

"Thank you," Carter said, his voice steadier than the emotion churning beneath his carefully composed expression. "This is..."

The words died in his throat as a familiar voice reached them both: Mary Cain.

"Hey, Deputy Chambers—Oh," she said, the single syllable hanging awkwardly between them when she noticed Carter. "Hi, Carter."

He noticed she wore a dark green coat that made her brown eyes appear deeper, her hair windblown from the walk across the parking lot. For a painful instant, their gazes locked—Carter's surprised, Mary's equally startled before sliding toward something unreadable.

"H-hey." His response came out as something between a cough and a greeting, his sudden self-consciousness made worse by Sam's presence.

Mary shifted her weight, glancing between them before settling on Sam. "I came to see my dad. Mom said he called about dinner."

"Perfect timing," Sam replied, either oblivious to or tactfully ignoring the tension. "I can take you to him." He turned to Carter with a grin. "Mary, you should've seen this kid today. Cracked the bicycle thief case wide open with photo evidence that would make CSI jealous."

Mary's eyebrows lifted slightly. "Really? That's... impressive." Her smile seemed genuine, if carefully measured. "Congratulations." Carter, still awkwardly trying to remain calm, missed the cues.

"Thanks," Carter managed, the single word emerging more normally. "It wasn't that big a deal."

"Don't sell yourself short," Sam insisted, glancing at his watch. "I should get Mary to the sheriff. You good to get home okay?"

Carter nodded, raising the badge slightly. "Thanks again for this."

"You earned it, Detective Thompson," Sam replied with a wink. "See you around."

Carter watched as Sam guided Mary through the door, her coat swinging slightly with each step. Just before disappearing around the corner, Mary glanced back over her shoulder, catching Carter watching. Instead of the embarrassment he expected to feel, a curious lightness spread through his chest when she offered a small, almost conspiratorial smile before continuing on.

Left alone on the sidewalk, Carter lifted the badge, feeling the weight, the metal catching the glow of the waning sky, transforming the surface into something almost glowing.

Detective Thompson. The title resonated in his mind, fitting with satisfying precision. Not a patronizing fantasy but recognition of capability. Sam had seen what others missed— Carter's true potential, his rightful place.

The moment stretched, perfect and pure, before shattering with the sudden panicked realization that he had left his backpack in the sheriff's office—the backpack that held his notebook that, if examined carefully, might reveal connections Carter needed to keep to himself, at least for now.

Carter turned sharply, heart rate accelerating as he reentered the station. Deputy Garrett still manned the front desk, her expression souring slightly at his return.

"I left my backpack in Sheriff Cain's office," he explained, forcing his voice to remain casual. "Can I grab it real quick?"

Louise's eyes narrowed slightly. "Sheriff's already left for the day."

"It'll just take a second," Carter pressed, injecting the perfect note of teenage awkwardness. "All my school stuff is in there. My grandmother will kill me if I lose another backpack."

The deputy sighed, the mention of his grandmother softening her resolve as he'd known it would. "Fine. But make it quick." She buzzed him through.

"Thanks," Carter said, already moving toward the sheriff's office, mentally calculating the odds. If the sheriff had noticed the backpack and grown curious enough to look inside... if he'd connected Carter's "observations" with details that hadn't been released publicly...

The bullpen buzzed with activity—deputies filing reports, phones ringing intermittently, the scanner providing a constant background of crackling static. Nobody paid him any attention as he slipped past desks toward the hallway where the sheriff's office waited.

The room was empty when he arrived, his backpack resting on the floor beside the visitor's chair, exactly as he'd left it. Carter exhaled in relief, crossing quickly to retrieve it. His fingers automatically found the zipper compartment where his notebook rested, confirming its presence with a touch.

As he slung the backpack over his shoulder, his gaze caught on a framed photograph on the sheriff's desk that he hadn't noticed earlier—Mary at about twelve years old, grinning beside a younger Carter, both holding up handmade "detective badges" cut from cardboard and covered in aluminum foil. The summer they'd formed their detective team, solving "mysteries" like Mrs. Johnson's missing garden gnome and who was leaving candy wrappers in the school yard.

Before his parents' accident. Before everything changed.

The memory pricked at him—the easy friendship they'd once shared, now replaced with the awkward dance of their current relationship. The lunches they occasionally shared in the library were glimpses of what had been, moments when Mary would laugh at his observations or share some detail of her day that made him feel, briefly, like he still mattered to her. Then would come the inevitable hallway encounters where she'd be surrounded by friends, offering only a quick smile or brief wave as she passed, leaving him standing alone as she disappeared into her group.

He'd told himself it was enough. He knew her better than any of them ever would—had seen the side of her that loved puzzles and asked hard questions and stayed up too late reading mystery novels under her covers. The others only saw the sheriff's daughter, the pretty girl with the infectious laugh.

Of course, that had been before he'd discovered how to see real patterns, and how to force everyone to see him differently.

Carter stepped back into the hallway, about to head toward the exit when realization dawned—this moment of invisibility was an opportunity. The station's attention was focused elsewhere; no one was monitoring his movements. He glanced down the corridor where evidence was processed and stored, a restricted area he'd never been allowed to enter.

The evidence from Jackson McKenzie and Ned Miller's cases would be there. Physical proof collected, cataloged and analyzed by professionals who had no idea how to really investigate a crime.

Decision made, Carter moved silently down the hallway, hugging the wall. Each step felt magnified in his mind, but years of moving unnoticed through Stillwater had taught him how to remain invisible when necessary. He passed closed doors—conference rooms, supply closets, the break room—until reaching a T-junction that branched toward the evidence lockers.

In the interrogation room, Mary perched on the edge of the metal table, her fingers intertwined with Sam's as he stood close in front of her. The overhead fluorescents cast harsh shadows across their faces, but couldn't diminish the tenderness in Sam's expression as he brushed a strand of hair from her forehead.

"We can't keep doing this here," Mary whispered, her voice low with both desire and anxiety. "If my dad found out..."

"I know, I know," Sam soothed, his thumb tracing her cheekbone in a gesture of intimate familiarity. "But I needed to see you today. After everything with Kilgore, the chase..."

"What happened?" Her hands moved to his face, fingers gentle against the bruising around his nose. "When you called, I was so worried."

"I'm fine," he assured her, leaning in for a kiss that she returned with equal fervor. "Everything's fine now."

Mary pulled away slightly, her eyes darting toward the door. "What about Carter? I saw you giving him something."

Sam shook his head. "Just my old junior detective badge. Kid solved the bicycle theft case. Figured he deserved some recognition." Mary flinched slightly at Sam calling Carter a kid. She knew they were only one year apart, which made her as much a kid as Carter.

Mary pushed the thought aside, and her expression softened into something complicated—fondness mixed with sadness. "He was always like that, even when we were young. Noticing things nobody else did." She sighed. "We used to be inseparable before his parents died. Now it's just... awkward.

She looked down at their intertwined fingers. "I feel guilty sometimes. We were best friends for years, and then when he probably needed me most, I just... drifted away. It was easier than dealing with how different he became after the accident."

"You were kids," Sam said gently. "Nobody expects you to carry that responsibility."

"Maybe. But I see how he looks at me sometimes. Like he's waiting for me to remember something important." She shook her head, pushing the thought away. "Anyway, it was nice of you to give him that badge."

"He's got the mind for it," Sam acknowledged. "Just needs to channel it properly."

Mary's hands moved to the front of Sam's uniform, pulling him closer. "Right now, I don't want to talk about Carter Thompson."

Their lips met again, bodies pressing together in the empty room, the two-way mirror on the wall reflecting their embrace in silent witness.

Boom!

A sudden, explosive sound shattered the moment, the noise reverberating through the viewing window with violent force, as if someone had struck the glass from the other side.

Mary jumped back with a startled cry. Sam instinctively pushed her behind him, his hand moving to his sidearm as he stared toward the two way mirror.

"What the hell?" he breathed, before moving toward the door.

"Sam?" Mary's voice trembled. "What was that?"

"Stay here," he ordered, pulling the door open and rushing into the hallway.

The observation room door stood partially open, the interior dark. Sam entered cautiously, hand still on his weapon, flicking on the light switch with his other hand. The room was empty— no intruder, no explanation for the thunderous sound that had interrupted them. Sam glanced to the window, the two-way mirror that allowed them to observe a suspect. Mary stood alone in the interrogation room, her heart still racing from the abrupt interruption.

Sam's eyes swept the small space, stopping at the table beneath the two-way mirror. There, placed deliberately in the center, sat the junior detective badge he'd given Carter less than ten minutes ago.

Sam's blood ran cold as realization dawned. He picked up the badge, its metal now cool against his fingers, understanding with sick certainty that Carter Thompson had seen everything.

And worse—had left this unmistakable message before disappearing into the night.

"Is everything okay?" Mary appeared in the doorway, her face pale with concern.

Sam closed his fist around the badge, mind racing through the implications. He slid it into his pocket before turning to Mary. "Maybe it was a sonic boom or something," Sam said, forcing a smile. "Nothing to worry about," he added. Mary nodded, not convinced, but unable to make a different conclusion.

"I better go," she said. "Get that nose checked out, please." She smiled warmly, then left. Sam pulled the badge back out, trying to evaluate the consequences that were about to fall upon him, or worse yet, Mary.

Outside in the dusk light, Carter Thompson adjusted his backpack and walked steadily away from the sheriff's station, his expression betraying nothing of the cold calculation taking shape within. The new information was just a trifle, something he could use for his own gain. He pushed down the pain it had brought to the surface, a loss similar to losing his parents, but this time of someone still alive, Mary.

He shook off the emotion, as he had done in the past. It was the work at hand that was important, not the silly drama of relationships that meant nothing to him. He could use it, but it would not distract him from the task at hand.

They had acknowledged him today, but they still didn't see him. Not really. Not yet.

Even Carter didn't notice the tears rolling down his cheeks as he pedaled away into the night.

TWENTY-THREE

Rays of an early October sun failed to fight through the canopy of low lying clouds and fog, leaving Stillwater Park in muted tones of gray and brown. The playground stood empty, metal slides and swing sets glistening with morning dew, the children who normally filled the space headed to classrooms on this Tuesday morning.

Carter sat alone on a bench facing the duck pond, his posture rigid, hands resting on his knees with a stillness that contradicted the anticipation running through him. His backpack leaned against his leg, containing his ever-present notebook and the carefully laid groundwork for today's conversation.

His breath fogged in the chilly air as he checked his watch—8:42 AM. Sam had received his message that morning, delivered via a note slipped under the windshield wiper of his department vehicle. The location and time were non-negotiable; Carter made it clear how important this was to Sam's future.

At precisely 8:45, footsteps approached from behind. Carter didn't turn around. Power lay in making others come to you.

Deputy Sam Chambers appeared at the edge of Carter's vision, his uniform jacket zipped against the cold, his expression arranged in a friendly smile that didn't reach his eyes. The bruising around his nose had faded to a yellowish purple, his department badge catching the meager sunlight as he moved.

"Carter," Sam greeted, his tone artificially upbeat. "Got your note. Cryptic."

Carter gestured to the empty space beside him on the bench. Sam hesitated before sitting, maintaining a careful distance between them.

"Beautiful morning," Sam tried again, rubbing his hands together against the chill. "Though you're missing school. Again."

Carter finally turned to face the deputy, his expression perfectly blank. No smile, no frown, nothing to telegraph his intentions. The lack of teenage awkwardness seemed to unnerve Sam more than any display of emotion might have.

Sam's forced cheer collapsed under that steady gaze. As Carter planned, the deputy would quickly come to the realization that he wasn't here for small talk.

"What's this all about, Carter?" he asked, voice lower now, glancing around casually to ensure no one was nearby. The park was empty, with only the two figures occupying the bench.

"I need a new case," Carter replied, his tone conversational despite the demand. "The McKenzie, Cooper and Miller murders."

Sam stiffened. "Those are accidents as far as the public knows."

"But not as far as the sheriff knows," Carter countered smoothly. "He's keeping it quiet to prevent panic. Smart, but ultimately futile."

"How did you—" Sam caught himself, jaw tightening. "Look, I appreciate your help with Kilgore, but I can't get you involved in an active murder investigation. It's too dangerous, and the sheriff would never allow it."

Carter tilted his head slightly, a scientist observing a specimen's predictable reaction. "I don't think Sheriff Cain would be too pleased to know his deputy is involved with his seventeen-year-old daughter either."

The color drained from Sam's face. He glanced around again before leaning closer.

"That's—you don't understand what you're talking about," he attempted, voice strained. "Mary and I are just—"

"Don't insult my intelligence," Carter interrupted, voice still eerily calm. "I saw you. In the interrogation room. And I've been watching since. The way you park three blocks from her house on Thursdays when her father works late. The texts—thirty-seven in the last two days, actually. The way she touches her neck when your name comes up in conversation."

Sam's expression cycled through shock, fear, and anger in rapid succession. "Jesus, kid, are you stalking us?"

"I would call it investigating you. I observe patterns," Carter corrected. "It's what makes me valuable to the department."

Sam ran a hand over his face, the reality of his situation sinking in. The kid was unbalanced, it was becoming obvious, but he was also dangerous, both to himself and Mary. "Ok, so what exactly do you want?"

"A complete copy of the case files. Everything you have on all three murders. By tomorrow morning."

"That's impossible. Those files are secure, confidential—"

"You have access," Carter stated, not a question but a certainty. "The sheriff trusts you."

Sam stared at him, recognition dawning in his eyes—not of blackmail, which had been immediately clear, but of something deeper and more troubling in the teenager before him. Something calculated and cold that no junior detective badge could explain away.

"Why do you care so much about these cases?" he asked, studying Carter with new wariness.

Carter stood, slinging his backpack over one shoulder in a single fluid motion. "Because patterns matter. There's a darker plan at play here, one it seems the sheriff is choosing to ignore, like he has so many times in the past. And I don't think this plan is finished yet."

The ominous words struck Sam, not for fear of more murders, but for the clarity in which Carter seemed to process the concept. This boy — no, this man — was smart, calculating… and determined. But what game he was playing Sam could not decide, except to know that Carter would not hesitate to use information he had to get what he wanted.

Carter turned to leave, then paused, glancing back at Sam who remained frozen on the bench. "Tomorrow morning. My locker at school. Number 237." He offered the ghost of a smile. "I trust you know how to break into a locker discreetly, Deputy Chambers."

With that, Carter walked away, his pace unhurried, leaving Sam staring after him. The deputy's face reflected the dawning realization that he'd completely misjudged the boy he'd patronized with a child's badge—a boy who now held the power to destroy his career with a few carefully chosen words.

Carter didn't look back, his steps light despite the weight of his backpack. Everything was proceeding according to plan. Soon, he would have official access, the authority's perspective on crimes they knew so little about.

And if Sam failed to deliver? Well, that would simply become another necessary adjustment to the pattern. Carter had learned long ago that people were ultimately predictable when properly motivated.

TWENTY-FOUR

Mary Cain walked down the uneven driveway leading to the Thompson house, stepping over ruts that seemed to have worsened since her last visit years ago. The house itself reflected similar neglect—peeling paint, sagging gutters, flower beds long since surrendered to weeds. A stark contrast to the meticulously maintained home she remembered from childhood, when Carter's mother had tended roses along the walkway and his father had spent weekends on home improvement projects.

Mary stopped by the rusting mailbox, its door hanging askew, still clinging to the aging siding. Her fingers tapped nervously against her leg as she gathered her courage. She hadn't been here since the memorial service after the accident, when the house had been filled with casseroles and quiet condolences. Her friendship with Carter had already begun fraying by then, her discomfort with his grief creating a chasm she didn't realize she herself was creating.

Now she was back, driven by a mix of guilt and concern that had slowly grown since seeing him at the station weeks ago. It wasn't lost on Mary that since that day Sam's opinion of Carter had changed. His pride at a young prodigy had disappeared, something had shifted. Sam hadn't made any comments, but his mood shifted whenever Carter's name arose, suggesting unresolved tension.

Mary crossed to the front door and climbed the porch steps, wincing at the creak of rotting wood beneath her feet. She knocked firmly, waiting for a response that didn't come. After a second attempt yielded similar silence, she tested the doorknob. It turned easily in her hand.

"Hello?" she called, pushing the door open slightly. "Carter? Mrs. Thompson?"

The house's interior was dim despite the afternoon hour, heavy curtains drawn against the daylight. Mary hesitated on the threshold, about to retreat when voices from the living room reached her.

"Who are you?" A woman's frightened, unsettled tone was shrill in the darkness. "What are you doing in my house?"

"Gran, it's me." Carter's voice, strained with a patience that sounded repeatedly tested. "It's Carter. Your grandson."

Mary froze, instinctively stepping back from the private moment she was inadvertently witnessing.

"I don't have a grandson," the elderly woman insisted, her voice rising with distress. "Robert? Robert, there's a strange boy in the house!"

"Dad's not here, gran. He died, remember? With Mom. There was an accident."

There was a pause, followed by a soft, confused whimper. "No, that's not right. Robert was just here. He brought me flowers."

"That was me, gran. I brought you the flowers from the yard. The dandelions you like."

Mary backed out of the house, heart twisting at the quiet desperation in Carter's voice. She pulled the door nearly closed, then knocked again, much louder this time, deliberately rattling the doorframe.

Footsteps approached, and the door swung open to reveal Carter, his expression transitioning rapidly from weary resignation to surprise to guarded suspicion.

"Mary?" He glanced past her to the empty porch, as if expecting others. "What are you doing here?"

She shifted uncomfortably, suddenly uncertain of her purpose. "I was in the neighborhood. Thought I'd stop by. See how you're doing."

His eyes narrowed slightly. "You live next door."

"Yeah, well, still… it's been awhile." She tried to smile. "I missed you at lunch. I came by the library — I just... I thought I'd come by."

Carter studied her for a long moment, his gaze analytical in a way that made her feel oddly exposed. Whatever he was seeing, he seemed to process it, deciding to accept her words and intentions; his posture relaxed fractionally.

"Sorry," he said, stepping back to allow her entry. "My grandmother's having a difficult day."

Mary followed him inside, the familiar layout of the house now transformed by neglect and dim lighting. Mrs. Thompson sat in a recliner before a flickering television, her thin frame swallowed by a cardigan several sizes too large. She looked up as they entered, her eyes vacant of recognition.

"Who's this?" she asked Carter, her tone simultaneously suspicious and fearful.

"This is Mary, gran. Sheriff Cain's daughter. My friend from school."

The elderly woman blinked, confusion evident in her features. "The sheriff's girl? Has something happened?"

"No, gran. Just visiting," Carter replied with practiced patience. "Why don't you watch your show? I'll make some tea."

He gestured for Mary to follow him to the kitchen, closing the living room door partially behind them. The kitchen was cleaner than Mary expected, dishes neatly stacked in the drying rack, counters wiped down, medication bottles orderly arranged on a shelf.

"Sorry about that," Carter said, filling a kettle with water. "She has good days and bad days. Today's..." He trailed off, the implication clear.

"I didn't know it had gotten so bad," Mary said quietly. "Carter, I'm sorry."

He shrugged, the gesture carefully calibrated to appear casual. "It's been getting worse for a while. The doctor says it's progressive. Nothing to be done except make her comfortable."

Mary watched as he methodically prepared three mugs for tea, his movements precise and economical. "Is there anyone helping you? Social services or home health aides?"

"We're managing." His tone made it clear the subject was closed.

Mary glanced around the kitchen, noting the budget grocery store brand foods, the carefully rationed supplies, the repaired appliances that should have been replaced years ago. "Carter, if you need anything—"

"We're fine," he interrupted, then softened his tone. "But thanks."

The kettle whistled, filling the awkward silence that followed. As Carter poured the water, Mary noticed his hands—steady, controlled, much older than his sixteen years should allow.

"Actually," he said, handing her a mug, "there is something you could help with."

"Name it," she replied, perhaps too eagerly.

"I've been working on something. For school," he added quickly. "A project on local history. I need to visit the spot where Jackson McKenzie was found, by the river. For research."

Mary's brow furrowed slightly. "The drowning victim? That's an unusual history project."

"It's for science class, I'm doing a paper on forensic analysis," Carter explained smoothly. "Examining how natural environments affect evidence collection. But I don't have a car, and it's a long bike ride."

She hesitated, unease flickering through her. "I'm not sure my dad would—"

"Your dad doesn't need to know," Carter said, then immediately softened his approach. "The scene has long since been documented. We wouldn't be breaking any laws. It's just for school, Mary. I was going to skip it, but since you're here..."

He gestured vaguely toward the living room, where the muffled sound of his grandmother talking to the television filtered through the door. The reminder of his situation—trapped in this gloomy house with a woman who doesn't recognize him—tugged at Mary's sympathies.

"Okay," she conceded. "But just a quick visit. I need to be home for dinner."

The Blackwater River glittered in the late afternoon sun, its surface deceptively peaceful as it curved through the woods outside Stillwater. Mary parked off the road just past the bend, pulling onto the soft shoulder.

"It's about a 100 yards that way," Carter said, already exiting the car, his backpack slung over one shoulder. "There's a trail."

Mary followed him into the woods, memories surfacing with each step. "Remember when we used to come out here to catch frogs?" she asked, ducking under a low-hanging branch. "Your mom would get so mad when we'd bring them home in jars."

Carter glanced back, the ghost of a genuine smile touching his lips. "She made us release every single one back exactly where we found them."

"Ecological responsibility," Mary quoted in a perfect imitation of Mrs. Thompson's stern teacher voice, drawing a short laugh from Carter.

The sound startled her—when was the last time she'd heard him laugh? The Carter she'd known before his parents' deaths had laughed easily, frequently. This Carter moved through the world with careful precision, as if one wrong step might shatter something irreplaceable, as if laughter implied weakness.

They emerged from the trees onto a rocky bank where the river widened into a deep pool. Yellow police tape, faded and tattered from months of exposure, still clung to several trees, marking the area where Jackson McKenzie's body had been discovered.

"This is it," Carter said, his voice shifting to something more focused, analytical. Two medical gloves appeared from Carter's pocket. A second pair was offered to Mary, who took them absentmindedly. Carter slipped the gloves on with practiced ease, and then extracted a small notebook from his backpack and began making notations, pacing the area with methodical attention.

Mary hung back, suddenly uncomfortable. "Should we really be disturbing a... you know, a death scene?"

"The police are done with it," Carter replied without looking up. "Unless you're superstitious, we aren't disturbing anything."

He continued his careful survey, measuring distances between landmarks, noting the river's current, examining the composition of the riverbank. His intensity was both familiar and strange—the obsessive focus she remembered from their childhood detective games, but now applied with adult precision.

"Here," Carter said suddenly, pointing to an impression in the mud. "This is where the fence panel that trapped him was anchored. It broke loose from this embankment and swept downstream, catching him as he was wading."

Despite her initial reluctance, Mary found herself drawn into his methodical examination. "How do you know that's where it was attached?"

"See these marks?" Carter indicated several indentations in the bank. "Post holes. And there's still a piece of metal embedded here. The rest was carried away by the current."

Mary crouched beside him, seeing the evidence he'd identified. Something about his careful analysis awakened memories of their childhood partnership—the hours spent creating elaborate mysteries for each other to solve, combing the neighborhood for clues, documenting their findings in matching spiral notebooks. She found herself slipping on the medical gloves herself, a part of the ritual she remembered so well.

"What about the victim's position?" she asked. "The current here looks strong. Would he have been standing or sitting?"

Carter's eyes lit with approval. "Standing. See how the water breaks around those rocks? That's the deepest wading point. He would have been right there when the fence broke loose."

For nearly an hour, they worked the scene together, Carter documenting and Mary questioning, challenging his conclusions, offering alternative theories. The tension that had characterized their interactions for years slowly melted away, replaced by the comfortable synchronicity of their childhood friendship.

"Check this out," Mary called, having wandered downstream a few yards. "There's something wedged under these rocks."

Carter joined her at the water's edge where she pointed to a dark object partially obscured by river stones. He crouched, carefully moving the smaller rocks out of the way. A piece of tangled old twine held the the leather object in place. Carter extracted a switchblade from his pocket, the sharp edge opening with a swish that surprised Mary.

The knife made her nervous, for some reason, the long blade sharp and carefully maintained. Something more likely carried by a street thug, not a 16 year old, and used with a comfort of practice, and familiarity. Carter positioned the blade, cutting at the twine until the item came free. Mary forced her focus back to the object.

It was a shoe—a heavy work boot, waterlogged and stained with river mud. The leather was worn but still intact, the laces tangled with debris.

"Is that...?" Mary's voice trailed off, the reality of what they were doing suddenly crashing back.

"Jackson McKenzie's," Carter confirmed, turning the boot over in his hands with clinical interest. "The police must have missed it."

Mary stepped back, a chill running through her that had nothing to do with the cooling evening air. "We should call my dad. That's evidence."

"Of an accidental drowning?" Carter raised an eyebrow. "It's just a shoe, Mary."

"But what if it wasn't an accident?" The words escaped before she could consider them, a half-formed suspicion she hadn't realized she harbored.

Carter went very still, his expression unreadable. "What makes you say that?"

Mary wrapped her arms around herself, suddenly aware of the deepening shadows as the sun lowered behind the trees. "I don't know. Just... there have been a lot of accidents lately. This, the farmer with the tractor, Mr. Miller. My dad seems worried."

"Your dad thinks these deaths are connected?" Carter's tone was carefully neutral, but his eyes had intensified, focused on her with unsettling precision.

"I don't know what he thinks," Mary admitted. "He doesn't talk about cases at home, at least not with me. But he's been distracted, working late. And I heard him arguing with a deputy about evidence protocols."

Carter placed the boot in a plastic bag, then shoved it into his backpack with deliberate movements. "I'll turn this in anonymously. Say I found it while hiking. No need to explain why we were out here."

Mary nodded, relieved by the solution but unable to shake her growing discomfort. What had started as a nostalgic reconnection now felt somehow wrong, as if they'd crossed an invisible boundary.

"We should head back," she said, already moving toward the trail. "It's getting dark."

Carter shouldered his backpack, now containing the grim relic of Jackson McKenzie's final moments. "Thanks for the ride, Mary. It was almost like old times."

"Yeah," she agreed, though the childhood innocence of their detective games felt impossibly distant now. "Almost."

As they walked back to the car in silence, Mary couldn't help feeling that something fundamental had shifted between them —not a healing of their fractured friendship, but the creation of something new and undefined. Something that, like the river current that had claimed Jackson McKenzie, might be stronger and more dangerous than it initially appeared.

TWENTY-FIVE

The station hummed with the quiet efficiency of mid-morning routines. Deputies filed reports, phones rang intermittently, coffee brewed in the small kitchenette. Outside Sheriff Cain's office, Deputy Sam Chambers paced, as if trying to will himself to enter but lacking the words he needed, or the conviction.

Three times he'd approached the door. Three times he'd retreated. The weight of his confession pressed against his chest like a physical burden. His relationship with Mary. Carter's blackmail. His complicity in providing confidential case files to a civilian minor. Each transgression stacked atop the others, a precarious tower of professional and personal betrayals.

Through the open door, he could hear the sheriff moving around the office. Cain had been unusually withdrawn since Gerald Cooper's death, his orders more terse directives, his mind occupied by the heavy burden of not just Cooper, but the multiple deaths in recent months. His office door, always open, was supposed to be inviting, but the staff knew better than to try and engage the sheriff when he was this way, focused, intense.

Sam moved away again, courage failing. He'd rehearsed the confession a dozen times, but the words disintegrated when he tried to form them. Mary's future, his career, the department's integrity—all hung in the balance of what he was about to do.

The silhouette in the office stilled, then moved purposefully toward the door. Sam froze as the sheriff appeared in the doorway, the weathered face, shadows under his eyes suggesting a series of sleepless nights.

"Either come in or go away, Chambers," the sheriff said flatly. "You've been haunting my doorway for ten minutes."

Heat rushed to Sam's face. "Sorry, sir. I needed to speak with you."

Cain stepped aside, gesturing him in with a brusque wave. "Then speak. I've got enough ghosts without adding you to my collection."

Sam entered, his prepared speech evaporating as he took in the state of the office. The normally organized space had transformed into an investigative nerve center. Crime scene photos covered the desk in methodical groupings. Maps of Stillwater marked with new colored pins dominated one wall. A timeline stretched across another, connecting dates, locations, and victims with red string.

Cain closed the door behind him, the soft click of the latch sealing them in with the evidence of Stillwater's new darkening reality.

"What's on your mind, Chambers?" Cain asked, returning to his desk chair.

Sam's throat constricted, the confession he'd planned now competing with the urgent visual evidence of the investigation surrounding them. "It's about Carter Thompson, sir."

The sheriff's expression sharpened, attention focusing with sudden intensity. "Carter Thompson," he repeated, as if testing the name for hidden meaning. "Interesting coincidence."

"Sir?"

Cain gestured to the chair across from his desk. "Sit. Tell me what's concerning you about the Thompson kid."

Sam lowered himself into the seat, the vinyl creaking beneath him. The office suddenly felt too small, too warm. "He's been... taking an unusual interest in our investigations. The bicycle theft case was just the beginning."

"Go on." The sheriff's voice remained neutral, but his eyes were focused with attention.

"He knows things, sir. Details he shouldn't have access to." Sam's fingers twisted together in his lap, anxiety crystallizing into physical tension. "About the recent deaths. McKenzie, Miller, Cooper." Sam wanted to admit that some of those details he had provided, but he also knew that Carter had an uncanny knowledge of the crimes, something he had before Sam had shared the case files with him.

Instead of surprise, Cain merely nodded, as if Sam had confirmed a suspicion rather than presented new information. The sheriff remained silent for a moment, then methodically began rearranging the photographs on his desk, grouping them into three distinct clusters.

"Three men," Cain said finally. "Three 'accidents.' Each involving equipment or structural failures." He tapped each cluster in turn. "McKenzie drowns when a fence post breaks loose and traps him in the river. Miller is impaled when his ladder collapses while changing a fuse. Cooper is crushed when his tractor rolls downhill despite the parking brake being engaged."

Sam nodded, uncertain where this was leading.

The sheriff reached into his desk drawer and withdrew a manila folder. From it, he extracted three additional photographs, placing each with its corresponding cluster.

"These weren't included in the official evidence logs," Cain explained. "I had Rivers take these, after something about these deaths started nagging at me."

Sam leaned forward to examine the new images. Each was a close-up detail from the respective death scenes—the broken fence post from McKenzie drowning, the fractured ladder leg from Miller's impalement, the severed brake line from Cooper's tractor.

"Look closer," Cain instructed. "What do you see?"

Sam studied the photographs, recognition dawning slowly. "They're not natural breaks. The fence post... it's been partially sawed through. And the ladder leg too."

"And the brake line was deliberately cut," Cain finished. "Just enough to ensure it would fail when pressure was applied, but subtle enough to pass as wear and tear to a casual examination."

"Deliberate sabotage," Sam breathed, the implications sending a cold wave through his body. "All three deaths were engineered to look like accidents."

"Engineered," Cain repeated, nodding grimly. "That's the word, Chambers. These aren't crimes of passion or opportunity.

They're meticulously planned, executed with precision. Almost... clinical."

The sheriff retrieved another folder, this one thinner than the first. "Now, about Carter Thompson." He withdrew several sheets of paper, sliding them across the desk. "These are his notes on the McKenzie death. The ones he provided as part of his 'investigation' into the bicycle thefts."

Sam scanned the pages, a chill settling in his stomach as he read. Carter's observations were exhaustively detailed—water depth at the scene, current strength, the precise angle of the fence post's break, the likely position of the McKenzie body when the panel struck him.

"He knew the depth of the water within an inch," Cain said quietly. "The exact position where McKenzie was standing. Details we never released to the public, details only the investigators and the killer would know."

"You think Carter...?" Sam couldn't complete the question, the suggestion too monstrous to voice aloud.

"I think a sixteen-year-old committing multiple homicides seems unlikely," Cain said, leaning back in his chair. "But I also think there's clearly more to Carter Thompson than meets the eye. His intelligence, his attention to detail, his obsession with detective work—all admirable traits in the right context."

"And potentially dangerous in the wrong one," Sam finished, his planned confession about Mary now seeming trivial compared to the darkness unfolding before him.

"You said he's been taking an unusual interest in our investigations," Cain prompted. "Tell me everything. When did this start? How has he been accessing information?"

Sam hesitated, the full truth hovering on his tongue—how Carter had blackmailed him, how he'd provided case files in exchange for silence about Mary. But fear closed his throat. If Carter was somehow connected to these deaths, what might he do if cornered? And if he wasn't, what damage would Sam's confession do to both their lives?

"He's been hanging around the station," Sam offered instead, the partial truth burning like acid. "Asking questions, volunteering information. I think he sees himself as some kind of consulting detective, like in those books he reads."

Cain's eyes narrowed slightly, as if sensing the omission. "And you believe he might have accessed case information? Files, photographs, evidence logs?"

"It's possible," Sam admitted, shame coiling tighter in his chest. "He's observant, resourceful. If there was a way to get information, he'd find it."

The sheriff gathered the photographs, returning them to their folders with methodical precision. "I want Carter Thompson monitored, but discreetly. No direct contact, no confrontation. If he's connected to these deaths, I don't want him spooked. And if he's not, I don't want to traumatize a kid who might just have an unusual hobby."

"Yes, sir." Relief and guilt warred within Sam. He'd been granted a reprieve from his confession, but it left a dull ache in his stomach.

"Was there anything else you wanted to discuss, Chambers?" Cain asked, his gaze piercing.

The question hung in the air between them, laden with opportunity. Sam's mouth went dry. This was the moment—to confess about Mary, to come clean about the files, to unburden himself of the secrets that were consuming him from within.

"No, sir," he said finally, the words like ash in his mouth. "Nothing else."

Cain studied him for a long moment, then nodded once. "Dismissed, then. And Chambers? Whatever's weighing on you —handle it. I need my deputies at a hundred percent right now."

"Yes, sir," Sam replied, rising from the chair on legs that felt suddenly unsteady.

As he left the office, closing the door behind him, Sam was struck by the terrible clarity of his situation. He'd entered intending to confess one betrayal, only to compound it with another. And somewhere in Stillwater, Carter Thompson continued his observations, gathering information, weaving himself deeper into an investigation that was increasingly pointing in his direction.

Sam moved through the bullpen toward his desk, the weight of his decisions pressing down like a physical burden. For the first time, he found himself wondering if he was merely a pawn in a game whose rules and boundaries he didn't understand—a game where a sixteen-year-old boy somehow was making all the moves.

TWENTY-SIX

The Stillwater Cougars' victory over rival Pinecrest filled the night with celebration, car horns and jubilant shouts echoing across town long after the final whistle. The game had been a nail-biter—tied until the fourth quarter when Jason Mercer's thirty-yard field goal secured the win that would carry them to regionals.

Jason, Dylan Foster, and Eric Tanner walked the darkened streets of Stillwater, their voices loud with the invincibility of teenage triumph, shoulders bumping as they reenacted the game's highlights. Emotional energy escaped from their bodies in the night air, letterman jackets unzipped despite the autumn chill.

"Did you see Coach's face when that linebacker went down?" Dylan crowed, his bulk impressive even among the athletic trio. At six-foot-two and built like the defensive lineman he was, Dylan's shadow stretched long and imposing across the sidewalk. "Thought he was gonna have a heart attack right there."

"Man nearly took your head off," Eric laughed, punching Dylan's shoulder. "Lucky for us you've got that concrete block on your shoulders instead of a brain."

"Better than your twig neck," Dylan shot back, shoving Eric. "One hit and you'd snap like a chicken."

Jason checked his phone as they reached the intersection of Maple and Pine. "Guys, I gotta roll. Sarah's waiting up." He held up the phone, showing a string of texts from his girlfriend.

"Whipped," Eric coughed into his hand, earning a middle finger from Jason.

"Whatever. You're just jealous because the only female who touches you is your mom."

"Brutal," Dylan laughed. "I'm heading south anyway. Got my dad's truck in the shop lot."

"Guess that leaves me solo," Eric said. "I'm looking at swiping a bottle from the old man and having a one-man celebration in the basement. Call if you get bored."

They bumped fists at the intersection, the trio splitting with casual promises to meet at Donna's Diner tomorrow. Jason headed east toward the newer developments, Eric continued north toward the middle-class neighborhood beyond the school, and Dylan turned south toward the river and the auto shop his father owned near the edge of town.

The adrenaline of the game still coursed through Dylan's veins as he walked, replaying his tackles, the perfect blitz that had forced a fumble in the third quarter. Football was his ticket out of Stillwater—scouts from state universities had been watching, his coach had said. A scholarship was within reach if he kept his grades up and his nose clean for the rest of the year.

The thought sobered him slightly. The "nose clean" part had been a pointed reference to the incident last spring—the confrontation with that weird Thompson kid in the alley. That old man that had broken it up must have told Coach about it at some point, and it was brought up at a spring practice. The one drawback of a small town, for better or worse, word got around fast. Coach hadn't said it outright, but the implication was clear: another disciplinary mark on his record would jeopardize everything.

It hadn't been his fault, not really. Thompson had been creeping around Mary Cain, and somebody needed to set him straight. The fact that Thompson's parents were dead didn't give him the right to stalk the sheriff's daughter. But Coach didn't see it that way, and neither had Principal Stevenson. One more incident, they'd warned, and his athletic future would be in jeopardy.

Dylan shook off the memory as he approached the darkest stretch of his route home—a block where budget cuts had left half the streetlights non-functional, bordered by two abandoned houses awaiting demolition. Most nights he'd cut around this section, but the victory high made him less cautious, more inclined to take the direct route despite the eerie emptiness.

A single working streetlight cast a sickly yellow pool at the center of the block. As Dylan approached, he noticed something in the dim circle of illumination—a shape on the ground, and beside it, the unmistakable silhouette of an overturned bicycle.

"Hello?" he called, pace slowing. "Someone there?"

No answer came, but as he drew closer, he could make out a figure sprawled beside the bike. A boy, it seemed, wearing jeans and a dark jacket. An accident, maybe—hit a pothole in the dark and took a spill.

Dylan approached cautiously, athlete's instincts warring with the natural concern for an injured person. When he reached the edge of the light, recognition dawned with a jolt of surprise.

Carter Thompson lay on his side, one leg bent at an angle that immediately suggested serious injury. His face was partially obscured by shadow, but there was no mistaking the worn backpack, the distinctive bike with its taped handlebars.

"Thompson?" Dylan's voice echoed in the empty street. "You okay, man?"

A low groan answered him. Carter shifted slightly, face contorting in apparent pain. "My leg," he managed, the words strained through clenched teeth. "I think it's broken. Can't move."

Dylan hesitated, conflicting emotions churning in his gut. This was the freak who got him in trouble, who almost ruined his future.

But even a freak with a broken leg needed help. And besides, maybe if he helped word might get around, and coach might cut him some slack.

"Hold on," Dylan said, fishing his phone from his pocket. "I'll call 911."

"Please," Carter whispered, his voice suddenly young and frightened. "It hurts. Can you help me sit up?"

Dylan crouching beside the injured boy, setting his phone beside him on the ground. Up close, Carter looked pathetic— pale face streaked with dirt, eyes wide with pain and fear. Nothing like the cold, calculating weirdo Dylan had confronted in the alley.

"Where's it hurt?" Dylan asked, reaching toward Carter's seemingly injured leg.

"Here," Carter gestured weakly.

As Dylan leaned closer, something shifted in Carter's expression—the pain vanishing like a mask being lifted, replaced by something focused and intent. Before Dylan could process the change, Carter's hand flashed upward from beneath his jacket.

The switchblade caught the streetlight's glow for a split second before plunging into Dylan's side, just below his ribs.

Pain exploded through Dylan's body, hot and electric. He fell backward, hand instinctively pressing against the wound, warm blood seeping between his fingers. "What the—"

Carter rose smoothly to his feet, all traces of injury gone. He stood over Dylan, the switchblade held loosely in one hand, his face in shadow from the harsh streetlight above. His expression wasn't angry or triumphant—just clinically interested, like a scientist observing an experiment.

"You were right, Dylan," Carter said, his voice quiet but perfectly clear in the silent street. "It wasn't over."

Dylan tried to speak, to call for help, but the pain transformed his words into a gasping groan. He pressed harder against the wound, blood pulsing between his fingers with each heartbeat. He reached for his phone, searching for it blindly on the ground. Carter casually kicked it away, out of reach.

He calmly wiped the blood off on Dylan's jacket, then folded the switchblade, returning it to his pocket before righting his bicycle. He mounted it with practiced ease, looking down at Dylan one last time.

"Football scholarships require a physical, don't they?" Carter observed with detached curiosity. "I wonder if a lacerated kidney might complicate that."

Through the haze of shock and pain, Dylan registered the absolute coldness in Carter's eyes—not the heated rage of a bullied kid seeking revenge, but something far more calculated and deliberate.

Carter adjusted his backpack, then pushed off on his bike, pedaling away with unhurried confidence. The darkness swallowed him within seconds, leaving Dylan alone under the yellow streetlight, blood pooling on the asphalt beneath him.

As consciousness began to waver, a distant part of Dylan's mind registered the terrible truth: this hadn't been chance or opportunity. Carter Thompson had been waiting. Planning. The entire scenario methodically arranged to ensure Dylan would be alone, would approach, would be vulnerable.

The realization followed Dylan into darkness as he slumped fully to the ground, the night silent except for the steady drip of blood against asphalt and the fading sound of bicycle wheels turning in the distance.

TWENTY-SEVEN

At night, the forest surrounding Stillwater seemed to breathe with a life of its own. Shadows stretched between ancient pines, blackness pooled in the spaces where moonlight couldn't reach. On a narrow dirt turnout half a mile down Sawmill Road, Mary's Honda Civic sat with its lights extinguished, engine idling softly, windows fogging slightly from the warmth of its occupants. Behind her, a sheriff's department vehicle parked, quiet and still.

Inside the Civic, Sam Chambers leaned against the passenger door, his uniform jacket discarded on the back seat, his face half-illuminated by the dim glow of the dashboard. Mary sat in the driver's seat, fingers tracing nervous patterns on the steering wheel, her hair falling forward to curtain her face as she absorbed what he'd been telling her.

"So my dad thinks Carter might be involved somehow?" Her voice was small, disbelieving. "That's... I can't even process that."

Sam ran a hand over his face, exhaustion etched in the lines around his eyes. "Not just involved, Mary. The evidence suggests he might know things about these deaths that only the investigators—or the killer—would know."

"But that's impossible. He's sixteen, Sam."

"I know how it sounds." Sam stared out the windshield into the darkness. "And your dad isn't making any accusations. We're just... gathering information. Being careful."

Mary turned to face him fully, pulling one leg up beneath her. "Is that why you were so eager to meet out here tonight? To warn me about Carter?"

Sam nodded, his expression grave. "That, and because I need to tell you something." He paused, swallowing hard. "I almost confessed everything to your dad today. About us."

A flicker of alarm crossed Mary's features. "But you didn't."

"I couldn't." Shame crept into his voice. "I stood there in his office, surrounded by evidence of three murders, and I choked. Couldn't get the words out."

"You're afraid of what he might do to you if he finds out."

"I'm afraid of what he might do to you," Sam corrected, reaching across to take her hand. "Your future. Your options. If this comes out—me, an officer, dating the sheriff's underage daughter—it's not just my career that implodes. It's your life that gets overturned too."

Mary squeezed his hand, her eyes softening. "I'm not mad, Sam. I get it. I'm seventeen, you're twenty-two. It's complicated."

"Complicated," he echoed with a hollow laugh. "That's one word for statutory rape charges and career suicide."

"My dad wouldn't press charges. He'd just kill you." A smile ghosted across her lips, but the attempt at humor fell flat between them.

Sam leaned his head back against the seat. "And with everything happening in town right now... it's just a bad time to create more problems for your dad."

"I understand," Mary said, though fear shadowed her features. "So what now? We keep hiding out in the woods? Sneaking around behind my dad's back until I turn eighteen?"

"I don't know," Sam admitted, rubbing his thumb across her knuckles. "I'm not even sure he'll be that open to us when you're eighteen. I'm still a deputy." Sam shook his head, realizing the depths of the situation. "But what I do know is that right now, I need you to be careful around Carter."

Mary frowned. "I still can't believe he could be involved in something like this. We were best friends for years. He's been through so much with his parents, and now his grandmother..."

"People change, Mary. Trauma affects everyone differently." Sam's voice grew softer. "When was the last time you spent any real time with him? Do you truly know who he is now?"

She thought about their trip to the river, the methodical way Carter had examined the scene, his detached interest in where Jackson McKenzie had died. She had seen glimpses of the old Carter, the friend she had grown up with, but it was as if those parts were only allowed to peek out before being quickly pushed down, hidden back in some deep pit in which Carter had relegated his childhood. She knew something had felt off about it, but she'd dismissed the feeling at the time as simple awkwardness between old friends who'd grown apart. But maybe there was more.

"I guess I don't," she admitted reluctantly. "Not anymore."

Sam squeezed her hand gently. "Just promise me you'll keep your distance until we know more. Promise me, Mary."

She nodded slowly. "I promise."

Sam leaned across the center console, pressing his lips to hers in a kiss that felt more like a farewell than a promise. Mary's fingers curled against his shirt, pulling him closer for a brief moment before they both withdrew.

The silence that followed was shattered by the sudden wail of a police siren—growing from the distance and moving fast. Headlights swept across the trees as a vehicle approached along the main road, the distinctive light bar of a sheriff's department cruiser sending red and blue reflections dancing through the forest.

Mary and Sam froze, watching as the patrol car sped past their turnout without slowing, emergency lights flashing. Within seconds, the forest returned to darkness, though the receding lights remained visible through the trees for another moment, the siren slowly absorbed by the darkness.

They looked at each other, the same question mirrored in their expressions.

Sam reached for the portable radio clipped to his belt, turning up the volume. Static crackled, punctuated by bursts of dispatcher's voice, but the signal was broken and unintelligible this far from town.

"—respond to—" The voice cut in and out. "—Maple Street—"

"—medical requested—"

More static swallowed whatever came next.

Sam lowered the radio, already reaching for his jacket. "I better go see what that is. Could be connected to our investigation."

Mary nodded, trying to ignore the cold dread settling in her stomach. "Be careful."

"Always am." He opened the passenger door, pausing with one foot on the ground. "Remember what I said, Mary. Stay away from Carter until we know more."

"I will," she promised, though even she doubted her own response.

Sam leaned in for one last brief kiss before slipping out into the darkness. Mary watched as he jogged toward his own vehicle. His engine roared to life and he backed out of the road, his own siren and lights blazing on as he accelerated away.

As Mary started her engine to head home, she couldn't shake the image of Carter in her mind—not the disturbed teenager Sam had described, but the small boy who had once helped her build a fort in her backyard, who had cried when they found an injured bird, who had held her hand at her grandmother's funeral.

If what Sam suspected was true, if Carter was somehow connected to the deaths in Stillwater, then Mary had to confront a terrifying possibility: That she'd watched him transform into something dangerous and done nothing to stop it—or worse, had contributed to his dark slide by her own inability to deal with his own grief.

The headlights of her Honda cut through the darkness as she pulled back onto the main road, illuminating the path ahead while leaving the forest on either side in impenetrable shadow.

Somewhere in that darkness, she sensed, answers waited—answers she wasn't entirely sure she wanted to find.

214

Somewhere in that darkness, she sensed, answers waited—answers she wasn't entirely sure she wanted to find.

TWENTY-EIGHT

The emergency room doors of Stillwater Memorial burst open at 1:17 AM, fluorescent lights reflecting off the worn aluminum of an ambulance gurney rushed through the entry toward the triage room with practiced urgency. Two paramedics flanked the patient, one holding an IV bag aloft while pressing gauze against a wound that had soaked through multiple layers. The other worked an air bag, pressing air into the victim's lungs.

"What have we got?" Laura Cain asked, meeting them at the entrance.

"Male, eighteen years old, stab wound to the right flank," the lead paramedic reported. "Heavy loss of blood. BP's 80/50 and dropping. Pulse weak and thready at 60. Found on Maple Street by a passing motorist. Unknown how long he was there before discovery."

Laura pulled the gurney into triage, her experienced eyes already assessing the pale, unconscious form on the gurney. Blood had soaked through the paramedics' temporary dressings, creating a stark contrast against the boy's t-shirt. His football letterman jacket had been pulled open and partially cut to allow access to the wound.

"Dylan Foster," she murmured, recognizing the linebacker from her daughter's high school. "Alright, on my count. One, two, three—"

The team transferred him from the gurney to the hospital bed with coordinated precision. Nurses swarmed around him, already connecting monitors, hanging new fluids, cutting away remaining clothing.

"Type and cross, but hang two liters of LR now," Laura ordered, snapping on fresh gloves. "Get four units of O-negative on standby. Page the attending and alert surgery. Trauma ultrasound, stat — we need eyes on the belly."

Doctor Sydney Stevens had been a trauma surgeon in Detroit before a nasty divorce had forced him to reconsider his career and his location. Stillwater had seemed a perfect place to start again, and though the town had welcomed him almost eagerly, he had remained single despite his best efforts. He found he enjoyed the peaceful surroundings of the small town, and the lack of gunshot wounds that came with a big city residency.

But tonight the mood was entirely different. Stevens rushed down the hall, wondering how in such a simple town a teenager could be knifed and left for dead. Memories of Detroit raced through his mind as he rushed into triage just as Laura activated the ultrasound. He met Laura's eyes, seeing the concern she felt, before grabbing the device from her and focusing. Steven's trained hands explored the wound. The stab was deep, angled upward beneath the ribs—not a random slash but a precise strike that suggested deliberate intent.

"Possible kidney involvement," he announced, reading the ultrasound screen as he moved the wand across Dylan's abdomen. "There's free fluid in the abdomen. He's bleeding internally. Let's get him to surgery now."

The room's controlled chaos continued as they stabilized the teenager for emergency surgery. Laura stepped back only when the surgical team arrived to take over, her scrubs now bearing more of Dylan's blood than his body seemed able to spare. Stevens watched them wheel the patient out, headed for surgery. He felt helpless, sure he could have done more, but knowing that only surgery would save the boy.

Laura pushed through the doors into the hallway, stripping off her gloves with a practiced motion, and nearly collided with her husband.

Martin Cain stood in the corridor, uniform rumpled from what had clearly been hours on duty, his face etched with the grim lines of someone bearing witness to too many tragedies.

"Martin," Laura said, surprise momentarily replacing her professional demeanor. "Did you find him?"

Cain shook his head. "Dispatch contacted me as soon as they identified the victim," he replied, eyes moving to the trauma room doors behind her. "How bad is it?"

Laura guided him away from the bustling corridor to a quieter corner. "It's serious. Stab wound to the right side, penetrating the kidney. He's lost a lot of blood, Martin. They're taking him to surgery now."

"Will he make it?"

The question hung between them—sheriff to nurse, not husband to wife—both of them falling into their professional roles even in this private moment.

"If they can control the bleeding in time," Laura answered carefully. "But he was out there a long time before being found. Hours, possibly. That's a lot of blood loss, severe hypovolemic shock, which leads to organ failure."

Martin nodded, absorbing the information with the detached analysis of someone accustomed to weighing terrible possibilities. "Have you spoken to Mary," he asked. "I checked before coming here. She didn't pick up."

Laura shook her head, reaching for her phone. "Let me try. I need to tell her—Dylan's in her grade, they must know each other..." She dialed Mary's number, but it quickly went to voicemail. She hung up in frustration.

Martin didn't hear her, his mind deep in analysis of the crime, despite a lack of any true facts. "Everyone knows everyone in Stillwater," Martin continued, his voice low with frustration. "Which makes it all the more baffling that we have no witnesses, no weapon, nothing to go on."

"What do you think happened?"

Martin leaned against the wall, suddenly looking every one of his forty-seven years. "Deputies are still processing the scene. Preliminary assessment is that Dylan was walking home from the football game. According to his friends he left them at the intersection of Maple and Pine headed to his dad's garage. He was attacked sometime just after that."

"A mugging?" Laura asked, though her skepticism was evident in her tone. "Was anything stolen?"

"His wallet was still on him. Phone was nearby, not on him." Martin shook his head. "Some of the deputies are suggesting it might have been one of the transients from the encampment by the river. Random violence, wrong place, wrong time."

"But you don't think so," Laura observed, reading her husband's expression with the familiarity of twenty years of marriage.

"Dylan Foster is six-foot-two, two hundred pounds of muscle, and defensive captain of a football team," Martin said. "He wouldn't be an easy target, even for someone desperate enough to try. He'd have to be surprised or—"

"Or what?" Laura prompted when he fell silent.

"Or tricked," Martin finished, the implication heavy in his words.

A nurse appeared at Laura's elbow, breaking the moment. "Dr. Patel's asking for the sheriff in OR 2. They've found something unusual about the wound."

The surgical observation room smelled of antiseptic and coffee, the harsh fluorescent lighting casting everything in a clinical paleness that made even the living look half-dead. Laura Cain stood behind the glass partition with her husband, watching as Dr. Patel and his team worked on Dylan Foster, their movements precise despite the urgency of the situation.

Dr. Abhinav Patel had been Stillwater Memorial's chief surgeon for fifteen years, recruited from Portland with promises of a quieter life and less demanding schedule. He had sought a surgical residency in Portland out of med school, particularly in emergency, but was talked into being a Medical Examiner, a position at the time that he thought would be an honor. As ME of a larger town though, he quickly found he had one of the busiest jobs on city payroll, and one of the least rewarding. He longed for treating patients, for saving them, as opposed to overseeing them when it was too late to help.

Stillwater seemed to be the answer. A surgical position where most days broken bones from skiing accidents, appendectomies, and the occasional complication from chronic conditions were the norm. Tonight was different. Tonight reminded him of his residency in the city, where knife wounds and gunshots had been routine rather than exceptional.

The intercom crackled as Dr. Patel spoke without looking up from his work. "Sheriff, good. Take a look at this." He gestured with a gloved hand to the monitor in the observation room as he maneuvered a camera to focus on where the wound in Dylan's side had been expanded for better access. "Unusual entry pattern."

Cain looked up, taken back by the close, somewhat gruesome image of the wound. "What am I looking at?"

"The wound track isn't what we typically see with impulsive stabbings," Dr. Patel explained, using a sterile probe to indicate the path the blade had taken. "Most knife attacks involve multiple strikes, frenzied and often shallow. This is a single puncture, angled precisely upward beneath the ribs, directly into the kidney."

A surgical resident carefully suctioned blood from the field, revealing more of the internal damage. Dr. Patel continued his assessment, his voice carrying the measured tone of scientific observation despite the grim subject matter.

"The blade was thin but rigid—approximately three to four inches in length based on the depth of penetration. Single-edged, I believe, given the tissue damage pattern on one side versus the other."

"A switchblade?" Laura suggested, mental images from countless study cases supplying the likely weapon.

"Possibly," Dr. Patel agreed. "But what's most concerning is the placement." He looked up briefly, meeting Cain's eyes through the glass. "This wasn't random. This was precisely targeted to cause maximum damage to the kidney. Whoever did this knew exactly where to strike."

Cain felt a chill run through him that had nothing to do with the hospital's aggressive air conditioning. "You're saying this was... anatomically informed? Deliberate?"

"I'm saying this exhibits knowledge beyond what we typically see in street violence or crimes of passion," Dr. Patel replied, returning his attention to controlling the bleeding vessel he'd been working to repair. "The entry angle avoided the ribs, navigated between major blood vessels that would have caused immediate death if severed, and instead targeted an organ that would cause significant damage without necessarily being immediately fatal."

"Someone who wanted him to suffer," Laura murmured, the nurse in her automatically cataloging the medical implications while another part of her mind—the part connected to being the sheriff's wife—processed the darker implications.

"Or someone who wanted him found alive," Dr. Patel suggested. "The kidney damage is severe, but survivable with prompt treatment. If the intent had been death, there were more efficient targets available."

The surgical team worked in focused silence for several minutes, closing damaged blood vessels, assessing the extent of the kidney injury. Cain watched, his mind racing with possibilities, each more disturbing than the last.

"One more thing," Dr. Patel added, not looking up from his meticulous work. "There's minimal defensive trauma. No cuts on the hands or forearms that would suggest he tried to fight off an attacker. No bruising that would indicate a struggle. Either he was completely taken by surprise..."

"Or he knew his attacker," Cain finished, the conclusion inescapable. "Someone he wouldn't perceive as a threat until it was too late."

Dr. Patel nodded, his expression grim beneath his surgical mask. "I've stabilized the bleeding for now, but he's lost nearly fifty percent of his blood volume. The next twenty-four hours will be critical. Even if he survives, there's a significant chance he'll lose the kidney."

"A college football scholarship with one kidney," Laura said softly, thinking of Dylan's future—the future that had seemed so bright just hours ago, and was now in serious jeopardy.

"Medical clearance would be challenging," Dr. Patel agreed. "Not impossible, but complicated. His athletic aspirations may be the least of his concerns right now."

Cain thanked the surgeon and stepped back from the observation window, the weight of what he'd learned settling heavily on his shoulders. He needed to process this—not just medical information but evidence that pointed toward a calculated, knowledgeable attacker rather than a random act of violence.

As Cain and Laura moved back into the quiet corridors toward the waiting area, Cain couldn't shake the unsettling feeling that Stillwater's troubles were far from random. The precision of Dylan's injury, the careful targeting of the kidney, the lack of defensive wounds—all suggested planning, knowledge, and purpose.

"So much for our quiet town," Laura said, trying to break the palpable silence.

The implication hung between them, unspoken but undeniable. Laura saw the calculation in her husband's eyes, the mental list he was already compiling of possible suspects, of teenagers with grudges, of social dynamics that might have led to this violent outcome. Laura stopped him with a touch to his arm.

"The precision of the wound, the knowledge it demonstrates... it reminds me of what you described with the other deaths. The deliberate weakening of the fence post, the ladder, the tractor brake. The same methodical approach. You think they're related? The deaths of three elderly men and the stabbing of a high school football player?" Cain shook his head, not in denial, but unwilling or unable to accept the obvious. He was trying to make sense of it, but knew there would be no sense to be found.

"I think Stillwater is too small for that many calculated attacks to be coincidence," Cain replied carefully. "And I've been thinking about a pattern for weeks now." Martin turned abruptly, pacing the small waiting area with contained energy. "Different methods, different victims, different apparent motives. What connects an eighteen-year-old athlete to three men in their seventies?"

"I don't know," Laura admitted. "But someone does."

"True. Someone who understands physical vulnerabilities—whether it's the structural weakness of a ladder or the anatomical vulnerability of a kidney."

Martin stopped his pacing, turning to face her with an expression that balanced professional determination with personal dread. "Someone knowledgeable. Someone calculating. Someone hiding in plain sight."

The hospital's overhead lighting flickered briefly, casting momentary shadows across the waiting room before stabilizing again. In that brief dimming, Laura caught a glimpse of true fear in her husband's eyes—not for himself, but for their community, for the invisible threat walking among them.

"What do we do now?" she asked, though she already knew the answer.

"We wait for Dylan to wake up," Martin replied, his voice hardening with resolve. "And then hopefully we find out who in Stillwater has the knowledge, opportunity, and motivation to orchestrate all of this."

Laura rose to join him, placing a steadying hand on his arm. "Be careful, Martin." Martin pulled her close, hugging her tightly, sharing a moment of familiarity and comfort in their quickly changing world.

"I should go tell Mary," Martin said, finally pulling away. "She'll want to know." Laura nodded, glad he came to that conclusion on his own.

"I think hearing it from you would be good."

They hugged, and Laura hurried back into the ER, leaving Martin alone in the quiet corridor. He remained there for several minutes, battling with questions in his mind, the weight of Stillwater's mounting troubles settling across his shoulders like a physical burden. He only needed one answer: Who could be creating this chaos in his town?

Deep down Cain knew, or suspected, but refused to admit it. His training told him to investigate, not assume, not jump to conclusions. But he was still a human, and like all humans his tendency was to assume the worst, to jump to a conclusion because it seemed so obvious. He knew that didn't make it true, but in this case, it just might be.

Carter.

Martin pushed himself away from the wall and headed toward the door, hating to leave but knowing he had to tell Mary first. As he reached the waiting room he found Deputy Rivers just entering.

"Carol, I've got to get home," Martin said. "Can you wait for Dylan's parents? They'll want an update. Find Laura. She can fill you in."

"Of course. I'll take care of it." Martin nodded, then left, a look of determination on his face, masking the fear that was growing in his heart for the town.

The Cain house stood silent in the pre-dawn darkness, a single porch light illuminating the front steps as Martin's Bronco pulled into the driveway. He cut the engine, sitting motionless for a long moment as fatigue washed over him in heavy waves. The digital clock on his dashboard displayed 2:48 AM in harsh green numerals—another night of broken sleep in a week full of them.

The walk from the driveway to his front door felt longer than usual, each step weighted with the burden of what he'd witnessed at the hospital and the news he now carried. He hesitated, looking next door to the home where Carter Thompson lived. It was dark, silent, and felt more so than the rest of the block, both from the lack of any exterior or interior light, but also because of his own dark thoughts around Carter. Martin thought about him and his 'investigations', wondering just how far a 16-year old might go for approval, or for revenge. He shook his head, trying not to let his own fears cloud his judgment.

His key turned in the lock with a click that seemed unnaturally loud in the quiet neighborhood. Inside, the house was dark except for the small night light in the hallway—a concession to Laura's late-night hospital shifts that often had her navigating the stairs in darkness.

Martin removed his jacket and gun belt, hanging them on the designated hooks by the door, a ritual unchanged in twenty years. He moved toward the kitchen, intending to pour a glass of water before heading upstairs, when his gaze drifted up toward Mary's bedroom at the top of the stairs.

He hesitated, torn between the desire to let her sleep and the knowledge that she'd want to hear about Dylan from him rather than through a chain of text messages or social media posts once morning came. The news would spread through Stillwater High like wildfire; better she heard the facts first, unfiltered by teenage speculation and rumor.

Decision made, Martin climbed the stairs quietly, the familiar creaks of the old wooden treads quietly telegraphing his approach. He paused outside Mary's door, listening for any indication that she might still be awake despite the hour. Hearing nothing, he gently turned the knob and pushed the door open.

Mary's room was a study in controlled chaos—textbooks and notebooks stacked precariously on her desk, clothes draped over the back of a chair, walls covered with photos of friends and artwork she'd collected over the years. In the center of it all, Mary slept curled on her side, one hand tucked beneath her pillow, hair spilling across her face in a dark tangle.

Martin approached slowly, lowering himself to the edge of her bed with care. For a moment, he just looked at her—not the defiant teenager who challenged his authority at every turn, but the little girl who had once climbed into his lap for bedtime stories, who had worn his badge for Halloween three years running, who had looked at him like he could fix anything broken in her world.

When had that changed? When had he become the obstacle rather than the protector in her eyes?

With gentle hesitation, he placed his hand on her shoulder, squeezing softly. "Mary," he whispered. "Wake up, sweetheart."

She stirred, eyelids fluttering against the disorientation of being pulled from deep sleep. "Mmm? What's wrong?" Her voice was thick with sleep, younger somehow without the defensive edge it usually carried.

"I need to talk to you," Martin said, keeping his voice low. "It's important."

Mary pushed herself up on one elbow, blinking in the dim light from the hallway. For a moment, she looked confused by his presence, then concern washed over her features.

"Daddy?" The childhood name slipped out unconsciously, a remnant of their relationship before its recent complications. "What's going on? Is it Mom?"

"Mom's fine," he assured her quickly, touched by the immediate concern for Laura. "She's at the hospital. There's been an incident, Mary. I wanted you to hear it from me first."

Mary sat up fully now, pushing her hair back from her face, sleep receding as alertness took its place. "What happened?"

Martin took a breath, choosing his words carefully. "Dylan Foster was attacked tonight walking home from the game. He was stabbed and left on Maple Street. Looks like a switchblade. Maybe a vagrant. We don't know yet. A driver found him and called 911, but he'd lost a lot of blood by then." Martin caught himself, afraid he had offered too much detail, his brain sometimes unable to stop the analytical nature of his job. But Mary didn't seem to notice, only accepting the minimal report as fact, to be processed.

"Dylan?" Mary's voice caught on the name, her eyes widening. "Is he—is he dead?"

"No," Martin said quickly. "He's in surgery. Mom's there with him and the surgical team. They're doing everything they can."

Mary's hand covered her mouth, tears welling immediately in her eyes. "That's why that call came in," she whispered, almost to herself. "After the game, when everyone was celebrating. He left early..."

Martin caught the odd phrasing but set it aside for the moment, focusing instead on the distress evident in his daughter's face. "I'm sorry, sweetheart. I know he's your classmate."

Without warning, Mary lunged forward, wrapping her arms around his middle in a tight hug that caught him by surprise. "Thank you for telling me," she mumbled against his uniform shirt. "For waking me up. For not letting me find out from Instagram or something."

Martin's arms encircled her automatically, one hand coming up to stroke her hair as he had when she was small. The familiar gesture felt both natural and strange after so many months of careful distance between them.

"I thought you'd want to know," he said simply.

Mary pulled back, wiping at her eyes with the sleeve of her oversized sleep shirt. "Can I see him? Is that allowed?"

"Not right now. He's still in surgery, and then he'll be in ICU, family only." Martin squeezed her shoulder gently. "Maybe tomorrow, if he's stabilized. Mom can let us know when he's able to have visitors."

Mary nodded, her expression somber. "We weren't close or anything, but... he's always been nice to me. Even when some of the other football guys were jerks." She pulled her knees up to her chest, wrapping her arms around them. "Who would do something like this?"

The question held no expectation of an answer—the natural response of someone confronted with senseless violence. Martin knew this, yet he still felt the weight of his inability to provide an answer, either for his daughter or himself.

"I don't know yet," he admitted. "But I promise you, I'm going to find out."

Mary nodded, accepting his promise with a trust he hadn't seen from her in months. In this moment, with sleep still softening her edges and shock rendering her vulnerable, she looked to him as she once had—as if his word alone could make the world right again.

"Try to get some more sleep," he suggested, standing from her bed. "I'll let you know if there's any news."

"Okay," Mary agreed, though her furrowed brow suggested sleep would be elusive now. "Dad? Tell Mom I love her. And... be careful, okay?"

The concern in her voice touched something deep in Martin's chest. "I will," he promised, moving toward the door.

"And Dad?" Mary called softly as he reached the threshold. "I love you too."

Martin paused, the simple declaration landing with unexpected weight. "I love you too, Mary," he replied, his voice rough with emotion he rarely allowed himself to display. "More than you know."

He closed her door gently, standing in the hallway for a moment to collect himself. The conversation had been a gift—a brief window into the relationship they'd once had, uncomplicated by teenage rebellion and parental fear. For a few precious minutes, they had connected without the tension that had defined their interactions for the past year.

As he moved toward his own bedroom, Martin found himself grateful for the small mercy of that connection, even as the circumstances that prompted it pressed heavily on his conscience. He vowed to work harder with Mary, to give her space and let her be a teenager. It was something he had sworn to himself before, but now, this time, he could see what he had lost for all his demands on Mary, and he realized it had no value. His daughter was a good person, doing well in the world. Her father's strict parenting was not helping, and instead pushing away one of only two things that mattered to him in the world.

But for now, just for this moment, he would hold onto the warmth of his daughter's embrace, the trust in her eyes, the

"Daddy" that had slipped unconsciously from her lips—small comforts against the darkness that seemed to be closing in around their town.

Back in Mary's bedroom, she lay quietly in bed, trying to get the image of such a brutal attack out of her mind. She knew she wouldn't be able to sleep. She hadn't been close to Dylan, but still. As she prayed quietly to herself, one detail lingered in her mind, floating back up through layers of sadness and fear.

A switchblade. She had only seen one in her life. Carter's switchblade from the riverside crime scene. She knew it would be considered circumstantial evidence, but the idea still danced enticingly close to her conscious thoughts. She knew Dylan didn't like Carter, warning Mary on a few occasions that Carter was stalking her. Mary always brushed it off. She knew Carter, Dylan didn't. But even if she knew Carter would never hurt her, what were the possibilities that he would hurt Dylan?

The idea seemed preposterous. But still, Mary couldn't seem to push it away. She would have to face it at some point, prove to herself that Carter wasn't the attacker. The idea let her mind rest a little, enough that she fell into a fitful sleep, if only for a short while before the sun rose on a different day, one already marred with more tragedy.

TWENTY-NINE

The morning arrived with the sluggish reluctance of a low tide dragging itself up a shallow beach. Sheriff Cain had managed less than two hours of restless sleep before his alarm pulled him back to consciousness. Mary hadn't been awake yet, or so Cain assumed, and he resisted checking in on her before he quickly left for the station. The coffee tasted bitter in his mouth as he drove, the rising sun doing little to dispel the darkening shadow that had settled over Stillwater since last night.

The sheriff's department was already humming with activity when he pushed through the glass doors at 7:30 AM. Deputies moved with purpose between desks, phones rang with the steady persistence of small-town emergencies, and the air carried the distinct tension of a department stretched beyond its resources.

Deputy Garrett looked up from the front desk, her usual professional smile replaced by a grimace as she caught Cain's eye and tilted her head meaningfully toward the bullpen. Following her gaze, Cain registered an unexpected scene that stopped him mid-stride.

James Kilgore stood at the property desk, hands splayed across the counter as Deputy Weathers methodically returned items in a plastic bag. Beside Kilgore, a thin woman in a rumpled navy suit consulted a clipboard with sharp, irritated movements of her pen. Cain recognized her immediately—Marianne Hewitt, public defender for Stillwater County, a woman whose determination was matched only by her perpetual glare.

"You've got to be kidding me," Cain muttered, striding toward the scene with barely contained anger. "Weathers, hold up."

The deputy looked up, relief evident in his expression at the sheriff's timely arrival. "Morning, Sheriff. Just processing Mr. Kilgore's release."

"On whose authority?" Cain demanded, positioning himself squarely in front of Kilgore, who remained surprisingly composed, his usual nervous energy replaced by something that bordered on smug satisfaction.

Marianne Hewitt stepped forward, inserting herself between Cain and her client. "On my authority as counsel representing Mr. Kilgore, and more importantly, on the authority of the law, which you're supposedly upholding, Sheriff." She thrust a document toward him. "Release order, signed by Judge Martinez at 6:45 this morning."

Cain took the paper, scanning it quickly. "This man is a person of interest in multiple ongoing investigations."

"Being a 'person of interest' is not grounds for detention beyond sixty days without charges in this state," Hewitt countered, reclaiming the document from his hands with a sharp tug. "You've held my client for 58 days on a bicycle theft allegation with insufficient evidence to file formal charges. Time's up, Sheriff."

"What about the assault charges," Cain countered. "He broke my deputy's nose and escaped custody."

"He wasn't in custody according to your statement," Hewitt said. "And your deputy decided not to press charges." Cain turned, locking eyes with Sam, who simply shrugged an apology. Cain knew it would be embarrassing for Chambers, to admit he was caught flat footed by a "person of interest." Cain shook his head then turned his attention to Kilgore, who had the decency to lower his gaze, though the ghost of a smile played at the corners of his mouth. "We're not finished, Kilgore."

"Actually, you are," Hewitt interjected. "Unless you'd like to arrest him right now, with evidence for a specific crime. Do you have new evidence connecting my client to anything beyond possible bicycle theft? Because if not, we're walking out that door, and any further harassment will result in a formal complaint to the county commissioner."

The bullpen had fallen silent, all eyes focused on the confrontation. Cain fought the urge to overplay his hand. Despite his suspicions about Kilgore's connection to the deaths in Stillwater, he had nothing concrete linking the man to the sabotaged equipment that had killed three elderly residents, and there was no way he could have attacked Dylan.

"Deputy Weathers," Cain said finally, not taking his eyes off Kilgore, "complete the release process."

Weathers nodded, returning to the task of cataloging Kilgore's personal effects—a wallet with seven dollars, a Swiss Army knife, a set of keys to unknown locks, and a cheap prepaid cell phone.

"Sign here," Weathers instructed, sliding a form across the counter.

Kilgore scratched his signature with deliberate slowness, then gathered his belongings, tucking them into the pockets of his weathered jacket. "It's been a pleasure, Sheriff," he said, his voice carrying an undercurrent of amusement that set Cain's teeth on edge.

"You can use my office to reach Mr. Kilgore, if you develop any actual evidence," Hewitt added, her tone making it clear how unlikely she considered that possibility. "In the meantime, I trust your department will respect his rights as a citizen."

"Absolutely," Cain replied with as much neutrality as he could muster, with just a hint of threat still in his voice. "We're all about respecting rights in Stillwater. We expect citizens to respect them as well."

Hewitt narrowed her eyes at the implied threat but chose not to engage further. She gestured for Kilgore to follow her toward the exit.

As they passed, Kilgore paused briefly beside Cain, his voice dropping to a near-whisper. "Heard about that football kid. Terrible thing. Town's getting dangerous." He shook his head in mock concern. "Might need to look closer to home, Sheriff. Sometimes the monsters aren't the ones living in the woods."

Before Cain could respond, Kilgore continued toward the door. At the threshold, he turned back, catching Cain's gaze one last time. With deliberate slowness, he winked—a gesture so uncharacteristic and unsettling that it sent a cold ripple down Cain's spine.

Then they were gone, the glass doors sliding closed behind them with a soft hydraulic hiss.

"What the hell was that about?" Sam asked, appearing at Cain's side, his voice low enough that only the sheriff could hear.

Cain watched through the windows as Kilgore and Hewitt crossed the parking lot, the public defender already on her phone, likely arranging transportation for her client back to whatever temporary shelter she'd established for him, or simply to the tent city at the end of Maple.

"I'm not sure," Cain admitted. "But I don't like it. That didn't feel like the relief of an innocent man being released. That felt like..."

"Victory," Sam finished, following Cain's gaze. "Like he'd accomplished something by being here."

Cain nodded, the unease in his gut solidifying into something more concrete. "I'll have Carol tail them. Discreetly. I want to know where he goes, who he talks to."

Sam hesitated, the coffee mug suspended halfway to his lips. "You think he's connected to Dylan Foster's stabbing?"

"I can't see how, but I also think nothing in Stillwater happens in isolation anymore," Cain replied, turning away from the windows to face his deputy. "And I think James Kilgore knows more than he's saying—about a lot of things."

Sam set his mug down on a nearby desk, his expression troubled. "If he is connected to these cases, letting him walk could be dangerous."

"Or it could be exactly what we need," Cain countered, lowering his voice as he led Sam toward his office. "Sometimes you have to let the fish swim to find the bigger predators in the pond."

"You still think he's working with someone else?"

Cain closed his office door behind them, ensuring privacy before responding. "I think Kilgore's not smart enough or motivated enough to engineer the deaths we've seen. He's a tool, not an architect."

Sam leaned against the desk, arms crossed over his chest. "So who's using him? And why?"

"That," Cain said grimly, "is exactly what I intend to find out."

The sheriff moved to the evidence board that still dominated one wall of his office, where photographs, timelines, and connections mapped the growing darkness in Stillwater. Three confirmed deaths. Cain wrote on a new card and pasted it in place: Dylan Foster. Add one attempted murder, and a pattern that suggested methodical planning rather than random violence.

"This came in earlier," Sam said, handing Cain a sheet of paper —a preliminary report on the stabbing, complete with medical diagrams indicating the precise nature of the wound.

"Still unconscious," Cain replied, looking over the report. "Laura called before I left. He made it through surgery, but he's not out of the woods yet. Even if he recovers, there's no guarantee he'll remember who attacked him."

"So we're back to evidence and witness statements," Sam concluded, the frustration evident in his voice. "Neither of which we have in abundance."

Cain studied the board, eyes moving from victim to victim, searching for the connection that continued to elude him. Jackson McKenzie, Ned Miller, Gerald Cooper, Dylan Foster

—four men with seemingly nothing in common beyond residence in Stillwater.

"Everyone's connected in a town this size," Cain mused, thinking aloud. "We're just not seeing the pattern yet."

Sam moved closer to the board, examining the photographs with renewed attention. "What about Carter? He seems to have a knack for seeing patterns others miss."

Cain turned to study his deputy, a flicker of something—suspicion, perhaps, or simple curiosity—crossing his features. "Do you mean as a resource, or a suspect?"

Sam shrugged. "Maybe both. He was spot on about Kilgore, at least so it appeared."

"I'm not so sure anymore," Cain said. "You found bicycle parts, but were they ever identified as parts from the bikes reported stolen?"

"No, though that was hard to determine. Parts are parts to a degree. The frames in that shed were old. The other parts too generic to be sure."

"As if they might have been put there, to lead us to a conclusion that was ultimately false if we looked close enough."

"Why wasn't that enough to hold Kilgore on suspicion," Sam asked. "Bike parts in his shed and a witness with images of that same person messing with bikes at the library." Cain shook his head, unsure of how this all made sense. "What about other evidence in the shed," Sam added. "Fishing line, a couple saws."

"We couldn't tie any of it directly back to any of the deaths. The line matched the type we found at the river, but it was such a common brand we couldn't definitively tie it in. Saws were clean, so no direct connection, at least none that we could determine here. I want to send them into Portland for a deeper forensic comparison to the cut posts and ladder, but that's going to take time. Ultimately, the evidence was all too convenient, almost obvious, but just vague enough to not lead us anywhere." Cain paused. "And so Kilgore walks free despite that evidence, however circumstantial," he pointed out. "Curious, don't you think?"

"What are you suggesting?"

"I'm not suggesting anything," Cain replied, though his tone implied otherwise. "I'm simply noting that Carter Thompson seems to be on the periphery of multiple investigations, always with information that's just useful enough to be credible but never quite enough to close a case. He knows a little too much for my taste."

Sam shifted uncomfortably, avoiding direct eye contact. "Are you thinking he's a suspect?"

"I think," Cain said carefully, "that nothing and no one in this investigation is above scrutiny. Including a sixteen-year-old with an unusual interest in detective work and a habit of knowing a lot about our crime scenes."

The room fell silent as Sam absorbed the implication. Outside, the morning continued to unfold—deputies filing reports, phones ringing, the routine of law enforcement proceeding despite the shadow that had fallen over Stillwater. But inside the sheriff's office, something had shifted—a new possibility added to an already complex equation.

"We'll keep an eye on Kilgore," Cain instructed, turning back to the evidence board. "But let's also take a closer look at Carter Thompson. His movements, his associations, his access to information about these cases."

"You really think a kid could be behind this?" Sam asked, disbelief evident in his voice even as he recalled the cold determination he had seen in Carter's face at the park, when he had blackmailed him.

Cain's expression remained grim as he studied the board outlining four men whose lives had been violently interrupted. "I think assuming limitations based on age or appearance is exactly how predators go undetected. And I'm done making assumptions about anyone in this town."

The declaration hung in the air between them, a new boundary established in an investigation that had already challenged everything Martin Cain thought he knew about the community he'd sworn to protect.

THIRTY

The library at Stillwater High occupied the northeast corner of the campus, a two-story structure with tall windows that flooded the reading areas with natural light. Unlike the cafeteria with its cacophony of competing conversations and clattering trays, the library maintained a hushed atmosphere even during lunch period—a sanctuary for students seeking quiet or solitude.

Mary Cain stood at the entrance, scanning the familiar space for a specific silhouette. She spotted him at his usual table in the reference section—a corner partially obscured by tall shelves that offered both privacy and a clear view of anyone approaching. Carter Thompson sat alone, a half-eaten sandwich and open book before him, his attention focused on the notebook where his pen moved with methodical precision.

Mary hesitated, her lunch tray balanced in one hand, backpack slung over her opposite shoulder. The conversation with her father that morning had left her unsettled, thoughts circling back to Dylan Foster's stabbing and the strange pattern of deaths in Stillwater. Sam's warnings about Carter echoed in her mind, but so did the memories of their childhood friendship—a connection that seemed increasingly distant yet somehow still fundamental.

Decision made, she approached his table, clearing her throat softly as she reached him. "Mind if I join you?"

Carter looked up, a smile flickering across his features before settling into a carefully neutral expression. "Free country," he replied, moving his backpack to make room.

"Or so they say," Mary replied, setting her tray down and sliding into the chair across from him.

"Tired of the constant climb of the social ladder," Carter asked, his tone hovering between teasing humor and practiced indifference.

"Something like that." Mary took a bite of her sandwich, chewing thoughtfully before continuing. "Actually, I'm not really up for the cafeteria today. Not with everything that's happened."

Carter closed his notebook, his movements unhurried. "Dylan Foster," he said, not a question but an acknowledgment.

Mary nodded, studying Carter's face for his reaction. "You heard?"

"Everyone's heard. It's all anyone's talking about." Carter's expression remained neutral, his voice even. "Stabbed walking home from the game, found half-dead on Maple Street. Critical condition at Stillwater Memorial."

The clinical detachment in his statement sent a small chill through Mary. No shock, no outrage, just a factual assessment delivered with the emotional investment one might give a weather report.

"He's still unconscious," Mary added, watching Carter carefully. "My mom's been with him in ICU. They don't know if he'll make it, or if he'll have permanent damage even if he does."

Carter nodded, taking a bite of his own sandwich before responding. "That's unfortunate."

"Unfortunate?" Mary echoed, unable to keep the surprise from her voice. "Carter, someone tried to kill him."

"And that's terrible," Carter agreed, though his tone conveyed minimal conviction. "But you have to understand, Dylan Foster isn't exactly someone I'm going to shed tears over."

"What does that mean?"

Carter met her gaze directly. "It means Dylan and his friends have made my life difficult since middle school. Shoving me into lockers, knocking books out of my hands, calling me 'freak' and worse." His voice remained steady, but something hardened behind his eyes. "Three months ago, they cornered me in the alley behind Maple Street. Three against one. If a resident hadn't heard the commotion and intervened..."

He trailed off, leaving the outcome unspoken but clear enough.

"I didn't know," Mary said softly, genuinely surprised. "Why didn't you report it?"

A humorless smile tugged at the corner of Carter's mouth. "To who? Teachers who look the other way? Administrators who say 'boys will be boys?' Or maybe to the sheriff, who'd see it as a popular student's word against the weird kid whose parents died?"

The bitterness in his voice was so unexpected that Mary sat back slightly. "You know my dad would take it seriously. That's not fair."

"Life rarely is," Carter replied, his demeanor shifting back to neutral with unsettling speed. "Look, I'm not happy someone stabbed Dylan. Violence is bad for any town, especially a small one like this. But I can't pretend to be devastated that he got hurt, even if the injuries are far more severe than he deserved."

Mary absorbed this, uncertain how to reconcile the cold pragmatism before her with the sensitive boy she'd once known. Her dad's mention of the switchblade brought Mary back to her reason for finding Carter. She shifted her tone, trying to match his clinical tone. "My dad says they don't have any leads yet. No witnesses, no weapon found. He says someone very smart orchestrated the attack."

"Interesting," Carter murmured, his eyes sharpening with renewed focus. Mary could almost sense a flash of pride, though she wasn't sure she was projecting the feeling. "What else did the sheriff share? Any theories about who might have done it?"

Mary felt a subtle shift in the conversation, like stepping onto ice of uncertain thickness. "Not really. Just that it seemed... deliberate. Not a random attack."

"The location would suggest that," Carter agreed, leaning forward slightly. "Maple Street between Pine and Cedar is poorly lit at night. The perfect place for an ambush, especially after a game when everyone's attention is divided."

"You've thought about this," Mary observed, keeping her tone casual despite the unease stirring in her stomach.

"I think about a lot of things," Carter replied. "It's how my mind works. Patterns, probabilities, scenarios. Like those other deaths the sheriff's been investigating."

The deliberate introduction of the topic sent Mary's mental alarms ringing. She took a sip of water, using the moment to compose her response. "I kinda heard about them. What's the connection?"

Carter's eyes narrowed slightly, a detective recognizing evasion. "No connection, just unfortunate coincidence. Jackson McKenzie, Ned Miller, Gerald Cooper. Three elderly men, three 'accidents' in close succession. Quite the statistical anomaly for a town this size, wouldn't you say?"

Mary maintained a carefully neutral expression. "I don't really know the details. Dad doesn't bring work home."

"Really?" Carter's eyebrow arched in polite disbelief. "The sheriff never discusses cases at the dinner table? Never makes phone calls you might overhear? Never leaves files where a curious daughter might glimpse them?"

"No," Mary replied firmly, meeting his gaze directly. "He's very professional about separating work from home. It's annoying," she added, trying to lighten the moment.

Carter nodded, conceding the point with surprising grace. "That's admirable. Though the Mary I knew would have been so curious about this type of thing."

"That was younger me. I've got other things to think about these days," Mary said, though the words felt hollow even to her own ears. She'd spent years trying to penetrate those very boundaries, eavesdropping on conversations, scrolling through his phone when he left it unattended, piecing together fragments of cases from overheard radio calls. She tried to reconcile it as innocent curiosity, but knew she held a level of morbid curiosity for crime, borne out of the seemingly innocent games she and Carter had pursued as amateur detectives years ago.

"Of course," Carter agreed, his tone suggesting he understood more than she was admitting. "Still, you must wonder about the connection. Four victims in a small town like Stillwater, all within a few months. The statistical probability is... significant."

Mary recognized the familiar pattern from their childhood—Carter laying out evidence, guiding her toward a conclusion while making it seem like her own discovery. The old dance of their detective games, but with stakes that now felt dangerously real.

"This reminds me of when we were younger," she said, deliberately trying to lighten the mood, to steer clear of too much darkness. "I loved how we took it so seriously, but I guess none of our 'cases' were that serious."

A genuine smile flickered across Carter's face, momentarily transforming him into the boy she remembered. "You were always better at interviewing witnesses. They trusted you more."

"And you were better at noticing details everyone else missed," Mary replied, returning the smile. "We made a good team."

The moment of connection hung between them, fragile but real. Mary found herself wanting to preserve it, to recapture something of the uncomplicated friendship they'd once shared. Yet beneath that desire lay a purpose she couldn't ignore—to understand who Carter had become, and whether Sam's warnings had merit.

"Maybe we still could," she suggested, keeping her tone light. "Be a team, I mean. Maybe we could look into some of these 'events' as you used to call them, I mean, discreetly." She almost held her breath, trying to casually take a bite of her sandwich to hide the tension building inside of her.

Carter studied her, his expression unreadable. For a moment, Mary feared she'd overplayed her hand, that he'd see through the transparent attempt to monitor his activities. But then his features softened.

"I'd like that," he said, surprising her with what appeared to be genuine enthusiasm. "There's actually something I've been wanting to check out. The Campbell property, where Kilgore was staying. I have a theory about some evidence that might still be there."

"The bicycle thief?" Mary asked, a sudden wave of anxiety washing over her. How did she know that name, after she had just told Carter her father never spoke about cases? She kept her face calm, hoping it would be missed.

Carter nodded, too excited to talk about the case to notice. "The same. Though I suspect there's more to his story than simple theft." He leaned closer, lowering his voice. "What if he's connected to what happened to Dylan? To the other deaths? An outsider, no connections in town, homeless, a ghost. Who would suspect someone so invisible?"

The theory sent a chill through Mary. It sounded plausible—exactly the kind of pattern Carter excelled at identifying. Yet something in his eagerness, the gleam in his eyes as he outlined the possibility, struck her as performative rather than genuine.

"That's... quite a theory," she managed, forcing a fascinated expression. She wanted to keep Carter on the hook, but worried about overplaying her hand. Yet she knew she had to. "When did you want to go? How about tonight?" Mary suggested, seizing the opportunity. "A weeknight is perfect—nobody would expect us to be out investigating."

Carter's enthusiasm visibly faltered. "I can't tonight. I have some... loose ends to wrap up."

"Loose ends? Sounds so adult," Mary laughed softly, unsurprised by a statement like that from Carter.

"Just some things I need to take care of," Carter replied, his tone suddenly cryptic. "Nothing interesting. What about tomorrow night instead?"

"Friday?" Mary frowned slightly. "That's the first football game since Dylan's attack. There's going to be a moment of silence and everything." She immediately regretted saying it.

Something flashed in Carter's eyes—irritation, perhaps, or something darker. Right. Of course she'd want to be part of the spectacle. The whole school coming together to pretend they cared about Dylan when most of them just enjoyed watching him torment kids like me, Carter thought. His opinion of Mary slipped for a moment, until she jumped in.

"Actually, that makes it perfect," she said eagerly. "Everyone will be at the game. Nobody would notice us slipping away with their collective grieving."

Carter's expression shifted, the darkness receding as he considered her logic. "That's... actually a good point. While the town is distracted..."

"We could get away unnoticed," Mary finished for him, secretly relieved her recovery had worked. "I'll drive us out there right after school."

"Perfect," Carter agreed, his enthusiasm returning.

The bell signaling the end of lunch period rang, startling them both. Students began moving toward the exit, conversations rising briefly before being hushed by the librarian's stern glance.

Mary gathered her things, an odd mixture of anticipation and dread settling in her stomach. She'd achieved her goal— gaining insight into Carter's thoughts about Dylan's attack and securing an opportunity to observe him firsthand. Yet she couldn't shake the feeling that she'd just agreed to something dangerous, that the game they were playing had rules she didn't fully understand.

"So, tomorrow night then," Carter confirmed, slipping his notebook into his backpack with practiced efficiency.

"Tomorrow," Mary agreed, shouldering her own bag. "Just like old times."

Carter smiled—a genuine expression that reached his eyes, transforming his face into something younger, more familiar. "Just like old times," he echoed.

As they parted ways in the hallway outside the library, Mary turned the opposite direction, glancing back at the receding shape of Carter, his demure form swallowed by the flow of students around him.

She'd learned nothing concrete about Carter's potential involvement in Dylan's stabbing or the other deaths in Stillwater. Instead, she'd committed to spending more time with him, potentially placing herself closer to danger if Sam's suspicions proved correct.

The unease that had led her to seek Carter out in the first place hadn't dissipated—if anything, it had intensified, crystallizing into something more specific. The careful way he'd questioned her about her father's investigation, the clinical detachment with which he'd discussed Dylan's attack, the eager anticipation in his voice when proposing their expedition to the Campbell property—all of it suggested a complexity to Carter Thompson that went far beyond the withdrawn teenager she watched disappear down the hall.

As Mary turned and headed toward her next class, she realized the true nature of their lunch conversation—a sophisticated game of cat and mouse, with both of them alternating roles. The question that troubled her, that sent a chill of uncertainty through her veins, was which of them had ultimately been the cat, and which the mouse.

And who would catch whom when the game inevitably ended.

THIRTY-ONE

The final bell's echo faded into a cacophony of lockers slamming and teenage voices rising in the relief of day's end. Carter moved through the hallways with practiced efficiency, navigating between clusters of students without engaging, a ghost passing through crowds unseen.

Outside, Stillwater High erupted into its daily afternoon ritual —yellow buses idling in neat rows, engines grumbling as they swallowed lines of younger students, upperclassmen jangling car keys and organizing carpools, athletes shouldering duffel bags as they trudged toward practice fields. A carefully orchestrated chaos that Carter observed with detached interest while unlocking his bicycle from the rack.

He pushed off into the stream of departing vehicles, pedaling with a steady rhythm. As the distance between him and the school increased, the noise receded like a tide drawing back from shore. First the shouts and laughter faded, then the rumble of bus engines, until finally he was left with only the soft whir of his bicycle chain and the whisper of tires against asphalt.

This transition—from the forced socialization of school to the peaceful solitude of his ride home—was Carter's favorite part of the day. These fifteen minutes belonged exclusively to him, a buffer between worlds where his mind could process, catalog, and plan without interruption.

Today's thoughts circled around Mary Cain and their conversation in the library. Her sudden interest in the crimes, her carefully casual questions about Dylan Foster, her suggestion that they investigate together—all data points forming a pattern he couldn't ignore. She was fishing for information, likely at her father's behest. The sheriff was closing in, beginning to see connections Carter had deliberately left visible.

Good. Everything proceeding according to schedule.

The residential streets of Stillwater unfolded before him, autumn leaves scattering in his wake. Carter was so absorbed in his thoughts that he nearly missed the subtle sound of an engine turning over behind him. A police cruiser pulled out from a side street, maintaining a distance of approximately two blocks—close enough to keep him in sight but far enough to avoid obvious surveillance.

Carter didn't turn to look, didn't alter his pace or trajectory. Instead, he focused on the reflection in a parked car's side mirror as he passed, catching a glimpse of the driver. Despite the distance he could see it was Deputy Sam Chambers.

So the sheriff had assigned his newest deputy to tail him. Interesting choice. Chambers was eager, probably more than willing to tail someone like Carter, but inexperienced enough to make mistakes. Like parking too close to the intersection where Carter would inevitably notice him. His patrol car stuck out like a sore thumb.

He allowed himself a small, private smile as he turned onto his street, the cruiser faithfully maintaining its distance. This, too, had been anticipated—though perhaps sooner than he'd expected. The game was accelerating.

He coasted to a stop in front of his house, dismounting with fluid grace and securing his bicycle to the porch railing with practiced movements. Throughout the routine, he gave no indication that he'd noticed his shadow. Let them think their surveillance was succeeding.

Inside, the house greeted him with its familiar mustiness—the scent of age and neglect that no amount of cleaning could fully eradicate. The television's muffled drone led him to the living room, where his grandmother sat in her recliner, gaze fixed on a game show whose questions she could no longer follow.

Carter stood and watched her grandmother for a moment. The shell that sat before him was nothing like what he remembered from his youth. Like Carter, who had suffered and changed after the death of his father and mother, the impact of those deaths had eventually taken its toll on her as well. For the first months she had been a strength Carter could count on, taking the place of his parents as best as she could, being the person he could confide in. But time caught up quickly, and age had no concern for such human needs. Her confusion and, clearly dementia, had grown at an accelerated pace. Now Carter barely recognized the woman that used to be his best friend.

So be it.

"I'm home, gran," he announced, placing a gentle hand on her shoulder.

She looked up, momentary confusion clouding her features before recognition dawned. "Carter. Good. Did you finish your homework at school?"

"Not yet," he replied patiently, though he'd completed all assignments during study hall. "I'll work on it later. Do you need anything? Water? Tea? Did you take your pills yet?"

She looked down to the two pills still sitting on her side table, confused. "I thought I did," she mumbled, reaching down with a shaky hand to pick them up and place them in her mouth. Carter helped her with her glass of water, preventing her shaking hand from spilling, and ensuring she swallowed both pills.

He waited with her for a minute, watching her attention wane and her eyes move back to the bright colors and flashing lights of the television. After a moment, she mumbled, "Your father will be home soon. We'll have dinner then."

Carter didn't correct her, merely nodded and retreated from the room. These slips had become so common that addressing them felt pointless, like trying to hold back the tide with bare hands. He took his backpack into the side room, a dim space with a small table where his grandmother used to sew. Setting out his school books and a notepad, he opened the books to pages from the day's lesson, and added a few new notes onto the pad. He emptied the rest of his backpack, setting the small stack of books remaining to the side. Satisfied, he left everything laid out, grabbed his now empty backpack and left the room.

In the kitchen, he glanced through the window and spotted Sam's cruiser now parked two blocks away, partially concealed by a large oak tree. The deputy remained in the driver's seat, occasionally lifting what appeared to be a phone to his ear.

Satisfied, Carter moved away from the window, heading to the basement door. He flicked on the light switch, illuminating the narrow staircase that descended into the cool darkness below. The stairs creaked beneath his weight, each sound a familiar note in the house's constant symphony of age.

The basement had once been his father's workshop, the walls lined with pegboards that still held the ghostly outlines of tools long since sold to cover bills. Now it served as Carter's private domain, a space his grandmother never ventured into due to her increasing difficulty with stairs. Here, he could work undisturbed.

Carter moved to a workbench in the far corner, spreading a clean cloth across its surface. From a drawer, he extracted a pair of latex examination gloves, pulling them on with practiced efficiency. The thin material clung to his fingers like a second skin as he began assembling the items he would need.

First, a model F-14 airplane, fully assembled but unpainted, its plastic components gleaming under the single overhead bulb. Carter handled it carefully, wiping each piece with a cloth with methodical attention before placing it in his backpack. Next came a set of fine-tipped paintbrushes, each cleaned and inspected before being added to the growing items in his bag, finished off with a collection of small model paint bottles.

From a shelf above the workbench, he retrieved two large bottles of rubber cement—one nearly new, its viscous contents clearly visible through the glass, the other half full, bearing the smudges and stains of frequent use. Carter dug out a plastic squeeze bottle, empty and unused, then poured the rubber cement into it, filling it to the top. He cut off the tip of the squeeze bottle, making the opening larger, then covered the opening with duct tape. Both empty original bottles and the now full plastic bottle were wiped down thoroughly before joining the other items in his backpack.

The final item came from a locked cabinet beneath the stairs— a spark striker, the kind used for lighting gas stoves and camping equipment. Carter tested it once, the metallic scrape producing a bright spark that momentarily illuminated his concentrated expression. After wiping it down, this too disappeared into his backpack.

Each movement was performed with surgical precision, leaving no trace of fingerprints or DNA. Not a single item went into the bag without first being carefully cleaned and inspected. Whatever he was planning, Carter was ensuring that nothing could be traced back to him.

With everything secured in his backpack, Carter zipped it closed and slung it over one shoulder. He slipped off the gloves, shoving them in his pants pocket before ascending the stairs. At the top he paused to listen. The television continued its monotonous drone from the living room, his grandmother's occasional responses to questions no one had asked the only indication of her presence.

Carter stepped into the hallway, setting down his backpack then moving to the living room doorway. His grandmother remained exactly as he'd left her, lost in the flickering world of the screen, her reality blurring at the edges as twilight deepened the shadows in the room. He took a breath, then stepped to his grandmother's side.

"Did you take your pills, gran?" His voice pulled her from her stupor, her glazed eyes moving up to his face.

"I don't remember." Carter nodded, then took her pill bottle, laying the lid to the side and feeding out six pills, placing them in her out held hand.

"Take these," he said, holding up her water glass. She looked at the pills in confusion, as if remembering something faintly in the distant confines of her mind. "You'll feel better if you take them," he added, answering the question that lingered on her face, masked by her confusion. She took the water and swallowed the pills. The now eight pill dose would take affect quickly, he knew. He dumped the remaining pills, half the bottle, into a small baggie and shoved it into his pants pocket. Time to get going.

"I'm going to work on a school project," he said, knowing she wouldn't question the vague explanation. "I won't be long."

She nodded without looking away from the television. "Don't forget your jacket. It's getting cold out there."

The comment—a flash of maternal concern cutting through the fog of her confusion—caught him momentarily off-guard. Carter swallowed against an unexpected tightness in his throat. "I won't." The thought of what he had just done bringing a subtle wave of guilt to the pit of Carter's stomach. "I love you, gran," he added, then pushed the guilt aside.

He retreated to the kitchen, which had darkened as evening settled over Stillwater. Moving carefully to avoid silhouetting himself against any windows, Carter peered out once more. The cruiser remained in position, its outline just visible in the gathering dusk. Inside, the dome light briefly illuminated as Sam appeared to check something.

Perfect. Exactly where Carter wanted him.

He backed away from the window, pulled on a coat. He reached into his pocket, feeling a pair of thin gloves he kept there for cold bike rides, before securing his backpack back over both shoulders. With silent, measured movements, he unlocked the rear door, disengaging the security chain with careful precision to avoid any noise. The door opened with the barest whisper of sound, revealing the darkened backyard beyond.

He slipped outside, easing the door closed behind him. The night air carried a sharp chill that promised frost by morning, but Carter seemed impervious to the cold as he moved across the yard. At the back fence, a loose board swung aside with a gentle push, creating an opening just wide enough for him to squeeze through.

Beyond lay a narrow alley that ran behind several properties, invisible from the street where Deputy Chambers maintained his vigilant, but ultimately futile, surveillance. Carter moved along this hidden corridor with confident familiarity, the shadows embracing him like old friends.

Within minutes, he had navigated a complex route through back yards and side streets, eventually emerging several blocks away at an intersection where no police cruiser waited. Carter Thompson had vanished into the gathering darkness of Stillwater.

Inside the cruiser, Sam shifted uncomfortably, the seat that had seemed perfectly adequate at the beginning of his shift now feeling like concrete beneath him. Over four hours of surveillance had yielded nothing more exciting than Carter Thompson arriving home from school and disappearing inside. No visitors, no suspicious activity, nothing to justify the growing stiffness in Sam's lower back.

He lifted his phone as it vibrated with an incoming call. Sheriff Cain's name flashed on the screen.

"Chambers," Sam answered, keeping his voice professional despite the tedium of his assignment.

"Anything?" The sheriff's voice was terse, preoccupied.

"Nothing so far," Sam reported, eyes fixed on the Thompson house. "He arrived home from school at 3:45, entered the residence, and hasn't emerged. Lights visible in what I believe is the living room. No unusual activity to report."

A sigh crackled through the connection. "Keep on it. If he really is a suspect, or knows something, we need to keep tabs on him. These patterns don't just stop."

"Yes, sir." Sam hesitated, then added, "How long should I maintain position if there's no movement?"

"Until midnight. Then Deputy Hargrove will relieve you." The sheriff's voice softened slightly. "I know it's boring as hell, Sam, but if we're right about this kid—" He didn't need to finish his sentence. Sam got it. "I have Weathers on Kilgore. He's at the homeless encampment by the river. Rivers will replace him at 8pm. Just running short of hands."

"I understand, sir," Sam assured him. "Whatever it takes. I'll call immediately if anything changes."

The call ended, leaving Sam alone with the hum of the cruiser's idle engine and the distant sounds of evening settling over Stillwater. He drummed his fingers against the steering wheel, mentally reviewing the evidence that had led to this surveillance assignment. Carter Thompson's detailed knowledge of crime scenes. His convenient appearance with information about James Kilgore. His access to the sheriff's office on multiple occasions. All circumstantial, but together forming a troubling pattern that couldn't be ignored. And then there was the blackmail. Another element only Sam knew of, but added to the mystery of who Carter Thompson really was.

Movement caught Sam's attention—not at the Thompson house, but at the Cain residence next door. A silver Honda had pulled to the curb, and Mary emerged, waving goodbye to her friend Amber before heading up the walkway. Sam watched as she unlocked the door and disappeared inside, the house remaining dark except for the kitchen light switching on.

Sam checked the time—7:45 PM. Sheriff Cain wouldn't be home for hours yet, tied up with the investigation into Dylan Foster's stabbing. He heard Laura Cain was working a double shift at the hospital. Mary would be alone in that big house, just as she often was during her father's extended investigations.

Before he could reconsider, Sam grabbed his phone and typed a quick message.

Sam: I'm nearby. You should join me.

He sent the text, using their private code rather than his name —"IT" for "Ice Tea," a joke that had started when Mary had texted her dad asking if he wanted iced tea and accidentally sent it to Sam instead. He'd replied "Yes please," which created an awkward drink delivery to her father, and the nickname had stuck. It was silly but innocuous enough to appear on her phone without raising suspicions.

Sam returned his attention to the Thompson house, but his focus had fractured. Part of him remained fixed on his assignment, while another part listened for the sound of his phone that would signal Mary's reply.

The phone dinged less than a minute later.

Mary: Where?

Sam smiled, a warmth spreading through him that had nothing to do with the cruiser's heating system. He flashed the headlights once, briefly, knowing she would see it from her kitchen window.

Mary: Are you crazy?? Dad would kill us both. I can't.

Sam's smile faded. She was right, of course. The risk was enormous.

Sam: You're right. Just missing you. Been sitting here for hours watching nothing happen.

Mary: Wish I could help. Dad will be home soon anyway. Tomorrow?

Sam sighed, typing his response with reluctant acceptance.

Sam: Tomorrow. Be safe.

He set the phone down on the passenger seat, forcing his attention back to the Thompson house. The living room light remained on, the flicker of a television visible through partially drawn curtains. Everything appeared normal—a quiet evening in a modest if not neglected home, a teenager presumably doing homework, a grandmother watching her shows.

Nothing to suggest that Carter Thompson was anything other than what he appeared to be. Nothing except the prickling instinct at the base of Sam's neck that had never steered him wrong during his brief law enforcement career. The same instinct that had prompted him to follow a suspicious vehicle during his academy training, leading to the discovery of a kidnapping victim in the trunk. The same instinct now telling him that something was very wrong with the seemingly ordinary scene before him.

Sam straightened in his seat, eyes narrowing as he scanned the house once more. The television flickered in the living room, casting moving shadows on the wall visible through the window. The kitchen remained dark. No movement on the second floor, where Carter's bedroom was presumed to be. Everything exactly as it had been for the past three hours.

Too still. Too unchanged.

Sam reached for the small pair of binoculars kept in the glove compartment. Raising them to his eyes, he focused on the living room window, adjusting until the interior came into better view.

Through the sheer curtains he could see the television was indeed on, its colors washing across the wall opposite the window. A recliner was positioned before it, the back of a head just visible above the headrest—gray hair, not Carter's brown. The grandmother, presumably. But there was no movement, no shifting, not even the minor adjustments a person normally makes when watching television.

Sam lowered the binoculars, unease building in his chest. Something wasn't right. He began to reach for his radio, then hesitated. What would he report? An elderly woman sitting too still while watching television? Sheriff Cain would think he was grasping at straws, creating excitement to justify his assignment.

But the sensation wouldn't leave him. Sam replayed the afternoon in his mind—Carter arriving home, entering through the front door with his backpack, and then... nothing. No movement at the windows, no comings or goings, no lights switching on upstairs.

What if Carter had found a way to conceal his actions? What if the boy Sam had followed home was smarter than they thought, and had found a way to operate beneath an unchanging domestic tableau?

Sam started to shut off the cruiser's engine, ready to investigate, then stopped himself. He couldn't break from his orders. Until he had more information, more facts, he would just have to wait, despite the gnawing feeling in his side that there was more to this picture than there seemed to be.

THIRTY-TWO

The homeless encampment at the far end of Maple Street existed in a strange limbo—close enough to town that its residents could access services when needed, far enough from commercial areas that Stillwater's business owners could pretend it didn't exist. Here, where the riverbank widened and city property blurred into county land, a makeshift community had taken root on the shore of the river that bore the town's name.

Carter approached from the south, having circled around to avoid any potential witnesses who might connect him to his destination. His hood pulled low over his face, he adjusted his posture and gait, shoulders hunching forward, steps becoming irregular and shuffling. The transformation was subtle but effective—the confident, precise teenager vanishing beneath the slouched demeanor of someone society had learned to overlook.

The encampment was quiet in the evening hours. A few small fires dotted the area, figures huddled around them seeking warmth against the deepening autumn chill. Most residents had retreated to their shelters—tents of varying quality, improvised lean-tos, and in one case, an old camping trailer with its wheels long since removed. No one paid particular attention to Carter as he made his way between these temporary homes, just another shadow moving through shadows.

Carter glanced down Maple Street, seeing the police cruiser parked back from the encampment. This was the deputy assigned to watching Kilgore. He smiled, enjoying his unique ability to occupy two deputies on the same night. He glanced at his watch as the hour struck 8pm. He knew their shift usually ended at 8, and he hoped this time was no different. After only a few minutes, the cruiser started its engine and pulled away quietly. Their replacement would be back in place soon. It was time for Carter to move.

He located Kilgore's tent near the eastern edge of the encampment, identifiable by the blue tarp stretched above it for additional rain protection and the small American flag pinned to its entrance—a remnant of the man's military service before construction work, before injury, before addiction had defined his existence.

Carter approached with deliberate noise, scuffing his feet against the dirt path to announce his presence rather than startling the tent's occupant.

"Kilgore," he called softly, keeping his voice low enough to avoid carrying to neighboring shelters.

Movement sounded from within, followed by the rasp of a zipper being drawn down. James Kilgore's face appeared in the opening, initial wariness giving way to surprise as he recognized his visitor.

"Jesus, kid," he hissed, glancing around nervously before focusing on Carter again. "What the hell are you doing here? The cops are watching me."

"I know," Carter replied, his voice calm and measured. "That's why I came. To thank you."

Kilgore's expression flickered between confusion and suspicion. "Thank me? For what?"

"For not telling them about me. About our arrangement." Carter maintained steady eye contact, his gaze betraying none of the calculation behind it. "They held you for a long time. You could have traded information for leniency. But you didn't."

Kilgore's laugh was bitter, barely more than an exhale. "Not much to tell that wouldn't incriminate me worse than the bike thing. Besides, it was like having my own apartment, free meals and a softer bed than here." He hesitated, then unzipped the tent further. "You better come in before somebody sees you."

Carter ducked inside, the confined space immediately filling his nose with the mingled scents of unwashed body, stale alcohol, and the distinctive undertone of someone in the early stages of withdrawal. Kilgore had arranged his small domain with military precision despite his circumstances—sleeping bag tidy, personal items organized in plastic containers, a battery-powered lantern casting shadows across the tent's interior.

"You shouldn't be here," Kilgore said, partially zipping the entrance behind them. His hands trembled slightly, skin pale and clammy despite the relative warmth inside the tent. "If they followed you—"

"They didn't," Carter assured him. He reached into his pants pocket, extracting the small plastic bag containing pills—round, white tablets marked with precise pharmaceutical identifiers. "As we agreed."

Kilgore's eyes fixed on the bag with naked longing, his Adam's apple bobbing as he swallowed hard. "You came through," he whispered, reaching for the medication with unsteady fingers.

"I keep my promises," Carter replied, relinquishing the OxyContin tablets. "We're done now. As long as you continue to keep our connection to yourself."

Kilgore clutched the bag to his chest, relief washing over his features. But beneath the gratitude, anxiety still lurked. "What if they come back? That sheriff, he's not stupid. He knows something's up with those deaths. Keeps asking if I was at the river when the old man drowned, if I knew anything about the ladder guy..."

"They have nothing concrete," Carter interrupted, his tone soothing yet firm. "They released you, which means they lack evidence. Just stay quiet, stick to the story about the bicycle thefts, and this will all blow over."

Kilgore didn't appear convinced, his gaze darting between the tent entrance and the precious medication in his hands. "Easy for you to say. You get to go home to a real house. I'm stuck here, exposed. What if they know more than you think?"

Carter considered the man before him—once strong and capable, now reduced to this nervous, addiction-driven shell. For a brief moment, something like compassion crossed his features. It faded quickly. He reached into his backpack, rummaging past the rubber cement bottles to extract the F-14 model airplane.

"Here," he said, extending the model toward Kilgore. "My dad and I made this when I was younger. I thought you might like it. Something to keep your hands busy when things get rough."

Kilgore stared at the offering, momentarily forgetting his anxiety. "A model plane?"

"It's stupid, I know," Carter said, a hint of teenage awkwardness entering his voice for the first time. "But you mentioned working on these jets, and I remembered you knew my dad, so..."

Kilgore accepted the model with surprising gentleness, turning it over to examine the details. It had been one of Carter's prized possessions, because it was one of the last things he and his dad had built together. He was proud of it, but now knew it would serve a greater purpose. Carter reached into his backpack and extracted the bottles of paint and paint brushes, handing them over. "I thought maybe you could finish it. Since you know how they really look."

Kilgore nodded, accepting them solemnly. "Thank you, Carter. This means a lot to me." He watched as Kilgore turned to place the airplane carefully on a plastic storage box that served as his nightstand, lingering with a moment of long forgotten memories of times past.

While Kilgore's back was turned, Carter's demeanor underwent a transformation. All traces of teenage awkwardness vanished, replaced by focused, methodical purpose.

From his backpack, he extracted the squeeze bottle of rubber cement. As Kilgore, his back still turned, delicately positioned the model, Carter removed the tape and began squeezing the bottle, applying the clear, viscous adhesive to the sleeping bag and surrounding blankets. He worked quickly, squeezing generous amounts onto the fabric where Kilgore slept, ensuring maximum contact with the materials.

The chemical odor spread rapidly in the confined space. Kilgore stiffened, sniffing the air before turning around. "What's that smell? Are you—" He turned back, his eyes wide as he registered what Carter was doing. "What the fuck?"

Before Kilgore could react further, Carter lunged forward, squeezing the bottle hard, spraying the thick liquid directly onto Kilgore's shirt and pants. The man recoiled, stumbling backward into the tent wall.

"What the hell are you doing?" Kilgore shouted, frantically trying to wipe the sticky substance from his clothing. "This stuff is flammable! Are you crazy?"

Carter didn't respond. His movements remained controlled and deliberate as he pulled the spark striker from his pocket. Kilgore's eyes fixed on the device, comprehension and horror dawning simultaneously on his face.

"No," he pleaded, raising his hands defensively. "Carter, don't. Please. I won't say anything, I swear—"

Carter crouched down, holding the spark striker close to soaked blankets. The scrape of metal against flint created a shower of bright sparks that landed on Kilgore's bedding. Ignition was immediate and devastating. Flames erupted from the floor, the fire spreading rapidly to Kilgore, licking up his legs, finding a trail of rubber cement that led quickly to the man's chest. It spread viciously to his arms, engulfing him. Even as he fought to beat the flame back, the cement simply spread, adding more fuel to the deadly fire.

Kilgore's scream tore through the quiet encampment, primal and agonized. He flailed wildly, attempting to extinguish the flames that now consumed his upper body. In his panic, he tripped, falling onto the sleeping bag and into the already raging bedding fire as it spread throughout the tent's interior.

Carter slipped backward through the entrance, moving with the same methodical efficiency that had characterized all his actions. The flames cast an orange glow over his expressionless face as Kilgore thrashed inside the burning tent, the man's screams already attracting attention from neighboring shelters. He watched for a beat, ensuring Kilgore was not going to escape, then Carter reached into his bag, throwing the now empty rubber cement bottles into the flame, followed by the plastic bottle and the medical gloves that were stuffed in his pants pocket. Finally, he casually slipped off his outer gloves, throwing them into the fire that was quickly consuming the tent.

Shouts and alarmed voices rose from around the encampment. A woman's voice called out for someone to call 911. Footsteps approached as residents rushed toward the source of the commotion.

Carter ducked behind the burning tent. He moved silently along the back perimeter of the encampment, staying in shadow as confused residents emerged from their shelters and gathered at the front of Kilgore's tent, now fully engulfed in flames, screams from inside overpowering the calls for help from outside. He moved through the darkness while chaos erupted behind him. The orange glow of the fire illuminated the trees, casting long shadows that provided additional cover for his escape. Kilgore's screams had stopped—the flames having most certainly overcome him.

As he reached the edge of the encampment, distant sirens began to wail—fire trucks and police responding to multiple 911 calls. Carter slipped into the dense underbrush that separated the homeless community from the nearest residential area, his footsteps making no sound on the forest floor.

Behind him, James Kilgore's tent collapsed in a shower of sparks, the fire beginning to spread to neighboring shelters as panicked residents attempted to salvage their meager possessions. The carefully orchestrated tragedy unfolded exactly as planned, eliminating a loose end, and to Carter's pleasure, simultaneously creating a diversion that would occupy Stillwater's limited law enforcement resources for hours.

THIRTY-THREE

The journey back to his house required more caution than the trip out. Carter reversed the journey, using side streets to reach the back of his house. Just two blocks away from his house he saw Deputy Chambers' cruiser in position, headlights off but the silhouette of the officer visible through the rear window.

Carter slipped through the loose fence board and crossed the backyard silently, his movements deliberate and unhurried despite the acrid smell of smoke that clung to his clothing. The house greeted him with silence. Muffled television sounds, no shuffling movements, nothing but the soft hum of the refrigerator and the occasional creak of settling floorboards. Carter moved through the house, sliding off his backpack as he slid into the downstairs bathroom.

He stripped down, depositing his backpack, smokey shirt and pants in the washer, dousing them with detergent. He added a healthy collection of his grandmother's clothes then ran the washer, letting the clothes soak, the fragrant soap removing the evidence of a crime from the wardrobe. He showered, washing any remnants of smoke from his body, then dressed in fresh clothes. When he was done he moved the items from the washer to the dryer, completing the task of evidence removal. As the clothes finished drying he stepped into the living room.

His grandmother remained in her recliner, positioned exactly as he'd left her hours earlier. Her head rested against the chair's back, eyes closed, hands folded peacefully in her lap. The television cast blue-white shadows across her face, illuminating the stillness that had settled over her features.

Carter crossed the room without hesitation, crouching beside the chair. He reached for her wrist, fingers pressing gently against the spot where a pulse should throb beneath paper-thin skin. Nothing. No rhythm, no movement, no warmth.

He held the position for thirty seconds, methodically confirming what he'd already known. When he finally released her wrist, allowing it to settle back onto the armrest, his expression revealed nothing—no grief, no shock, only the quiet acknowledgment of an accomplished task.

Carter rose, turning off the television that had been playing to a lifeless room. He stood motionless for a moment, looking down at the woman who had helped raised him. Her face appeared younger, the constant confusion that had clouded her features in recent years finally absent.

Without ceremony, Carter returned to the kitchen. He flicked on the light, its harsh fluorescence a stark contrast to the shadows that had enveloped the house. He lifted the phone from its cradle, dialing three digits with steady fingers.

As the call connected and a dispatcher's voice answered, transformation overcame Carter Thompson. His shoulders hunched forward, his breathing became rapid and shallow, and his voice—when it finally emerged—trembled with the panic of a frightened teenager.

"My grandmother," he gasped, perfectly mimicking the shock of unexpected discovery. "I think there's something wrong. I don't think she's breathing!"

He provided the address with appropriate difficulty, voice breaking at all the right moments. "Please hurry," he begged, the performance flawless. "She was fine earlier, I don't understand what happened!"

Carter hung up the phone and immediately began the next phase of his performance. He paced the kitchen with agitated steps, ran a hand through his hair repeatedly to create appropriate dishevelment, and even splashed cold water on his face to simulate the physical manifestations of distress. He heard the dryer finish, and removed his backpack from it, filling it with the extra books he had set aside, then leaned it against the leg of the study table.

He then returned to his grandmother's side, kneeling beside her chair, taking her cold hand in his—the tableau of grief perfectly arranged for when emergency responders would arrive.

Next door, Mary Cain sat at her kitchen table, textbooks spread before her in a half-hearted attempt at studying. The house felt too quiet with both parents absent—her father working late again, her mother covering another night shift at the hospital. She'd turned on music to fill the silence, but it only emphasized her solitude, she wished for the raucous company of her friends and their dramas.

The sudden intrusion of flashing lights through the kitchen window and the harsh sirens of an ambulance startled her from a paragraph she'd read three times without comprehending. Red and blue pulses painted the walls, accompanied by the distinctive wail that quickly cut off as vehicles came to a stop.

Mary rose from the table, moving to the front door with growing concern. An ambulance and emergency response vehicle had pulled up outside the Thompson house. Even as she watched, EMTs rushed a gurney up the walkway, disappearing through the front door that stood open like a dark mouth in the white-painted facade.

Without conscious decision, Mary stepped onto her porch, drawn by the unique human instinct to move toward crisis rather than away from it. From her vantage point, she could see directly into the Thompson living room, where Carter stood with his arms wrapped around himself, watching as medical professionals crouched over a still figure in the recliner.

His grandmother. Mary's stomach tightened with dread. The elderly woman's declining health had been evident during her recent visit—the confusion, the vacant stares, the frailty that seemed to have accelerated in recent months.

A police cruiser pulled up behind the ambulance, its lights also flashing but no siren sounding. Mary recognized it immediately —the same vehicle she'd seen from her kitchen window earlier, the one Sam had invited her to join him in. He emerged now in full professional mode, adjusting his uniform belt as he approached the house with purposeful strides.

Sam glanced in her direction as he passed, their eyes meeting briefly across the lawn that separated their properties. A flash of greeting, of shared concern, passed between them, but neither acknowledged the other beyond that momentary connection. Sam continued into the Thompson house, duty overriding any personal considerations.

Mary remained on her porch, arms crossed against the evening chill, watching as the drama unfolded through the open doorway. The EMTs movements were measured and deliberate —a shift out of emergency response that signaled death rather than rescue.

Carter stood speaking with Sam, his posture conveying distress and confusion. Though Mary couldn't hear his words, she could read the narrative in his gestures—pointing to the recliner, then the back room, then to his watch. Explaining when he'd last seen her alive, what he'd been doing, how he'd found her.

One of the EMTs lifted something from the side table next to the recliner—an orange prescription bottle, holding it up for Sam to see. Carter's explanation continued, his hands moving in helpless circles, the universal gesture of a teenager trying to convey complicated circumstances to authority figures.

Mary could fill in the blanks without hearing the words. The grandmother's confusion about her medication. Carter's efforts to manage her doses. The inevitable failure of a system that relied on a sixteen-year-old to provide medical supervision for a deteriorating elder.

The EMTs began preparations to remove the body, their movements respectful but efficient as they transferred her from recliner to gurney. Carter watched, his face a study in grief— eyes wide, lips pressed tightly together, shoulders rigid with the effort of maintaining composure.

It was familiar body language to Mary, who had seen it three years earlier at his parents' funeral. The same controlled pain, the same measured reaction in the face of loss. Something about it had seemed off then, as it did now—too composed, too managed for genuine grief. But perhaps that was simply Carter's way, his particular method of processing trauma.

The gurney emerged from the house, a sheet drawn over the still form it carried. Carter followed to the threshold, watching as his grandmother's body was loaded into the ambulance. Sam remained beside him, a hand resting briefly on the teenager's shoulder in what appeared to be genuine sympathy.

As the ambulance doors closed and the vehicle prepared to depart, Carter turned back toward the house. For a brief moment, his gaze drifted across the lawn, to where Mary stood watching from her porch. Mary tried to raise her hand, to let him know she was there for him, but his eyes drifted by, her gesture unacknowledged.

Mary lowered her hand, her heart twisting with conflicting emotions—sympathy for his loss, unease at the timing, confusion about the boy who had once been her closest friend and was now a stranger wrapped in familiar skin.

The ambulance pulled away, its lights still flashing but the siren respectfully silent. Sam spoke a few more words to Carter before returning to his cruiser, presumably to file a report on what appeared to be a natural death or accidental overdose.

And then Carter Thompson was alone, standing in the doorway of an empty house that used to hold every member of his family, a family he had lost one by one. He remained there for a long moment, silhouetted against the light behind him, before stepping back and closing the door with quiet finality.

Mary returned to her kitchen, the textbooks still open to pages she could no longer concentrate on. Though she tried, she couldn't make herself sit down, to re-engage on something so trivial as school work. Despite her uncertainty, she knew she needed to go see Carter.

She turned back to the door, hesitating only a moment with her hand on the doorknob, before pulling it open.

THIRTY-FOUR

As Mary walked out of the side door, she glanced to the Thompson house. With it's dilapidated exterior and heavy aura of loss, it exuded an uncomfortable, dark silence. Mary walked around the hedge, then up the cracked concrete path that led to Carter's front door.

She hesitated there, hand raised to knock, uncertainty freezing her in place. What would she say? What comfort could she offer that wouldn't sound hollow, perfunctory?

Before she could decide, the door opened. Carter stood in the threshold, his face drawn and pale, eyes reflecting the porch light like dark pools. He didn't seem surprised to see her.

"I saw you watching," he said, his voice steady despite the circumstances. "From your porch."

"I'm sorry," Mary replied, though whether she was apologizing for watching or for his loss remained ambiguous. "I... I wanted to make sure you're okay."

A ghost of a smile touched his lips. "Okay is relative." He stepped back, opening the door wider. "Do you want to come in?"

Mary nodded, crossing the threshold into a house that felt immediately, palpably different from when she'd visited just days before. The absence of Carter's grandmother—her television shows, her confused questions, her very presence—had transformed the space into something hollow.

"Can I get you anything?" Carter asked, the automatic politeness of a host at odds with the circumstances. "Water? There might be some soda in the fridge..."

"I'm fine," Mary assured him. She glanced toward the living room, where the empty recliner now seemed to dominate the space. "Carter, I'm so sorry about your grandmother."

His shoulders slumped slightly, the first genuine display of emotion she'd seen from him. "She's been slipping away for a long time. Tonight just made it official."

The clinical assessment should have seemed cold, but Mary recognized it as Carter's way of processing—his retreat into analytical thinking when emotions threatened to overwhelm him. She'd seen it after his parents' deaths too, the way he'd recited accident statistics and survival rates rather than simply crying like other children might have.

"Still," she said gently, "it's a lot. And you've been taking care of her alone all this time."

Carter moved to the kitchen, Mary following behind. The space felt preserved in amber—washed dishes in a dish rack by the sink, medication organizers laid out on the counter, a calendar on the wall with doctor's appointments meticulously noted in Carter's precise handwriting.

"I don't really want to be down here," he said suddenly, gesturing vaguely to the living room. "Do you mind if we go upstairs? To my room?"

Mary hesitated only briefly. "Of course not."

They climbed the stairs in silence, the old house creaking beneath their feet. Carter led her to the door at the end of the hallway—his bedroom, a space Mary hadn't entered in years, not since they were children working on science fair projects together.

The room surprised her. She expected a meticulously organized space, but Carter's bedroom reflected a different kind of order —walls covered with newspaper clippings, photographs, and handwritten notes, all connected by string that created a web of information too complex for Mary to immediately comprehend.

"Sorry about the mess," Carter said, quickly moving to clear books from the single chair beside his desk. "I haven't had visitors in awhile."

Mary's eyes swept across the walls, taking in fragments of headlines—"LOCAL MAN DROWNS," "TRAGIC ACCIDENT CLAIMS ELDERLY RESIDENT," "TRACTOR DEATH SHOCKS COMMUNITY." Police reports, or what appeared to be copies of them. Maps of Stillwater with locations marked in red.

"What is all this?" she asked, unable to keep the unease from her voice.

Carter glanced at the walls as if seeing them for the first time. "My investigations. Patterns I've been tracking." He shrugged, an attempt to project a casual tone that didn't quite succeed. "Your dad isn't the only one who notices things in this town."

Mary moved closer to one section of the wall, where Jackson McKenzie's drowning was documented in disturbing detail— water depth measurements, current calculations, diagrams of the broken fence post that had trapped him.

"This is... thorough," she managed, torn between admiration for the methodical analysis and concern about the obsessive quality it suggested.

"I've always been good at seeing connections," Carter replied, sitting on the edge of his bed. "Patterns other people miss." His voice dropped, taking on a weariness beyond his years. "Not that anyone cares. Your dad's deputies think I'm just a weird kid playing detective. No one takes me seriously."

The vulnerability in his tone drew Mary's attention away from the wall. She turned to find Carter staring at his hands, shoulders hunched forward, the picture of defeat. In that moment, she caught a glimpse of the boy she'd once known— the one who had built elaborate theories about neighborhood mysteries, who had stayed up all night reading detective novels under his covers with a flashlight, and had been comfortable being vulnerable with her.

"I enjoyed when we would investigate together," Mary said gently.

A genuine smile touched his lips. "Like when we figured out it was Principal Stevenson's cat that was getting into Mrs. Abernathy's garden? Everyone thought it was raccoons."

"We tracked those little paw prints through three yards," Mary laughed, the memory warming her. "And set up that stakeout with your dad's video camera."

"My parents thought we were crazy," Carter said, the smile lingering despite the mention of his loss. "But they supported it. Bought me that detective kit for Christmas, remember? With the fingerprint powder and the magnifying glass?"

"You were so excited you couldn't even wait until morning to open it," Mary recalled. "Your mom called our house at, like, six AM because you insisted on coming over to dust my room for prints."

They both laughed, the sound strange but welcome in the somber house. For a moment, the years between them seemed to vanish—the awkwardness of adolescence, the drift of different social circles, the recent suspicions all temporarily suspended.

Carter's laughter faded first, his expression growing serious. "It's been hard without them," he said quietly. "My parents, I mean. And watching gran slip away bit by bit..." He shook his head. "I just wanted to make them proud, you know? To show someone that I was good at something. That I mattered."

The raw honesty in his voice caught Mary off guard. This wasn't the calculated, clinical Carter she'd come to expect, but something more authentic—a sixteen-year-old boy who had lost everyone who mattered to him, who was desperately seeking validation in the only way he knew how.

"You always mattered, Carter," she said softly. "To them. To me."

"To you?" His eyes met hers, skepticism and hope warring in his expression. "We've barely spoken in years, Mary."

"I know," she said, guilt washing through her. "And that's on me. After your parents died, I didn't know what to say, how to act around you. It was easier to just... drift away."

"Easier for you," Carter said, but there was no accusation in his tone, just a statement of fact.

Mary moved from the chair to sit beside him on the bed, close enough that their shoulders nearly touched. "I'm sorry," she said, the words inadequate but sincere. "I should have been there for you. Especially knowing what you were dealing with at home, with your grandmother..."

Mary's hand found his, fingers intertwining with a familiarity that belied their years apart. "I'm here now," she said simply.

The contact sent an unexpected warmth through Mary—not the nervous flutter she felt with Sam, but something deeper, a connection to a shared history that had shaped them both. She looked up to find Carter watching her, his gaze more open and vulnerable than she'd seen in years.

Something shifted between them, the air in the room suddenly charged with possibility. Carter leaned closer, hesitant but purposeful, his intent clear in the way his eyes dropped to her lips. For a moment, Mary found herself leaning in as well, drawn by the gravity of their shared past and the revelation of the boy she'd once known still existing beneath the analytical exterior.

Their lips nearly touched before Mary pulled back, reality crashing in like a cold wave. This was Carter Thompson—the boy Sam had warned her about, the teenager who had detailed knowledge of suspicious deaths, whose room was decorated with the evidence of obsession. The boy who had carefully questioned her about police investigations, who had shown disturbing detachment about Dylan Foster's stabbing.

"I'm sorry," she whispered, drawing her hand from his. "I can't —this is—"

"Too much, too fast," Carter finished for her, retreating to his analytical shell with practiced ease. "Of course. My grandmother just died. The timing is inappropriate."

The clinical assessment made Mary flinch, but she nodded, grateful for the excuse. "It's been an emotional night."

Carter stood abruptly. "I should get you some water," he said, his voice regaining its careful neutrality, though his body language still carried a nervous edge. Perhaps he was embarrassed, Mary thought, and just needed an excuse to break the moment. "And I need to get my grandmother's medications from the bathroom. The EMTs said I should have them ready for when the medical examiner follows up tomorrow."

Before Mary could respond, he'd left the room, his footsteps receding down the hallway. She released a breath she hadn't realized she was holding, the tension in her shoulders easing slightly with his absence.

Alone in Carter's room, Mary's attention returned to the walls covered in his investigations. She rose from the bed, moving closer to examine the web of connections he'd created. What had seemed like obsessive documentation at first glance now revealed itself as something more methodical.

Her gaze settled on what appeared to be the focal point of his investigation—a section dedicated to Jackson McKenzie, Ned Miller, and Gerald Cooper. Three elderly men, three "accidents" that her father had begun to suspect were deliberate. Carter had drawn the same conclusion, it seemed, his notes indicating the specific mechanical failures that had led to each death.

Mary's unease returned, stronger now. How had Carter determined these details? Some appeared to be public knowledge, gleaned from newspaper articles or gossip. But others—the precise angle of cuts in Ned Miller's ladder, the detailed analysis of Gerald Cooper's tractor brake—seemed too specific, too technical for a sixteen-year-old to have deduced independently.

A photograph partially obscured on Carter's desk caught her attention—not part of his murder wall but hidden, as if for more personal contemplation. Mary moved closer, pulling the corner of the picture to reveal it, her breath catching as she recognized herself in the image. It showed her leaving the library with Amber and Heather, laughing at something one of them had said. The angle suggested it had been taken from across the street, the grain and slight blur indicating a telephoto lens.

She picked up the photograph, hands trembling slightly. Beneath it lay another—Mary sitting alone on a bench outside school, reading a book, unaware of being observed. And another—Mary getting out of her mother's car in their driveway, grocery bags in her arms.

Half a dozen photographs of her, captured at different locations around Stillwater, all taken without her knowledge. The unease that had been building in Mary's chest crystallized into something sharper, colder.

In her shock, Mary's elbow bumped a small container of paperclips, sending them scattering across the desk and floor. She knelt quickly to clean up the mess, her mind racing to process what she'd discovered. As she reached under the desk to retrieve fallen clips, her palm rested on a board, which moved slightly under her weight. Mary glanced back to the door, listening for the creak of the stairs warning her of Carter's return. Hearing nothing, she pulled up the board, moving it aside to reveal something—the edge of a book, concealed beneath the floorboard.

Curiosity overriding caution, Mary reached in, her fingers feeling a leather-bound journal wedged into the space beneath. She glanced toward the door, listening for Carter's return once more, then carefully extracted the hidden book.

Unlike the meticulously organized investigation materials on the walls, this journal appeared more personal, the handwriting varying between Carter's usual precise script and a more hurried, almost frantic scrawl. Mary opened to a random page, eyes widening as she took in the contents.

Detailed plans for Jackson McKenzie's death. Not theories or post-event analysis, but pre-execution planning—calculations of water depth and current strength, analysis of fishing line strength, diagrams showing exactly where and how to weaken the fence post to ensure catastrophic failure when pressure was applied, a timeline for implementation that ensured no witnesses would be present.

With shaking hands, Mary turned the pages, finding similar plans for Ned Miller and Gerald Cooper. The ladder, the tractor brake—both sabotaged according to Carter's precise specifications, designed to appear as accidents while guaranteeing fatal outcomes.

A page outlined various substances and their properties; acid, rubber cement, aerosols. Her heart racing, she quickly paged through the book, finding more plans—future targets, she realized with growing horror. Deputy Sam Chambers was there, with notes about his routine, the layout of his house, his relationship with her carefully documented. And her father— Sheriff Martin Cain, whose patterns and vulnerabilities Carter had studied with the same methodical precision he'd applied to his previous victims.

Mary was so absorbed in the horrifying discovery that she failed to notice the shadow that fell across the hallway outside the bedroom door. Carter stood motionless in the corridor, glass of water in hand, watching as Mary crouched beside his desk, his private journal open in her trembling hands. His expression shifted—surprise giving way to cold calculation as he assessed the situation with clinical detachment.

She had found it. She knew everything. The secrets he had so carefully preserved were now exposed, the patterns he had meticulously constructed now visible to someone else. To Mary.

For a long moment, Carter remained perfectly still, weighing options, calculating outcomes with the same methodical precision he applied to all his endeavors. Then, silently, he withdrew from the doorway, retreating several steps down the hall before deliberately making a floorboard creak beneath his weight.

At the sound, Mary quickly returned the journal to its hiding place, sliding the floorboard back into position and rising just as footsteps approached the door.

She turned toward the door just as Carter appeared, carrying a glass of water, his face a mask of casual normality that betrayed nothing of what he had witnessed. "Sorry that took so long. Gran's medications were a mess."

"It's fine," Mary managed, taking the glass with hands she forced to remain steady. Carter studied her, his head tilting slightly in what appeared to be casual curiosity but was actually precise assessment. "You okay? You seem... different."

Mary forced a smile. "Just tired. And worried about you, being here alone."

"I'll be fine," Carter replied, his own smile not quite reaching his eyes as he watched her—watching her perform, watching her lie, cataloging every micro-expression that confirmed what he already knew. "I've been pretty independent for a while now, with gran's condition."

An uncomfortable silence fell between them, the room suddenly too small, too full of secrets both exposed and concealed. Mary set the water glass down, searching for an excuse to leave without raising suspicion, oblivious to the fact that her performance had already failed its audience of one.

"I should probably get home," she said, gesturing vaguely toward the door. "It's getting late, and you need to rest."

Carter nodded, stepping aside to clear her path to the door. "Before you go," he said, his voice betraying none of the adjustment happening behind his eyes, "I was thinking about tomorrow. Our investigation at the Campbell property?"

The invitation hung in the air, loaded with implications neither fully acknowledged. Mary immediately felt an internal battle between avoiding suspicion and protecting herself. She couldn't know that Carter was offering a test—one whose outcome would determine her place in his carefully constructed world.

"We don't have to go," Mary said, watching every flicker of emotion across his face. "I understand if you'd rather not do that right now."

"No," Carter replied, his voice steady. "No, I think it's a good idea. Take my mind off things." She forced a smile.

"Ok. I'll pick you up after school, like we planned."

Carter allowed relief to wash visibly over his features, shoulders relaxing in an intentional display that concealed the calculations continuing beneath. "Great. Something to look forward to."

They moved toward the stairs, Carter following close behind her. The pair descended in uncomfortable silence, each step bringing them closer to the front door and the moment they would separate—Mary believing she carried a secret, Carter knowing that there were no secrets left between them.

At the door, Mary turned to Carter, her performance admirable despite its futility. "Try to get some sleep," she said softly. "I'll see you tomorrow."

Before she could reconsider, she leaned forward and placed a quick kiss on his cheek. Carter's eyes widened slightly in genuine surprise, the calculated mask briefly slipping to reveal something more authentic—a moment of connection that complicated the cold equations forming in his mind.

"Thank you for coming over," he replied, voice warm with an emotion that wasn't entirely performance. "It means more than you know."

As Mary stepped over the threshold into the cool night air, she couldn't help looking back at Carter. He stood framed in the doorway, a solitary figure in an empty house, watching her departure with an expression that mixed longing with something darker.

"Goodnight, Mary," he called as she reached the sidewalk. "Sweet dreams."

What Mary couldn't see, as she hurried home through the darkness, was the way Carter's expression transformed once she was beyond view—the mask of humanity falling away completely, replaced by cold, methodical purpose. He closed the door with deliberate care, then returned upstairs to his room.

Kneeling beside the desk, he moved to the loose floorboard, extracting the journal Mary had discovered. Opening to a fresh page, Carter began to write with calm, measured strokes—adding a new name to the book.

Mary Cain.

The name stood alone on the otherwise blank page, a unique if not somewhat unexpected detail in the unfolding drama. Carter knew Mary would play an integral part in this story, but he didn't expect her role to expand so quickly. If anything, it made the trip tomorrow that much more… interesting. The Campbell property would be a test—his final opportunity to demonstrate her place in his carefully planned scenario. By the end of the day, Mary, Sam Chambers and Sheriff Cain would all understand their own roles in the Carter Thompson story, and just like the way Sheriff Cain forever changed his world on the night of his parent's death, tomorrow would change his.

THIRTY-FIVE

The homeless encampment smoldered in the early morning darkness, charred remnants of tents and possessions scattered across the riverside clearing like debris from a war zone. A thin layer of smoke hung in the air, acrid and chemical, clinging to everything it touched. Emergency vehicles lined up along the street bordering the river, their lights cutting through the lingering haze in rhythmic pulses of red and blue.

Sheriff Cain stood at the edge of what had been Kilgore's tent, hands on his hips as he surveyed the destruction. The fire had spread quickly through the makeshift community, consuming five shelters before the fire department managed to contain it. One fatality confirmed—James Kilgore, found at the epicenter of the blaze, his body burned beyond recognition but for the dog tags that had survived the inferno, identifying the remains.

Sam's cruiser pulled up to the police line, tires crunching over gravel and ash. The young deputy emerged, slipping his hat on as he approached the scene. His gait betrayed his exhaustion— shoulders slightly slumped, movements less crisp than usual after what had clearly been a long night.

"Sheriff," Sam acknowledged, ducking under the yellow tape that fluttered in the morning breeze. "Got here as soon as I could."

Cain nodded toward the blackened remains of Kilgore's tent. "Medical examiner confirms it's him. Preliminary cause of death is smoke inhalation, followed by extensive thermal injuries."

Sam surveyed the scene, professional assessment momentarily overriding his fatigue. "Witnesses?"

"A few. Most residents were in their tents when it started. Those who were outside report seeing the fire begin in Kilgore's tent, then spread rapidly." Cain's expression remained neutral, though the tightness around his eyes betrayed his frustration. "Too rapidly for anyone to help him."

Sam took this in, processing the implications against what he already knew. "Sir," he began carefully, "are we thinking this is connected to our other cases?"

"What do you think, Chambers?" Cain replied, turning to study his deputy's reaction.

Sam hesitated, weighing his response. "The timing is suspicious. Kilgore gets released, potentially could talk about what he knows, and within the day he's dead in a fire. And it looks like it was enough to conveniently destroys any evidence as well."

"Agreed." Cain began walking along the perimeter of the scene, Sam falling into step beside him. "The question is who did it? And how?"

"Carter Thompson," Cain continued, his voice low enough that only Sam could hear. "He's been involved from the beginning —bringing us information about Kilgore, showing detailed knowledge of the deaths that shouldn't be available to a civilian."

Chambers shook his head slightly. "Timeline doesn't work. Carter was at home discovering his grandmother's body roughly around the same time the fire started. Confirmed by the 911 call and the EMTs who responded." Cain, frustration evident in the set of his jaw, stopped.

"Unless he somehow managed to be in two places at once."

Cain frowned. "I was watching his house right up to the 911 call," he admitted. "Didn't see him leave."

"A back door?" Cain pressed. "Could he have slipped away unnoticed?"

The implication hung between them—a gap in surveillance, a window of opportunity that couldn't be confirmed or denied. Sam's frown deepened as he considered the possibility.

"Even if he somehow slipped out without me seeing," Sam continued, "it's a tight timeline. Set the fire, get back home, discover his grandmother, call 911... all within what, an hour?"

"Possible," Cain allowed. "Not probable, but possible. But what about his grandmother? Was it just a coincidence that he found her dead and called 911 at the perfect moment needed to give him an alibi?" Chambers shook his head in disbelief.

"That's pretty dark," he said. "Either she was already dead, or…" He stopped himself, unable to even speak the words that they both were thinking.

They continued walking in silence, circling the perimeter of destruction. Fire investigators in turnout gear sifted through the debris, methodically documenting and collecting evidence from the scene. The smell of wet ash and melted plastic permeated everything, a tangible reminder of lives disrupted and one extinguished.

"Sir," Sam ventured after a moment, "what if we're looking at this wrong? What if Carter isn't working alone?"

Cain paused, turning to face his deputy fully. "Go on."

"The precision of these deaths, the methodical planning—it suggests someone with experience, maturity. Carter's smart, but he's still just sixteen." Sam's eyes tracked a fire investigator who was carefully photographing a segment of the scene. "What if he's the apprentice, not the mastermind?"

The sheriff considered this, the theory clearly aligning with thoughts he'd already entertained. "Kilgore had the practical skills—construction background, knowledge of structural integrity. But not the intelligence or patience for the long game we're seeing. And he definitely had no motive."

"So maybe there's a third party," Sam suggested. "Someone directing both of them. Someone we haven't identified yet."

Before Cain could respond, Deputy Carol Rivers approached from the investigation zone, evidence bag held carefully in her gloved hands. Her expression was professionally neutral, but the slight furrow between her eyebrows suggested she'd found something significant.

"Sheriff," she greeted them, holding up the bag for inspection. Inside was a charred plastic bottle, its label partially melted but still recognizable as rubber cement. "Found this in the tent."

Cain examined the evidence without touching it, eyes narrowing as he studied the container. "Rubber cement?" He looked to Rivers.

"A very good accelerant, could easily catch on fire, and these tents are filled with flammable fabrics," Rivers said. "We also found these." She produced a second evidence bag containing several small paintbrushes, their bristles melted and handles charred.

"Are those model paint brushes? He was painting a model?" Cain was puzzled. "Is that a thing you'd expect a homeless man to pursue?"

"Wasn't he former military," Chambers asked. "Maybe a hobby that reminded him of better days?" Even Sam thought the idea far fetched.

To Cain it seemed like a mistake by an arsonist, an unbelievable element that stood out, but maybe one that was meant to do just so.

"Or maybe it was planted," Cain suggested. He glanced around as if looking for the culprit nearby. "I think we're being manipulated. Someone is playing with us. Leaving breadcrumbs they want us to follow."

They all fell silent, each weighing their limited options. The investigation had reached a critical juncture—three elderly deaths disguised as accidents, a football player stabbed and barely alive, and now Kilgore eliminated before he could possibly provide any useful information. If these were all connected, then someone was playing a game, one where the rules were still unclear to most of the players. Cain knew the only thing they could do was not take any possibility off the table.

"We need to proceed carefully," he decided finally. "Rivers, continue processing the scene. I want every piece of evidence documented, every witness statement cross-referenced. If there's a connection to our other cases, we'll find it."

Rivers nodded, returning to the investigation with renewed purpose. When she was out of earshot, Sam turned to Cain, his voice dropping to ensure privacy.

"And Carter," the deputy asked.

"We watch him. Closely. But from a distance." Cain turned back toward the smoldering remains of the encampment, his expression hardening as he surveyed the destruction. "If he's involved in this—in any of it—I want irrefutable evidence before we move. No mistakes, no procedural errors that could jeopardize prosecution."

"Yes, sir," Sam acknowledged, though uncertainty lingered in his tone. "And if he makes another move before we can gather that evidence?"

The question hung between them, laden with implications neither wanted to voice aloud. Cain's jaw tightened, the only outward sign of the conflict raging within him—the sheriff's duty to protect his community, his friends and family, against the need to follow evidentiary rules. He knew deep down the decision he would make, if it came to it.

"Then we do what's necessary," he replied finally, words carefully measured. "Whatever that entails."

The ambiguity of the statement wasn't lost on Sam, who nodded once in solemn understanding. They stood together in silence, watching as rays of moonlight broke through the night haze, casting cool light on the destruction. Muted figures, residents of the homeless community, lurked in the darkness, secretly interested in the charred remains, but equally eager to stay hidden in the shadows.

Cain scanned the crowd, looking for someone that might show some sign of involvement, following the age old adage that criminals often returned to the scene of their own crime. But he knew the person he was playing this game with would not follow any such obvious rule. They were too smart for that. All he could do now was stay vigilant, and hope this serial murderer would make just one mistake.

That's all Sheriff Cain needed.

THIRTY-SIX

The early morning mist lingered in Riverside Park, turning the familiar landscape into something ethereal and strange. Dew clung to benches and playground equipment, the sun was just starting to brighten the very edge of the horizon, not yet enough to burn away the moisture that had settled in overnight. At this early hour, the park stood empty save for a solitary figure seated on a bench overlooking the water.

Mary pulled her jacket tighter against the cold, her breath forming small clouds that dissipated in the damp air. Her backpack sat next to her, filled with books for classes, forgotten for now in the chill around her. She'd received Sam's text at 5:30 AM—urgent, asking her to meet him before school. She had no idea what he needed to meet about, but trusted him, and didn't hesitate to agree.

Headlights swept across the parking lot, illuminating the mist in ghostly patterns before cutting off. Sam's personal vehicle— not his cruiser—rolled to a stop in the empty lot. He emerged, glancing around before crossing to where Mary waited, his uniform replaced by jeans and a worn leather jacket that made him look younger, less official.

"Thanks for meeting me," he said as he approached, the dark circles beneath his eyes testament to a sleepless night. He remained standing, too restless to sit, hands shoved deep in his pockets against the morning chill.

Mary nodded, studying his face with growing concern. "What's going on, Sam? Your text sounded serious."

"It is." He glanced around once more, ensuring they were truly alone before continuing. "There was a fire last night at the homeless encampment by the river. James Kilgore is dead."

The news landed with the weight of a stone dropped into still water, ripples of implication spreading outward. Mary's expression shifted from surprise to concern in rapid succession.

"The bicycle thief?" she asked, though she already knew the answer. "The one Carter identified?"

Sam nodded, watching her reaction carefully. "Kilgore gets released from custody, and within hours he's dead in a fire that conveniently destroys any evidence he might have provided about his connection to the other deaths."

Mary absorbed this, the pieces fitting too neatly with what she'd discovered in Carter's room the night before. She wanted to tell Sam but she was afraid, not just of his reaction, but the fear of voicing the horrible discoveries she made would seal her friend's fate. "You think Carter was involved."

"I think it's possible," Sam agreed, careful not to overstate his suspicions. "The timeline is tight, but not impossible. The fire started around the same time Carter was supposedly discovering his grandmother."

"Supposedly?" Mary caught the qualifier immediately.

Sam sighed, running a hand through his hair. "We have no way to verify exactly when his grandmother died, or when he actually found her. Just his 911 call and the EMTs' arrival time."

Mary stood, suddenly needing to move as her thoughts raced. "I was with him last night," she admitted, the confession bursting forth with unexpected urgency. "After they took his grandmother away. I went over to see if he was okay."

Sam's expression tightened. "Tell me everything," he said, tone carefully neutral despite the concern evident in his eyes.

The story poured out of Mary in a rush—her sympathy visit, Carter's room with its walls of investigation materials, the photographs he'd taken of her without her knowledge, the hidden journal containing detailed plans for each death.

"He had everything documented, Sam," she concluded, voice shaking slightly as she relived the discovery. "Not theories or after-the-fact analysis, but actual plans. Calculations. Diagrams. Things he couldn't have known without being involved."

Sam listened without interrupting, only the set of his jaw indicating his reaction to the damning evidence. When Mary finally fell silent, he remained perfectly still for a long moment, processing the implications.

"And after you found the journal?" he asked finally. "What happened?"

"I put it back before he returned. He didn't know I'd seen it." Mary wrapped her arms around herself, a chill shaking her despite her jacket.

Sam's expression suggested he wasn't convinced. "And then?"

"We talked. He asked if we were still on for today— investigating the Campbell property after school. It's something we talked about yesterday, at lunch." Mary's gaze dropped to the dew-dampened grass beneath their feet. "I said yes."

"You what?" Sam's neutral façade cracked, alarm breaking through his professional composure. "Mary, you can't possibly be considering going anywhere alone with him after what you found."

"I had to say yes," she defended. "I didn't want him to suspect that I knew anything. I needed time to tell my dad, to figure out what to do next."

Sam closed the distance between them, his hands coming to rest on her shoulders. "Listen to me carefully. You are not going anywhere with Carter Thompson. Not today, not ever. He's dangerous, Mary. If he's done these things, if he's behind these deaths—"

"Don't tell me what to do," Mary interrupted, shrugging out of his grip. Her voice rose with a flash of defiance that reminded Sam uncomfortably of her arguments with her father. "I'm not some helpless child who needs protection. I know Carter better than anyone. I can handle this."

"This isn't about your capability," Sam insisted, frustration bleeding into his tone. "This is about a sixteen-year-old who has potentially orchestrated multiple murders with disturbing precision. Who has been stalking you from a distance long enough to amass a collection of photographs."

"You think I don't understand how serious this is?" Mary demanded. "I'm the one who found the evidence, Sam. I'm the one who's known him since we were children. I'm the one he —" She stopped abruptly, unwilling to complete the thought.

"The one he what?" Sam pressed, something in her hesitation triggering a deeper concern.

Mary looked away, the memory of Carter's near-kiss flashing through her mind. "Nothing. It doesn't matter."

Sam studied her, professional assessment temporarily overriding personal connection. "Did something happen between you two last night? Something you're not telling me?"

"No," Mary answered too quickly, then sighed at Sam's skeptical expression. "We almost... he tried to kiss me. I pulled away."

The admission hung in the air between them, heavy with implications neither was prepared to fully address. Sam's expression darkened, his jaw working again as he processed this new information.

"All the more reason you need to stay away from him," he said finally, his tone softening despite the firmness of his words. "Mary, please. Promise me you won't go with him today."

"Why do you care so much?" Mary challenged, though the question lacked real heat. "Is this the deputy speaking, or something else?"

Sam hesitated, the professional and personal blurring dangerously before him. He glanced around once more, confirming their privacy, before meeting her gaze directly.

"Both," he admitted quietly. "I care about your safety as a deputy. And I care about you because..." He faltered, the words he'd never spoken aloud suddenly difficult to voice. "Because I love you, Mary. And the thought of you in danger—with him—it terrifies me more than anything I've ever faced."

The declaration hung between them, unexpectedly raw and real in the misty morning air. Mary's expression softened, her defensive posture melting away as she absorbed the significance of what he'd said—the first time either had used that words, crossing a threshold in their relationship that could never be uncrossed.

"Sam," she whispered, moving toward him, only to stop as the distant sound of a car door slamming reminded them of their public location.

Reality crashed back upon both of them—the inappropriateness of their relationship, the danger posed by Carter, the complicated web of loyalty and duty that entangled them both. Sam stepped back first, professional distance reasserting itself despite the emotional vulnerability he'd just displayed.

"Promise me you won't go with him today," he repeated, his tone gentle but insistent. "For me. For your father. For your own safety."

Mary hesitated, conflicting impulses warring within her. The evidence against Carter was damning, yet part of her still struggled to reconcile the methodical killer described in that journal with the boy who had once been her closest friend, who had shown genuine vulnerability when discussing his loss.

"I promise," she said finally, the words carrying the weight of a vow. "I'll make an excuse. Tell him I can't go."

Relief washed over Sam's features, though something in his eyes suggested he wasn't entirely convinced of her commitment, but he knew he couldn't question her, not now. "Thank you," he said simply.

Mary glanced at her watch, reality intruding once more. "I should go."

Sam nodded, though reluctance was evident in his posture. "I'll walk you to your car."

They moved across the damp grass in silence, the early morning light strengthening around them, burning away the mist that had provided cover for their meeting. Sam rested his hand on her shoulder, trying to show some affection, some support, despite their fear of discovery. At Mary's car, Sam paused, one hand resting lightly on the door as she unlocked it.

"Be careful today," he said, the words carrying layers of meaning beyond their simple caution. "If Carter suspects you know anything..."

"I can handle Carter," Mary assured him, though the confidence in her voice wasn't quite convincing. "I've known him my whole life."

"That's what worries me," Sam replied softly. "You think you know him. I'm not sure anyone does. Not really."

Mary opened her car door. Sam helped her slide off her backpack, his hand moving across the open main pouch. She tossed her backpack onto the passenger seat. "I'll text you after school. Let you know I'm safe at home."

Sam nodded, stepping back to allow her entry. "Drive safely," he said, closing the door with a gentle push.

Mary started the engine, offering a small smile through the window before pulling away from the curb. Sam watched her departure, standing motionless until her taillights disappeared around the corner at the park entrance.

Only then did he allow his calm mask to fall, concern etching deeper lines in his young face. He glanced down at his phone, opening an app that displayed a small red dot now moving steadily along the streets of Stillwater. The tracking device he'd slipped into Mary's backpack was functioning perfectly, its signal strong and clear.

The deception sat uneasily with him—the violation of Mary's trust, the doubt of her promise. But as he returned to his own vehicle, Sam couldn't shake the conviction that Mary Cain, despite her assurances, had no intention of avoiding Carter Thompson today. The determination he'd seen behind her eyes, the curiosity that had always defined her, the sense of loyalty to her former friend—all suggested she would pursue the truth regardless of the danger.

And if she wouldn't protect herself, Sam would do it for her, even if it meant betraying her trust to ensure her safety. Because a world without Mary Cain was not a world he was prepared to face, no matter what the cost to their relationship might be.

He started his engine, the small red dot on his phone screen a constant reminder of what was at stake as the new day dawned over Stillwater—a day that would bring answers, one way or another, to the questions that had haunted the town for months.

THIRTY-SEVEN

oving with purpose through the subdued light of pre-dawn, Carter Thompson approached Sam's modest Craftsman from the rear, having cut through several backyards to avoid the street. The neighborhood still slept around him, windows dark, only the occasional porch light breaking the cool early morning light with its amber hue.

Carter wore dark clothing, a knit cap pulled low over his hair, thin latex gloves that did nothing for warmth but insured the absence of fingerprints. His footsteps were deliberately placed, avoiding dried leaves and loose gravel that might betray his presence. In his pocket, a small tool kit clinked softly with each careful step, its contents assembled with methodical precision for the task ahead.

The storm doors leading to Sam's basement stood slightly raised from the ground at the rear of the house, secured by a padlock that had likely been in place since the previous owner. Carter crouched beside it, extracting a set of lock picks from his jacket. The tools felt familiar in his hands, hours of practice on test locks had him working the mechanism with ease.

The padlock surrendered in less than thirty seconds, the metallic click barely audible in the quiet morning. Carter removed it carefully, setting it aside before lifting one of the metal doors. The hinges protested slightly, a whisper of metal against metal that made him pause, listening and looking for any notice from a neighboring house. When none came, he continued, creating an opening just wide enough for his slim frame to slip through.

The basement air greeted him with the distinctive mustiness of old houses—damp concrete, aging wood, the mineral scent of stone foundation walls that had stood for nearly a century. Carter used the dim light filtering through small ground-level windows to orient himself, avoiding the flashlight that would announce his presence to any early-rising neighbors.

As his eyes adjusted to the darkness, he surveyed the space with clinical interest. Typical unfinished basement: exposed ceiling joists, aging electrical panel, laundry area in one corner. His gaze settled on the ancient boiler and the maze of pipes running along the ceiling—copper, galvanized steel, and the distinctive black iron pipe of a gas line.

A smile curved Carter's lips, barely visible in the dim light. His research of the house and it's construction through the city office had paid off. Everything was just as he had planned.

Carter moved silently to the wooden stairs leading up to the kitchen. The treads creaked slightly under his weight, but he had expected this, having studied the common structural weaknesses of houses this age. He tested each step before committing his full weight, navigating the creaks and groans of old wood with careful precision.

At the top of the stairs, he examined the door. A simple interior door, never designed to provide real security between living spaces. He turned the knob slowly, finding it unlocked as expected. The door opened onto Sam's kitchen, still muted in the early morning hours, the deputy's absence confirmed by the silence of the house around him. Carter was tempted to explore, to see what kind of life Sam Chambers lived. He knew

Sam was meeting with Mary, most likely coming up with some plan to thwart him. He had at least 30 minutes.

He only needed 10.

Carter turned back to the door. Working quickly, he examined the door's latch mechanism with practiced eyes. Using a small set of files extracted from his pocket, he carefully shaved down the angled edge of the latch bolt—the part that would normally retract when the door closed against the strike plate. With methodical precision, he altered the angle just enough that it would still allow the door to close and latch normally, but would resist opening from the basement side without significant force.

Next, he bent the metal strike plate on the door frame slightly inward, creating a stronger catch that would grip the modified latch more securely. The adjustments were subtle, visible only under close inspection, but would transform the door into a one-way barrier—easy to pass through from the kitchen to the basement, nearly impossible to exit from below without breaking the door itself.

Satisfied with the modification, Carter left the the door open slightly, then descended back to the basement, footsteps precise and calculated on each creaking tread. In the dimness below, he moved directly to the black iron pipe that carried propane gas from the exterior tank into the home's heating system.

From his pocket, he extracted a small drill with a bit no wider than a pin. Working with the focused concentration of a surgeon, Carter selected locations along the side of the pipe— areas hidden from casual observation, spaced at irregular intervals to create an appearance of natural deterioration rather than deliberate sabotage.

One by one, he drilled tiny holes in the pipe, each barely large enough to permit the slowest of leaks. Nothing immediately dangerous to Carter, nothing that would create a noticeable odor right away. Just enough to allow propane—heavier than air — to gradually accumulate in the basement's lowest points over the next few hours.

With each hole, Carter paused, listening for any sound from above or outside that might indicate discovery. The neighborhood remained quiet, the house empty, as he completed his work with the same methodical detail that characterized all his actions.

Finished with the gas line, Carter turned to a water line. With less precision and care he punched a small hole in a copper pipe, creating a harsh stream crashing against the cement floor.

Carter returned his tools to his pockets and performed a mental inventory to ensure he'd left nothing behind. He surveyed the basement once more, eyes lingering on the modified door at the top of the stairs, then the nearly invisible perforations in the gas line that would slowly fill this space with invisible danger.

The physical alterations were minimal, but their potential impact was precisely calculated. A deputy trapped in a basement filling with propane gas. A faulty exit route blocking escape. A house with an old boiler that used a spark and a flame to heat water. All these items, except perhaps the door lock, would seem natural, undetectable, after an explosion tore the house apart.

Another pattern adjusted, another variable controlled.

Carter slipped back through the storm doors, carefully lowering them into place. He replaced the padlock, ensuring it appeared undisturbed to casual observation. Then he melted into the shadows between houses, his dark clothing blending with the early morning light as he made his way back toward Stillwater's center.

THIRTY-EIGHT

Friday afternoon descended on Stillwater with the familiar rhythms of small-town life asserting itself after a week of tension and tragedy. The sun had broken through morning clouds, casting warm light across Main Street where storefront windows displayed handwritten signs for weekend specials and upcoming holiday festivals. American flags hung limply from lampposts in the still fall air, occasionally stirring with passing traffic.

At the diner, the after-school crowd had claimed their usual territory—the corner booths filled with cheerleaders in uniform, the central tables occupied by debate team members arguing good-naturedly over shared plates of fries, the counter stools hosting solitary students with textbooks open beside chocolate shakes. The jukebox played something from the early 2000s, a song about small towns and escaping them that felt ironic in this setting.

Waitress Ellie Hargrove—mother of Deputy Mike Hargrove and Stillwater High lunch lady for twenty years before exchanging school lunches with diner fare—moved between tables with practiced efficiency, remembering orders without writing them down, calling students by name, asking about assignments and upcoming games with genuine interest.

"Amber Wilder, don't think I don't see you trying to sneak that milkshake to Jason's table," she called out, not even turning around as Amber froze mid-mission, caught in her attempt at flirtation. "You know the rules—no fraternizing between tables during rush hour."

Outside the diner windows, life continued its forward momentum. On the practice field behind the high school, football players ran drills in the afternoon sun, their movements lacking the usual cockiness but carrying a new determination. Coach Brenner's voice carried across the field, pushing them harder than usual, preparing them for the night's game that would now be dedicated to their injured teammate.

"Move like you mean it, Peterson! Foster's counting on you to fill his position! Make him proud!"

The players responded with renewed effort, aware of the empty space in their lineup where Dylan Foster should have been— the defensive captain whose absence left a void larger than his considerable physical presence. The team had visited him that morning, squeezing into his hospital room in small groups, awkwardly offering encouragement to their still unconscious teammate.

Outside Stillwater Memorial, a makeshift shrine had grown throughout the week—flowers piled against the brick wall, handmade cards propped among stuffed animals, "Get Well Soon" balloons tugging at their anchors in the afternoon breeze. Students and teachers had contributed throughout the week, the initial shock of the attack transforming gradually into determined support.

A banner stretched across the hospital entrance, signed by nearly every student at Stillwater High: "STAY STRONG DYLAN #84 COUGAR STRONG." Beneath it, visitors passed in and out, nodding respectfully at the display of community solidarity.

In the midst of this pastoral scene of small-town resilience, Mary Cain gripped her steering wheel with white-knuckled tension as she drove through town and toward Carter's house. Her promise to Sam echoed in her mind—a promise she was breaking with every inch closer to Carter's front door. Sam had insisted on seeing her that afternoon, but she had texted an excuse to him an hour earlier, claiming a last-minute study session at the library. She knew he would be disappointed, and most likely suspicious, but she was determined she could handle this encounter with her childhood friend, and refused to let anyone tell her differently.

Pulling up to the house, Carter emerged before she could honk, locking the front door behind him. He wore jeans and a dark blue hoodie, a small backpack slung over one shoulder. Nothing about his appearance suggested a teenager who had lost his last living relative less than twenty-four hours ago. Nothing suggested he was a dangerous killer, someone that would hurt Mary. The dark shadows beneath his eyes, visible even from a distance, gave away his lack of sleep, and perhaps something else, though Mary could not be sure what.

"Hey," he greeted, sliding into the passenger seat with casual ease. "Thanks for still doing this. I wasn't sure you'd come."

Mary forced a smile, hoping the thundering of her heart wasn't audible in the confined space. "I said I would." She backed out of the driveway, focusing on the road to avoid meeting his eyes. "How are you holding up?"

Carter's shrug was visible in her peripheral vision. "As well as can be expected. The funeral home called this morning. Apparently there's a lot of paperwork when you're sixteen and suddenly have no legal guardian."

The clinical detachment in his tone sent a chill down Mary's spine despite the afternoon warmth. This was the Carter she'd glimpsed in his room—analytical, removed, processing human tragedy like data points in an equation.

"I'm sorry," she offered, the words feeling hollow despite their sincerity. Part of her—the part that remembered building forts with him as children, sharing ice cream cones on summer afternoons—genuinely mourned for the lonely boy who had lost everyone. The other part remembered the journal beneath his floorboard, the methodical plans for murder, the photographs taken without her knowledge.

"Thanks." He turned to look out the window as they passed the town limits, heading toward the county road that would take them to the abandoned Campbell property. "Did you hear about the fire last night? At the homeless camp?"

Mary's grip tightened on the steering wheel, her pulse accelerating. "I heard something about it this morning. On the news."

"Kilgore died," Carter said, his tone neutral, as if discussing the weather. "The bicycle thief I identified for your dad. Burned to death in his tent."

"That's terrible," Mary managed, focusing on maintaining an even speed, on keeping her breathing steady. "Do they know what happened?"

Carter shrugged again. "The news said something about flammable materials. Rubber cement or something. Apparently he was doing crafts in his tent."

The deliberate mention of rubber cement—the exact material Mary had read about in Carter's journal—was too specific to be coincidental. Was he testing her? Gauging her reaction to see if she knew more than she let on?

"Crafts?" she repeated, injecting an appropriate amount of skepticism into her tone. "In a homeless camp?"

"People find comfort in strange things," Carter replied, his gaze still fixed on the passing landscape. "Especially those living on society's edges. Model airplanes. Toys. Journals. Photographs. We all have our methods of making sense of the world."

The pointed references couldn't be accidental. Mary's throat tightened, her palms growing damp against the steering wheel. He knew. Somehow, Carter knew she had discovered his secrets. The realization settled in her stomach like ice, even as she maintained her outward composure.

"I suppose we do," she agreed, voice remarkably steady despite her racing thoughts. "Are you sure you want to do this today? After everything with your grandmother, it might be better to take some time—"

"This is exactly what I need," Carter interrupted, turning to face her fully for the first time since entering the car. "Distraction. Purpose. Something to focus on besides empty rooms and funeral arrangements."

His eyes held hers for a moment too long before she returned her attention to the road. There was something different in his gaze now—a focused intensity that hadn't been there before, assessing and calculating with precision that made Mary deeply unsettled.

"I understand," she said softly, and part of her did. The need to escape grief, to find purpose amid chaos—these were human impulses she recognized. The problem was that Carter's purpose seemed to involve methodically ending other people's lives.

The road narrowed as they left Stillwater proper behind, tall pines closing in on both sides, dappling the pavement with shifting shadows. The Campbell property lay another fifteen minutes ahead, down a gravel road that hadn't seen regular maintenance in years. Mary's phone signal had already begun to weaken, the bars diminishing with each mile away from town—a detail she'd failed to consider when formulating her ill-advised go with Carter.

Silence settled between them, heavy with unspoken truths and concealed intentions. Mary focused on her breathing, on the mechanical act of driving, on formulating a plan to extract herself from the situation if things went wrong. Carter seemed content with the quiet, his expression peaceful as he watched the forest slide past.

"Almost there," he said finally as they approached a weathered sign indicating the turnoff for Campbell Road. "Turn left here."

Mary complied, the car bouncing slightly as they transitioned from asphalt to gravel. The engine's sound seemed suddenly louder in the stillness of the forest, the crunch of tires on loose stone unnaturally amplified. She glanced at her phone—one bar of service left, flickering uncertainly as if it might disappear at any moment.

"It's beautiful out here," Carter observed, his tone conversational yet somehow wrong in its casualness. "Isolated. Peaceful. The perfect place to have a private conversation, don't you think?"

Mary's heart hammered against her ribs as she navigated around a particularly deep pothole. "What kind of conversation did you have in mind?"

Carter smiled, the expression not reaching his eyes. "I thought we might discuss what you found in my room last night. Under the floorboard."

Mary's hands jerked on the wheel, the direct confirmation of her fears momentarily shattering her composure. She corrected quickly, forcing steadiness into her voice. "I don't know what you're talking about."

"Come on, Mary," Carter said, disappointment coloring his tone. "We've known each other our whole lives. You've never been a convincing liar." He turned in his seat to face her fully. "You found my journal. You know what I've done. What I'm still doing."

Mary kept her eyes fixed on the rough road ahead, mind racing through options that grew more limited with each passing second. "What journal," she said, realizing how silly she sounded. She changed her tack. "If I did, why would I be alone in a car with you, driving into the middle of nowhere?"

"That's the fascinating question, isn't it?" Carter replied, genuine curiosity evident in his voice. "At first, I thought you might be recording our conversation. Wearing a wire for your father, gathering evidence." He leaned closer. "But you're too smart for something that obvious. No, I think you came because you had to know. Had to understand. It's the same curiosity that made you a good detective when we were kids."

The gravel road curved ahead, the abandoned Campbell house just visible through the trees—a dilapidated structure sagging under the weight of years of neglect. Mary slowed the car, buying precious seconds to think.

"And what if I did find it?" she asked finally, abandoning the pretense of ignorance. "What happens now, Carter?"

He leaned back in his seat, something like relief crossing his features. "Now? Now we have an honest conversation. No more games, no more pretending. Just truth between old friends."

Mary brought the car to a stop at the overgrown driveway in front of the house, cutting the engine but leaving the keys in the ignition. The sudden silence felt oppressive, the trees around them watching like indifferent witnesses.

"Truth," she repeated, finally turning to meet his gaze directly. "Like the truth about Jackson McKenzie? Ned Miller? Gerald Cooper? The truth about James Kilgore?"

Carter's expression remained unchanged, neither confirming nor denying her accusations. "The truth about patterns, Mary. About a world that makes more sense when you control the variables instead of being controlled by them."

In Carter's eyes Mary saw something she'd never noticed before—a cold emptiness where emotion should be, a void masked by performance so convincing she'd never recognized its deception until now.

"You killed them," she said, the words hanging in the still air between them. "All of them. And you were planning to kill my father. And Sam."

Carter tilted his head slightly, considering her statement. "Kill is such a limited word. I adjusted patterns. Created order from chaos." His gaze intensified, focusing on her with unsettling precision. "You're part of that pattern, too, Mary."

The implication hung between them, Mary suddenly acutely aware of how isolated they were, how far from help, how completely she had walked into a situation she might not be able to control.

"What happens now?" she asked again, her voice steadier than she felt.

Carter smiled, the expression almost gentle despite the coldness in his eyes. "Let's go for a walk." He reached into the back seat, grabbing Mary's bag and pushing it to her, as he grabbed the keys from the ignition and got out of the car. Mary, unsure of her next play, tried to steel her nerves. She quickly picked up her phone and typed out a fast text to her dad, one word that might save her, as Carter was looking away. She didn't have time to see that it sent though. She shoved the phone back into her bag just as Carter moved around to open her door.

She knew Carter was too calculating to simply kill her. There had to be a plan, and maybe she could stop it, help prevent another needless death.

Preferably her own.

THIRTY-NINE

Sheriff Cain frowned at the quiet phone sitting on his desk. He looked up, through his open door to Deputy Hargrove at his desk across the room, talking on the radio. He sensed the sheriff's eyes on him, turning and shook his head as he set down the radio. Sam should have reported to work hours ago, yet nobody had seen him or could reach him. He picked up his own cell phone, dialing his deputy, just another of more than a dozen tries he had made through the morning. Voice mail clicked on—Sam's professional greeting offering no clue to his whereabouts.

"Chambers, it's Cain. Call me when you get this. Immediately." He ended the call, setting the phone down with more force than necessary. He had left the same voicemail half a dozen times, as if more than one might shake Sam free of whatever was keeping him hidden.

Rising from his desk, Cain moved to the bullpen where Deputies Rivers and Weathers were reviewing evidence from the fire scene, photographs spread across a desk between them.

"Either of you seen Chambers today?" he asked, interrupting their discussion.

Rivers shook her head. "Not since last night at the fire scene. I released him around three or so."

"Wasn't he supposed to be watching the Thompson kid?" Weathers added, looking up from a photograph of the burnt tent remains.

"I took him off that assignment after what happened with the grandmother," Cain replied, unease growing in his gut. "But he should have checked in for his shift hours ago."

The deputies exchanged glances, both recognizing the unusual nature of Sam's absence. The young deputy was notorious for his punctuality, often arriving early for shifts and staying late to complete paperwork.

"Maybe he went back to the Thompson surveillance," Rivers suggested. "You know how focused he gets. Could have lost track of time."

Cain shook his head. "I specifically ordered him to end that surveillance. And he's not answering his radio or cell."

"Want us to swing by his house?" Weathers offered, already reaching for his keys. "Could be something simple—dead battery, overslept."

"Not Sam," Cain muttered, more to himself than his deputies. Something was wrong—the same instinct that had served him through his years of law enforcement was sounding alarms he couldn't ignore. "Carol, call dispatch. Have them ping his phone location. Dale, see if you can track his movements after the fire. I'm going to his house to check there. Let's make this a priority."

As the deputies moved to comply, Cain returned to his office, unease hardening into genuine concern. He picked up his phone again, this time dialing his home number. When no one answered, he tried Laura's cell, reaching her at the hospital.

"Have you seen Mary?" he asked without preamble when she picked up.

"Hello to you, too," Laura replied, the sounds of the hospital evident in the background. "She should be at school. What's going on, Martin?"

"School let out an hour ago. She's not answering her cell."

A pause on the line, Laura clearly picking up on his concern. "Maybe she's with friends? Or at practice? I can't keep track of her schedule these days."

Cain moved to his window, staring out at the street below where normal small-town life continued, oblivious to his mounting anxiety. "I think Sam Chambers is missing too."

The implications of that statement hung between them, unsaid but understood. Laura's voice lowered, professional calm replacing casual conversation. "What do you need me to do?"

"Call her friends. Check if anyone's seen her since school let out. I'll handle things from this end."

"Martin," Laura said, hesitation evident in her tone. "Do you think this has something to do with the cases you've been working? The deaths?"

Cain closed his eyes briefly, the weight of his suspicions pressing down like a physical burden. "I don't know. Hopefully I'm just being paranoid, but either way I intend to find out."

He hung up, then stood and, grabbing his coat, rushed out of his office, stopping in the bull pen. "If Deputy Chambers reports in, have him call me immediately. I'm on my cell." The room nodded in silence, the sheriff's concern spreading like wildfire.

As he headed toward the exit, Rivers intercepted him, her expression suggesting news he wouldn't like. "Sir, dispatch couldn't get a lock on Deputy Chambers' phone. Either it's powered off or..."

"Or somewhere without service," Cain finished, the implications sending a chill through him. Stillwater was notorious for bad radio reception, and cell phones were just as bad. But he knew this was something different, something more sinister.

"I'm headed out," Cain announced, already moving toward the exit with renewed purpose. "I've got a bad feeling. Let's all try to find Sam, ok?" The deputies nodded, sensing the urgency, picking up on the sheriff's concern.

He pushed through the station doors into the afternoon sunlight, a wave of fear propelling him forward. Something was coming unraveled in Stillwater, and whatever had been unfolding in the shadows was accelerating toward a conclusion he couldn't yet see, but feared with every fiber of his being.

As he slid behind the wheel of his Bronco, his mind allowed the terrible thought that Sam's disappearance and Mary's absence weren't coincidental, were somehow connected. The engine roared to life as Sheriff Cain pulled away from the curb. If his suspicions were correct, if Mary and Sam were in danger, he had to find them before Carter could complete his plans, whatever they might be. He had to find him, break the rules of his game, before it was too late.

And he had no intention of giving anyone—especially not a sixteen-year-old boy who might be a murderer—the chance to change the rules, again.

FORTY

The forest closed around them as the trail Carter followed led he and Mary deeper into the woods. It quickly narrowed until their shoulders occasionally brushed against low-hanging branches, snagging on Mary's shirt like grappling fingers in the dark. Afternoon sunlight filtered through the pine canopy in dappled patterns, creating an almost peaceful atmosphere that stood in stark contrast to the tension vibrating between them.

"I thought we were going to the Campbell property," Mary said, glancing over her shoulder at the increasingly distant car they'd left parked at the driveway.

Carter continued forward without breaking stride, his eyes fixed on the path ahead. "The cabin isn't important anymore."

Mary's pulse quickened, though she maintained an outward calm. This deviation from their stated destination wasn't random—nothing about Carter ever was. Each step taking them further from the road, from potential witnesses, from the possibility of easy escape, she knew was deliberate and calculated.

"Where are we going, then?" she asked, keeping her voice steady despite the fear beginning to coil in her stomach.

"Patience was never your strong suit," Carter replied, a faint smile touching his lips as he glanced back at her. "Always rushing ahead to a conclusion before examining all the evidence. That's why I was the better detective, even back then."

Mary bristled at the assessment despite herself. "Is that what all this has been about? Proving you're the better detective?"

"Partly," Carter admitted, ducking beneath a low-hanging branch. "At first, anyway. Why shouldn't I seek some validation? After my parents died, all of that just... stopped. The praise, the attention, the sense that someone was proud of me. It all disappeared overnight."

The candid admission caught Mary off guard. Carter rarely spoke of his parents' accident, and never with such raw honesty. The forest path before them blurred as sudden, unbidden images flooded her consciousness—not her own memories, but scenes she had constructed from fragments of stories overheard, from newspaper articles, from the collective whispers of Stillwater about the day Carter Thompson lost everything.

Mottled sunlight streamed through the car windows, breaking through the parting clouds that had dropped heavy rain on the area only minutes ago. The light beams created dancing patterns across the backseat where twelve-year-old Carter sat, a book open on his lap. His hair shorter, his face rounder with childhood, his eyes bright with an innocence that would soon be extinguished.

In the front seat, Robert Thompson glances back at his son through the rearview mirror, pride evident in his expression as he says something that makes Carter smile. Sarah Thompson turns in the passenger seat, her auburn hair catching the light as she laughs at something her husband has said, her hand reaching back to ruffle Carter's hair.

Carter's focus shifts from his book to his parents, observing their interaction with the analytical interest that already defines his personality. His father's hand leaves the steering wheel momentarily to gesture as he speaks, the car drifting slightly toward the center line before he corrects.

Sarah playfully swats her husband's arm, reminding him to watch the road. Robert exaggeratedly straightens in his seat, pantomiming excessive attention to driving that makes both Sarah and Carter laugh. The family unit, complete and whole, sharing a private moment of joy.

Then—a deer darts into the road ahead.

Robert Thompson's face transforms from laughter to alarm in an instant. He jerks the wheel, overcompensating. The tires lose traction on the rain-slick curve of Sawmill Bridge Road.

Carter's book flies from his hands as the car lurches. His mother screams. His father wrestles with the steering wheel, trying to regain control as the vehicle slides across the pavement. Carter's body is held in place by his seatbelt, but his head whips forward, then back.

Time slows as the car leaves the road entirely, becoming airborne for a horrifying moment before the front end connects with a massive pine tree at the edge of the forest. The impact is catastrophic—metal crumpling, glass shattering, the sickening sound of bodies violently thrown against unyielding surfaces.

Silence follows. The kind of absolute silence that only exists in the aftermath of chaos.

Carter blinks, disoriented, tasting blood from where he's bitten his tongue. The world tilts at an unnatural angle as the car has come to rest partially on its side. He hangs awkwardly from his seatbelt, which has left an angry red line across his chest and shoulder.

Carter unbuckles his seatbelt, carefully bracing himself to avoid falling. He climbs over the center console into the front of the car, calling for his parents in a voice that sounds distant to his own ears.

What he finds sears itself permanently into his memory, altered his perception of reality forever.

His father, impaled by a branch that has punched through the windshield and into his chest. Blood bubbles from Robert Thompson's lips with each shallow, failing breath. His eyes are open but unfocused, seeing nothing as life drains from him.

His mother has been thrown forward without the protection of a seatbelt. Her head has shattered the windshield, leaving a spider-web of cracks radiating from the point of impact. Her body is unnaturally still, neck at an impossible angle, blood matting her long hair.

Carter reaches out, his hand touching his mother's shoulder. No response. He turns to his father, calling to him. Robert's eyes briefly focus on his son, recognition and something like regret flickering in his gaze before the light fades completely.

Outside the shattered vehicle, the forest continues its indifferent existence. Birds call. Wind rustles leaves. The world remains stubbornly, insultingly alive while inside the crumpled metal shape, Carter Thompson watches his childhood end in blood and stillness.

Later, as emergency vehicles surround the crash site, their lights painting the forest in alternating red and blue flashes, Carter stands apart from the activity. Paramedics work on his parents inside the vehicle, their urgent movements and professional terminology a pantomime of hope when Carter already knows the truth.

A thermal blanket hangs from his shoulders, ignored. A female EMT kneels before him, examining a cut on his forehead, her lips moving with words he doesn't process. His gaze remains fixed on the car, on the stretchers now being prepared, on the body bags waiting on the ground.

Sheriff Martin Cain approaches, his face somber beneath his department hat. He crouches before Carter, speaking softly, one hand reaching out to rest on the boy's shoulder in a gesture of comfort.

Carter flinches away, his first display of emotion since the crash. His face contorts with rage, with grief too vast for his twelve-year-old frame to contain. He shouts something at the sheriff, his body rigid with rejection of the offered sympathy.

The sheriff tries again, but Carter backs away, arms wrapped tightly around himself, building the first layers of the walls that would eventually encase him completely. His eyes, which had been wide with shock, now narrow with something harder, colder—the first glimmers of the analytical detachment that would become his shield against a world that had shattered beyond repair.

As paramedics lift the black body bags containing what remains of Robert and Sarah Thompson, Carter watches with unblinking intensity. A paramedic tries to pull him away, to shield him from the horrific image, but Carter fights, refuses, remains focused on the view, the last of his parents as their bodies are loaded into an ambulance. His expression transforms, grief giving way to something more calculating as he observes the procedures, the protocols, the methodical handling of death.

In that moment, standing alone beside Sawmill Bridge Road while the adults move around him in a choreography of emergency response, Carter Thompson begins to disappear— the laughing child in the backseat with his book replaced by something else, something formed in the caldron of sudden, violent loss.

The images faded, returning Mary to the present moment—to the forest path, to the details that now colored her perception of the boy who had become a killer simply to be seen in a world that had taken his audience from him in a single, catastrophic moment.

"So you staged the murders," Mary said, the words feeling surreal as they left her lips. "Created crimes you could solve. For attention?"

Carter paused at a fork in the trail, considering the path to the right before shaking his head slightly and continuing left.

"For recognition. For acknowledgment of my abilities. My grandmother was already slipping away mentally when my parents died. She couldn't even remember who I was most days, let alone appreciate anything I accomplished."

A piece clicked into place for Mary—the desperate need for validation that had driven Carter's increasingly elaborate and dangerous "investigations" over the years.

"You've been doing this since your parents died, haven't you?" she asked, seeing the pattern now. "Creating problems just so you could solve them. Small things at first. Neighborhood vandalism you could 'investigate.' Missing items you would miraculously find. Each time, people would express gratitude, admiration. It was... addictive. But eventually that wasn't enough," Mary concluded, horror dawning as she understood the progression.

"The rush faded with each success," Carter confirmed, his voice detached despite the personal nature of his confession. "I needed more complex scenarios, more significant stakes. So I evolved my approach."

"Into murder," Mary said flatly, unable to keep the revulsion from her voice.

"Into carefully controlled experiments," Carter corrected, his momentary vulnerability vanishing behind clinical terminology. "Each one designed to challenge my abilities while showcasing them to others—particularly your father and his department."

"Why elderly men?" she asked, gathering information even as part of her recoiled from the conversation. "McKenzie, Miller, Cooper—what made them suitable... variables?"

Carter seemed to appreciate the question, his pace slowing slightly as he considered his response. "Routine. Predictability. Each followed established patterns, and performed regular tasks that could be subtly adjusted to create fatal outcomes that appeared accidental. And when I would provide insights into their deaths, people would listen. They would value what I had to say."

"But they weren't accidents," Mary pressed. "They were murders. You murdered them for validation you could have found in healthier ways."

Carter shook his head, a flicker of irritation crossing his features. "That word again. Murder. So limited in its scope, so lacking in nuance. I adjusted patterns, Mary. Created order from chaos. And in doing so, I made myself necessary. Important. Someone people couldn't simply forget or abandon."

The pain underlying his justification was palpable, revealing a wound that had never healed—the trauma of losing his parents and effectively his grandmother in such a short span, leaving him invisible in a world that had once seen and valued him.

"You took their lives," Mary insisted, refusing to let him hide behind clinical terminology or childhood trauma. "For what? To feel seen?"

"That's the fascinating thing," Carter replied, his irritation giving way to something closer to genuine reflection. "It evolved. What began as a need for recognition became something more complex. I started to see patterns beyond the individual scenarios—connections in the community's response, in your father's investigation techniques, in the way fear rippled outward from each event. I became not just the solver of mysteries, but their creator and conductor."

The growing sound of a waterfall began to reach them: Stillwater Falls. Mary became suddenly aware of how the sound of rushing water would mask any noise—a cry for help, a scream, a struggle. Another calculated choice in their journey, perhaps.

"And Dylan?" she asked, steadying herself against a tree trunk as her foot slipped slightly on a moss-covered stone. "Where did he fit into your need for recognition?"

Something darkened in Carter's expression—a flicker of genuine emotion breaking through the controlled façade.

"Dylan Foster was different. An annoyance. A distraction. Someone who deserved what happened to him for entirely separate reasons."

"Because he bullied you," Mary concluded, the pieces falling into place.

Carter's mouth tightened into a thin line. "He never saw me as a person. Just a target. A way to entertain himself and his Neanderthal friends. When I tried to get recognition through academic achievement, through my investigations, people like Dylan made sure I remained insignificant, ridiculous, the weird kid no one took seriously."

"So you stabbed him," Mary said, the brutality of the act hanging between them. "That's different from your other methods. More direct. More personal."

"As I said, he was an anomaly. Outside the primary pattern." Carter stepped over a fallen log. As Mary followed, her foot slipped on the damp surface. Carter reached out, grabbing her hand to support her. "But useful in creating confusion, in diverting attention from other activities while still contributing to my larger purpose."

Mary was acutely aware of his strength as his fingers closed around hers. This simple contact—once familiar, now laden with threat—reminded her of their childhood connection and the twisted path that had led them here, deep in the woods, discussing murder as casually as they once discussed comic books.

"You needed people to see how clever you were," she said softly, understanding dawning fully now. "After your parents died, you lost the audience that mattered most to you. The people who naturally celebrated your intelligence, your observations."

Carter released her hand once she was safely across, something vulnerable flickering in his eyes before being submerged once more beneath calculated control. "When you lose the people who see you—really see you—it's like ceasing to exist. I refused to disappear."

"So you made yourself impossible to ignore," Mary concluded. "Through increasingly dangerous and elaborate scenarios that would showcase your abilities."

"And it worked," Carter said, a hint of pride creeping into his voice. "Your father started paying attention. The deputies began to respect my insights. Even you came back into my life, after years of pretending I didn't exist."

The admission was a knife twisted in Mary's conscience—the recognition that her abandonment of their friendship after his parents' death had contributed, however indirectly, to the path he'd chosen.

"Things got out of control, didn't they?" she suggested, searching for a vulnerability, an opening in his methodical narrative.

Carter's expression shifted, something like genuine reflection crossing his features. "Not out of control. Patterns expanded in scope and complexity."

"And where do I fit into these patterns?" Mary asked, the question that had been hovering between them since they'd left the car. "What's my role in your grand experiment?"

Carter turned to face her fully, his eyes meeting hers with an intensity that made her breath catch. For a moment, the mask slipped further, revealing something raw and genuine beneath the calculated exterior.

"You were never supposed to be a variable, Mary," he said softly. "You were the constant. The fixed point around which everything else revolved. The one person who used to see me clearly, whose approval mattered more than anyone's after my parents were gone."

The admission hung in the air between them, more disturbing in its twisted affection than any threat might have been. Mary felt a chill that had nothing to do with the forest shadows creeping across the trail as afternoon began its slow transition toward evening.

"That's why you took the photographs," she realized. "Why you kept them separate from your murder wall. I wasn't just another investigation to you."

Carter resumed their walk along the narrowing trail. "I've always seen you more clearly than anyone else. Just as you've always seen me." He glanced back at her, something almost wistful in his expression. "At least, until recently. Until you joined the others in looking past me, through me."

Mary followed, mind racing to understand where this path—both literal and figurative—was leading. Carter wasn't taking her into the woods simply to kill her; that would be too direct, too unrefined for his methodical approach. He had something more elaborate planned, something that fit the patterns he'd been constructing with such care, something that would finally bring him the recognition he'd been desperately seeking since losing his parents.

"Where are we going, Carter?" she asked again, more directly this time.

"To show you what no one else has seen," he replied, pushing aside a branch that blocked their way. "The culmination of everything I've been working toward. The final piece of the pattern that will make it impossible for anyone to ignore what I'm capable of."

"And after you show me?" she pressed, her voice steady despite the fear coiling tighter in her chest. "What happens then?"

Carter simply smiled. He offered his hand again as the trail narrowed further, the gesture at once courteous and controlling. Mary hesitated before accepting it, her mind working frantically to identify options, escape routes, ways to delay whatever was waiting at the end of this path.

The forest shadows lengthened around them as the roar of Stillwater Falls began to demand their attention. Mary shivered at the cooling temperatures, and at the coming revelation she wasn't certain she would survive.

FORTY-ONE

Sheriff Cain pulled his Bronco to the curb outside Sam Chambers' modest Craftsman, the knot of unease in his stomach tightening at the sight of Sam's department vehicle parked in the driveway. The cruiser's presence confirmed Sam was home—or at least should be—yet he hadn't responded to radio calls or his cell phone for hours.

Cain scanned the property as he approached. Nothing appeared immediately amiss—no signs of struggle, no broken windows, no evidence to easily explain what had happened. Just a quiet house on a weekday, curtains drawn against the afternoon sun.

"Chambers?" Cain called, rapping his knuckles against the front door with official authority. "Sam? It's Sheriff Cain."

Silence answered him. Cain tried the doorknob—locked—then moved to peer through the front window, shielding his eyes against the glare. The living room beyond appeared undisturbed, if slightly cluttered with the organized chaos of a young bachelor. No signs of a struggle, no indications of trouble.

Cain circled to the side of the house, checking windows as he went. Kitchen—empty, dishes in the sink. Bedroom—bed unmade but otherwise normal. Nothing to explain Sam's silence or absence.

As he rounded the rear of the house, Cain's eyes fell on the storm doors rising slightly from ground level—the entrance to the basement Sam had mentioned needing repairs. An ancient padlock secured them shut, its metal gleaming dully in the afternoon light.

Inside the basement, Deputy Sam Chambers kneeled beneath the small ground-level window, his face positioned carefully at the end of a makeshift breathing apparatus he'd constructed from pieces of flexible dryer ducting. The contraption extended from his position to a small vent in the foundation wall, providing a tenuous connection to fresh air in a space now saturated with invisible danger.

The propane had begun leaking hours ago, the tiny holes in the gas line releasing the heavy vapor that now filled the basement. Sam had spent hours taking a deep breath through the hose, then looking for a way out, one that wouldn't cause a spark or friction and potentially set off the gas. The modified door latch at the top of the stairs was forceable, he felt, but it would take his entire weight thrown at the door jam to break the latch, and he worried the violence might cause unforeseen results in a room filled with highly flammable gas.

As Sam stayed low enough to access the breathing tube, he glanced at his department radio laying a few feet away. He was grateful for his time at the fire academy. It was a career path he had abandoned in favor of police work, but the training had saved him: He knew that an older radio could cause a spark, igniting combustible gas in a concentrated environment, the exact situation he found himself trapped in. Though he desperately wanted to use it, to reach out for help, he had shut it off immediately. The risk was far too great. His cell phone, without signal in the basement's concrete confines, had been shoved back into his pocket, useless.

Sam had returned after his meeting with Mary, exhausted and convinced Mary would not keep her promise. He knew he needed to talk to the sheriff, not only about the information she had learned, but also about their relationship. The danger posed by not speaking up was too great, and Sam could not reconcile his fear of his own culpability in the affair with any loss of life, especially Mary's.

He would face the consequences, but he would do everything he could to protect her.

It was with these thoughts Sam had returned home that morning, decided a shower would help wake him up before heading into the office to face the sheriff. As he climbed into the stall and turned on the water, only a gurgle escaped.

"Damnit," he said, knowing another pipe had broken. He quickly dressed again and headed into the basement.

Even as he opened the door at the top of the stairs he could hear the sharp sound of a water leak. He padded down the steps, absentmindedly pulling the door shut behind him. He barely registered the click of the door closing.

At first the smell of gas was limited, but as Sam continued further down the stairs it became much stronger, making Sam choke and pull up his shirt to cover his nose and mouth. Quickly, Sam turned to head back up the stairs, knowing he also had a gas leak, but found the door jammed or strangely locked. He banged his shoulder against it but it didn't move, leaving him to realize his predicament.

It only took minutes of basement exploration, showing him without a doubt he was trapped, for Sam to conclude he needed an airway, and he quickly fashioned something that worked well enough, a dryer hose through a small grated window vent. Sam could get no signal on his cell, and his radio was a dangerous alternative. He was relegated to waiting until someone came to find him.

By four in the afternoon, as the sun began to set and the temperature dropped, he glanced over to the ancient boiler. The pilot light had been replaced by the previous owner with an electronic ignition, the simple fact which had saved his life so far. But he knew if the temperature dropped too far, the spark from the ignition, as it turned on the boiler, would ignite the gas around him. Sam found himself regretting a plethora of errors in his life, and hoping at the same time for a chance to reconcile them.

Movement outside caught Sam's attention—a pair of uniform-clad legs passing the window. Relief surged through him as he recognized the sheriff's distinctive gait.

"Sheriff!" Sam called, his voice emerging as a croak after hours of breathing through the tube. "Sheriff Cain! Down here!"

The legs paused, then changed direction, moving closer to the window. Cain's face appeared, bending to peer through the decorative but sturdy security mesh covering the small opening.

"Sam?" Confusion and concern mingled in the sheriff's voice as he took in the deputy's prone position and the strange tubing arrangement. "What the hell?"

"Propane leak," Sam explained, keeping his voice calm despite the desperation of his situation. "Basement's full of it. I'm trapped—door latch is jammed and I can't risk creating a spark trying to break it open."

Cain's expression darkened with understanding. "How long have you been down there?"

"Since this morning. After I met with—" Sam caught himself, professional instinct momentarily overriding the urgency of his situation. "After I got home from an early errand. Found the basement door wouldn't open from this side, then smelled the gas."

The sheriff straightened, already reaching for his radio. "Dispatch, this is Sheriff Cain. I need backup at 427 Maple Street. Notify utilities." He tried to peer down into the basement, the smell of gas already reaching out through the small grate.

His heart raced, realizing the danger they both were in. His gaze shifted to the storm doors he'd noticed earlier. "What about your cellar doors? That's your way out."

"Should be, but it's locked from the outside. I've been meaning to fix that."

"I'll be right back," Cain said, already moving toward his vehicle. "Hang tight."

Sam almost laughed at the unintentional pun, hysteria bubbling beneath the surface of his professional calm. He watched through the mesh as the sheriff's legs hurried away, disappearing from his limited field of vision.

Minutes that felt like hours passed before Cain returned, bolt cutters clutched in his hands. Sam could see the sheriff's legs approach the storm doors, then the metallic snip of the cutters severing the padlock.

"Sam!" Cain called from outside as he yanked open the storm doors. "Come on!"

Sam took a deep breath, then pulled away from the tube and moved to the storm door.

"Coming out!" he called, moving carefully toward the now-visible rectangle of daylight.

In the corner of the basement, a small solenoid connected to the base of the boiler activated. The cool fall afternoon had dropped the temperature enough in the house to trigger the heat. The electronic ignition clicked as it attempted to generate a spark, to ignite the boiler.

The sound froze Sam in place, horror washing over him as he realized what was about to happen. From his position, he could almost imagine the tiny spark, the flow of gas—could almost visualize the flame appearing.

Time slowed as Sam lunged for the stairs, taking them two at a time as Cain reached down to grab his arm. The spark appeared, the tiny flow of gas from the boiler overwhelmed by the saturation of propane in the basement. The rush of flame rolling out from the corner of the basement created an inhuman roar.

Cain's strong grip closed around Sam's forearm just as the air behind him ignited. The explosion wasn't the dramatic fireball of action movies but something more insidious—a rapid pressure wave accompanied by a whooshing scream as the gas combusted, racing through the basement and up the stairs behind Sam's fleeing form.

The blast caught them just as Sam cleared the doors, propelling both men across the yard with terrifying force. They landed hard on the lawn in a tumble of arms, legs and debris. Behind them, windows shattered as flames erupted from the basement, rushing to consume the oxygen now available through the broken glass and open storm door.

For several moments, they lay stunned on the grass, ears ringing from the explosion. Cain recovered first, pushing himself to a sitting position to assess the damage. The house was already engulfed in flames, fire racing up the walls with unnatural speed as the old, dry wood eagerly welcomed the firestorm.

"Sam?" he called, turning to his deputy who remained motionless beside him. "Chambers!"

Sam groaned, his eyes fluttering open. "Sheriff," he managed, then gasped as he tried to move. "My leg—"

Cain's gaze dropped to Sam's lower body, where a jagged shard of wood—part of a support beam blown apart by the explosion —had embedded itself deeply in the young deputy's calf. Blood pulsed around the foreign object in a rhythm that immediately set off alarm bells in Cain's mind.

"Don't move," he ordered, already removing his belt with practiced efficiency. "It's bleeding pretty bad."

Sam lifted his head enough to see the injury, his face paling beneath the soot that covered it. "That's... not good."

"Could be worse," Cain replied grimly, wrapping his belt around Sam's thigh, above the injury. "Could have hit your femoral. This we can manage."

With the practiced movements of someone who'd received medical training, Cain fashioned a makeshift tourniquet with his belt, tightening it just enough to slow the dangerous bleeding without completely cutting off circulation. Sam hissed through clenched teeth as the pressure increased.

"Sorry," Cain muttered, securing the belt. "Better than bleeding out."

In the distance, sirens wailed—the backup Cain had requested before understanding the danger they were facing.

"This wasn't an accident," Cain stated, eyes narrowed as he surveyed the burning structure. "Someone tampered with your gas line, rigged your basement door so you couldn't escape."

Sam nodded, fighting through the pain to focus. "Carter Thompson. Has to be. He's been one step ahead of us this whole time."

The sheriff turned to Sam, his expression hardening. "Mary is missing, too. She should have been home from school hours ago, but her car's gone and she's not answering her phone."

The statement hit Sam with more force than the explosion had, the compartmentalized concern he'd been suppressing now rushing to the forefront of his mind. His hand moved automatically to check his pocket, confirming the phone was still there despite the blast.

"That's the other thing we need to talk about," Sam said, dread settling in his stomach. "Mary's with Carter Thompson. She went with him to the Campbell property after school."

"What?" Cain's voice went dangerously quiet, the kind of calm that experienced officers recognized as preceding a storm. "Why would she do that?"

Sam took a deep breath, recognizing that the moment for partial truths had passed. "Because she said she found evidence in his room last night—a journal documenting how he engineered the deaths of McKenzie, Miller, and Cooper. She went to confirm her suspicions, to get him to talk."

"And you let her go?" Incredulity and anger battled in Cain's tone. "Knowing what she suspected, what he was capable of?"

"I tried to stop her," Sam defended, wincing as a wave of pain shot through his injured leg. "I made her promise not to go. But Mary is... determined. When she sets her mind to something—"

"She's just like her mother, or me," Cain finished, a mixture of pride and frustration in his voice. "But that doesn't explain how you know where she went, or why you didn't tell me immediately."

The moment of truth had arrived. Sam straightened his shoulders, meeting his superior officer's gaze directly despite the pain threatening to overwhelm him. "Because Mary and I have been seeing each other. Romantically. For the past three months."

The confession landed between them like a physical object, heavy with implications both professional and personal. Cain's expression cycled through shock, disbelief, and anger in rapid succession.

"You're twenty-two," he said finally, voice dangerously quiet. "She's seventeen."

"I know, sir." Sam didn't flinch from the accusation implicit in those facts. "It's complicated. And Carter Thompson found out, used it to blackmail me into providing him with case files about the investigations."

"Jesus Christ, Chambers." Cain ran a hand over his face, smearing the blood from a cut on his forehead in an unconscious gesture. "You compromised an active investigation because you were sleeping with my underage daughter?"

The arrival of the first fire truck spared Sam from immediate response, red lights washing over them as firefighters leapt into action, unrolling hose lines and shouting commands. The house had become a fully involved structure fire, flames now visible through the roof as years of careful savings and hard work transformed into heat before Sam's eyes.

"We don't have time for this right now," Sam said, pulling his phone from his pocket with hands that trembled slightly from blood loss. "What matters is finding Mary before Carter does whatever he's been planning."

"And how exactly do you propose we do that?" Cain demanded, professional focus returning despite the personal bombshell Sam had dropped. "Unless they are waiting at the cabin for us to arrive, the Campbell property covers fifty acres of forest. They could be anywhere out there."

Sam activated his phone, opening a tracking app. A small red dot pulsed on the screen, its position several miles outside town. "Because I put a tracker in her backpack this morning. I knew she wouldn't keep her promise to stay away from him."

Cain stared at the phone, then at Sam, emotions warring across his features. "This is all so wrong."

"I did what was necessary to protect her," Sam replied simply, his voice weakening as the blood loss began to take its toll. He squinted at the screen, focusing through the growing lightheadedness. "They're moving away from the cabin... heading toward Stillwater Falls."

Alarm sharpened Cain's features. They both knew the threat to Mary was increasing by the minute. There was no time to waste.

Without responding, Cain reached into his pocket and extracted his own phone. He unlocked it and held the screen toward Sam, displaying a single-word text message from Mary that had arrived approximately an hour earlier: "Campbell."

"This makes more sense now," Cain said, eyes never leaving Sam's face.

Sam stared at the message, understanding dawning through the haze of pain. "She was trying to tell you where she was going. The Campbell property. And my tracker confirms that."

A paramedic approached them at last, medical bag in hand, her expression professional but concerned as she took in Sam's bloodied leg and the makeshift tourniquet.

"I need to go after them," Cain said, rising to his feet with sudden urgency. "He's taking her to the falls."

"We need to go," Sam corrected, attempting to sit up before the paramedic gently but firmly pushed him back down.

"You're not going anywhere except the hospital," she stated with the authority of someone accustomed to dealing with stubborn patients.

"She's right," Cain agreed, his tone inviting no argument. "You've lost too much blood already. You'd slow me down, and time is something Mary doesn't have."

Sam wanted to protest, to insist on accompanying the sheriff despite his injury, but the growing weakness in his limbs and the tunnel vision creeping at the edges of his consciousness confirmed the truth of Cain's assessment. He was in no condition to hike through forest terrain to Stillwater Falls.

"Take my phone," Sam said, offering the device with its tracking app still active. "Follow the signal. But be careful— Carter's too methodical to leave anything to chance. He'll have contingencies, backup plans."

Cain accepted the phone, tucking it securely into his pocket. "I've been tracking killers since before that boy was born," he reminded Sam, his voice low and dangerous. "If he hurt my daughter, there won't be a pattern in the world that will save him."

The paramedic had begun cutting away Sam's pant leg, exposing the full extent of the injury. "This might need surgery," she informed them, preparing to stabilize the embedded wood shard for transport.

Cain nodded, his attention already shifting toward the gathering first responders. Deputy Rivers rushed up to Cain and Sam.

"Carol, Sam's been injured," Cain said. "We've got a situation up at the old Campbell cabin and Stillwater Falls. I need to go after my daughter."

Rivers didn't waste time with questions. "What do you need from us?"

"Coordinate fire response, get Sam to the hospital, and keep this situation contained," Cain ordered, already moving toward his Bronco. "No radio chatter about my location or Mary's situation. This stays between us for now. If you don't hear from me in an hour, send backup."

Sam reached out, grabbing Cain's ankle to get his attention, his voice weaker than he would have liked. "I know you don't want to hear it, but I love your daughter. Save her."

Cain paused, looking back at his injured deputy. A complex mixture of emotions crossed his features—anger, concern, determination, and something harder to define that might have been forgiveness, or at least its possibility.

"We'll discuss your situation when I get back," he said, the statement both a promise and a warning. "In the meantime, don't die. That's an order, Deputy."

"Yes, sir," Sam managed, the edges of his vision darkening as the blood loss took its toll.

Cain nodded once, then disappeared into the waiting SUV. The vehicle peeled away from the curb with a squeal of tires, lights flashing but siren silent as the sheriff raced to intercept his daughter and her captor.

As paramedics worked to stabilize his injury for transport, Sam fought against the encroaching unconsciousness, his thoughts fixed on Mary—on her determination, her courage, and the terrible danger she now faced because of his failure to protect her. His last conscious thought before the darkness claimed him was a prayer to whatever power might be listening that Sheriff Cain would reach his daughter in time.

Behind them, the house continued to burn, flames consuming the structure that represented Sam's first real attempt at permanence in Stillwater. Like so much else in the past twenty-four hours, it had been sacrificed to Carter Thompson's methodical campaign of destruction—a campaign that was now racing toward its deadly conclusion at the edge of Stillwater Falls.

349

FORTY-TWO

The hike to Stillwater Falls had gotten more challenging in the final stretch, the trail narrowing as it wound through increasingly rocky terrain. Mary's breath came in short gasps, legs burning, though her physical discomfort paled against the growing dread that accompanied each step closer to their destination.

Carter moved with disturbing ease ahead of her, seemingly unaffected by the long walk. His movements remained fluid and controlled, as if this hike were merely a casual afternoon stroll rather than what Mary increasingly suspected was her final journey.

"Almost there," he called back, voice light with an anticipation that chilled her more than any threat could have. "You can really hear it now."

The distant rush of water reached her ears—Stillwater Falls, the town's namesake and natural wonder. In the summer, tourists gathered at its base to marvel at the six hundred and twenty foot cascade tumbling down the mountainside. But it was the precipitous drop from the falls' edge that made Mary's stomach clench in terror. No one ventured this close to the lip during the wet season, when the rushing waters made the surrounding rocks treacherously slippery.

The tree line remained thick as they approached the summit, sunlight barely breaking through the canopy to illuminate their path. Passing through a final thick stand of trees, they emerged onto a flat outcropping that formed a natural viewing platform at the edge, where the river flowed over the falls. Mary staggered slightly as she stepped into the open space, legs unsteady after the long walk, lungs working to recapture her breath.

Just yards away, the world simply ended—the stone shelf gave way to a heart-stopping void where water tumbled into misty oblivion. The falls roared below, water crashing against rocks on its long journey to the river that would eventually wind through the town.

"Beautiful, isn't it?" Carter observed, his voice carrying easily over the water's constant thunder. His expression was peaceful, almost reverential as he gazed out over the epic view spread before them—miles of forest canopy, distant mountains hazy on the horizon, the town of Stillwater unseen, miles away downstream.

Mary remained near the tree line, instinctively maintaining distance between herself and both Carter and the precipitous drop. "Why are we here, Carter?"

The question seemed to amuse him. Without responding, he circled around, blocking Mary's escape, then reaching into his pocket to withdraw something that caught the late afternoon sunlight—the metallic flash of a switchblade, its blade snapping open with mechanical precision.

"Have a seat, Mary," he said, gesturing toward a flat rock with the knife. The command was delivered with the same casual tone he might have used to offer her a chair at a study session, but the blade eliminated any pretense of choice.

Mary complied slowly, lowering herself onto the indicated rock, mind racing through diminishing options. No one knew where they were. No one would hear her scream over the falls' constant roar. No one would find them in time.

"What's happening?" she asked, struggling to keep her voice steady. "What are we doing here?"

Carter glanced at his watch, a slight smile tugging at the corner of his mouth. "I think by now your boyfriend is experiencing an interesting chemical reaction in his basement. Propane gas and oxygen, with just the right spark to bring them together. Or maybe just simple suffocation. That's a strong possibility as well."

The cryptic statement took a moment to register. When understanding dawned, Mary felt as if the ground had dropped away beneath her. "Sam? What did you do to Sam?"

"Nothing complicated," Carter replied, the clinical detachment returning to his voice. "Just some minor adjustments to his gas line. A few strategic holes, a modified door latch to ensure he couldn't escape the basement. He really should have removed that padlock from the outside of his storm doors." He examined the knife blade with professional interest.

"No," Mary whispered, the horror of his casual description overwhelming her. Tears welled in her eyes, spilling over before she could stop them. "You're lying. You couldn't have —"

"I assure you, I could and did," Carter interrupted. "It was actually quite simple. Your beloved deputy wasn't nearly as security-conscious as he should have been for someone in law enforcement."

Mary stared at him through her welling tears, truly seeing him perhaps for the first time—not the childhood friend who had suffered tragic loss, not the awkward teenager seeking connection, but something else entirely. Something cold and calculating that merely wore Carter's face like a mask.

"Why?" she managed, the question encompassing not just Sam but everything—the murders, the manipulations, this final act of cruelty.

"Because he was in the way," Carter stated simply. "A variable that needed adjustment. He took what was mine."

"I was never yours," Mary shot back, grief momentarily giving way to anger.

"No?" Carter tilted his head, studying her with disconcerting intensity. "We were inseparable once. Two parts of a whole. The only person who truly understood me." The knife glinted as he gestured with it. "And then, when I needed you most, you disappeared."

Mary's tears flowed freely now, the bitter truth of his accusation impossible to deny.

"I'm sorry," she whispered, the inadequate words all she could offer. "I was young. I didn't know how to help you."

"And yet you found time to help everyone else," Carter observed, a hint of the old pain breaking through his cold exterior. "The class pet projects, the volunteer work at the hospital, the endless social causes. Everyone but me."

Before Mary could respond, Carter stiffened, head turning slightly as if listening. After a moment, he smiled—a genuine expression that transformed his face into something almost boyish, a ghost of the child he'd once been.

"Right on schedule," he murmured, reaching for Mary's backpack which lay on the ground beside her. "Your father has excellent response time."

Mary's heart leapt at the mention of her father, hope flaring briefly before freezing into new terror. Carter had been expecting him. This wasn't an interruption of his plans; it was part of them.

Carter reached deep into her backpack and extracted a small black object no larger than a thumb drive. He held it up for her inspection—a tracking device, its tiny LED blinking steadily.

"Your deputy boyfriend really should be more creative with his surveillance techniques," Carter remarked, turning the device in his hand. "I knew it was there, even without seeing it. Sloppy work, really, but useful for my purposes."

Understanding dawned like ice water down Mary's spine. "You knew. You've known all along."

"Of course I knew," Carter replied, as if her surprise was both expected and slightly disappointing. "Just as I knew you found my journal. Just as I knew you would try to play detective one last time, to confirm your suspicions while maintaining the pretense of sympathy." He tucked the tracker into his pocket. "Predictable patterns, Mary. Everyone follows them if you know how to look."

A faint sound reached them—the snap of a twig, the rustle of undergrowth. Carter's posture shifted instantaneously, all casual pretense vanishing as he moved behind Mary, one hand gripping her upper arm forcing her to stand, the other bringing the switchblade to rest against her throat.

"Come out slowly, Sheriff," he called out, voice carrying through the clearing. "Unless you want to test how quickly I can open an artery." The blade pressed lightly against Mary's neck, her eyes widening in fear.

From the tree line at the trail's end, Sheriff Cain emerged, service weapon drawn and aimed. His face was streaked with soot, uniform singed at the edges—evidence of his recent proximity to the explosion at Sam's house. His eyes moved rapidly between Carter and Mary, assessing the situation with professional detachment betrayed only by the tension in his face.

"Let her go, Carter," he commanded, voice steady despite the fear evident in his eyes. "This is between you and me."

"Is it?" Carter questioned, tightening his grip on Mary. "I'm not so sure about that. Put the gun down, Sheriff. Toss it over here."

Cain's aim remained steady. "You know I can't do that, son."

"I'm not your son," Carter responded, voice hardening as he pressed the knife more firmly against Mary's skin. A thin line of red appeared as the blade broke the surface. "And I'm not asking. Gun down, now, or I finish what I started with your daughter."

Mary met her father's gaze, trying to convey both apology and warning. She felt Carter's breath against her ear, his body tense but controlled behind her. The knife at her throat was held with practiced steadiness, the slight sting of the initial cut a promise of what would follow if her father refused to comply.

After what seemed an eternity, Sheriff Cain slowly lowered his weapon. Keeping his movements deliberate and non-threatening, he tossed the gun toward them.

The service weapon skidded across the rocky surface, coming to rest a few feet from where Carter held Mary. With surprising agility, he dropped into a crouch, bringing Mary along, as he snatched up the gun without releasing her, the switchblade never wavering from her throat.

"Thank you for your cooperation, Sheriff." He backed up slightly, the need for a human shield diminished, but his control over Mary unwavering, all while increasing the distance between them and Cain. "I've always appreciated how seriously you take your duty to protect and serve."

"What do you want, Carter?" Cain asked, hands now away from his sides, open in the universal gesture of non-aggression. "What's your play here?"

Carter smiled. "Isn't it obvious? I want you to experience what I experienced. To understand what it feels like to watch your family die while you stand helpless to prevent it."

The brutal honesty of the statement hung in the air, clarifying the horror of Carter's intentions beyond any doubt. Mary felt something brush against her cheek—not the knife, but a tear. Carter's tear, falling unbidden as the memory of his parents' death broke through his carefully constructed facade.

"Your parents' accident wasn't your fault, Carter," Cain said softly, taking a cautious step forward. "And it wasn't mine. What happened that day on Sawmill Bridge Road—it was a tragedy. But it was an accident."

"Stop!" Carter shouted, his composure fracturing momentarily. The hand holding the gun rose, aiming directly at Cain. "Don't come any closer. And don't pretend you understand what happened that day."

Cain froze, hands still raised. "Then help me understand. Talk to me, Carter. Whatever you're feeling—"

"Feeling?" Carter let out a harsh laugh that held no humor. "That's the problem with all of you. You think this is about feelings. About emotions I couldn't process, trauma I couldn't handle." The gun remained steady, aimed at Cain's chest. "This isn't about feelings. It's about patterns. About cause and effect. About restoring balance to an equation that's been unsolved for three years."

Mary could feel Carter's heart pounding against her back, his breath coming faster despite his attempt at controlled speech. For all his talk of patterns and equations, raw emotion was bleeding through—the abandoned twelve-year-old seeking redress for losses he couldn't comprehend.

"Carter, please," she whispered, feeling the knife still pressed against her throat. "This won't bring them back. It won't fix what happened."

"No," he agreed, his voice soft against her ear. "But it will complete the pattern. And you, Mary—you disappointed me most of all."

The pain in those words cut deeper than any blade could have. Mary closed her eyes briefly, accepting the truth of his accusation. "I know," she admitted. "I abandoned you. I was a coward, and I'm sorry."

"And then you fell in love with him," Carter continued, as if she hadn't spoken. "With Chambers. The newest, shiniest deputy in your father's collection. The perfect replacement for the broken boy next door."

Mary's eyes found her father's. His expression confirmed what she'd both hoped and feared—that her father knew. In a moment she realized, for better or worse, that she was relieved he knew. If Sam died after unburdening himself, then she would take the rest of the burden for him.

"Tell him," Carter urged, the knife pressing slightly harder against her skin. "Tell your father how you feel about his deputy. I want him to know exactly what he's losing today."

Tears streamed down Mary's face as she looked at her father— this man who had protected her, raised her, loved her unconditionally despite the distance that had grown between them in recent years. "Dad," she began, voice breaking. "Sam means everything to me. I love him. I'm sorry you had to find out like this."

Cain's expression softened despite the danger, years of parental love overriding even the shock of the revelation. "I know, honey," he said simply. "We'll talk about it later. Right now, I need you to stay calm."

"How touching," Carter observed, beginning to back toward the edge of the falls, dragging Mary with him. The mist rising from below dampened their clothing, making the rocky surface treacherously slick. "A family reconciliation just before the end. Almost poetic, isn't it?"

Cain tensed, clearly preparing to lunge forward despite the gun aimed at him. "Carter, don't—"

The crack of the gunshot was deafening, eclipsing even the roar of the falls for a split second. Cain cried out, collapsing to one knee as blood bloomed across his thigh, the bullet finding its mark with devastating result.

"Dad!" Mary screamed, struggling against Carter's grip, heedless of the knife at her throat.

"Predictable," Carter commented, the gun still smoking in his hand. "Always the hero, ready to sacrifice himself. But I need you alive, Sheriff. I need you to watch." Carter turned to Mary, his voice deep and heavy against her ear. "He'll live," Carter assured her, tightening his hold until she could barely breathe. "That's the point. He'll live with the knowledge that he failed to save you, just as I've lived with the knowledge that I couldn't save my parents."

They were at the very edge now, the misty abyss yawning behind them. Mary could feel the spray on her back, the thunderous roar of the falls vibrating through the stone beneath their feet. Cain pressed a hand to his bleeding thigh, teeth clenched in pain but eyes alert, watching for any opening to intervene despite his injury.

"Carter," Mary gasped, feeling the knife ease slightly as his attention divided between her and her father. "This isn't you. This isn't who you really are."

Mary's hand moved slowly upwards, taking his wrist lightly, holding his hand at bay. "I see you," she whispered. "I've always seen you, even when I wasn't there. That's why I came today. Because I remembered the boy who was my best friend."

Something flickered in Carter's expression—doubt, perhaps, or a momentary connection to the child he'd once been. The knife wavered slightly, the gun lowering a fraction of an inch as conflicting impulses battled within him.

It was all the opening Mary needed. With a sudden twist, she wrenched herself sideways, forcing the knife away from her throat. The gun clattered to the ground as Carter dropped it, struggling to maintain his grip on her. Mary fought with desperate strength, feeling the blade slice across her palm as she grappled for control of the weapon. The blade clattered to the ground, skidding away on the slick stone.

"Dad!" Mary screamed, hoping he could somehow intervene despite his wounded leg.

Carter's face transformed into a mask of rage as his carefully constructed plan dissolved into chaos. With unexpected strength, he seized Mary by the throat, choking her. She gasped for air as he dragged her the final few steps to the edge, the misty void now directly behind them.

"That's enough, Mary. Time to face the inevitable."

Through the spots darkening her vision, Mary saw a blur of movement from the tree line—a figure launching toward them with reckless speed. For a moment, she thought it was her father, somehow overcoming his injury through sheer paternal determination.

Then recognition hit, along with paralyzing horror.

Sam.

His uniform was torn and bloodied, the hastily applied bandage on his leg already soaked through with crimson. His face was pale from blood loss, features tight with pain, but his eyes burned with focused intensity as he charged across the clearing toward them.

"Sam, no!" she tried to scream, but Carter's hands around her throat reduced the warning to a strangled whisper.

The impact when Sam crashed into them was like being hit by a truck. The three bodies collided with bone-jarring force, Carter's grip on Mary's throat finally breaking as Sam's momentum pushed them apart. They fell to the ground and Sam, with one powerful shove, tried to throw Mary clear of the edge, but her body only slid on the wet stone.

"Mary, go!" Sam shouted, grappling with Carter. Despite his weakened condition, adrenaline and protective rage lent him temporary strength as they fought for control.

Mary turned back, unwilling to leave Sam alone in the fight. "Sam!" she cried, scrambling toward the struggle at the falls' edge.

The fight was brutal and swift. Carter, pinned to the ground, enduring Sam's rage filled punches, found the switchblade, and it flashed suddenly forward like his own punch, sinking the metal into Sam's abdomen. The deputy gasped, momentarily freezing as the blade penetrated flesh and muscle.

"NO!" Mary screamed, the sound tearing from her throat. She scrambled closer, desperate to help Sam, to save him, no longer aware of the edge of the abyss just beyond the fight.

Carter and Sam seemed to rise to their knees together, Sam trying to pull away from the blade, and Carter pushing it deeper, ensuring it did its damage. But Sam wasn't finished. With a roar that seemed to rise from the very core of his being, he drove his fist into Carter's face, a powerful blow that sent the teenager spinning backward toward the precipice, the blood-soaked blade pulling from Sam's stomach, clattering to the rocks. Carter slid to the ground, slipping toward the edge, stunned by Sam's attack and struggling to stop the inevitable motion toward the falls.

Mary scrambled toward Sam, hoping to reach him, to find a way to save him despite the damage done by Carter's blade.

Carter's feet dangled over the very edge, hands grasping for purchase as he fought for balance on the slick stone. At the last moment, as his body began to slide backward into the abyss, his hand shot out, fingers closing around Mary's ankle as she attempted to reach Sam.

Mary screamed as she felt herself being dragged toward the edge. Her fingers clawed at the stone, only finding loose dirt and smooth rock that did nothing to weaken Carter's grip. Behind her, she heard her father's shout as he tried to drag himself into the fight, his wounded leg preventing him from reaching her in time.

Sam, his left hand gripping his stomach wound, summoning one last surge, and lunged forward, his right hand gripping a rock. He slammed it down with furious force, connecting with Carter's arm as it grappled with Mary's ankle. Something cracked—bone giving way beneath the fierce blow, and his grip on Mary's ankle weakened. Sam dropped the rock, then punched Carter in the face, forcing him back, allowing Mary to pull free, to scramble away. Carter, ignoring his broken arm, turned his attention to Sam, grabbing at him as he cried out in pain and fury, dragging him to the edge.

As Mary turned, she saw Sam and Carter sliding over the brink —two figures silhouetted against the misty void beyond. Sam turned back, found Mary's eyes, something passing between them in that final instant—love, perhaps, an apology, or simply acceptance of what was to come.

Then they were gone, disappearing over the edge into the thundering mist below.

"SAM!" Mary's scream tore through the clearing. She crawled to the edge, heedless of the danger, peering desperately into the misty abyss below. "SAM!"

Nothing but tumbling water and obscuring mist answered her cry. The falls continued their eternal journey downward, indifferent to the human tragedy that had just unfolded at their brink.

Strong arms encircled Mary from behind, pulling her back from the edge. Her father's voice, tight with pain yet steady with authority, whispered in her ear. "He's gone, Mary. You can't follow him. You can't."

She collapsed against him, sobs wracking her body with seismic force. Together they huddled on the wet stone, a father and daughter united in grief, clinging to each other.

"I loved him," Mary whispered between sobs. "Dad, I loved him so much."

"I know, sweetheart," Sheriff Cain replied, his own voice rough with emotion as he held his daughter close, her tears falling to mingle with his blood on the stone where they knelt. "He loved you, too. He told me." Mary, gripped her father tighter.

The sun began its descent toward the western horizon, casting long shadows across Stillwater Falls as emergency responders, led by Deputy Rivers, finally reached the falls. They found the sheriff and his daughter still locked in their grief-stricken embrace, unwilling or unable to leave the place where Sam Chambers had made his final sacrifice.

Below, the search for survivors began, though all involved knew the task was likely futile. The falls were deep, the currents treacherous, the rocky basin at their base a graveyard for anything—or anyone—that made the fatal plunge from above.

Yet still, Mary Cain hoped, because that was all she had left.

FORTY-THREE

The heavy scent of carnations and lilies hung in the air, mingling with the earthy smell of recently turned soil. A gentle breeze stirred the arrangements surrounding the polished mahogany casket, carrying the priest's final words across the cemetery where a substantial crowd had gathered to say goodbye to Deputy Sam Chambers.

"Ashes to ashes, dust to dust." The priest's voice carried the weight of ritual, of words spoken over countless graves throughout human history. "We commend our brother Samuel to the earth from which we all came, in the sure and certain hope of resurrection to eternal life."

As the final prayer concluded, the mourners began to disperse, moving in small, somber groups toward waiting vehicles. The sheriff's department had turned out in full force, uniforms crisp, badges wrapped in the black bands of mourning. Deputies clustered together, exchanging quiet words and memories of their fallen colleague. Laura Cain moved among them, offering comfort with a touch or word, her own grief evident but controlled as she fulfilled her role as the sheriff's wife and the community's unofficial caretaker.

Mary remained beside the casket, her hand resting lightly on its polished surface, unwilling or unable to join the departing crowd. She wore a simple black dress, her hair pulled back in a loose ponytail, her face pale but composed. The rawness of her grief had been replaced by something quieter, a sadness that seemed to have settled into her bones.

Sheriff Cain stood beside her, one hand on her shoulder, his other gripping a cane that supported his weight on the side where Carter's bullet had torn through muscle and tissue. The wound was healing well according to the doctors, but the limp would likely remain for months, perhaps longer—a physical reminder of that day at the falls, as if any of them needed reminding.

"It was a nice service," Cain said finally, breaking the silence between them.

Mary nodded, fingers tracing the grain of the wood beneath her palm. "I think he would have been embarrassed by all the fuss. He was always so... understated."

A ghost of a smile touched Cain's lips. "True. But he deserved every bit of recognition. He saved both our lives."

They stood in comfortable silence for a moment, shared grief creating a bridge between them that had been absent in recent years. The distance that had defined their relationship since Mary's entry into adolescence had vanished, burned away in the crucible of near-death and devastating loss.

"Did I ever tell you," Cain said, his voice softening, "that even while Sam was lying there bleeding after the explosion, his first concern was for you? Not himself, not his injuries. You."

Mary looked up at her father, tears gathering in her eyes. "Really?"

Cain nodded, his own eyes bright with emotion. "The paramedics were working on his leg, and he was fighting to stay conscious long enough to tell me where you were. To make sure I got to you in time." He swallowed hard. "That's the kind of man he was."

"He was so special, Dad," Mary whispered, the tears spilling over despite her efforts to contain them. "I know you didn't approve—our relationship, the age difference, all of it—but he was truly special."

"I know that now," Cain admitted, pulling her closer as her tears fell faster. "I think I always knew it, really."

Mary leaned into him, grateful for his strength as her own seemed to desert her. "I'm sorry we didn't tell you. That we went behind your back. That you had to find out the way you did."

Cain sighed, the sound heavy with regret and acceptance. "It doesn't matter now, honey. None of that matters anymore. What matters is remembering him for who he was, for the good he did, for the lives he touched—especially yours."

They began walking slowly toward the cemetery entrance, Mary matching her pace to her father's careful steps. The day was beautiful—clear blue sky, bare trees and a feeling of snow in the air. Birds called to one another from branches overhead. The kind of day that made death seem like an impossibility, a mistake in the natural order.

"I've been thinking about Carter too," Mary said after a while, her voice hesitant. "Not about the falls, or what he did to Sam, or any of the murders. About before. When we were kids."

Cain glanced at her, surprise evident in his expression. "That can't be easy."

"It's not," she admitted. "But there was good there too, you know? Before his parents died, before everything changed. He was kind once. Funny. Brilliant in a way that made me want to keep up with him." She paused, collecting her thoughts. "Sometimes I wish we could have a funeral for him too. For that Carter, the one I knew before."

Her father was silent for a long moment, considering her words. "We found Sam, so we might still find Carter's body," he said finally. "Downstream, or when the water levels drop in summer. The search teams haven't given up."

Mary nodded, though something in her expression suggested doubt. "I know. But the falls are so deep, and the current so strong..."

"Nature has a way of revealing its secrets eventually," Cain replied, his tone gentle but containing the certainty of a man who had seen many investigations reach their conclusion, even when hope seemed lost. "If he's there, we'll find him."

They reached the sheriff's department SUV, where Laura waited patiently beside the passenger door. She embraced Mary tightly before she climbed in, then helped Cain into the vehicle, taking his cane and stowing it in the back seat before walking around to the driver's side.

As they pulled away from the cemetery, Mary gazed out the window at the rows of headstones passing by—monuments to lives completed, stories ended, journeys concluded. Among them now was a marker for Sam Chambers, a placeholder for a man who meant so much to them all.

And somewhere out there lay what remained of Carter Thompson—the boy who had been her best friend, the teenager who had become a killer, the broken soul whose desperate need for recognition had led him down a path of destruction that had claimed not only his victims but ultimately himself.

What if he didn't die?

The thought surfaced unexpectedly in Mary's mind, a whisper of doubt she couldn't quite suppress. Carter had been methodical in everything, had planned each detail with precision, had always maintained control of the variables. Could his final act have been planned as well? Could he have survived what Sam, with his greater size and strength, had not?

She pushed the thought away, recognizing it as the confusion of grief, the mind's reluctance to accept finality. No one could have survived that fall, that impact, those currents. It was impossible, a fantasy born of trauma rather than reason.

And yet, as the cemetery receded behind them and Stillwater's familiar streets came into view, Mary couldn't shake the feeling that patterns, once established, tended to continue—and Carter Thompson had always been exceptionally good at recognizing patterns, at manipulating variables, at planning for contingencies others couldn't even imagine.

She said nothing of these thoughts to her parents, instead resting her head against her father's shoulder, taking comfort in his solid presence, in the knowledge that whatever happened next, they would face it together. The Thompson house stood empty now, the grandmother having passed away, the final resident presumed dead. Soon it would be sold, its grim history becoming just another Stillwater ghost story shared on dark nights around campfires.

Life would continue. Grief would ease, though never disappear completely. The patterns of daily existence would reassert themselves, routines forming new shapes around the absence of those who had been lost.

And if sometimes, in the darkest hours of night, Mary found herself watching the shadows, aware of the strange variables of the world around her—well, that was simply the price of surviving, of being the one left behind to remember, to wonder, to watch for the patterns that others might miss.

The End

ABOUT THE AUTHOR

John Parenteau is an accomplished writer and filmmaker, having worked in the entertainment industry for over 30 years. After writing many screenplays yet selling few, he decided it was time to convert his unsold screenplays into novels. "Stillwater" is a story borne from his childhood desire to be a detective, set in a small town similar to the one he grew up in, Silverton, Oregon.

John currently lives in Los Angeles with his wife Maggie and his belligerent cat, Sebastian.

Thank You for Reading

If you enjoyed *Stillwater*, the best way you can support it is by telling others. Reviews help readers discover new stories, and they mean the world to authors like me.

It only takes a minute to leave your thoughts—short or long, it all helps.

You can leave a review here: bit.ly/41G8Rwp

Thank you for spending your time in Stillwater. I hope we meet again in the next story.

John